The
White Pavilion

by

Ruth Fox

THE WHITE PAVILION

Copyright 2022
Hague Publishing
PO Box 451
Bassendean, Western AUSTRALIA 6934

Email: contact@haguepublishing.com
Web: www.haguepublishing.com

ISBN 978-0-6488346-5-6

Cover by Jade Zivanovic
http://www.steampowerstudios.com.au/
Original image used under license from Shutterstock.com.

Typeset Text: Garramond 12/14

The White Pavilion

When Imre falls dancing the Dance of a Thousand Steps, she is summoned to the Citadel by the Principe Regent, certain she is to be punished.

But the Regent is both more and less than he seems, and Imre must now discover why *Tierra Méjor* is being ripped from its Core.

But on a broken world that moves to the ticking of the Pendulum and the spinning of the Wheel, can Imre prevent her world from being torn apart?

Chapter One

It was the dawn of the Festival de Tiemp, and the Greatest City rose as the light of la Grulla tipped over the horizon.

My sisters and I had been awake for an hour. Some of us even longer – it was always difficult to sleep the night before. Like the children we'd once been, we stayed up late, sharing stories and sipping *espiritu*. It was the one night of the year Maestra Tinir permitted us to do so.

"You are all good girls," she had told us last night, kissing each of our cheeks before bed. It was rare for a compliment to fall from her lips, and we didn't take it for granted. "Tomorrow you will dance beautifully. It will be the greatest Dance the City has ever seen!"

This morning, we were barely contained bundles of energy and nerves. We clamoured and laughed and chatted and yelled over one another as we fought for space before the bathroom mirrors, exchanged kohl pencils, and argued over the best hairstyles to complement our costumes.

"I've lost my mask!" Ketra fretted, and we all rolled our eyes. Every year, she lost something.

I turned to Yui, my dark-haired sister, whose almond-shaped eyes always seemed full of tears just about to spill over. She sat next to me, leaning in close to the mirror to pat her make-up dry. "She'll find it under her bed."

It was Yui's first time in the Dance of a Thousand Steps, and she was wide-eyed and breathless. I wasn't much different, for though it was my third time in the Dance, it was the first I had ever been cast as 'la Grulla', the Crane. The most important role in the whole dance – and especially so, this time, for this was the Year Five Hundred. Everyone's eyes would be on me, all the way from the steps of the White Pavilion to the gates of the Citadel.

"Imre, little sister, you look stunning!"

This was Carla, who had just come in from our shared bedroom. She was carrying my costume, and it looked – it looked beyond incredible. The white feathers fluttered from the skirt like the wings of tiny birds, and the bodice was edged with fine white piping. It was very old, having been worn by every girl who'd played the Crane for at least three decades, but it was still crisp and white and perfect.

"Here," Carla said. "You must put it on, or we'll be late."

I stood up, and Rehina instantly took my place at the mirror. "I just can't get my lips to look red enough!" she pouted, pressing her flawlessly coloured lips into an unattractive moue.

I slipped out of my shift and allowed Carla to hold the dress while I wriggled into it. She pulled it up, her fingers deftly tugging it over my bare skin.

Carla was playing 'Viento Cósmico', the Cosmic Wind. "You and I," she whispered as she buttoned the back, "will render the crowd speechless."

She knew, as I did, the importance of our roles. Though it was la Relojero, the Clockmaker, who led the Dance, and la Oráculo who followed in her wake, guiding the entire procession as if they walked again those Thousand Steps that signified the creation of our world, Tierra Mejór, everyone looked for the Cosmic Wind and the Crane. Their costumes are dazzling, their movements unique. It was said among the sisters that those roles are much harder than the two leads.

"Do you think I can do this?" I asked her as I turned, a note of panic in my voice.

"Imre," Carla put her hands on either side of my head, pressing her masked forehead to my as-yet-bare one – I could feel the ticking of her *metrónomo* against my temple, and she could probably feel mine, "you know as well as I do that you were born to dance the Crane."

***

The children came first, as they always did, bright-eyed with excitement and the lack of sleep. They giggled and shouted as they poured into the streets, singing their *parabra* in high little voices, off-key and unfinished, the words hopelessly muddled.

Their parents, grandparents, older siblings, and neighbours followed, no less enthusiastically, and already sipping from cups of strong espiritu. Others had indulged in their own vices, such as the little paper cups of white-powder the street vendors sold, which made them joyous – at least for the moment. Soon, the avenues were full.

And we danced the *Dance of a Thousand Steps*, for the five hundredth time. The day was alive with music, and caught in the magic of the celebration, we danced to the glory of the Pattern.

Only the heralds, the men of the Brotherhood of the Pattern, were missing; they, and their novices. They celebrated the day in their own, sombre celebration, locked inside, deep in prayer. Every other woman, man, youth, child, grandmother, and old man was on the streets, mirroring our movements in their own less formal version of the dance, shouting and laughing, toasting the health of Tierra Mejór and each other in newfound and unfortunately short-lived comradeship. From each Tier they came, from the Fourth to the First; it was the one day when the lock gates were open to all, to pass freely as they pleased.

Factories and shops closed their doors. There would be no carrier pigeons sent or received today. Of all the machines, only the shuttle-trains continued to run, bringing those who could afford the price of a ticket from the Wheel to the Spindle to witness the spectacle.

Fireworks dazzled their eyes, reflected by the sequins of our glittering costumes. "To la Relojero!" they called. "To la Grulla!"

Oh, how we danced! My feet flew across the road, as if I'd been born knowing the movements. The music seemed to guide my steps. I danced as well as Maestra Tinir, my teacher; I danced as well as Vahn, who was *favourito* of Senora R. I twirled and leaped, I spun and slid, unable to keep the smile from my face or the laughter from my lips. We danced through the cheering crowds; we danced along the road, the watchers throwing coloured streamers and confetti in our wake. We danced the *Dance of a Thousand Steps*, from the doors of the White Pavilion, around the spiralling streets, through the lock gate from the Second Tier to the First, to the front gates of the Citadel.

"Oh," breathed Yui, who was just behind me. "Look!"

I looked. As la Grulla, I was in the front ranks, where I had a view uncompromised by the whirling forms of my sisters.

Ahead of me, before the Citadel, the throng was so thick, it seemed a sea made of human faces. The *vigilar*, in their black uniforms, had lined the Plaza de Lágrima to hold open a space for us. Dizzy with exhilaration, I felt no weariness, only a deep-seated longing to dance, and continue to dance forever. I drank in the Citadel spires, gold against the grey sky; the Reloj de pie, the giant clock in its enormous tower, both its slender hands positioned perfectly at twelve, and thought it had never looked so beautiful.

But though we'd reached our destination, the dance was far from over. I glided to my post, opposite Carla, who was so utterly, gloriously at home playing the part of Viento Cosmico, the Cosmic Wind. Counterpart and complement to the Crane, we would ever circle one another; one flying ahead of the other, at times supporting, at times acting as adversary; the other battling, flagging, gathering strength and flying onwards.

Carla had been right that I was meant to dance this part. In this moment, my earlier doubts were nowhere to be seen. I ducked and wove around Carla, kicking the long white skirt with my feet so that it billowed and swished. The sleeves of the costume hung long, like feathered wings, and I raised them elegantly above my head – about to take flight – then lowered them as the West Wind whirled past, halting my passage in a flurry of glittering blue. Behind her mask, Carla's eyes twinkled.

Ahead of us, la Relojero, played by Vahn, and la Oráculo, played by Ketra, danced in unison. Their movements stately, they stepped out the time-laden story. La Relojero was visited by la Oráculo. He gave to her a key, ancient and mysterious, that had once enjoyed some other purpose; he gave to her a heart, made of glass; he gave to her a flute; and he gave to her a message, which was that the Old Earth was dying, for the people had neglected and wandered from the true path, the intrinsic Pattern of Life.

As it is written in the Sacred Text, la Relojero had gone before the people and said, 'Listen! We are facing our last turnings here. Will you help me?'

But the people were afraid. The world burned under the merciless sun, the protective veils of the atmosphere stripped away, and they were in the middle of a war. They did not hear her.

So, she worked for a thousand turnings upon her masterwork, which was Tierra Mejór. She launched it into space, setting it between the stars.

'Look!' she said to the people, who had at last stopped fighting, their amazement finally overshadowing their fear and anger. 'Will you follow me now?'

And they said that they would, but how were they to reach this great new world?

And so, la Relojero went to work again. Another fine work she created, and this was the Crane, which she fitted with the glass heart that beat with the rhythm of her great wings. And on whose back the Companions, those seven men and women who believed strongly enough to put aside their fears, would ride.

They were plucked from the disparate guilds of life. The Poet. The Architect. The Tinker. The Physician. The Smith. The Gardener. And Aurelia, the Whore.

They had climbed between her great wings, and Aurelia played the mercurial flute la Oráculo had given her, and so harnessed the Cosmic Wind, which would bear them to their new home.

It had taken one thousand days to reach Tierra Mejór, and it was a long and arduous journey full of many pitfalls, traps, hardships, and horrors. Finally, when la Grulla's strength was flagging to her last reserve – here, I swayed, my steps slowing – the clouds had parted, and la Relojero had seen the world she had created.

She, along with her Seven Companions, and la Oráculo, had tumbled from la Grulla's back, and looked around them in wonder. For here was a world filled with order and rhythm; a world where the Pattern could thrive. It was a stark place, and living would not be easy; but it was clean, new, untouched, unsoiled by those human hands which had so marred the beauty of the Old Earth.

Here, there would be no disharmony.

But the Viento Cósmico, the Cosmic Wind, which had borne them on her breath, was disquieted. The world was not yet alive. The waters in the wells were still. The clouds, made from the condensation gathering on the metal surface, sat static in the sky. The fronds of green moss, which grew in the ruts where water gathered, would not sway.

And so, la Relojero, tired as she was, took her leave of the company. Alone, she ventured far from their landing place, to where she had left open a long passageway. Down she went into the Core of the World. There, among the fire and fury of the great engines, was a keyhole. Here she fitted the key la Oráculo had given her, and wound it ten times. And the planet spun. The Spindle, which was made of rotating tiers. The Wheel, which circled around it, creating gravity and equilibrium. And the weighted Pendulum, attached by the Tether, which governed the subtle shifts and inner balances, regulating the weather and forming the murky clouds that made the atmosphere.

The air warmed and cooled according to the position of the Pendulum, and life-giving rain fell from the pipes on the underside of its weighted tip. Thus did the seeds of the Sacred Tree, brought by Nuru, the Gardener, begin to grow amid the moss. Among these plants, the first moths were born, small, ghostly white creatures, shedding dust from their wings as they fluttered like petals on the wind, eating and spreading the pollen of the plants. The other flowers, shrubs, and grains followed, and soon there were beautiful, lush gardens. Animals were born, rats and foxes and fish and spiders and wasps; and the world began to feel alive.

All this we danced, our metrónomos keeping perfect time.

And then, suddenly, a harsh sound. "Hold!" cried a strident voice.

I turned, shocked that such a command should be shouted at all, let alone now, as we were reaching the next phase of the performance. The cheers died away, the music missed a beat, and for a moment, the dance faltered as we peered ahead.

A man stood before the statue of la Oráculo, conspicuous with his hat tied with a green band, the symbol of the rebels.

"Hold!" he shouted again. "What do you dance for? Why do you cheer? The dark days are coming, and you have forgotten!"

"Remove him!" Someone – a tall man, wearing a grey shirt and the gold emblem of the *guardia* on his shoulder – strode forwards, gesturing to the nearest of the vigilar. When they did not move, he barked: "Now!"

There was a moment of confusion, a tussle, I saw through my mask, as the vigilar took the man by his arms and straightened one behind his back, twisting it mercilessly until he was doubled over in agony. His green-banded hat dropped to the ground, trampled by the swarm of black uniforms.

"Listen!" he yelled, even as they lifted him off his feet and carried him, kicking and bucking. "The Queen is not herself! I speak the truth. The Queen! Look to the Queen! La Rebelde does not lie!"

In moments, he was gone, and the music picked up as if it had never faltered. We, who had been trained to continue a dance even when our feet bled and our dinner had long gone cold, did not miss a beat. Even though, in the distance, we heard his screams.

Ketra, as la Relojero, raised her hands.

Around her, the flowers bloomed – dancers who shed their dull grey cloaks to reveal brightly coloured costumes underneath – and the crops flourished – sisters dressed in gold and green who swayed from side to side as wheat and corn under the breath of the wind.

Thus Tierra Mejór was born.

La Grulla should soar, here, as the world came to life, her glass heart beating as the planet turned, and Time began as we would know it for the next five hundred years. La Grulla, by whom we measured our days and months and years, as she waxed and waned, shining in the day and fading in the night. La Grulla, who would always watch over us, her people, as surely as she had carried us on her back across the vast regions of the Unknown.

La Reloj de pie struck once. Twice, thrice. Around me, the sisters dipped and swayed, then raised their hands to la Grulla. We were an image of perfection, our timing impeccable, our movements precisely measured by our ticking metrónomos. The crowd looked on as we told the story for the five hundredth time in this, our ancient city. Tens of thousands rejoiced as we celebrated our place on Tierra Mejór.

La Reloj de pie struck the fourth time, the fifth.

A great cheer went up. I turned my eyes to the Clocktower. Below the large face of its clock – it must have been as wide across as the room I shared with my sisters – was a balcony with a railing of iron lacework. There a door opened, and here she was, the beautiful Queen, *la Reina*. In a gown of green velvet, with her silver-blond hair curling around her perfect cheeks, she raised a hand, and more cheers resounded. It was too far to see her features, but I imagined she smiled.

La Reloj chimed the sixth.

I stepped forward, to the base of the statue of la Oráculo. I would pirouette seven times around it, standing, each time I leaped, on one of the symbols etched at precise intervals; one, two three – I twirled, my white skirts flying – four, five – again, faster – six, – and now I stopped before the outstretched hand of la Oráculo. La Reloj de pie struck the final time. Seven. I landed on the final cobblestone, marked with Aurelia's symbol, the crescent moon, and only just big enough for the toe of my slipper. I plucked a feather from my skirt, and skipped ahead, raising my arms – my arms, which were wings – ready to place the feather in the statue's stone palm.

In the distance, beyond the music and the cheers of the crowd, a pistol went off.

And before these countless watching eyes, I fell.

Chapter Two

To recognise moments in which history is made is a skill I have never mastered. To me, they have always slipped past amid my own personal anguishes.

I wish I had the skill of the poets. To spot these moments that should be recorded, and to capture them as Ante, the Poet, captured the sight of the first dawn on Tierra Mejór:

'In those bright shades of red and gold as la Grulla rose, we saw the Pattern as we had not before, unshrouded, clear. And distance was no longer that which could not be crossed, but that which proved a child, starving, orphaned, and alone, would be denied nourishment never, so long as he could take one final step."

But how had Companion Ante known, as he penned those words, that they would survive until this turning, recorded in the *Texto Sagrado,* where I would read them with such awe, under the guidance of my grandmother? How had he known how important that one sight would be for all the people who would live after him on Tierra Mejór? For surely, the rising of la Grulla was often something I reviled, wishing only to turn over and return to sleep for another hour, or two. I would never think to write of it, even if I had the skill. But what if that single moment was one which would change the course of my life? What if, in rolling over in my bed and ignoring the first breaking rays, in wishing I was somewhere else, in another time, I missed something vital?

This time was no exception. Something had changed, but I wanted nothing more than this moment to pass, for things to settle back into their normal equilibrium. But that is not the way of the Pattern, as I have come to learn. And so, I will do my best, now, to put it into words; I will seek to tell it as truthfully as I can.

***

Pain. It woke me, a tight knot in my stomach. *Strange.* It was my foot I had injured, after all, not my abdomen; yet that was where the pain was, like a rock lodged in my belly.

A blurred face appeared before me.

"Oh, Imre," it gasped. "Oh, dearest!"

Ketra. Her features twisted in sympathy that did not quite reach her eyes. I tried to speak, but couldn't manage an intelligent sound.

"She's awake! Imre, don't try to speak. The healer gave you herbs for the pain . . . they said they will make you drowsy and confused."

"I can speak," I replied indignantly, but the words came out wrong. I reached for my mask, but of course, it was no longer there. Instead, my fingers grazed the slightly raised metal of my metrónomo, from the corner of my left eye, up to my left temple. It throbbed steadily, pulsing with the beat of life, but there was a faintness to the beat, I was almost sure. Ketra pushed my hand back and ran delicate fingers over my golden hair. I tried to shake away her touch, but in my current state could do nothing but endure it.

"What have you got there?" a soft voice murmured, prodding at my hand. My fingers were clenched tightly around something small and soft. A feather, a white feather, the feather I was to carry to the end of the dance. Every year for four hundred and ninety-nine years, a feather had been placed in the hand of the statue of la Oráculo, to be left where it would vanish minutes, or hours, or days later as the wind bore it away.

Every year but this one, thanks to me.

"Give it to me, Imre. You don't need it anymore."

I clenched my fist, and they did not press me.

"Daughter."

Maestra Tinir, crouching by my side. Her touch was gentle, but firm. I tried not to. I couldn't help it. I started to cry.

"Do not." There was no sympathy in her voice. It was a command, a statement of the futility of such an action. Her next words were warmer. "You never did do things by halves."

"I'm sorry," I whispered. "I'm so sorry."

She waved a hand dismissively. "There's nothing to be done now."

"But the Festival de Tiempo . . . I've ruined everything . . ."

She pinched her lips. "You danced well, Imre. No one can dispute that. You felt the spirit of the Crane herself, my little one, did you not?"

"Yes." I nodded earnestly. I *had* felt it, for those glorious moments of the Dance.

"That is a gift of the Pattern, an eternal gift."

"I will do better next time," I promised her. "I will do better!"

She smiled, and it cut my heart to pieces. It was the wrong kind of smile. The smile of regret, of untold truths. I felt so numb and cold. I didn't dare ask her. I turned my head away into the pillow, and they left me alone. I tucked the feather under my pillow. I slept.

***

When I was a very small child, my grandmother gave me a present. It was the only thing I kept from my childhood when I came to the Pavilion. I could still remember my *abuela*, her old, frail hands pressing this gift into mine, and how carefully I had unwrapped it.

It was a small porcelain statue of a woman wearing a blue robe and hood. She was kneeling, her lovely face bowed. She looked a little like the statue of la Relojero in the Templo.

"Mary," Abuela explained. "Her name was Mary, and she was worshipped by many people on Old Earth for being the mother of a very important man."

I tried to imagine a world where a woman could be worshipped for carrying only one son, but my six-year-old mind could not fathom it. I loved that figurine, however, with its chipped, worn paint. It fit perfectly into my fist as I'd grown, and I'd carried it everywhere for many years, imagining that she accompanied me on all my adventures, this small, blue-cloaked woman; until at last, I came to the Pavilion, where she found a home beneath my pillow.

I felt, now, as if I was the size of that statue, frozen, unable to move, while some great hand had tipped my world on its head.

***

I had never been allowed such luxury as I have in the turning that followed. In the wake of my accident, every previously held law was suspended; even the dawn regimen took place without me. And for once, I would have given anything at all to drag myself from sleep and the comfort of bed to walk with the others to the courtyard, to feel the chill of morning and the burn of waking stretches, to listen to Reloj de pie ring seven times through the streets and remind us of our numbered turnings, to speak my parabra under my breath and hope the Pattern would hear it.

I could hardly taste the food I ate: when I was finished, the meal sat in my stomach like a stone and I wished I could vomit. Later on, I did.

I heard noises beyond the curtained door, footsteps, voices, the daily sounds of life in the White Pavilion. It was a taunt, a reminder that everything went on without me. That I was so unimportant, *this* changed nothing.

It changed everything.

Chapter Three

"This is the child?"

I was startled that the voice was not the one I had expected. I had thought it Maestra Tinir, or one of the *concerjes* come to deliver another bowl of stew. I blinked up at the stranger. Shock reached its cold fingers around my heart. I lay very still, conscious of the thin sheets covering my body, offering little protection from the raking gaze of a pair of ebony eyes.

He was tall and slender. His pale skin contrasted sharply with his charcoal hair, and a neatly-clipped beard joined with his moustache, framing his mouth, making his cheeks seem shallower, his jaw narrower. Lines at the corners of his eyes. I was only distantly aware that Maestra Tinir stood at his shoulder, until she said:

"This is Imre."

What was I supposed to do? I could not curtsy! I could not even stand! I lowered my eyes and held my breath.

"Imre," he muttered. From beneath my lashes, I peeked, despite myself. "A strange name."

A moment passed in which he did nothing but stare at me. I shifted my gaze about the room, but his eyes never wavered. Then, abruptly, he turned on his heel. "When she is well enough to be moved," he said, "you will bring her before my Liege."

And that – apart from a glimpse of Maestra Tinir's unsmiling face – was all I got before the door closed and I was alone again.

***

I had much time to ponder on the strangeness of this visit, to wonder what it meant. And oh, my imagination was most active. I decided, eventually, that it could only have meant I was to be punished in some way, but that it could not happen until I had healed.

There was only one punishment for a daughter of the White Pavilion. I would be asked to leave. Cast out, my reputation ruined. My metrónomo removed. If I ever danced again, it would be in a show, or at a market. I wept in humiliation.

A group of my sisters came to see me. They gathered around the bed and chattered like a bunch of carrier pigeons, all relaying their messages at once.

"Don't worry about a thing, Imre." Firreli smiled. "Remember when Sharquen broke her wrist? It was . . ."

"Oh, and we all know how that happened!" interrupted Rehina, inducing a fit of laughter from all but quiet Yui, who stared at her hands.

"She'll never tell, will she?" burbled Vahn. "She swears it was a fall."

"Oh, indeed a fall, but from where?"

"Councillor Horoth, they all say he has a propensity for the rougher kind of love."

Laughter, raining down like glitter confetti.

"Sharquen might be the one petitioned by the Senor, then." Vahn winked. "I suspect he's one who might suit her tastes. Glowering and scowling like that . . . You can tell he enjoys the *darker* arts."

"Oh, Vahn!" exclaimed Rehina. "Do you think in all honesty . . ."

"Why else would he have come?"

"Do you pay no attention at all? When has the Principe Regente's most trusted adviser ever entered the doors of the Pavilion, let alone strode it halls with a glower upon his face, looking as if he's about to murder someone?"

"He had close words with Maestra Tinir. Perhaps he petitions on behalf of another?"

Firreli gasped. "You cannot mean the Prince?"

Vahn shrugged, and laughed. "Can you imagine?"

"Never. He has a hundred concubines. A Principe has never entered the doors of the White Pavilion."

"Not during your time."

"Oh yes, his father came regularly, in disguise. I've heard Senora R. speak of it . . ."

It had taken me a while to connect the man they referred to as the Senor to my taciturn visitor. They could not have known he had come into my room, or they'd never have let it alone. Even more frightened of what this meant now that I knew he was the Prince's adviser, I kept silent.

"We bought you something." Firreli leaned closer to me, producing a small paper box. I had smelled it as they walked in: coffee biscuits. "They're not just the ordinary ones –"

"Though of course we know they have miraculous powers where you're concerned on any ordinary turning!" Rehina burst out.

"— no, these are imbued with the magical ability to make you well," Ketra finished. "And you must eat every last crumb, or they won't work at all."

I had no heart to tell them I had no desire to touch them. Lying here in bed, how could I justify eating them? What if I grew too fat to dance? Such were the evil thoughts that began to prey on my mind.

My next visits were from the Concerje, coming to change the sheets and take away the uneaten biscuits. He was a strong man, and lifted me easily into a chair while he worked briskly.

"My son is lamed," he told me. "Fell from a balcony, he did, while drinking more goldwine than he should."

"Lamed," I repeated weakly, wondering if this was supposed to be a comfort.

The Concerje turned a wide grin on me. "He gets about with crutches."

The emptiness inside me gaped a little wider.

"He's married. Three kids. You don't stop living, do you?"

He seemed to expect a response, so I shook my head. You don't stop living until you're dead. But if my mother had taught me one thing, it was that you can certainly stop *wanting* to.

The healer came again, and again. She hummed and hah-ed, turning my foot, prodding it and stroking it, like an unruly pet. Finally, she said, "You will walk again. And soon."

It was a ridiculous thing to say to a grown woman, a statement as seemingly superfluous as informing someone that, in a moment, they must take another breath. But how those words scared me! As horrible as my enforced captivity in this bed may have been, how much more terrifying to face the possibility that I might stand – and fall?

***

I woke after the evening meal. Everything was quiet. I could imagine the others getting ready for the night petitions in the upper chambers. There would be laughter and chatter as my sisters ran about, avoiding Maestra Tinir and the Concerje, who would tell them to calm themselves; *mecenas* came for the company of fine women, not babbling children.

I slipped from my bed. The pain in my ankle nearly made me scream, but the knot in my stomach was worse. I made myself stand upright and take one step, then another. If I could touch the door, I promised myself, I could rest. I could turn back at any moment. But once I'd reached that landmark, I told myself the end of the hall would do as well; then the stairs. Before I knew it, I was at the stone archway leading into the Room of Roses.

Harp music tinkled through the air and sent a shiver down my spine. I peered around the aperture and saw the night's mecenas gathered there. My gaze swept over them. Tall men, short men, some dressed in silk and velvet finery, others in cheaper crepe-like fabric, clearly borrowed or hired for the night. Some stood at ease, nursing their glasses of goldwine and chatting up their companions, gambling at the tables, roaring when they won and roaring louder when they lost. Others were edgy and nervous, glancing about at the smooth marble walls, the opulent crystal chandelier, the colourful tapestries which depicted the Crossing, the pillars, which rotated as the themed rooms above moved.

There were tables laid out with gaming chips and cards, presided over by rundown automata. The servitors buzzed about, boxy things of indeterminate shape with mismatched wheels, laden with trays full of fruits and crackers and little square pieces of moth-meat, discretely sucking up dust and dropped crumbs through their bottom vents. The Concerje walked among them, ensuring that the play was fair, and that no trouble was roused, stopping to talk occasionally to this man or that. There were even a few women, come as companions, or out of curiosity as to what the Pavilion might offer their men – women, indisputably, were excluded from patronage.

How many times had I stood here, crouching with my sisters as a child, then a young woman, wondering which mecenas I would choose when I passed my initiation? Or which one I would make my first, when I reached eighteen years? The tall, dark man with the angular face? The one who strode with such ease and surety that his purse surely bulged with coin? The small, balding one with the stomach that flopped over his belt? (Here we would nudge one another and giggle.)

A man turned, and in an instant, his eyes locked with mine. There was something strange about his mouth. I squinted, peering closer, but he must have noticed me, for he winked. I drew back quickly, ashamed that he had seen my face unmasked.

I tore myself away. Soon, my sisters would arrive in their glittering gowns and feathered masks and the music would change to a dancing tune. They would glide among the petitioners, dancing, serving goldwine and titbits, before choosing their mecenas. I didn't want any of them to spy me here.

I limped down the quiet, cold hallway towards the kitchens, but soon had to duck into a side room as a servitor whirred past with a laden tray. The knot in my stomach tightened as I caught the scent of river salmon and goat cheese. The small amount of food I had managed to keep down had been an accomplishment. I wondered if I would ever be able to eat again.

Rather than risk going down the hallway, I crossed the room to the far side. A small door here led onto a tiny terrace. There was no egress from this narrow balcony, which is why it was often overlooked and rarely locked. Even the gardeners did not bother to trim back the leaves that grew over the lintel.

Outside, I gulped the fresh air like a person who had surfaced from a near-drowning. It was so cold and clean, it felt like it was scouring my insides. The chill bit through my thin shift, but I did not stop.

Climbing the railing was difficult with my ankle, though the drop was barely more than an arm-span. But the healer told me I must walk, and I had done this many times. My arms supporting most of my weight, soon my bare feet touched the grass. I wanted to run. I would have, if I was whole, but instead, I hobbled, bracing myself against the white walls. Overhead, the turrets and towers soared, and I could not repress a sudden surge of respect and love for the White Pavilion; my home.

The Pavilion was reached by a wide thoroughfare called the Calle del Corazón, the Street of the Heart. This circled the Greatest City from the gates of the Citadel, down to the Second Tier and the Pavilion, where it ended in a wide loop for the autocarriages and rotor-trams that passed this way. The small lights of a passing servitor blinked through the dark trees as it swept the rubbish from the paving. As a child, before I had become a Daughter of the Pavilion, I would climb the stairs from the Third Tier to the Second, and sit at the side of the Calle, looking towards the tall white towers, wondering and dreaming.

The Pavilion grounds were beautiful, laid out in concentric half-circles with the white building at the centre, each ring larger than the one before. The rings held a variety of trees and plants, and there was even a small eddy-lake crossable by an ornamental bridge. The last level backed onto the banks of the Reservoir.

Here, where the water sat like a black glass plate, even when the creeper-fish edged their blind way through its depths, the gardens met with an older ground, one cultivated here since the founding of the Ciudad; here, the Abbey was built. Some say the place where the first stone was laid was where la Nuru knelt and took a sip from the Reservoir (which in those times was clear and not in need of filtering), thus ending the long thirst of the Seven Companions.

I descended the steps through two rings, until the sparkling reflections of stars on the water greeted me through the vine-covered trees. I started a little at a rustling in the grass, but it was only a street-fox, looking at me with shining green eyes.

Ahead, a winding path led to a small building, and this was my destination. The Templo de las Siete, the Temple of the Seven, had always been my favourite place to seek solitude and peace, and it did not disappoint me now.

Only five shallow steps led up into the interior. The bare stone floor had been polished to a gloss by years of feet and knees of the faithful. Several wooden pews shored up the sides, but the centre was open all the way to the altar, on which sat a simple marble statue of la Relojero, the Clockmaker.

The Temple of the Seven was older than the Pavilion, and perhaps older than the Iglesia, built upon the weighted tip of the Pendulum, though no herald or novice would ever admit it. It had been rebuilt after a sudden fire a decade ago, but many of the original features remained. This statue was one of them, and it differed from the depictions of la Relojero in more modern Temples.

This Relojero kneeled, her head bowed. Her hair was unbound, instead of hidden by a veil. Her eyes were lowered, but she didn't look down, as she did in other depictions; instead, she looked up, just slightly, from under her lashes, and there was a slight upwards tilt to her lips, as if she had seen something that amused her. I had come across this look before on women as they flirted with a man. It made me think that this Relojero was not the staid and distant figure the heralds would make her out to be, but rather mischievous, young, and impetuous.

I limped towards the altar and lowered myself to my knees. My ankle hurt, but it was my stomach that burned and twisted. I bowed my head.

"By the Pattern," I began my parabra. "I come to you with head bowed and heart open wide."

I waited, and saw the candles flicker. My heart skipped a beat, but a second instant told me that the flicker had been caused by a movement behind me. I turned to find a figure in a long dark robe.

"Oh," I put a hand to my heart. "You startled me."

"I see that." The speaker moved into the candlelight. His face, previously hidden in the shadows of his half-cowl, was young, made younger as it showed no sign of a beard. His blood was Ruedan, from his father's side; the man had come from the Wheel, and a hairless face was the norm for that part of Tierra Mejór. But Tomas did not have the stature of their men. His blood was diluted by his Ciudad-dweller mother. "Forgive me for intruding on your prayer, Sister. I thought the Temple would be empty, as it is time for the night's assignations."

He took a few steps closer – close enough to see my tears, even though I ducked my head to hide them. He pushed back his half-cowl, revealing his shoulder-length hair, the same colour as my own, and kneeled next to me, taking my hand. "What's wrong, Imre?" His voice lapped against my ear, softer now, the formal edge gone.

"Oh, Tomas," I gasped, and slumped sideways into his arms. He gathered me to him like a father cradling a small child, and I buried my face in his shoulder. Everything I had been holding inside began to spill out. I sobbed desperately. "I'm so afraid."

"I heard what happened," he murmured into my hair. "I didn't see it. Otherwise . . ."

I knew what he would have wanted to do, if he hadn't been cloistered in the Abbey, speaking parabra. He would have carried me back to the Pavilion himself; though how he would accomplish such a feat, with his wiry body and spindly arms, I have no idea. But he would have been by my side, of that I had no doubt.

But he was a novice of the Brotherhood, and a soon-to-be herald. He would wear the black tattoo of a wheel on his neck, and, when he had proven his devotion, the long black robes that covered him, head to foot, with a full cowl across his face. To attend the festivities would have been a violation of his vows, not to mention touching a Daughter of the Pavilion. As he held me now, in the darkened Temple, I felt his heart race. If we were caught, he would be punished, perhaps even banished from the Brotherhood. It tore at my soul, but I pulled away from him, sitting so that my ankle was straight before me.

"They're sending me away," I told him.

He said nothing. I couldn't read the expression on his face; his eyes focused on la Relojero's likeness, and reflected the dancing candlelight. He had changed, I realised, in the past few months. The days when we had played together as young children, sneaking away from our respective duties to meet in the chicken yard or by the fountains in the bottom gardens, to play games with string and carved wax figures, were gone. Now, we were all but grown into our chosen roles.

I wanted him to tell me he wouldn't let them take me. That I couldn't go. We had been together for most of our lives, sharing dreams, and fears, and misadventures. Once, we had stolen apples from the orchards behind the Pavilion. We'd run, jumping the fence, and crouching behind a gardener's shed, we'd counted out our goods. I had wolfed down half of one before I noticed it was full of worms. It took only minutes for the first cramp to seize my belly. I vomited, and my bowels let go.

I was horrified. But Tomas had held my hair out of my face and wiped me clean with his own shirt. He hadn't left my side except for a brief moment when he ran to pinch a shift from the washing lines for me to change into.

I was so horribly embarrassed. But he had teased and joked – "you look as green as those apples!" – until I could do nothing except laugh along with him. Only then did he lead me back to the Pavilion. We parted ways at the lowest garden – he heading for the novice's quarters in the Abbey by the Reservoir, me, creeping back up to the Pavilion and discarding my ruined dress along the way. He didn't raise the matter again until I did, when enough time had passed that I had forgotten my humiliation.

I wanted him to do that again. To find some way to make things right in this world that had been skewed so horribly.

"Don't be afraid," he said at last. "I will come here every evening at this time and speak the parabra for you."

"You will?" I asked him, unsure if I was grateful or incredulous.

"For as long as I'm able." He looked at me sideways, and reached out a finger towards my temple. A familiar gesture, the tracing of my metrónomo, it never failed to send shivers rippling through my body. But instead, he drew back, and closed his eyes. When he opened them, they were fixed firmly on the altar. "I am to be a herald, Imre. What else can I possibly do?"

I did not want to think I imagined it; the sorrow in his voice, that he was to lose me; the sorrow that he couldn't say everything he ached to. That he loved me.

I did not want to think he had finally, truly come to believe the doctrine of la Boca, who had been High Priest of the Brotherhood for the past three decades: that, of the Seven who rode across the Unknown, it was Aurelia, the Whore, who did not deserve her place upon the Crane's back.

Rehina often scorned the novices. "Do you know they believe in the literal word of the Texto Sagrado, and think we literally were born from the Seven Companions? 'And from each of the Companions, seven children were born.' They believe that we were conceived –" she raised her hands, palms upwards – "Spontaneously! Just like that! If it's true, then we're all brothers and sisters, living in the shadow of Chaos – can they not see how hypocritical that sounds? And, somehow, even the men, like Neru and Artemu, gave birth!" She would trill that infectious laugher of hers until tears came to her eyes, and we would laugh with her. I would always go to bed those nights wondering how the Brotherhood could believe such things, but knowing in my heart of hearts that the Texto Sagrado was our guide, and for us, as Daughters of the Pavilion, to question it was blasphemy. Still, my mind wandered. It could not be the literal truth, for we were *not* all brothers and sisters, and men could *not* give birth. Not unless magic was involved somehow! But where, then, did we come from? It always left me uneasy, this surety that something vital was missing from our history. And dismayed, more than a little, knowing that Tomas was, as he spent more and more time at his training in the Abbey, losing his ability to question such things. Or, at least, his courage.

I bowed my head. "Thank you, Brother."

I didn't turn to watch him leave, but I listened to his footsteps until they had faded completely.

Chapter Four

Carla woke me. The room was dark – it was long past midnight. In ordinary circumstances, I would have been dancing in the Room of Roses, enticing a mecenas to part with his coins in exchange for a night of gambling and pleasure.

I shook my head to clear it. My hair hung limp and greasy; I had not cleansed myself properly for the three turnings since the Festival. The idea of a bath seemed an insurmountable endurance. But looking at Carla, her eyes rimmed with kohl, her russet dress flowing about her as she kneeled by my bed, I felt a hideous wreck.

"Imre dearest," she said, and I caught sight of the tears in her eyes. "The Senor has come. Maestra Tinir is talking to him."

I sat up. "Already?" My heart seemed to crack. The pain in my stomach blossomed.

Carla slipped onto the bed beside me, leaning her head on my chest. "He came only moments ago, demanding that you be brought out immediately. He seems in an awful hurry."

Her hair, the colour of straw, tickled my chin as I clung to her, my sister. "I don't want to go."

Taking my hand in hers, she kissed it. "I don't want you to go. I hate it every time one of us leaves. If I had my way, we'd all stay here forever."

But the others who leave, I wanted to remind her, they leave of their own choosing. And they know where they are going. To the houses of a rich mecenas who has paid their price to Senora R. They know what their lives will be: they know of the comfort they will enjoy, the favour of their men, and the scorn of their men's wives; the teaching of his children, and the bearing of other infants, if he so chooses; the knowledge that every turning, they will live to serve as working parts of the Pattern of the universe. Some of them, the luckiest of them, leave to dance the Dance of Love with their chosen partner as his one and only companion.

"Why did this happen to me?" I could not hold back. I fairly shouted the words, but they had no strength for my throat had tightened. "I didn't do anything wrong!"

"Do things happen for a reason?" My sister shook her head. "I don't know. I don't think we can ever know."

"It's not fair."

"It's not fair," she affirmed, and folded herself against my turned back, her head on my shoulder, holding me while I sobbed. "But if it is the Pattern's wish, Imre, then perhaps there is something you are meant to do, or see, or find, out there, beyond the doors of the Pavilion. Please stay strong, my hermana, my sister. I am certain you will dance again."

Maestra Tinir interrupted us. She was holding a green dress. It was my dress, one I hadn't worn in a long time, made of floating silk layers.

"Maestra Tinir?" I asked in a small voice.

She seemed worried. Tinir has a calm face, and every nuance shows upon it like ripples in a pond. It frightened me, and I trembled with the loss of Carla's reinforcement as she slipped from the bed and stood, as if an anchor had been cut loose.

"It is out of my hands, child," Maestra Tinir said. "But you must hurry. He has little patience."

I didn't need to ask her of whom she spoke.

Both of them helped me dress, and as I did so, I slipped the white feather, rather shabby and squashed now, into one of the pockets. "What are you still carrying that thing for?" spoke Maestra Tinir. "The costume has been stowed away for next year, as is proper; that useless feather should have been thrown out."

"I just wanted to keep it," I said in a small voice that sounded so forlorn that Maestra Tinir's face creased with pity and she turned her attention to my hair. "Oh, what shame that we have no time!" she cursed. "Your hair should be loose, the way it looks best; but we'll have to put it up and hide the tangles."

I couldn't say anything. I didn't ask the questions that burned in my throat because I didn't want to know the answers. If I didn't know anything for certain, I could imagine that things weren't so bad.

When Tinir was done, she turned me to face the mirror. I stared at my gaunt face, my hollow eyes, my hair, my one beauty, brushed to shining gold – and the elegant shape of my metrónomo pulsing beneath my skin – they belonged to a stranger.

Ketra hugged me tightly once more, and Maestra Tinir steered me out of the room. Her pace was brisk despite my limp. I did not complain, for I barely felt the pain.

At the corner of the corridor, Maestra Tinir suddenly stopped. She faced me, her mouth set into a grim expression. "Child," she said. "You have passed your initiation. I know you have yet to reach your eighteenth birthday, and your first time, but you know the Dances."

My mouth dry, I nodded miserably. "I know them," I assured her.

Maestra Tinir's hard stare didn't waver. "You will not shame the Daughters of the Pavilion, this I can tell." With a sharp nod, she led me onwards.

It was to one of the private audience chambers that we headed – the Flower Rooms, we called them, located on the second floor of the main building, radiating around a central atrium like petals, and decorated with every type of bloom and blossom in Tierra Mejór. They were reserved for the more affluent noblemen and women, more comfortable than the rooms used for regular meetings, but not as opulent as the Blue Rooms above, or, Pattern forbid, the Tower Rooms. Senora R. earmarked these highest chambers for those whose patronage was most valued.

The Concerje stood outside the door, his forbidding expression even more dire than usual.

Maestra Tinir paused to tuck a strand of my hair back into place. In the next moment, she nodded to the Concerje to open the door.

I stepped inside, and found myself inspected by Senora R., who sat in an opulent chair by the window, resplendent in a dress of deep red and gold silk layers and her usual abundance of jewelled rings. She had once been a Daughter of the Pavilion herself, one of its best dancers, but now her figure was shorter and rounder, her skin sagging around her jowls and mouth. Still, you could tell she had once been beautiful.

It was not her my gaze fell on, but the familiar figure opposite her: the dark man. He had his arms crossed, and he stood straight and tall. His chin was hidden by a dark goatee, and his eyes were slightly angled, giving him an exotic appearance. He wore a simple grey shirt over black trousers, and belted at his waist was a sheath, from which protruded the worn platinum hilt of a short sword.

Senor Grath, the Adviser to the Principe Regente of Tierra Mejór.

All sensibility vanished and I would have fallen if Maestra Tinir had not been holding me.

"Senor Grath," she said. "Allow me to present to you Daughter Imre."

I tried to curtsy, but Tinir pulled me straight. Indeed, I couldn't have made the gesture look any less graceful, and she did not want me to discredit myself, or her. Instead I lowered my eyes and spoke an inward parabra.

The man said nothing for a while. Then, in that quiet, measured tone: "Thank you, Maestra Tinir. I must apologise for the haste. Will you allow me to beg your leave? I'm afraid I don't have time to waste."

"A pleasure, Senor. Your carriage awaits."

"But —" I piped in. My voice was thin and shaky. "Please. I have not packed my things."

Maestra Tinir fixed me with her hardest glare, but Senor Grath said, "They will be sent."

"Of course," Tinir said with a smile. "Please, this way." She motioned towards the stairs, and together, we followed the man. The main staircase swept from the central chamber down to the entrance hall leading into the Rose Room, like the stem of the flower that gave it its name, well-planned to show the vastness of the building, as one descended past a myriad of open galleries and appreciated the distance of the ceiling many, many spans overhead, before at last landing on the tiled floor amid the sculptures, and paintings, and carvings. I had rarely had occasion to use it until this, my final farewell.

Maestra Tinir had deliberately chosen this route, probably suspecting she might entice Senor Grath to return and petition. It would be a hard man who was left unimpressed by the beauty of the Pavilion and what it offered within. And it seemed every Daughter, not otherwise occupied, had found occasion to be passing, waiting at the balustrades, or crossing through the atrium: Firelli, wearing red and orange and walking with Carla; Vahn, her pale skin as white as la Grulla herself; Sharquen, with her dazzling eyes; dark-skinned Rehina, who had somehow convinced quiet, staid Yui to join her for an unplanned, innocent stroll. They were dressed in their finest silks, their hair pinned in intricate, delicate styles, and they were all looking at Grath, and whispering behind their hands. But whether Grath was impressed or not, he gave no clue, descending at an even pace, as if he had no thought other than reaching the door and completing this business.

He certainly gave no glance back towards me, who felt every step I took as a step closer to my doom.

Chapter Five

It had begun to rain.

It was a steady rain, cool and clean, drifting down in slanted ribbons from the Pendulum high above. It made the wide Calle gleam.

Waiting for us at the bottom of the wide steps was an autocarriage.

I had never seen one up close, and though I was intrigued, when I realised that this was to be our conveyance, my curiosity turned very quickly to wariness. It looked harmless enough – just like a small rotor-tram, though it did not run on tracks. The paint was a deep black, and the roof made of leather, so the interior could be opened to the air. The windows were glass, tinted so dark I couldn't see in from the outside, and the wheels were thick, made of rubber, and their spokes were shining chrome.

The strange acrid smell of oil fumes filled my nostrils as we reached street level. I was only wearing thin slippers, and my toes curled against the dampness. A large man had been waiting by the open rear door of the conveyance, and he stepped up to offer his hand, taking my weight from Maestra Tinir's shoulders as easily as if he had just picked up a piece of paper. Beneath his black suit, he must have been very strong, and his bulk was a welcome shelter from the rain.

Senor Grath ducked his head as he slid gracefully into the car. The man who carried me placed me gently in after him, folding my legs like a child's.

The black leather of the seat felt cold through my thin shift. Senor Grath did not look at me, and the big man shut the door behind me. Instinctively, I reached for the handle. There was none.

My stomach twinged.

In the front of the car were two seats, one of them occupied by a second man who wore a hat. I couldn't see much in the dull light, only his silhouette against the rain-streaked window.

The big man who had carried me walked around to the front of the car and opened the second door, sliding into the seat beside the driver.

Senor Grath tapped a finger on his knee. His sleeve slid up, revealing an expensive-looking wristwatch, with several ticking dials made of crystal. "All haste, please, Feval." He sighed. "I've wasted enough time this night."

Feval moved. There was something strange in the motion – a jerkiness, and as his hand passed through a beam of reflected light, it shone silver. It struck me then that he wasn't a man at all, but an automaton. He fiddled with one of the controls on the panel before him, and the motor started; it sounded like a cough, then a roar, and the whole thing vibrated with the power of that mechanised magic underneath the hood. My hands tightened on the leather seat, trying to find a grip, some kind of assurance.

Feval must have put his foot down – should I be thinking of it as a he? After all, automata are not quite the same as servitors – for the car slid forward. The wheels hissed on the wet pavement. A rubber blade flicked back and forth across the windshield, clearing the raindrops in a perfect arch. I felt myself driven back in my seat, but, surprisingly, the motorcar felt comfortable, as if travelling at speed was precisely what it was meant to do, and it gloried in achieving its purpose.

I leaned my head back and tried to breathe evenly.

Senor Grath was shifting in his seat. His whole being seemed to radiate agitation, as if he wanted to be anywhere else in the Tierra Mejór apart from here.

Anywhere than with me.

I turned my head to watch the Calle de Corazón slide past as the rain smeared the globe-lights. Though the glass has seemed dark from the outside, from within, it was clear. I could see patrons gathered under the awnings of night-cafés and taverns marvelling at the passing autocarriage. They must have known it belonged to the Citadel. Did they try to make out who was inside? Did any of them imagine it was me?

I touched the glass, leaving behind misty imprints of my fingers.

Since arriving at the White Pavilion, I had never once wished my life was anything other than what it was. I had fulfilled my dream. But now, looking at those people going about their ordinary business, my stomach twisted painfully.

"What do you know about the Principe Regente?"

Pulled back to my immediate surrounds, I turned to Senor Grath. His eyes were fixed on me, unblinking. How long had he been watching me?

"Should I repeat the question?" he asked impatiently. Reaching into a pocket of his jacket, he withdrew a box of matches and a slim packet of cigarillos, and tapped one of each into his hands. He placed the thin white stick between his lips and with a practiced gesture, lit it with a match. The tip of it glowed bright orange, like a miniature star in the darkness.

"I – I – no, Senor. I simply . . . I'm not sure. I know what everyone knows, I suppose."

"And that is?" He raised an eyebrow, taking a deep draw from the cigarillo. The smoke curled around his face. It smelled rich and earthy, unlike any smoke I'd smelled before.

"He is fair-haired," I said. "He gave a speech at the Cámara de Justice, when he was," I tried to calculate his age, "twelve years old. He had come from the Estate, out on the Wheel, for his official recognition as La Reina's son. From that day on, he has resided in the Citadel, to learn the governance of Tierra Mejór, and the business of the Conclave, while he awaits the time he will be officially named as her heir. He will then take over the throne in an official capacity, and be named Principe Verderaro, in preparation to becoming el Rey, the King . . ."

Senor Grath yanked the cigarillo from his mouth. "I did not ask for a civics lesson," he snapped.

Stunned into silence, I felt tears prickle my eyes. How was I supposed to answer his question? I sat for a moment, dumfounded, as the car slid onwards through the night. Finally, the Senor sighed.

"He is a . . . troubled man," he said in a tone much quieter than I'd heard him use so far. "He doesn't go out in public often, and when he does, it's only for the sake of his duty. He is . . . whimsical."

Whimsical. What did Grath mean? "Why are you telling me this?"

"Because," Senor Grath tapped his cigarillo so that the ash fell to the floor, "you are one of his whimsies. If you follow the rules and humour him, you will soon be forgotten. Do not expect anything more; you are simply a plaything, a new toy. It won't last."

The knot in my stomach twisted. A plaything, a toy. There was a small part of me that was not surprised. There were many who thought the Daughters of the Pavilion nothing more than overpaid prostitutes. We usually laughed about it in our rooms; we knew the truth, and that was all that mattered.

But here, hearing it from this man, I didn't think this was what he meant. The way he said it made it sound as if the Prince was a greedy child. That he had seen some glittering toy, and it had caught his attention, and now he wished simply to own it for the sake of owning it. He had meant to degrade me, to shame me, and he had also meant it as a warning. *Don't imagine you're anyone special; don't cause any trouble for me.* But Senor Grath did not know he had given me a valuable gift with this information, one I grasped firmly with barely-disguised hope and tentative delight. When the Prince had no more need of me, surely, he would send me back to the Pavilion. He would send me home.

***

Having informed me that I was inconsequential – to him, to the Prince, and to the world –Senor Grath finished his cigarillo in silence. The regular swishing of the wiper blades and the hiss of the tires and the throbbing of the engine filled my ears, but I didn't have time to relax.

We passed along the Calle, pausing only once to wait for a lock gate to switch into place. The Pavilion is but one Tier lower than the Citadel, meaning that once every twenty minutes, the two halves of the street align. Some gates are larger than others, for the passage of autocarriages, servitors, or rotor-trams. Many of these on the First Tier are guarded by vigilar, to ensure those passing through have legitimate business, but there are smaller, pedestrian gates, often hidden in back streets and forgotten. Lower Tiers locked only once every six hours or so; here, the wait was barely a minute.

All too soon, the Citadel loomed up ahead.

If the White Pavilion was the realm of the night, the Citadel was a house of daylight. Its walls were built of yellow stone, turned golden with the reflected lights of the city. The tall towers reached into the heavens, la Reloj de pie the highest of all. The last time I'd seen it, I'd been dancing in the Plaza de Lágrima. I closed my eyes as we passed the space, unable to bear seeing the open square lined with cobblestones, and the fountain in the centre, carved as la Oráculo kneeling in his cloak, as tears washed down his cheeks endlessly, spilling into the glittering basin below. The Place of Tears. How fitting a name!

Once we had rounded the fountain, all I could see was the Citadel. The gates were thick iron bars topped with spikes. As the car approached, two vigilar came forth, very official in their guard uniforms: black tunic with black breeches, black boots, and steely looks in their eyes.

At their belts were the bulky shapes of revolver-pistols.

Feval rolled down his window with the same jerky motion. I saw, just before he turned his head, that he had only one, blinking eye.

"Ah!" said one of the vigilar. "Feval, my friend! Back on chauffeur duty?"

From Feval's mouth came a grating and clicking noise. The bulky man in the passenger seat leaned across him. "Feval's the best for the job," he said briskly. "Though his voice-box needs repairing. Just let us through, would you?"

The guards peered into the car through the windows on both sides. One of them asked something, motioning towards me, and Senor Grath pushed himself forward. "Ask the Prince if he'd like to be kept waiting," he growled impatiently, and this seemed to do the trick; the guards stepped back and one of them pulled a lever that made the heavy gates swing open soundlessly.

We passed through the arch into a tunnel that went the entire length of the wall, which was much thicker than it looked from the outside; a hundred paces, at least. Then, finally, we emerged into an open courtyard, paved with stone. A huge circular garden filled with exotic, if rain-sodden, plants took up the centre, and the car rounded this to stop in front of the steps.

I was inside the Citadel.

Chapter Six

After this, it was a blur; I was lifted from the car by the same man who had placed me in it. He carried me easily, and quickly, up the stairs and through the door. Though the entrance was cavernous, and beautifully ornate, I would come to learn this was only one of many ways in, and each was constructed for different purposes or occasions. This was one customarily used for those who came to the Citadel on business.

I let myself rest in the guardsman's arms. Despite the situation, I felt very safe while he held me, and wondered: had my father ever carried me this way? With such effortless care? He smelled surprisingly pleasant, which cut through the stale tang of Senor Grath's cigarillo smoke in my throat.

We followed a winding path, up and down several sets of shallow steps, around corners, past many rooms whose uses I couldn't guess, and finally on a short trip in a velour-lined lift-car that was faster and smoother than any I'd ever experienced. There was even a chair in the corner of the cabin, and mirrors fastened to the backs of the doors; my wan reflection stared back at me over the guardsman's shoulder.

"Can you stand?" the man's soft voice startled me.

"Yes," I said, though I wasn't convinced of this myself. My legs swayed under me as he sat me on the floor, but his steady hands held my shoulders, and under his guidance I managed to brace myself against the wall as we slid downwards.

Senor Grath looked at the ornate globe fitting on the ceiling rather than me. When we drew to a stop, he motioned me impatiently ahead into a large receiving room, decorated opulently with red velvet drapes, gold hangings, sofas piled high with cushions, and, on the marble floor, a rug woven with the most intricate design. The walls were lined with bookshelves and the windows stretched up to meet the ceiling.

Along the walls were several men, dressed in the black uniform of the vigilar. They all carried revolver-pistols at their belts.

At the far end, where a fire burned brightly in a hearth, was a large leather armchair.

It was here that he sat.

***

I kneeled on the polished marble floor before his chair, my head lowered and hands clasped. Grath hovered over me like a scowling cloud.

"Tell me why you fell."

My gaze flicked up to him, alight with the instant spark of fear as I recalled what I had done.

"Well?" he demanded, annoyed and disappointed.

"My Prince," I breathed. "Please, I did not mean to . . ."

"I didn't ask for an excuse, I asked for a reason."

"I – I –" But what was I to tell him?

"Did you injure your tongue as well?" the Prince sighed.

"I didn't trip on purpose!" the words burst out of me. I was instantly aghast. The Prince raised his eyebrows in surprise, an odd wash of delight sweeping through him. Mistaking his gaze for a rebuke, I stuttered, "I mean, my Prince, it was an accident, and I . . ."

"What is your name?"

I hunched lower, hoping the floor would take me into itself and let me fade away.

"This is Imre," said Senor Grath, speaking for the first time since we'd entered the room.

The Prince considered this. "How many years have you been dancing, Daughter Imre?"

"Since my first memory, my Prince. I was accepted into the Pavilion when I turned thirteen."

"And the *Dance of a Thousand Steps*? It was your first time?"

"My third."

His eyebrows arched. "And you were chosen as the Crane?"

"Yes, my Prince."

This seemed important to him, and I wondered how it could possibly have significance to anyone other than me. The Dance was my life. I'd put everything I was into cultivating its perfection, every effort I could possibly exert into that one allowance of glory. And I had failed. There would never be another chance for me to dance the *Dance of a Thousand Steps*.

"There are Twelve Dances," the Prince went on.

I nodded, reciting by heart. "The Dance of Birth, Death, Warm-season, Cold-season, Harvest, New Growth, Metal, Rock, Earth, Air, the Thousand Steps, and Love."

"Love," repeated the Principe Regente.

"We perform that one least often." My voice dropped, involuntarily, to a whisper.

"Why are you crying?"

His voice startled me. "I am not, my Prince," I returned, and knew he would see it instantly for the lie it was, since my cheeks were wet.

I ducked my head and pressed my forehead to the floor. The cold stone was blessed relief on my heated skin, the solid floor my only anchor against the whirling torrent of fear in my veins.

"You fascinate me."

I looked up and found myself impaled by his gaze. And I saw him then, as I had seen him only once before; but he was no longer a small boy of twelve, viewed through my thirteen-year-old eyes. His long brown-blond hair bound loosely at the nape of his neck, the strong line of his jaw, the intensity of his eyes. In that moment, it wasn't impossible that he could see my thoughts flickering inside my head. I couldn't do anything except stare back at him.

"Grath!" he snapped abruptly. "Take her away. I've grown tired; I think I will go to bed."

"My Liege." Senor Grath bowed. "Where shall I put her?"

Please, by the Pattern, I begged silently. *Please tell him to take me home.*

"With the other women in the Den," the Prince said. "Let them take care of her for now."

"She will need to be tended, my Liege," spoke another voice, and though I couldn't see him, I recognised the rumbling of the large guardsman who had carried me. "Her ankle. She is injured."

"Ah, well," the Prince said. "Send Oren in first thing tomorrow. Since you are so concerned, *guardia*, I suppose you might watch over her until then. Take over *sentinela* duty at the Oak Door."

And so it was that I was lifted to my feet by Senor Grath and led, with somewhat greater gentleness than I had expected from him, out of the reception chamber.

***

What was I expecting? I cannot say. But the Den, the women's quarters, was a world unto itself.

I was led by the silent Grath. I couldn't look at him, for I felt in my very bones how he despised me, and did not know why. The big man trailed behind, his gaze on my shoulders. I could tell he was worried I would fall, but I was determined I wouldn't give Grath the pleasure.

"Is the Prince always so . . ." I spoke in a quiet voice, not sure I should even be asking this question.

The man answered me in a similarly low voice. "Best not ask such questions, my Lady. The Prince is what he is, whether it's by his own doing or not." I tried to work out what he meant. Something in the Prince's gaze had been off, hadn't it? As if he wasn't truly present in the room. I wondered if he were drunk.

I was soon lost in the maze of corridors and passages. We came to a stairway that moved, the steps juddering downwards next to a handrail made of a great belt threaded alongside on wheels; we crossed a bridge that soared between two towers, while a cold wind blasted up from below; we passed through three clockwork doors requiring keys to open, which Senor Grath had on a ring hanging from his belt. I stumbled with exhaustion, my poor wounded ankle protesting painfully, before finally, we arrived at our destination.

It was a door carved with intertwining oak trees. This was guarded by a bronze sentinela. It looked slightly the worse for wear, with two large dents in its abdomen, and gave a rusty squeak when it lifted its arm to tap the butt of a long spear against the floor.

"Two-seven-oh-six," the big man said quietly. "Dismissed. Return to the Racks."

The sentinel bought the spear to its chest with a clang, then marched away with a sound like a tin can blown along an empty road by an errant breeze.

"You will be here until morning, *Sargento* Miguel," said Grath. "I'll have the Generalo arrange a replacement for you during the dawn hours."

The big man nodded and took up the vacant post, crossing his arms over his chest. It was only then that I noticed he was dressed in a grey shirt and black trousers, and on his shoulder glinted the golden wings of the guardia. A heavy metal-link belt circled his wide girth. From this hung a revolver-pistol in a leather sheath, the sight of which filled me with apprehension. Given my past, weapons were something I always viewed with cold fear.

"Very well, Senor," Miguel rumbled.

Senor Grath pushed open one-half of the great door and beyond this, sprawled a dark room. It was like stepping into a hole. Moments passed before I could make out the forms of furniture. Long, low couches had been dragged haphazardly about, causing the elegant rugs to buckle.

The air was thick with incense smoke, the scent overpowering as it mingled with a plethora of flowery perfumes.

There were women here – a dozen or so, dressed in long flowing dresses that were loose enough to reveal glimpses of thighs, arms, breasts. Some lay on the couches, others sat on the floor. Two had fallen asleep in one another's arms. Others fanned themselves with feathered fans.

They looked up at me with blank eyes, not so much curious as hostile; like drain-rats, sizing up an intruder and evaluating whether the newcomer would take a place as an underling.

"Well, well," said a woman who sat on a nearby sofa. She was tall and thin, perhaps ten years my elder, with jet-black hair hanging loose over her shoulders. She had a cigarillo in one elegant hand. "What have you bought us, Grath?"

Grath let go of my arm. "This is Daughter Imre. You're to care for her at the Principe's request."

"This is the falling dancer?"

Evidently, my arrival had been expected; perhaps that was why they were all out of their beds at this late hour. There was a tinkling of laughter. I tried to meet the woman's hard gaze with a friendly smile, but my lips trembled.

Senor Grath did not answer. He bowed, turned, and closed the door. Though it was unlocked, I felt as if my last escape was cut off; with the burly Miguel on the other side, I surely could never escape.

Not knowing what was expected of me, I curtseyed as best I could. My ankle ached.

The woman raised an eyebrow and turned to her companion, standing just behind her sofa. This one was petite, a slip of a girl in a long silver dress that contrasted strikingly with her long sable tresses and dusky skin. She was incredibly pretty but for her downturned mouth.

"Such manners they teach them in the Pavilion!" said she.

"Indeed," drawled the first, tapping her fingers on the back of the sofa. Her dress rippled as she moved, and I saw it was covered with tiny scales. "Can she twirl a baton, or swing on a trapeze like a circus monkey, too? Dance for us, girl," ordered the woman with a cruel grin. "I'm so bored. Entertain me."

I bowed my head, mostly to hide my burning cheeks. If I could run . . . But the heavy door had shut behind me. There was no retreat.

"I –"

"Hush, Jardine," another voice cut in, this one sounding close to my age. As was the speaker, sitting at a table in one corner, a book in hand. She motioned with it towards my ankle, pointing out the bandage. "Obviously, she's injured."

Jardine's wicked smile did not shift, but my rescuer abandoned her book on the table and stood. She was quite plain compared to the others, with her simple purple dress, modestly cut, and no jewellery to speak of. "You'll need to know where the bathrooms are," she said. "This way."

Seizing on this unexpected kindness, I followed her through the couches and cushions, trying desperately not to limp; every eye scrutinised my contortions.

This room was an entrance chamber or common room, beyond which was a cluster of smaller rooms in no particular order. Through these we travelled. In one, a running fountain burbled, the ceiling open to the sky. Two girls sat on the stone edge of the pool, in the half-light of a globe-lantern, heads bowed, whispering furiously, while raindrops splashed into the water behind them.

They paused in their conversation to look at me.

My guide ignored them.

A dark, shadowed room beyond, lit with coloured globe-lanterns, proved to be the bathroom. A sunken bath, like a pool, was set into the centre.

"You'll find clean towels on the shelves," my escort said. "The servants will replace them."

I nodded. "Thank you."

"Thanks are not necessary," she returned shortly, spinning on her toes and leaving me to my devices.

There was no door to the room. Even as I stood there, two of the women I'd seen in the common room arrived and stripped. Though they didn't look my way, I was sure they'd only chosen this hour for a bath because I was here.

"Such a shame, they all said." One of them laughed, loudly. "But honestly, did anyone truly expect they would be allowed to continue their disruptions? Trade is being delayed, and other services are suffering. It was time for something drastic."

"Of course. But the way that woman carried on," said her companion. "You would think it was her own son."

"I suppose he must have a mother, somewhere?"

"If so, she will never be able to claim the body."

They were paying no attention to me, so I removed my gown and bathed carefully, washing as best I could with limited mobility, and trying to keep my bandaged ankle out of the water. I rinsed out my hair and dried myself on the soft towels, then dressed again.

All the while, the two women chattered on about the execution of the Green-band. I paid scant attention – the man had practically invited trouble, the way he'd shouted like that, and there was no point in speculating further. I'd heard stories about what happened to those who spoke carelessly about la Rebelde and his followers in public. I had no desire to join their hypothesising.

Then, at a loss, I wandered back through the maze of rooms. I would soon learn that there were no locks on any of these doors, but that some belonged to certain women, and should never be entered without their permission, whereas others were designated as common areas. Finding the room with the open ceiling, empty now of its previous occupants, I sat on stone lip of the fountain.

This place was beautiful. A shrub grew in every corner, and a gentle night breeze blew through the cross-shaped hole in the ceiling. The sky was dark as black velvet, and when I tilted my head back, cold rain touched my face. I let myself be at peace.

***

Peace did not last long in the Den.

"You got any cigarillos, sugar?"

I had dozed, sitting upright. And now blinked. Light was beginning to fall through the ceiling. I had slept through the dawn regimen.

I opened my eyes to see the petite girl with the dark skin. She sat next to me on the edge of the fountain.

"I'm sorry." I shook my head.

She pouted and flicked her loose black locks over one shoulder. "You don't smoke?"

I tried to gauge her tone. Was she being friendly? Sarcastic? I resolved to keep quiet for now.

She heaved a sigh. "I suppose you're far too grand for that sort of thing, coming from the Pavilion. Look at that fine skin. Your pearly teeth."

"But my hair is no match for yours," I told her truthfully.

She preened and I knew I'd said the right thing. I counted it as one small victory for the night.

"Imre." She leaned in close enough for me to smell her perfume. "I must warn you. Being in the Den is like swimming in waters infested with creeper-fish." She looked around pointedly; whoever might be listening didn't stay her words. "They're hungry for blood, and they can smell fear. And, sugar, you smell like a beautiful, exotic dinner."

I wondered whether she was teasing me, but the predatory glances of the women in the common room hadn't been imagined.

"I don't know what to do," I said, helplessly.

She smiled, then stood, moving towards the door. "Oh, that's easy enough. You stick with me. I'll see that you're cared for."

"Thank you." I didn't have to fake my gratitude, which she accepted willingly as she stood. "But wait –" I called after her. "Your name. I don't know it."

"Bethery," she said over her shoulder. "Find me later, sugar. I'll be waiting for you."

Chapter Seven

As la Grulla rose, chasing away the wispy remnants of the clouds left over from last night's rain, the women drifted into the common room, yawning and stretching languorously.

I followed, keeping my hobble as quiet as I could, and took a space in the shadows. Presently the Oak Door opened, and as well as offering a glimpse of Miguel, still standing just as I'd last seen him, admitted two large, whirring servitors carrying food trays. They clicked their way into the middle of the room and sat idle.

My stomach gave an embarrassing rumble, drawing more attention to me than I would have liked. It was clear, however, that no one could help themselves as they chose. There was a hierarchy to be followed, and I was on the lowest tier.

I was used to holding my own among the women of the Pavilion. Rehina would often try to get away with stealing my affects, or tripping me in a rehearsal, or cutting in on a potential assignation when we were entertaining the mecenas in the Room of Roses. Vahn had a sharp tongue, and wouldn't hesitate to haul any of us over her viciously barbed words if we crossed her. Even Yui was fiercely competitive in her own quiet way. But the animosity permeating the Den was of an altogether different nature.

The trays were picked over first by Jardine, who arrived late, with two younger girls trailing like sentinela in her wake. It seemed she was the queen here in all but name; no one moved until she had sampled the tastiest dishes, sometimes picking things up with her fingers, and returning half-eaten morsels to the plates. When she had eaten her fill, she snapped her fingers and several other women moved in.

There was a lot of jostling and bickering among them. When they were finished, there was not much left at all, and what there was looked unappetising. The remaining few came forward. They were the shortest, the least glamorous, and the youngest; I was shocked to realise three were children, two girls and a boy. The girls looked to be perhaps five and ten, and the boy no more than three. I couldn't tell whom they belonged to, if anyone; in any case, they seemed to know their place, and took the remaining bowls to one corner, where they shared their spoils without complaint.

The plain girl who had showed me to the bathroom last night was also among these last, but I suspected it was by choice on her part. Perhaps she simply wasn't hungry, for she took only a few biscuits and retreated to her table and her book. Despite my earlier hunger, my appetite matched hers by this stage, as the knot in my stomach grew tight again.

I did not see Bethery at all.

***

I did not go looking for her, as she'd bade me to. I had been restlessly seeking a way out into the gardens, or at least a balcony or open window. I found none. The rooms were winding and dark, the windows deliberately covered by thick drapes or tapestries, and thick with smoke. It wasn't just cigarillo smoke, either, but a thicker, syrupy kind that smelled so sweet, it made me lightheaded. Maestra Tinir had always warned us about the dangers of white-smoke, and how some Daughters, tempted by over-indulgent mecenas, had lost their way to it, ending up in the Red Houses, but I hardly needed the lecture. I knew the evil effects firsthand and had no desire to breathe it.

Bethery appeared from nowhere. I would come to learn this was a habit of hers. She caught my elbow and laughed when I jumped.

"Sugar, you're too much," she said. "Little sweet thing! Just like a mouse!"

I smiled to humour her.

"Come this way." She tugged me along behind her down an arched hallway and into a suite. Here were three beds of varying sizes, one just a mattress on the floor. The bedclothes were silk and fine cotton, but they were rumpled and scattered as if they'd been swept about by a storm. Pillows lay strewn around here and there, some stained with food or drink. The ash trays overflowed with cigarillo ash, and more ash littered the chest of drawers and various vases, ewers, and globe-light holders. Like all the others, this room was dark, but there was one window set high in the wall, a single pitiful star shining through it.

Bethery towed me over to the largest of the beds. She sat on it and patted the sheets beside her. I took the offered seat with trepidation.

"I want you to tell me about life in your Pavilion," she said sweetly.

"What would you like to know?" I asked her.

She sighed. "Tell me what you do with your mecenas."

"Well," I hedged. "That depends on what is asked."

Bethery sighed again. She leaned back on her elbows, her breasts straining at her dress as she looked up at me from under her long lashes. "Well, then," she said. "Pretend I am one."

"I'm sorry?" I wasn't sure I'd heard her properly.

"Pretend I'm your patron. Enter the room and pretend I have offered you a price of . . . shall we say . . . seven hundred coins. Hm?"

I laughed, and she smiled indulgently, then motioned that I should stand. I did so, feeling a little unsure. But evidently this was what she wanted, and perhaps, if I just played along, she would soon give up this game.

I moved to the door, acting as if I had just come through it. I lowered my eyes to the floor as was proper. With my half-veil on, it meant only my hair and forehead were visible, my metrónomo showing to full advantage. *I am a Daughter,* was the meaning behind this. *First and foremost, I serve the Pattern.*

I crossed the room in seven steps. Every room in the Pavilion was marked with seven symbols on the floor, so a Daughter could time her paces accordingly, but now I had to step over strewn clothes and some empty tins of power and kohl, all under the watchful gaze of Bethery.

When I reached her, I kneeled on the floor, my head still bowed. "In the name of the Pattern, I offer my body. For Aurelia's glory, I will dance. What is your will?"

"My will?" Bethery said. "I get to choose?"

"Yes. The mecenas chooses the dance."

"Very well. I choose not to choose. Imre, I choose your choice."

I looked up at her then. I couldn't help myself. Why was she doing this? Certainly, she wasn't honouring Aurelia; this wasn't the way of the Pattern.

"Come on," whispered Bethery. Her lips glistened in the dull light, and something stirred inside me – a longing to kiss them, to feel their softness under my own.

I stood, holding my ankle carefully. Then I began to dance.

It has always been easy for me to dance to the glory of Aurelia. Her song flows through me, and the steps I have learned come easily. I turned, stepped, lifted my arms, and turned again. I danced the Dance of Harvest for Bethery – the fading warmth of Tierra Mejór, the slow lengthening of the nights as la Grulla waned towards the cold-season. I danced for the slow ticking of the cooling metal plates far beneath the ground and the gradual changing of the light as the stars, night by night, adjusted their position. I danced as the Pattern told its children to prepare for longer nights and shorter days as each turning stretched into a new phase; a time to rest and gather strength, and wait for the warm-season, and the time of business and growth.

With every turn I made, I faced Bethery. That languid smile on her beautiful lips did not falter until, in making a step, I put too much weight on my ankle. It twisted, and I overbalanced with a cry of pain. At once, Bethery caught me.

She was strong, but not strong enough to hold my weight. We fell, together, onto the bed, with her atop me. I caught another strong whiff of her perfume. Her jet hair trailed messily across my face, igniting a bright fire in me. It kindled in my stomach, at the heart of that knot, and spread outwards through my blood. She kissed me, then, and again, and again, and her kisses were exquisite.

I had kissed my sisters. As practice, as an experiment, to learn the ways of the Dance. But none of them had made me burn this way.

When Bethery's kisses hardened, I pushed back. I wrapped my hands in her hair to pull her closer; I wanted her with such passion, it hurt.

She reached down and tore my dress from me. I didn't care; I just wanted my skin next to hers, and when she stood back to remove her own gown, I saw that her body was as beautiful as her face. Her breasts were high and firm, larger than mine, and so smooth. As she returned to the bed and straddled me, I cupped them in my hands. She pushed my hands aside, then pinned my wrists to the bed, leaning over me so that her dark nipples danced over my chest. She kissed my neck, working her way across the curve of my collarbone, then down my sternum, across my belly, and finally reaching my centre.

It had been so long since I had been touched there that it was a shock. I squirmed away, but she held me fast by my wrists as her tongue went to work. Again, it was like what I had done with Ketra, with Vahn, with Rehina, but so vastly different; it was a burning need, a desire so deep, I wasn't sure how my body could contain it. In the end, it could not. I climaxed, again and again, in crashing waves, until I felt everything had been drained from me, and I lay insensate.

Bethery crawled back up my body and lay atop me for long minutes.

"Well, sugar," she said at last. "It seems we've both Danced tonight."

***

Had I but known it then, as I lay there beside the woman who, I suppose, was now my lover, that in a basement beneath a building I had once known well, on a lower Tier, in an area I hoped never to see again, a meeting was taking place.

They were men and women both, and they came from a myriad places, Tiers, guilds, and fortunes. They all wore hats, and around the hats were green ribbons.

They paused at the entrance to this basement; a door in a nondescript wall, partly overgrown with vine-weed, and said the password. "Catastrophe."

One by one, they went down the long stairs and into a dimly lit room. The smell of damp was powerful, but not so sharp as the scent of danger.

"Alen," they greeted one another.

"Jornel."

"Davique."

"Nathuin."

"Greida."

And so forth: there were twenty-six, in all, and, long-practiced at this, they took their seats on benches and leaned against the wall, turning their gaze to the front, where a youth with a scarred lip stood.

"Greetings," said he. "What news?"

"A spillage of oil," said one man. "In the leather factory. It ran into the waste drains. It will need to be pumped out before it is lost, but I cannot find a pump in working order. It might already be alight, burning in the sump, and causing untold damage to the sewers."

"Another a cut in wages, this time to a pen maker's apprentices on the Third Tier. The master says he can't afford to do otherwise. It may be so," another man said dubiously. "For I suspect his own allowance was cut."

"A man has killed his wife," said yet another. "His mind was gone. He was shot by the vigilar. The neighbours were dreadfully shaken."

"More instances of this illness," a woman spoke up. "An acquaintance of mine was found dead in the street last night, his skin blanched, and something bulging from his mouth. The body was sprayed with oil and burned, but people refuse to walk over the spot where he lay, lest they catch this sickness."

To all of this, the youth listened. Finally, he held up his hand. "We know what we must do. Spread the word. Create a fuss. Cause a ruckus. Don't be afraid. Fear is the only enemy greater than the dark figures of authority."

One of them spoke, then, a woman who looked older than her years.

"My son," she said woodenly.

The youth bowed his head – so did they all.

"Your son," repeated the youth. "Greida, your son spoke something very true, if they chose to shoot him rather than let him be heard."

Here he looked up, fixing all those who met his gaze with a look hard as steel. "We must honour his memory and continue our fight. Seek the truth. Spread the word. We will not be silenced."

The men and woman nodded to one another, shook hands, their eyes bright, and drifted away into the night.

Chapter Eight

This was how it was to be.

I belonged to Bethery, from that first evening forwards. I slept in her bed that night, and I discovered what it was like to be reviled, for there were three other girls in that room and they all had prior claim to Bethery's affections. When they drifted in, they fixed me with hateful glares, as if I had deliberately supplanted them.

Bethery saw to it that I was among the first to feed at mealtimes, after Jardine had taken her pick; she would collect a plate and fill it with food – a vegetable stew, usually, or a soup with floating chunks of moth-meat, with a few slices of unbuttered bread – bringing it to me as I sat meekly to one side. At times, she even fed me herself, holding out small bites and allowing me to take them from her fingers. She delighted when I wrapped my lips around her fingertips.

It was a double-edged blade. For Bethery's favouritism bought me enemies as surely as it bought me her protection, and soon I knew how much I needed that shield. As dangerous as men can be, women are a thousand times more cunning and ruthless.

At first it was small things. A sharp pin in the bodice of my dress that pricked me when I pulled it on in the morning. Light shoves when I passed the others in the hallways. An accidental kick of the foot that sent my towel into the water while I bathed.

Before you think that it was my only choice, let me assure you, I could have done otherwise. Certainly, it was clear that there were other women as strong or stronger. I was approached more than once by these others – a thin woman named Audren, and a plump, dark-haired one called Misthra. But even they seemed reluctant to press the issue once I'd made it clear I wasn't interested.

For none of the other women had a window in their room.

So, I chose to show my loyalty to Bethery. For at least with her, I knew what to expect, and knew that it would bring me favour. While I did not try to make friends with Bethery's other girls, I did complement Xith on her shawl, and I poured Harette a drink, and even offered to brush Minich's hair. Each time my attempts were met with frosty glares. They stuck together, these women; though competition among them was fierce, they were united against me, the intruder.

True to his word, Miguel arranged for a healer to see me. He was the only man I ever saw enter the Den. He was tall and thin, with a lined face and serious eyes. Like Senor Grath, his hair was silver, but he wore small round glasses that glittered in the globe-light.

Bethery led him into our room.

He approached the bed, and placed a small black case on the floor. Kneeling, he retrieved a long tube with a silver disc attached to the end. He reached for the coverlet, which I'd pulled up to my chin, and I jerked back. He huffed an impatient sigh.

"I'm a healer, child. My name is Oren. You need not worry about decency; I've seen everything you've got under there a thousand times."

From the doorway, Bethery sniggered. "Now, now, sugar! You choose this moment to be a prude?"

I blushed.

"I need to check your heartbeat," Oren went on. "Will you allow me to do that?"

There was an element of sarcasm in his deference, but still I suspected that if I refused, he would have assented to my wishes and left me alone. No doubt he had a dozen other calls to make that afternoon.

Slowly, warily, I nodded. He pulled the coverlet down just a little. Despite my shift, which was one of Bethery's, I felt terribly naked under his piercing eyes. He placed the disc against my collarbone, then slid it down under my shift to my left breast. It was cold, and my nipples tightened; I wondered if he cared, as they were clearly visible through the thin white fabric of the ill-fitting garment. Oren's gaze might appear clinical, but one thing I had learned as a Daughter of the Pavilion; that all men had appetites, no matter their profession.

He removed the stethoscope, frowning. "Is – is something wrong?" I asked.

"Hm?" he turned his head, as if he'd forgotten I was in the room. "Oh. Not at all." He bent to place the device back in his bag. "Strong heart."

He propped my ankle up on a pillow, then, and poked and prodded it, asking if I could feel anything. I nodded, and he twisted it back and forth.

Finally, he unwrapped it, cleaned away the congealed balm the healer had rubbed over it at the Pavilion, then rewrapped it with deft fingers.

"You need to walk," he pronounced. At my incredulous expression, he snorted through his nostrils. "The bone and surrounding muscles will never heal strongly if you lie around or make only short ventures. You need to walk."

"But . . . it hurts."

Oran levelled his gaze at me, his glasses shining. "You have a metrónomo."

I raised a hand to my temple, tracing the fine pattern down to the corner of my eye.

"Did it cause you pain?"

I remembered the feeling of the heavy bronze cup in my hands. The strong, bitter scent of the espiritu. The heat as I took my first sip. The hard, stone floor of the Temple against my thin body, the coldness as all my warmth was leached from me. Dizziness as the espiritu began to take effect, and fear as Maestra Tinir and the *tecnico* leaned over me, a blade in his hands, and then – something beyond pain lancing through my head. Something beyond numbness, something close to pleasure. Beyond, certainly, any type of human feeling.

And how could it not be? For how often do we look into the heart of the Pattern?

When I woke, the metrónomo was there, ticking just below my skin, and it was just as perfect as I had imagined it to be.

Oren nodded. "Sometimes the pain is worth the end result. Do not ignore it, but do not let it deter you from movement. If you wish to dance again, you must keep the muscles strong."

I nodded, chastened. "It would help," I said, "if I were allowed out of these rooms."

Oren raised his eyebrows. His glasses glinted. "I will see what can be done." Then, he packed up his bag and left me.

"Oh, sugar." Bethery crossed the room and climbed onto the bed, one knee on either side of my hips. Her hair tickled my forehead. "You look so darling, lying there, injured and helpless. Shall I help relieve your pain?"

And she did.

***

I took Oren's words to heart. Back and forth across Bethery's room I walked, with my halting gait. It made me feel like a fat old woman, breathless and worn-out, but I refused to stop. My fear of my muscles wasting kept me at it. I had discovered a new passion for pushing past the pain, into that blank white space where I could abandon thought.

It reminded me of dancing.

But when I lay down, my heart racing and my ankle throbbing, oh, everything came back. And here I wallowed in my worries.

If I couldn't dance, what would I do? If Maestra Tinir would not take me back into the Pavilion, would I be left here, forever? Around and around my head these unwelcome thoughts chased one another, and I realised that I had never considered this before: that I was nothing but a dancer. I was nothing.

Chapter Nine

My constant pacing annoyed the girls. Harette, who had tripped me several times, finally threw a globe-lantern at me. It struck my elbow before falling heavily to the floor, cracking one side. "For the sake of the Pattern, Imre! You'll drive us all mad."

It was possibly the least vindictive thing she'd ever said to me. I glanced at Bethery, who was drowsing on her own bed. She blinked slowly and said nothing in my defence, so I took it as a sign that she was in one of her taciturn moods and left the room. I wandered the Den until I found myself in the common room, facing the Oak Door. I traced the carving of the titular tree with my fingers, wondering how closely it matched the one on the outside: and then, with a surge of courage, I pushed it open.

Outside was Miguel. Had he even left, since delivering me here?

I tried not to look at his revolver-pistol.

"Senor?" I said, tentatively.

He turned, saw me, and bowed his head. "Yes, Mistress."

"Please, call me Imre," I begged him. "Mistress" was the term for a woman who dwelt in the Red Houses – where she plied men with pleasure, but did not worship the Pattern with her steps – and I might be facing that title soon enough. "Am I a prisoner?"

He looked shocked. "No, of course not, Mistress." Then, catching himself using the unwelcome term, he waved a hand. "Pattern forgive me."

"Then why must the doors remain always closed? If I'm not a prisoner, why can't I leave? Why can't others?"

"Imre." He rolled the word on his tongue. "It's an unusual name."

"Is it?" I replied blandly.

He sighed. "I have orders, Imre. I can't let you wander the Citadel. No one is allowed to, not unchecked. The safety of la Principe Regente is at stake. And my job would be forfeit."

It was my turn to sigh. I couldn't ask the man to endanger his position. "Talk to me, then. Could you?"

He raised his eyebrows. "Talk? About what?"

"Anything!" I took a step into the hallway, but he tensed, and I said, "I'll go no further, I promise. Please. Will you sit with me?"

He looked wary at first, but then his face softened. I was pleased to see that he was not in fact a human rock; that the man I had sensed under all that muscle, as he carried me that first night so gently and carefully, was hidden not so deeply beneath the surface.

I shut the door behind me and sat on the floor. Miguel lowered his own bulky form opposite me, careful to leave a respectable distance between us.

It was a sensible precaution, I suppose, to protect his reputation, one that didn't annoy me; instead, it made me smile to think that others might imagine that I, one of the youngest Daughters, and certainly not the most confident, would have the wiles and skill to charm this giant man.

For a while, we simply sat, regarding one another across the hallway. I was thinking of all the things I could have said to him, the opening lines from Maestra Tinir's lessons about how to make conversation with a mecenas: if he wore a Guild suit or belt, I should begin by asking his specialty, for men who worked as *artistas,* masons, or healers would always enjoy talking about their work. If the man looked as if he was well-built, you could assume he was a labourer, and compliment his physique; such men liked to be flattered, and assumed that any woman would be impressed. If he was finely dressed, ask him if he often visited the Pavilion, and if not, entice him with soft words of the pleasures that could be offered, so that he would return and pay more coin. If he looked like he was in a hurry, I should begin with a friendly, playful glance, then the first steps of the dance, and nothing more. It would tempt him to return and spend more time – and coin – in the future.

None of these were helpful in this situation, and I felt again a pang in my stomach. I didn't want Miguel to think I had nothing to say, and assume there was no point talking to me again. I desperately didn't want to be alone.

But in the next moment, Miguel reached into his pocket, and pulled out a small tin. I thought it was a cigarillo case at first, but when he opened it, a handful of battered cards spilled free. "Do you play Julepe?"

I shook my head. I'd never played myself, though I had stood at the tables as the automata dealt the cards, so that the mecenas could try their luck.

Miguel fanned the cards out, then began to shuffle them expertly.

"The winner needs to have the highest value card, or the highest card of the suit played by the first player," he explained. "At least two tricks should be gained in game in order to earn chips towards your pot. If the opponent makes less than one, the chips wagered by this player will be subtracted from his pot. The name of the game is *hacer julepe* which means 'Make the whist', which is done by winning at least two tricks during the game."

"Oh, I see," I said faintly, watching those cards flick back and forth in a blur of red and black.

He leaned forward, dealing the cards onto the floor between us. He placed them face-up, stopping when he got to a particular card.

"Ah, the *palo de Oro*. The Coin suit." He dropped this onto my pile, then gathered them up again. "You deal."

I was confused, but at his urging, I gathered the cards and dealt five each between the two of us, rather more slowly than he had done. "You must now choose," he said. "Whether this will be a Blind Wager or a Normal Wager game."

I laughed. "I don't know what either of those are."

"Then the choice should be easy," he said.

"Very well. Normal," I decided.

"What will you wager?"

I spread my hands. I had nothing at all in the Citadel; my belongings were all back in my room at the Pavilion. My dresses, my jewellery, my favourite blanket, my little figurine of Mary. I knew they were unlikely to be delivered, as had been promised. Even if they were, how would I keep anything safe from the quick hands of the other women?

"Think creatively," Miguel suggested. "Value can be assigned to the most unlikely things."

I smiled. "A kiss."

Miguel gave a small laugh. "Very well. Then my wager is a walk. I will ask permission. I will find a way to take you out of this room. Worth playing for?"

I nodded eagerly.

"Then you must deal three more cards." He placed the deck between us and turned the top card face-up. "This is the *triumfo*, the trump suit. Any card of this suit will now beat a card from any other suit. This is a three of spades. A three or an Ace has special rules, thus, you can take this card, and you become –" here, his eyes twinkled, "– the *postre*. The dessert."

A smile crossed my face, and with that moment, everything changed. Miguel and I fell into an easy banter as I played, very badly, through the first round. The postre takes on the condition that he or she will win three tricks, as opposed to merely hacer julepe. Otherwise, the dealer must Fall, not having met the conditions. A Fall was when a player did not meet the bid made previously, with a Widow, or did not win any hands. This player must place an amount equal to the total amount of wagers made in that round into the collective wager pot.

We took turns dealing our cards, and Miguel taught me that I could either pass or play, depending on what cards I held.

The game was intricate and complicated. At first I was terribly confused, but soon I started to see the patterns emerging. Though Miguel won the first hand, by the end of the second round, I had picked up enough to win. Proud of myself, I dealt the cards once more.

"Do you play often, Senor Miguel?"

"Miguel," he corrected. "If I'm to call you Imre, you must call me Miguel."

I nodded my assent, and smiled.

"You look different," he said. "When you smile."

I arched an eyebrow. "I do?"

"You should do it more often. While we've sat here, the lines of concentration on your face have deepened. There are many in the Citadel with those lines. Not enough smiles."

I think my smile must have dazzled him somehow, for not long afterwards, I won the trick.

"Don't feel too badly," I told him. "Perhaps next time you'll win a kiss."

He ducked his head. "I don't know what my wife would think about that."

I laughed, and realised that the whole time we played, I hadn't felt a single twinge in my stomach.

"Guardia!" The voice shocked us both, and the cards fell to the floor like leaves when the cold-season approaches. Miguel threw himself up, grabbing his spear, and looking flustered.

"Forgive me, Senor –"

I looked towards the door. Senor Grath. At his most acidic.

"You're neglecting your post."

"Well, not exactly," Miguel protested, and then, seeing the rage on his master's face, lowered his head. "Yes, Senor."

"He's supposed to be guarding me. That's exactly what he's doing," I said.

Senor Grath turned his steely gaze on me, and I wished I'd said nothing.

"Sargento Miguel. You have disobeyed orders," he snapped, his eyes still locked with mine.

"So, I *am* a prisoner," I said.

"A guest," Senor Grath replied. "For now. Guardsman, you are relieved. I will appoint a sentinela to take over the duty for the night."

My heart dropped as Miguel left. I went to gather the abandoned cards as I stood, but Senor Grath took my arm and pushed me back through the doorway. "Listen to me very carefully," he hissed. "Don't think you can use your seductive techniques to beguile my guardsmen. If you do something like this again, I won't hesitate to find . . . less pleasant quarters for you."

I looked down. Was I to apologise? Or would he think I was speaking out of turn? I wasn't even sure what I would be apologising *for*. It had just been a card game.

And so, I said nothing.

"I won't warn you again." And with that, he whirled and slammed the door shut.

I picked up the cards and threw them, ineffectually, at the closed door.

***

"Why are you crying?"

The voice startled me. I had sunk to my knees, so found myself looking up into a familiar face. It was the girl I had met when I entered the Den, the one who defended me against Jardine. She carried a book under her arm, just as she had that night.

"I'm not." I wiped my sleeve across my face. My shift was starting to stick to me, caked with perspiration and smears of Bethery's make-up, after turnings of use.

The girl dropped something onto my lap. It was a lacy handkerchief.

"You don't want the others to see you weeping," she said in a quiet voice.

"Why do you care?" I shot at her angrily.

She shrugged. "Maybe I don't. But you do."

I dabbed at my eyes with the handkerchief, then patted my nose. "Thank you," I said at last. "I don't know your name."

"I've got several," she said. "In this place, I go by Laisa."

"Why do you have more than one?"

She shrugged again. "Imre, isn't it?"

I nodded.

"You shouldn't be here."

I blinked. "I'll go –"

"No, that's not what I mean," she said. "You're just too . . . different. It's no wonder you've gathered such interest."

"Interest?" I prompted after a moment, but she shook her head.

"Bethery was very smart to take you first," she warned me. "If it had been Jardine . . ."

"I don't understand," I said desperately, and she laughed.

"Of course you don't! Just look at it this way. We are all –" she swept a hand to encompass the Den "– here because the Principe Regente saw something in us that he wanted to keep. We come from the Red Houses, or taverns, or places our Prince has spent slumming. Then you arrive, from the Pavilion, of all places!"

"But that wasn't my choice," I huffed. "I was brought here."

"Ah, but think about it! *Why* were you selected by him?"

Incredulously, I said, "Because I fell?"

She nodded. "We are here because we were the best, the prettiest, the ones who offered the most pleasure. In the outside world, many of us would find ourselves begging for food or shelter, or at least living in far less . . . comfortable . . . situations than your fine Pavilion. *You* are here simply because you made a mistake. Can you see why they might hate you for it?"

I shook my head, and she sighed, clutching her book to her chest.

"Where did you get the book?" I asked quickly, before she could leave, and curiously, for I'd seen no bookshelves in all the winding rooms.

"Oh! We're allowed to request small things from time to time. Well, perhaps not so much allowed as . . . we slip a note into the servitor trays after the meals are done. Sometimes a coin too, or a trinket or bauble. Then, the kitchen staff or one of the vigilar may send what we ask for."

"If I asked for a new dress, would they send it?"

She smiled, and despite her plain face, it was the most heartening expression I'd seen in the Den. "I'll give you one of mine so you won't be swimming in Bethery's old garb. We're almost the same size. Save your requests for things you truly want."

"I would love a book," I admitted.

"The Great Library has any title you can think of. But you might not get the one you want." She flipped hers over to show me the cover: *Cultivating Fruit Trees in Rueda.* "Divon, the Library's automata, might have had his workings upgraded, but his skills in comprehension are still a little lacking. He tends to loan out odd choices, and they're rarely the thing you're looking for. Sometimes I'd give anything to be able to go down there myself and choose."

"I've heard of the Great Library." I would, seeing as how Tomas had spoken of it with such awe. "Is it true the Sacred Texts are kept there?"

Laisa nodded. "And many other treasures besides." She sighed. "In any case, there is no use in dreaming. We must make the best of our lot, Imre, and truly, it's not so bad."

Before I returned to my room, she leaned me a spare gown, as promised; and I tucked the playing cards I'd gathered into one of the pockets, along with the battered white feather. She also loaned me her book. Despite the dry subject matter, I accepted it gratefully; starved of the written word, I couldn't wait to learn everything there was to know about orchards on the Wheel.

Chapter Ten

In the Den, we were cut off from the rest of the world. I couldn't observe the dawn regimen, for the girls in our room would sleep through until noon if they could, so I took to mouthing my parabra under my breath as I listened to Bethery's soft breathing at my shoulder. 'I seek to walk in the footsteps described by the Pattern. I strive to follow the true path of the Pattern. I love as I live, with every breath; I live that I might serve the Pattern.'

But even these words were half-hearted. Through the thick walls, I could barely hear the seven peals of Reloj la pie as la Grulla rose, and at times found myself waking so late that light was already streaming through the small high window.

***

Sometimes, visitors came.

"Relatives," Laisa informed me, the first time I found a group of unfamiliar women in our room, talking eagerly to Xith and Harette of a party they had attended at a night-café. "Relatives and friends are allowed to visit, though most don't. They are content to receive the stipend that is paid to them for the lease of their daughters, mothers, sisters, and forget where it came from."

She, it seemed, was one of the latter; no niece nor cousin nor friend came for her.

These women brought news of the outside world, grasped upon hungrily by all of us. What new clothes could be purchased, and at what price; what new drink was being served at a night-café on the Eastside; what someone's brother had done with someone's niece, and whether or not there would be a wedding.

And sometimes, they told news that was not good.

"A flood rose up right through the basement," a woman was saying to Audren as I passed by. "It just kept fountaining up out of some broken pipe, on and on, until it was running down the street. They had to get a man from the Architectural Guild to dive into one of the sewer tanks and turn-off the valve. The building is condemned."

"But how will they live?" Audren gasped, a hand covering her mouth. "That carrier-pigeon cleaning business of Hulot's is ill-advised, but every penny he has is lodged in it, the fool!"

"There's nothing that can be done. The equipment he had is mostly ruined, not to mention some customer's valuable birds – and whatever wasn't swamped shows mildew from the damp . . ."

There was talk, also, of instances of a strange illness that had struck down several men and women in the Lower Tiers. "Incurable," one visitor said. "And the symptoms quite horrible." Exactly what the symptoms were, I did not find out, however – not, at least, until much later.

Another time, I heard of a shuttle-load of moth-meat from Rueda that was discovered to be entirely spoiled. It was unknown whether the workers had loaded it knowing it was defective, hoping no one would notice, or whether it was a simple oversight. Yet another told of carrier pigeons going missing over certain areas, or turning up lost, or with their messages garbled into nonsense; and of servitors breaking down, leaving the streets filled with rotten rubbish; of plants dying, or food full of toxins, or cracks appearing in the streets.

And there was plenty of talk of la Rebelde, of course. "The vigilar raided a house in Third Tier last night," I overheard a girl say to Jardine. "They're holding nine people under suspicion of supporting la Rebelde. The last time they took a group in, they weren't seen again."

Jardine waved her hand. She always seemed to have an opinion on matters she had no personal involvement with. "Do they honestly think they will catch him? After all this time?"

"He is getting bolder. Did you hear, he painted the side of a shuttle-train? With the words 'The Pattern Unravels', no less!"

"Who does he think he is?" Jardine snorted derisively.

"They are Scions of Chaos," another woman spoke darkly, and after that, there was silence.

Sometimes, it was men that came.

Mostly, they were noblemen, wearing fine suits and mixed expressions of hauteur and guilt, which I recognised all too well from the mecenas – no doubt they had wives at home awaiting their return. Fewer than these were the guildsmen and their apprentices: clockmakers, masons, metalworkers who had found favour with the Citadel officials, and were claiming their reward. Fewer were vigilar, in their black suits. These vigilar, I would learn, had been given special privilege for some service or promotion, and, as Bethery whispered to me once, "they thought their cocks had grown seven inches."

At least they did not wear their gun-belts in the Den.

The arrival of a man was signalled by a bell which chimed, summoning all women to the common room, no matter where they were. We filtered into the common room readily, for excitement was thin in the Den, and the yearning to be chosen strong. Getting out of the Den, even for a few hours, to be spent in the company of some lascivious man, was a prize worth fighting for. There was jostling for space on the couches, posing and preening. The men, forbidden to cross through the doorway, would call their choices from the threshold.

"I suppose you must be used to it," Bethery said to me. "This is how it works in the Pavilion, no?"

It was not. "We dance with the men," I told her, rather stiffly. "The choice must be consensual, or the act is unworthy of the Pattern."

"How is that different from this?" Her tone was bored, and I couldn't tell if she was actually interested, or simply hoping I would rise to the bait.

As always, I bit hard on the barbed hook.

"La Oráculo said to la Relojero, 'fit together those parts which work in unison.' Those were the words of the Pattern! This impersonal choice has no harmony. That is why a Daughter of the Pavilion is different from a Red House whore."

I turned my back on her, and refused her teasing touches while the men at the door looked over their wares.

It's hard to say what living in such an environment did to the three young children. Certainly, they seemed used to it, this being the only life they'd ever known. In any case, perhaps they weren't aware of it at all, for the women took pains that they were always out of the room when the bell sounded, occupied somewhere or other. I wondered if the Principe Regente minded that some of his women were being used by other men – which made me wonder whether he had danced with them all, or kept some in reserve, like bedsheets in a linen closet, saved for a future date.

There were small lozenges made of herbs, Bethery told me, to prevent unwanted children; they were just like the ones we took in the Pavilion, also curbing our monthly flows if we chose. I took them out of habit, gladly, for I didn't welcome the idea of dealing with blood-stained rags in the very public environment of the Den.

But I was never chosen by the men.

It pained me, for being chosen would have been my sole way to get out of those rooms and away from the women and their glares and whisperings. But after seven different men had come and left with their chattel, I accepted that there was no chance I would be somehow picked by mistake.

"Sometimes they just want to talk," Xith said as she preened after returning from a liaison with a rather handsome young man, the son of a First Tier milliner. "He was telling me about a reservoir that had run suddenly dry, and for no reason. He'd been tasked with the descent, and was fairly shuddering with the horror of it! I all but laughed at him for being such a girl! When I tried to touch him, he practically leaped onto the ceiling! But he did give me this shawl." She shook it out and smoothed the fabric. It was white, embroidered with orange and purple designs, and fringed with blue tassels. It was very finely made, and I couldn't resist reaching to touch it along with the others.

"It's truly beautiful," I told her, and she sniffed, but looked inordinately pleased that she had a possession I envied.

The next time the chime signalled that a man had come to choose, I slipped away back to Bethery's room. No one noticed my absence, and the quietness of the empty rooms was bliss to me. It was after dark, and a ray of la Grulla's distant light shone through the high window. I climbed up on Bethery's bed, and when I stretched on my tiptoes, I could just see over the sill.

It was difficult to balance – my ankle still wouldn't take my full weight, and on the uneven surface of the mattress, I teetered dangerously. Still, my desperation drove me onwards. I fumbled blindly for the latch, and found it at last, but it was stiff from disuse. I prodded and pulled it, finally working it free, and even then, pushing the pane outwards was hard work. I looked at the narrow gap dubiously. I wasn't sure I'd even fit through.

My dancer's body served me well, even after turnings of languishing and idleness. My arms lifted my weight easily, and I perched on the sill with my knees; through the narrow gap, I couldn't even see the ground.

But I could see la Grulla, her waning, distant face shining like a beacon. I longed to stand in that silver light, to speak my parabra to la Relojero, and know I had not forgotten the Pattern.

I let out a long, slow breath, and then I lowered my feet through the narrow gap. This time, there was no thought in my mind that anyone might catch me. In fact, I don't remember thinking anything, except how beautiful the night seemed.

I landed softly, on my good foot; again, I thanked Maestra Tinir's thorough training.

The stone of the terrace was cold under my feet, which, I noted belatedly, were still bare; but the rough surface felt pleasant, and my ankle lodged no protest. I walked to the balustrade, which was carved with circles and crescents, and overgrown with a sweet-smelling vine, the scent of which conjured memories and longings which I could not pin down. Beyond, rose the yellow walls of the myriad other wings and towers of the Citadel. Lights sparkled from many of the windows, but just as many were dark. And below – ah, below! The gardens!

The terrace on which I stood overlooked a courtyard. It was filled with a dozen trees providing shade for the flowerbeds, which seemed to contain more plants than they could handle, for leaves and blooms spilled over their edges, encroaching on the edges of the paths. These were lined with brick, cobbles, stones, moss, or grass. They wound here and there and every-which-way.

At either end of the terrace, there were steps leading down into that verdant paradise. My feet took me to the right, and before I knew it, I was wandering amidst those incredible flowers, inhaling their heady scents and revelling in the sight. Their blooms were folded closed for the night, but that only made them more graceful and ethereal; I could only imagine how beautiful this place must be during daylight.

For a long time, I walked slowly, letting the winding paths draw me along. I stepped, once, into the golden light spilling from an open window at ground level, and saw figures moving within.

Later, I would know these men as Chancellor Dahrn, Councillor Horoth, Guildsman Ollander, and Secretary Allius. They were the last men left from the Conclave which had adjourned earlier, having failed to come to any conclusions, seeing as the Principe Regente had fallen asleep during a request to upgrade the lock gate on Camino de Muchos Giros. In fact, they were the men to whom the running of Tierra Mejór had fallen, given the Principe's recent reluctance to attend to any matter beyond his immediate pleasure.

As it was, I saw into the semicircular chamber, the mostly-empty seats rising around a central table, giving the sense of equality to every person seated within, even when that equality was merely an illusion.

It was a strange and sudden reminder that I wasn't alone in this place, but still, I felt removed from the world inside those walls, even when I heard their muffled voices.

" . . . will certainly not be long before . . ."

" . . . effects are varied . . . can only hope it . . . enough . . ."

" . . . slow, but patience is advised . . ."

And then, one sentence rang out clearly: "Oren will never discover it, even if she should wake up."

The man who had uttered this stood up from his chair at that central table, leaning back against it, his arms folded. "How much longer can we keep up this charade? La Boca has sent an official message; the carrier-pigeon arrived only this afternoon. I didn't have time to raise the issue earlier, while we were dealing with those reports of the spreading illness."

"Or perhaps you prudently waited," said another man with a sigh. "We can discuss how to handle this without interruption."

"Senor Grath will have to be informed. The delegation will be arriving in two days."

"Yet another disaster." The first man turned, and looked straight through the window at me. Or so it appeared; for a moment, I stood stunned, before I realised that he probably couldn't see me, shrouded as I was in darkness.

He squinted, and took a step closer. I heard a question from one of the other men, and glided smoothly aside. The leaves of a nearby bush provided cover. The man shook his head, turning back.

Terrified to further risk discovery, I took another path, deeper into the garden, and here found a small bower set in a grove, shadowed by a large tree adorned with trailing fronds. Below, almost hidden by the delicate leaves, was a statue of la Grulla, the Crane. Some working parts whirred gently inside her as her wings raised themselves to the heavens, then folded back down again, over and over. At a right angle to her, sat a simple wooden bench. For the first time since I'd arrived at the Citadel, I felt as if I belonged.

It was as I perched here that I saw movement. At first I thought it was a vigilar, or a member of the guardia, and then I thought it was the man who had glimpsed me through the window. My heart froze, and I stood abruptly. But a moment passed, and then another, and there was no shout of discovery or anger; the figure simply stood there.

He was tall, and his hair was long. Unbound, it fell just past his shoulders, and was slightly tousled. His features were very fine, as if they'd been moulded from porcelain. I couldn't see his eyes for they were deep in shadow, but made out a long shirt, belted at the waist, yet askew and with the buttons undone at the neck. His vest was falling from one shoulder.

My heart stuttered in my chest. I knew, oh I knew who he was. The last time I'd seen him, he had been sitting in that leather armchair, unbearably smug and regal; now the Principe Regente looked like nothing more than a vagabond.

"Are you a dream?" he slurred gently. I realised then; he was drunk.

I was suddenly aware that I wore nothing but the same thin white shift I'd had on for the past five turnings. The fabric was not enough to hide my shape, which, in the chill air, was all too visible. My own hair was a mess, half-bound in a plait, half-falling free and blowing in the breeze.

I was frozen, unable to speak. Beside me, the Crane lifted her wings and lowered them again, rustling the leaves of the nearby bushes.

Suddenly, a shout echoed from atop the distant walls, and while I couldn't make out the word, the Prince's head whipped around, and he cursed, and then he was gone, his uneven footsteps fading into the sounds of the night.

Chapter Eleven

Getting back through the window was easier than getting out, for I found a heavy cement flowerpot which I shifted a few inches to the left, allowing me to step up and balance on the edge while I gripped the window ledge. It would make things easier if I ever managed to escape again.

Bethery was sitting on the bed, waiting for me. Apart from her, the room was empty.

"Where've you been?" she asked me, pretending petulance, but her slow smile was already spreading across her lips.

"In the garden," I answered honestly.

"In the garden?" She looked slightly puzzled.

"The air is so close in here," I told her. "I just wanted to get out for a bit."

"Am I not giving you enough exercise?" She patted the bed, indicating that I should climb up beside her. She turned her head and nuzzled at my neck. Her breath tickled through my hair. "You must be careful, sugar. I sent the others away on errands, so they wouldn't notice the open window, or see your return. But had they found out, they would have reported you immediately. If you're caught – I don't want to lose you."

I pulled back from her, shocked at her sincerity. I enjoyed lying with Bethery, I must admit, but I hadn't counted on it involving any deeper feelings on her part.

"Is that what you want?" she asked, her level gaze unwavering. "Do you want to be away from me?"

"No!" I said quickly. "No, not at all. But I have – there is someone, and I wanted –"

"Someone on the outside," she said, with her usual sly intuition. "Someone you wish to see."

I nodded, and she wrapped her arms around me. My metrónomo pulsed between us. "I hate to share you," she whispered. "But if you take me with you, I promise I will cover our absence."

***

Bethery was good to her word. The following evening, she told Xith and Harette that they were not to bother us. They shared glances, and I knew this did not bode well, but my mind was focused on what was to come, so I didn't trouble myself with worrying about it. Inside the room, Bethery shut the door firmly and we waited until the grey sky showed the first touches of purple, and then I slipped through the window.

Bethery did not have my grace. It was the first time I had seen her movements so clumsy, yet even as she flopped to the stone terrace, she gave a sardonic smile.

"Well," she whispered. "That was amusing. Which way?"

Of course, I had no idea, but I pointed to the left. We took the stairs down into the maze-like garden, keeping to the straightest path I could find (which was not at all straight) following the wall of this wing of the Citadel.

Lights were coming on inside the rooms, but no one paid any attention to the leaf-filled gloom outside the windows. We moved quickly, my metrónomo ticking the minutes away.

"What in the Tierra Mejór would anyone want with all these plants?" Bethery grouched as we pushed our way past an overgrown bush. "By the Pattern, if I had so much land around me, I'd turn-off the irrigation systems and let the earth remain bare. It's far less messy."

I said nothing. The garden looked just as beautiful under the fading purple glow of evening as it had under the night sky. I wondered if I could ever find the statue of la Grulla again, and hoped so; nothing had seemed more perfect than that small grove.

We reached a corner where this wing of the Citadel ended. There was an iron gate covered in delicate vines. Their trumpet-shaped flowers were closed tight for the night, but I caught a hint of their heavenly scent as I tried the handle.

It was not locked.

When we walked through, we found ourselves in a narrow, arched walkway between two towering buildings. Someone walked across a bridge above our heads, and Bethery grabbed my hand, squeezing tight – I caught a glimpse of an excited smile on her face – but they did not look down, and we crept along the worn stone pathway until we reached a wooden door set deep into the wall. It was locked with a heavy iron bolt, but as I slid this back, the door swung open – and we were looking out at a city street.

"I didn't think it would be this easy," I whispered.

" 'Take what you are freely given, and save your questions for the given time'," Bethery quoted. I was shocked that she would know this line from the *Words of the Oracle,* but she was right; this was not the time for questions. I pulled the door carefully behind us.

The street was more of an alley, but it funnelled straight down into the Plaza de Lágrima. People were gathering here, craning their necks to look upwards. It wasn't just the Reloj de pie that was attracting their attention; an airship was lowering into the dock. The biggest I'd ever seen, and from its belly fluttered unfamiliar pennants.

" . . .how long they'll stay," someone said. "Or whether or not we'll see them."

"Should there not be a great parade?" another asked. "Surely a spectacle should be made! After all, we pay for their airships, their food and clothing, and what do we get in return? How often do they deign to cross . . ."

" . . .I've no doubt there will be a ball held in their honour, but it won't be for the likes of us!"

Bethery, who was wearing a shawl, pulled it up over her hair. I had to make do with ducking my head and hoping my hair would cover my face, but even as we crossed the Plaza, I realised that no one was paying us the slightest attention. I looked up at the brightness of the waning la Grulla and thanked the Pattern.

As we passed the statue of la Oráculo in the fountain, I almost shut my eyes again, hoping to block out the memory of my fall. It had happened just there, as I'd completed the last step. I could almost see the exact spot. One cobblestone, the crescent moon, looked a little crooked there – or was it my imagination? A second later, a group of carousers shifted, hiding the spot from view.

We walked to the Calle del Corazón.

"Oh!" Bethery pulled me to one side suddenly. "We must go in here!"

I protested, but it was no use. And no one turned at Bethery's loud voice; why would they? In the shadows, I dared hope that no one would recognise me at all.

The haberdasher's was a large shop, lavishly decorated with dried flower arrangements and silks. While I looked around in wonder, Bethery oozed satisfaction. We weren't the only customers. It seemed many women were out hunting for new dresses tonight.

Racks of clothes were hung from the ceiling, which rotated on tracks around the shop. If you wished for a particular item, you pulled on the appropriate lever, and the rail would whizz across for your perusal. Bethery demonstrated its use gleefully, and soon had several racks of the most expensive designer lines arrayed before me.

"This," she said, with a tone of authority, as she removed a silky dress in a shade of blue that I swear, I had never seen before, "is the latest thing from Hillier. The neck is too modest for my liking, but it's passable. Here, you *must* try it on."

She chivvied me into a fitting room, which seemed like a miniature luxury suite, with gold-edged mirrors that twisted slowly from side to side to show you from all angles, a comfortable armchair, in case one became over-whelmed by the task ahead, and a small waterfall trickling in the corner, for no reason I could see save ambiance.

The dress was lovely – and the neckline, far from being too high, showed plenty of cleavage. I pulled the curtain aside, to show Bethery.

"Oh, wonderful!" she called from the fitting room next to mine; she emerged a moment later, twirling in a sheath of saffron gauze. "What do you think, Imre?"

I plastered a smile on my face. "It is beautiful."

"Oh, you speak like a man," she giggled. "Tell me I look breathtaking. Remarkable. *Divine*. Beautiful is such a plain word."

An assistant, dressed in a fine silk tunic, approached us then, asking if we required assistance.

"No." Bethery sniffed. "Nothing here really suits us. We'll move on to Vitarain's, won't we, dear?"

She linked arms with me, and, unable to contain ourselves, we almost fell over as we left the shop, unable to contain our giggling.

A rotor-tram was just pulling up outside a busy night-café, and we slipped aboard with a group of drunken young men and women – students, I guessed, for none of them wore Guild colours yet. They made so much noise that not even the tram-operator noticed that we hadn't paid. I settled into a seat next to the window and let the chill night air ruffle my hair as the tram rolled along its tracks, taking the reverse of the journey that I had travelled . . . how long ago? A turning? Two? I wasn't even sure anymore.

Bethery still clutched my hand, and I was glad for that anchor to the here and now. "It's all so different," she breathed. "There's a new bakery on the corner. And – no! Aben's Millinery is quite gone!"

I looked at her sideways. "How long has it been since you've left the Citadel?"

"Oh." She frowned. "Seven years. I was thirteen when I last walked along this street."

Seven years. I was incredulous, and it must have shown on my face, because she laughed and pinched my chin lightly. "Don't look like that, sugar! What is here for me? I don't have the money to spend in the bakery or a place like Aben's, do I? And I didn't even before the Principe Regente found me in a night-café, drinking coffee made from what tasted like recycled machine oil. They'd hired me to catch the rats in their cellar, did you know that?"

I shook my head dumbly and accepted Bethery's gentle kiss on my cheek as a signal I need say no more.

Soon the Pavilion rose out of the darkness, its white towers lit with the light of la Grulla. We slipped off with a few passengers – two of them in what had to be their finest suits, obviously mecenas heading to the Room of Roses for a night of entertainment. I turned my head away, though neither was one I'd ever Danced for. They laughed and joked, jostling one another playfully and bickering over the dancers they would petition. Another man followed just behind them, not joining in their banter. He wore a black hat pulled down tight over his ears, and kept his head bowed. There was something not quite right about him.

"Where has he been the past three years? On the Wheel?" Bethery whispered in my ear, and I had to laugh. His clothes were outdated; far too colourful, and they hung from him stiffly, as if they were all brand-new. He must have heard Bethery's comment, for he turned slightly, and saw us watching him; he had a pale face with a narrow nose and a dark, neatly trimmed moustache.

Bethery sniggered, and he glanced away, picking up the pace as he hurried after the others.

I pulled Bethery by the hand, into the shadows, then through the darkened gardens, down the steps to the Templo de las Siete.

"So *this* is our destination?" As usual, I couldn't tell if Bethery was truly unimpressed or if she was simply adopting the apathetic demeanour that was her habit, so I didn't answer. Instead, I led the way up the steps and into the darkened interior.

It looked the same as it ever had, and for this I was glad. Inside, the statue of la Relojero waited, smiling slightly, as if she was pleased to see us. And before her kneeled a hooded figure.

"Tomas," I breathed. I was so glad to see him, I ached to run down the aisle, but I held myself back.

He turned, startled from his prayer. Upon seeing me, his eyes went wide. "Imre!" He got to his feet and, when I reached him, pulled me into his arms. He seemed to have grown over the past few turnings – was that possible? My head nestled against his chest, the soft, heavy material of his habit brushing my cheek, my metrónomo matching his heartbeat. All too soon, he pushed me back, a troubled expression crossing his face, one couldn't read at all.

"It's so strange." I pitched my voice low. "The Citadel! It's so grand – you would love to see it. To think that I sleep underneath the the Reloj! And the Great Library. I haven't seen it, but there is a way to borrow texts. Can you imagine?"

I looked at Tomas, trying to gauge his expression beneath his dark hood, but his eyes skated away from mine.

"But how can you be here?" he asked. "Has he – has the Principe Regente –"

I shook my head. "I've seen him only once. I don't know if he remembers me at all. But I'm living with the women he keeps at the Citadel . . . and, oh, Tomas, I've missed you so much!"

"I've missed you too, dearest." He smiled slightly. "I've kept my promise, though, see? Every evening, I come here."

"There is a way out of the Citadel. I can come here, every evening, too, and meet you. I could bring you books," I nattered, my enthusiasm bubbling over. "I could bring them here for you to read. They aren't missed – one of the other girls –"

I wished he would say something, that he would speak to me, but there was no reaction.

"Tonight –" My voice wavered, and rose. "As we left, we saw the *biggest* airship. I don't know where it's from, but I think –"

"Imre," he said at last. "It's nearly time."

"Time?" I frowned, puzzled. "For what?"

He sighed. "I'm taking my Vows tomorrow. I won't be able to come here and meet you. I won't be able to leave the Iglesia for seven turnings. And after that . . ."

Despair washed through me as the unfinished sentence rang in my ears. *After that, to talk with you will be blasphemy.*

"La Boca is here," he said. "Did you know that? He has actually come to the Ciudad." His eyes sparkled. "He is meeting with the Prince to discuss matters of grave importance. I think he is lobbying for change. He thinks we have strayed too far from the Pattern."

"Oh." I took a step back.

"Imre, this is what I've worked for. I've devoted my life to the Brotherhood, just as you've chosen the way of the Daughters. And to become a Brother now! It is time for change, and I can help bring it. You of all people must understand."

Tears choked in my throat. *I did not choose to give you up*, I wanted to say. *I would never do this.*

"Imre," he went on. "Look at you. Look at what you're doing." He waved a hand towards the door, and for the first time since I'd seen him, I remembered Bethery. She lingered in the doorway, her hand on her hip, a lascivious smile playing across her painted lips, her gown cut so low, I could see the gap between her breasts. I wondered suddenly how *I* must look to Tomas, in the company of this woman, and reeking of cigarillo smoke and lavish perfumes. "You don't belong here," Tomas said. "You know it. Things have changed, and it's all . . ."

Don't say it, I begged him silently. *Please don't say it.*

But he did. "It's all different now."

He stepped forward, took my shoulders, and bent to kiss my forehead – the briefest of touches, and then he walked away, down the aisle, passing Bethery without a second glance, and on, into the night.

I was terrified it would be the last time I would ever see him.

***

"I'm guessing that didn't go according to plan." Bethery clutched my shoulder with one hand. I shrugged away from her touch. I truly didn't want to feel anything right then.

"Sugar, this is a beautiful place," she said softly, and there was no trace of the usual affectation in her voice. "But we shouldn't linger here. Xith isn't known for her patience, and if she finds us gone, there will be no sneaking away for either of us in the future."

Numbly, I nodded, and we made our way back through the city, which was quieter now; across the Square, where the Reloj was chiming eight, and the great airship still hung; through the door, which we bolted behind us, and through the garden paths.

At one point, I stopped, holding up a hand to Bethery.

"What?" she whispered, and I hastily shushed her. I had thought I'd seen a man standing there, his back to us, and in that instant wondered if it was the Prince. But when I looked again through the dark leaves of a shrub, I could see nothing, and was almost sure I was mistaken.

Bethery's re-entry through the window was no better than her exit, and she flopped onto the bed in a fit of giggles. Despite, or perhaps because of my despair over Tomas's rejection, I couldn't help sharing her mirth as I dropped down beside her. I laughed as I had not for a very long time, and felt the relentless knot in my stomach ease, just a little.

Bethery wrapped me into her arms with a silk sheet, and that was how they found us, the others, when they finally burst in through the door.

I was treated to many a black stare after this, which I supposed I deserved. They thought I was taking their places, and they were right. Bethery and I shared something none of them were a part of.

***

The jealousy of the others was a palpable thing. There was a change in the quality of the pranks. I found my dress, the one given to me by Laisa, covered in something foul-smelling when I got out of bed one morning. I think it might have been water from a vase of flowers that had gone rotten, for there were a few of those in one of the sitting rooms, that were only removed when they became too smelly to bear; still, it left a muddy stain. I took it to the fountain to wash it out, and as I crouched there, I felt the shape of Miguel's playing cards in the pocket. They were crumpled, but they'd escaped the water. The feather was stained brown at the tip, but I placed it lovingly alongside the cards; my precious treasures, and, since my belongings had never arrived, possibly the only things I owned in this world.

As I was wringing it out, watching the drifting bits of dirt swirl away through the drains at the bottom of the stone pool, I felt eyes on my back, and turned to see one of the children – a girl, whose name I'd never learned.

Her hair was curly and blond, her nose pushed in, her cheeks round, in the way all childrens are before their features are truly defined. She held a ragged toy made of cloth. Stuffing spilled from a hole in its side and one eye was missing.

"Hello," I said after a moment of silence.

"Hello," the girl echoed in a soft voice.

"Are you searching for someone?" I asked her.

She shook her head and clutched her toy tighter.

"He's a fine-looking fellow," I said at last, at a loss. Children weren't something I had a great deal of experience with.

But this seemed to have been the right thing to say. A smile spread across her small face like sunshine breaking through dark clouds. "Scothe." She held him out to me.

I took the thing gingerly, for it looked about to disintegrate. "I'm very pleased to meet you . . . Scothe." I danced him through the air, and his ears flopped from side to side.

"You're hurt." The girl pointed to my ankle. I peered down at the bandage. It was stained now, with dirt and sweat.

"Oh, it doesn't hurt anymore." I tugged at it, and it came free. The skin underneath looked tender, but Doctor Oren's ointment had been washed away in the bath. I wasn't lying. It didn't hurt at all now, but yawning between the joints was a weakness that hadn't been there before.

The little girl sat down beside me. I thought she would grow bored and soon move on. Instead, she picked up one of the playing cards and flipped it in her fingers. Then, with a thoughtful look, she picked up another and balanced them so they formed a tiny tent. She did the same with three more, and then laid others across the top. Soon she'd added an extra level, and another, of perfectly balanced cards.

I watched her until a sudden breeze knocked them over. I looked up and saw Jardine standing there, a strange look on her face.

"Pressa," she snapped suddenly. "I was going to read you a story, do you remember?"

I expected the girl to be upset, but she simply rose, waved to me, and followed Jardine away.

I felt a strange sense of loss as I watched her go.

Chapter Twelve

My dress was clean, but the stain lingered, a faint comet-shaped reminder that I was hated. And by no means did my trials end there; next was the dart-spider.

It wasn't unusual for the women to receive gifts. They were brought into the rooms by the servitors, or left on the tables just inside the main door. Harette had asked for new make-up, and had received a tin of iridescent paint over which she and the others all but swooned. When she carried it back to our room, she insisted on applying it to Bethery.

"You must!" she said. "Above your green eyes, it will look as if you are born of la Grulla above . . ."

I shrank back, knowing their invitation was not for me, but for an unfathomable reason, Xith pushed the shawl I had so admired into my arms. The beautiful soft fabric felt warm to the touch, but it was light as a breeze and the swirling designs seemed to shift and shimmer as I held it.

The others gathered around the mirror. I retreated to Bethery's bed, for I knew I wasn't welcome, and was glad to have a moment to myself. I wrapped the shawl around my shoulders. I hadn't had any new clothes since I'd walked through the doors of the Den, and the shawl felt wonderfully luxuriant compared to the plain fabric of my gown. I was settling back on the pillows when I felt a movement next to my skin, and a sudden hot pain, as if something had hit me very hard in the crook of my elbow.

I gasped, but the sound was too soft to attract the attention of the others. I pulled the shawl away from my arm, and as I did, some small thing scuttled free. It was the colour of old parchment and barely as long as half my finger, but panic filled me at the dreaded sight of the eight slender legs and the curved tail tipped with a sharp barb.

A dart-spider.

I felt sick to my stomach even before I registered the true stinging pain. The room darkened and grey spots danced before my eyes. I had read enough to know what would happen next. The poison would spread through my veins, my own racing heart pumping it around my body. Already my fingers and toes were tingling and growing numb.

I opened my mouth, trying to speak. The others were only blurred shapes now, their voices distorted, as if they came from deep underwater.

" . . . looks divine . . ."

"Truly the most . . . colour . . ."

"Must request some for myself . . ."

And then, suddenly, very clearly, Bethery was before me. Her beautiful eyes were rimmed with glittering green. Her perfect lips parted: "And what do you think, sugar?"

"You look like la Grulla Herself," I replied, feeling faint and breathless.

And then, I felt nothing at all.

***

I woke, and beyond a veil of greyness, Bethery's face bent low over me. She was saying something. Behind her there were murmurs of protest, and a mocking laugh that echoed in my ears.

I faded again.

I woke, and the veil had turned bright red. Pain blazed through every joint, every limb. I was surely dying. And then, above me, was a pair of dark eyes, and they looked into mine so deeply. Strong arms wrapped around me, keeping me safe and still against the rising tide of nausea and dizziness. I was lifted . . .

I faded again.

I woke, and I was bathed in sweat, and covered with cotton sheets, every fibre cool against my heated skin. I drew in a breath, and it was like drinking after a long thirst – delicious and pure and fresh.

The dimensions of the bed were wrong and I came fully awake in a sudden panic; where was I? This bed was not mine! Had I fallen asleep after tending a mecenas? Maestra Tinir would kill me!

My eyes opened on a cloud of soft, white, gauzy material. I pushed myself up, and realised it was the canopy of a bed larger than any I'd ever seen in my life. The coverlet, which I had crumpled in my oblivious sleep, was thick and heavy, also white, patterned with intricate designs in indigo. The rest of the room was done in whites and blues, which made it seem clean and warm at the same time: a rug over the polished floorboards beside the bed, a chair, and thick heavy drapes covering two windows, one to my right, and one in the wall behind the bed. And a solid oak door, opposite the bed, which was closed.

I shut my eyes for a minute. By the Pattern, I prayed. *If I open my eyes and find this was all a dream, I will still think it the nicest one I've had in a long time.*

Chapter Thirteen

"Oh, you got those pretty eyes open at last," said a voice.

I turned my head to see a woman with a kindly, much-lined face. She was wearing a white skirt and blouse, and a white cap on her dark hair.

"I –"

"You bin deep in a fever a long time," she informed me brusquely in a heavy Second Tier accent as she folded the sheet down over my chest. Over my *naked* chest. I wondered, dazedly, how this occurred. "Where is my shift?"

"Oh, that old thing." She huffed. "It weren't too nice to look at. I believe Oren took it to be burned."

"No!" I exclaimed, struggling to sit up. "I need it!"

"There's no shortage of dresses in the Citadel, child," the woman said, faintly exasperated, as she tried to push me back down onto the bed.

"There were things in the pockets –" I protested, my voice trailing off as I realised I sounded utterly pathetic. "My things."

The woman gave me a level look, then turned her head. I saw, sitting on a low table beside the bed, the crumpled julepe cards, and my white feather. There was also the beautiful scarf that Xith had passed to me, just before . . . just before what?

"Now," she looked at me pointedly, "you keep yourself calm. It were a nasty bite."

"A bite," I repeated dumbly, and only then did I remember the dart-spider. What had happened to it? Sudden panic seized me. "Bethery!" Again, I jolted upright.

The woman seized my shoulders and clucked her tongue. "Now, what I tell you about calm? Sit you back, there."

"But –"

"No one else was harmed by the thing," she soothed me. "There was precious little left of it after one young raven-haired woman was done."

I gave a small laugh and flopped back on the soft bed. The pillows let out *whuffs* of air. I could just imagine what a mess Bethery would have made of that monster. Nothing intimidated her, and a dart-spider would be no exception. But how had the thing ended up in the shawl in the first place? Dart-spiders weren't indoor creatures by nature – they preferred the full light of day, the warmth of metal and earth, and they certainly wouldn't seek out the dark, humid space of the Den.

"But how did she call for help?" I asked, remembering the kind eyes and strong arms that had lifted me in my dreams.

"How?" The woman looked puzzled.

"The women of the Den – they aren't allowed through the Oak Door."

"Oh, but they rapped on it until the sentinel heard. Honestly, though, I've not seen any man tend to a woman's needs so quickly," she went on. "I've no idea what importance you are to him, but he was quick as lightning to fetch Doctor Oren when he heard."

Miguel. It must have been Miguel who rescued me. There was no other man in the Citadel who would give a honeyed fig whether I lived or died.

"Now, Oren'll be back in to see you before dark. He's set your ankle to rights – what you were doing to it, I've no clue. Until then, you're not to move from this bed." Something in her tone warned me that if I did, she would dole out a severe punishment.

There was a noise from outside the door, and a second later, a brisk knock sounded.

"Come on in," she called, and a smaller, younger woman wearing a white cap and an apron over a grey dress bustled through, carrying a tray that seemed far too large. She almost tipped it over, spilling the covered plates and jug to the floor, but caught it just in time with a rueful smile.

"You're awake, then!" she said cheerfully.

"Only just," muttered my nurse. "Well, then. She could use some food. Thank you, Adina."

My gaze, however, was on the space behind the girl. Through the open door I caught sight of a man in guardia uniform. He was facing the hallway, away from me, but I knew him all the same; Miguel.

Suddenly I felt a lot safer.

The serving girl – Adina – set the tray on a table, and went across to the wall on my left to draw aside the drapes with a quick sweep of her arms. Sunlight flooded the room, and I blinked. It had been a long time since I'd seen unfiltered daylight.

"Hold your protests, Hanna!" the girl said cheekily as my nurse rounded on her. "The girl is pale as a white moth. She'll be lacking her vitamins, and you know what Oren will say about that."

I was too busy staring out the window to pay much attention. It showed a view of the city as I had never seen it before; rooftops and chimneys stretching as far as the horizon, where the world dropped away to the Lower Tiers. Carrier pigeons winged their way across the distant clouds.

"One of the nicest rooms," Adina said expansively. "The others on this floor – much too grand. This," she returned to the tray and picked it up again, the plates clattering and jangling, "sedate and comfortable, if you ask me."

It didn't surprise me that they hadn't wasted one of the grander rooms on me, but if this was one of the less luxurious ones, I couldn't begin to imagine what the rest of the Citadel must be like. I scooted back in the bed as Adina placed the tray on my lap and removed the lids from the plates. Steam wafted out, and the most delightful scent of cinnamon and butter. There was a stack of pancakes, a small dish of butter, a bowl of strawberries, some kind of syrup in a small jar, and a pitcher of cream. The jug was full of spicy tea, and Hanna poured a measure into a delicate white teacup. After the plain pickings I'd had in the Den, it looked like a feast.

"Now, you make sure to eat all of this," the girl said with a smile. "Don't leave a crumb. You'll need all the strength you can to heal properly." She nodded towards my ankle.

My cheeks burned in sudden shame, and I ducked my head. "Does –" My voice came out soft and cracked. I tried again. "Does everyone know? Who I am, I mean? The whole Citadel?"

"Oh, child," Hanna murmured over Adina's shoulder, a sympathetic set to her wrinkles. "Your name is known, I admit it. But don't fret. There be worse things have happened, and worse things that will happen in times to come. It will be hard, but you've the look of a strong young woman. You'll bear it."

I wasn't so sure. I turned my eyes to the food instead, wondering if I could possibly eat it all, as the Adina insisted I must.

"Come now, girl. We'll leave the lass to it," Hanna said. Adina looked like she wanted to stay, but she obeyed the older woman's shooing gesture.

"Wait," I called, stopping them before they reached the door. "Thank you. Both of you."

A smile creased the old woman's face; Adina was already smiling, but she shared a look with Hanna that I couldn't decipher.

Hanna nodded. "I'll be back later with the Doctor. Otherwise, just ask Miguel if you need anything, won't you? You can trust him."

And then they were gone. The door shut behind them, and I looked at the tray. For once, the knot in my stomach didn't clench at the thought of eating; I picked up the silverware and cut into the pancakes. The smell of cinnamon filled my nostrils and made my mouth water. I scooped up the strawberries and poured cream over them. I shovelled a forkful into my mouth, and the taste exploded over my tongue like fireworks. Even the small portions of food I'd managed in the Den had been nothing like this. This was heaven.

I devoured every morsel on that tray, and washed it down with the spicy tea. It was the best meal I'd ever eaten in my life and soon, feeling full and heavy, I pushed the tray to the side and lay back down, wondering what Maestra Tinir would think if she knew the volume of food I'd just consumed. Cream, syrup, and sugary pancakes. 'You'll be too fat to dance' – her disapproving voice worried at my conscience.

What did it matter? I thought back as I put a hand on my taut belly. *What difference did it make?*

The tears came, then, and I cried until the thick, fluffy pillows were damp.

***

Oren did come, as promised, and examined me with as much impassivity as he had the first time. My ankle was twisted and turned, poked and prodded, and then, finally, slathered in more ointment and bound in more cloth. My elbow was treated similarly, though the pain of the sting was already fading. Before he left, the healer sniffed, and told me: "Something that will aid the healing process is general cleanliness. Your injury will not prevent you from washing, if you wish to partake of a bath."

I stared at him for a moment. "I would love a bath. Am I then to go back to the Den?"

"Heavens, no. You will not be going back there for the time being, I care not what anyone says. The risk of infection through shared facilities is too great. You have a private bathing chamber here." He pointed to a door in the wall to my right. "But don't use it alone. I'll have Hanna help you. I won't have your health suffering the ill humours associated with poor hygiene."

***

Once he was gone, I struggled out of bed. I felt dizzy and weak, but at least the bulk of my pain no longer centred on my ankle. Instead, it was my arm that felt fat and heavy. Gritting my teeth, I tottered to the window, where I leaned on the sill and took in the city.

How strange it was, to gaze across those gables, over the tops of the shops and taverns, the spires of the carrier-pigeon stations, towards the White Pavilion; my home. Since arriving at the age of thirteen, I'd never been away from it for this long. What would my sisters be doing now? What jokes were they laughing at? What dances did they practice? An ache bloomed in my heart, and the ever-present knot in my stomach twisted.

I will be home once more, I told myself. *Back with Vahn, Rehina, Firrelli, laughing, helping with hairstyles, happily lost in the clatter of endless footsteps and chatter and movement.*

I turned away and hobbled towards the door. The knob twisted easily in my hand, and found myself facing the bulky guardsman. Miguel still had a revolver-pistol against his hip, but he was such a welcome sight to me now, I didn't mind it.

His stony expression didn't change. "Imre." His voice was low and gravelly. "You should not leave your room."

"But I had to thank you," I said. "For coming, for carrying me out of the Den. I owe you my life."

He looked at me in surprise. "But it wasn't me at all. It happened during my absence. Until I heard the talk in the kitchens, of the Dancer girl stung by a dart-spider, I didn't know it was you. It was only then I asked to be transferred, that I might continue to guard you."

"Then – who?"

"That I do not know. I assume the sentinela on duty raised the alarm, after one of the women came to him."

I was glad Miguel had asked to stay with me, but the identity of the man who had carried me became a puzzle. To whom did those dark eyes belong? No stranger had ever looked at me with such concern and tenderness. If they were not Miguel's – and they were not, I realised, looking at his bright blue irises – whose were they?

***

I wandered my room and discovered all its secrets. Behind the second set of drapes, there were doors set with glass panes that led out onto a small balcony. Beyond this was a small courtyard, filled to overflowing with flowers, and edged with glorious vines. I longed to step through and breathe the scents of that place, but when I tried the handle, I found it locked.

The door to the bathing chamber was open, revealing a cream-tiled room with a wondrous bath, a basin, and a commode, all which ran off a complicated series of pipes. I would have to wait for Hanna, for I had no idea how to work the knobs and levers.

As darkness crept in, it hit me that I had nothing else to do except sleep. I slipped into that incredible bed, and I slept well, despite everything. At this point, I might imagine that I dreamed, and in my dream, I saw the Prince.

I did not see his face. I had never seen his face, at least, not close enough to know his features; but I knew it was him, in that way a person knows things in dreams. He walked with a brisk step down a long hallway. It was badly lit, but he seemed to know where he was going, and didn't stop until he reached the end.

Here, there was a door, made of thick oak panels held together with heavy iron bands. His confidence seemed to falter at that, and his steps slowed. He stopped just before it, and raised his hand to the knob, but paused again, as if he couldn't quite bring himself to complete the task.

For a long moment, he stood there while I watched him. Then, all at once, he whirled, and my heart quickened, for in the dream I was sure he'd seen me. But he blinked, and shook his head, then began the long walk back through the shadows of the hallway.

I woke feeling strange, as if I'd left something of myself behind in that dream.

Chapter Fourteen

True to her word, when Hanna came with my dinner, she gave many horrified exclamations. "I would have offered to help you earlier, if I'd been at all aware you weren't bathing by choice."

I laughed at this, slightly ashamed. "Conditions in the Den were less than ideal for hygiene. I bathed when I could, but the sweat and heat soon made me clammy once more."

She sighed. "I bin afraid of that. Is there anything worse than so many bodies cooped up in a small space?"

And, to my delight, she walked across and used a key to unlock the door to the terrace, which she left open while I swung my legs over the edge of the bed and took the tray onto my lap.

The scents of the garden were heady and made me long to stretch my legs. As it was, I felt significantly cheered, and decided I would not give up my freedom to wander once more. While her back was turned, I leaned over and took one of Miguel's playing cards from the bedside table. I folded it into the latch, bending it over to hide it from view.

Three maids came to my room after this; one of them was Adina. The others looked at me with shy glances. I was sure I didn't cut a very intimidating figure even when I wasn't laid up in a bed, pale, my hair messy, and dressed in a very crumpled shift, yet they seemed in complete awe.

"Hello," I said tentatively, and was rewarded with shocked glances. Then Adina curtseyed. The others followed her example, and I raised my hands. "Please, there's no need. But, what are your names?"

"Oh!" said Adina. Her voice was richer than usual for someone so young. She couldn't have been older than fourteen. "This is Elen and Paje."

I nodded to them and smiled. "My name is Imre. And please, don't address me as Lady, or Mistress, or I might scream."

Adina let out a sudden laugh, the sound completely honest, and of them all, I liked her best.

They led me into the bathing chamber, and Paje turned some wheels and pulled levers with practiced grace. Steam hissed, and wonderful warm water filled the air in streams. The pipes were fitted with rotating nozzles, which whirled as the pressure passed through them. There were other taps which released scented soap, and bubbles that made the water froth like clouds.

I stripped off my garments happily. The shift smelled stale and even the cool air of the room felt better on my skin than the worn-out fabric. The other maids averted their eyes, though I could see them glancing at me with barely-concealed wonder. Adina, however, made no secret of her admiration. Her eyes danced across my pale breasts, slid down my frame towards my thighs, then alighted on my navel. When she met my gaze, it was with a frankness I approved of. In the Pavilion, I bathed with my sisters, changed clothes with them, and slept naked alongside one another during the hot nights of summer. To find shame in one's unclothed body was an affront to the Pattern, who had designed ourselves so skillfully.

I stepped into the jets of water eagerly, and found the massaging streams of moisture just as wonderful as they'd promised. I breathed in the heady scented steam and let out a sigh of delight.

The maids, keeping out of the path of the water, scrubbed me with sponges and lathered my hair, pouring jug-fulls over my head to rinse it clean. As the steam filled the room, and they grew more certain I wasn't actually the prim, proper lady they were used to servicing, they began to chatter.

"Your hair is as fine as silk." Elen lifted a strand, running her fingers through it. "And so golden! Is it your mother's gift, or your father's?"

I did not want to think about my mother, and so I smiled. "Neither. But it is far too flat and straight."

"I would give anything for hair like yours," Elen disagreed. "Do the men like it?"

I blinked at her through the rainbow bubbles.

"Your . . ."

"My mecenas?" I asked her with a smile to show I wasn't insulted. "Some do. I suppose they don't choose me for my hair, though."

She blushed a terrible red, but a moment later she asked, "What do they look for, in a woman, then?"

I tried to guess her age. She must be older than me, but only by a few years. Twenty? Had she truly not bedded a man yet?

"The mecenas who come to the White Pavilion are not looking for a woman with which to spend the rest of their lives," I said. "They are looking for the one who will offer them what they want in that moment. We give them that for a price, and the proceeds are directed into the city coffers. If they are pleased, they will pay more, and Cuidad thrives. This is in service to the Pattern."

Paje looked away, her lips pursed, and I could tell she found the subject distasteful. I wondered if she had been listening to the speeches of la Boca, and whether she believed his words.

But Elen persevered. "They say that you were bought here by the Principe Regente."

"I was," I confirmed.

She seemed troubled by this, and I took the opportunity to press her. "I've gotten the impression the Principe often invites women to stay at the Citadel."

"Oh, yes," said Adina carelessly. "This isn't the first time we've been asked to attend to them, either."

"But you must know," Elen added quietly, glaring at Adina, "that people move through the Citadel like brown moths in warm-season. Guests come and go. There are meetings, and there are dinners, and functions, and ceremonies; dignitaries, guildsman, mercenaries."

"But there are other women," I said. "Others like me."

"Oh, not at all like you," Adina assured me. "The last was a terrible bitch! She pulled my hair when I dropped her necklace."

Elen hid a giggle behind her hand. "You slapped her, Adi!"

Adina grinned. "It wasn't even her necklace. It was borrowed; she was supposed to return it before she went into the Den. I suspect she wanted to hide it in her bodice and give it to her lover to pawn when he came to visit her. As if the stipend wasn't enough! But with the jewel hopelessly shattered, she wouldn't have gotten a penny."

So, this was how it was – just as Senor Grath had told me. The Prince brought women here, and when he grew bored with them, he sent them to the Den. There they lived out their lives, cloistered and forgotten.

"You needn't worry, Imre," said Elen. "You would be best to enjoy your time here while it lasts. If nothing else, you will have a story to tell the other ladies when you go back to the Den, no?"

I nodded at her. Her words didn't lessen my dread at returning to the Den, to the other women who had been put aside, but I appreciated them nonetheless.

Finally, when I was completely soaked and warm, my skin felt heavy with moisture. Adina, Elen, and Paje came forward with towels. But before they could wrap them around me, I shivered from a sudden breeze, and saw that the door to my room had opened.

We hadn't bothered to close the one to the bathing room, since Miguel knew why the maids had come and wouldn't intrude. But this man was not Miguel.

I looked into the face of the Principe Regente.

I was dripping wet; droplets of bathwater splashed onto the tiles. My hair was knotted, and my cheeks flushed, and my skin glistening. I had never been so naked as I was then.

He stared at me for a long minute, his eyes roaming over my bandaged ankle, my abdomen, the thatch of hair between my legs; he carefully noted my breasts, my jutting collarbone, the trailing strands of hair across my shoulders. They settled at last on my eyes. I wondered if he remembered me from the garden. If he even knew where he was at all. Finally, he said, "Forgive me."

It was only then that I noticed Senor Grath standing just behind his shoulder. His gaze had followed the same path as the Prince's, but with a coldness so palpable, the steamy warmth of the room chilled.

"Forgive me," the Prince repeated, though he certainly didn't sound in the least bit sorry. "I did not mean to intrude." And with a swift turn on his heel, he strode away. Senor Grath followed him closely.

Miguel peered around the edge of the door. "I'm sorry, Imre. I told him you were bathing."

I waved him away. I knew nothing Miguel could have said would have stopped the Prince doing as he pleased, though why Senor Grath had to take a peek when, even clothed, I disgusted him so, I had no idea. I turned to my stunned maids, who hurried to wrap me in the towels.

I wasn't sure how I was supposed to feel about the encounter. In one of the Blossom Rooms, I would have been proud to have a man look at me so. The Prince had all but asked me for a dance, and such a man would have inspired competition from my sisters; I would have been exhilarated to have him choose me. But here in the Citadel, everything was different.

Still, I couldn't keep the glowing smile from my face. I was so fresh and clean, I thought I would float away, but then, they produced a nightgown so soft, it felt like it was woven from feathers, and I thought if I raised my arms, I might just fly away, just like la Grulla, into the sky.

"Thank you," I said, and both Elen and Adina looked pleased. Paje did not return my smile.

***

Doctor Oren was right. After my bath, it seemed all my ill humours had washed away, and both my ankle and my elbow ceased to pain me so much.

I slept and woke. The maids had left me a clean dress. It wasn't new, but it was clean and in good repair.

Chapter Fifteen

If I thought the next turning would be any different, I would have been disappointed. Hanna brought me food, and chattered away as she set it down. This time, it was moth-meat cooked with herbs and pepper, juicy grilled tomatoes, salty crackers with white cheese, and hot milky coffee.

I ate gratefully, then slipped out of bed to look through the window over the city. When my ankle began to twinge, I went back to bed, where I lay down and toyed with my battered white feather and Miguel's cards, arranging them in lines, shuffling, dealing, and attempting to play hacer julepe against myself.

Hanna returned with more food at midday.

"Does everyone in the Citadel eat this well?" I asked her.

She smiled. "Oh, surely you are served such delicacies at the Pavilion."

But I shook my head. "We eat plain fare. 'Give to those who have nothing the food from your table, and you will serve the Pattern.'"

Hanna's smile thinned.

"We may eat as we choose," I said quickly, lest she thought the Daughters were deprived. "But of course, if we are to dance to the glory of the Seven, we are better to eat as they did. And so, the choice is limited."

"It's no wonder you're as thin as a rake." Hanna shook her head. "Tell me this. Do the mecenas eat as you do?"

"Of course not," I said. "They are given whatever they desire."

Hanna fixed me with a gaze which I could not quite read, then stood up abruptly. "Eat. You will serve the Pattern with the nourishment and pleasure you find in this food."

I ate.

***

That night, I sank into a wondrous sleep. My dreams folded over me like melted butter, and I was drawn into places where I felt comfortable and warm. But I woke all too soon, and it was to an empty room, darkness, and shadows.

My ankle barely twinged as I slipped out of bed, but my stomach clenched as I looked around the room. As wonderful as it was, it was not mine, and I would always be a stranger here.

The drapes were drawn over the window, so I walked instead to the glass doors that led out onto that beautiful balcony. Starlight splashed my skin as I pressed against the glass.

I felt as if I was still in my dream as I tried the handle. The playing card fluttered free – it had done the trick, preventing the door from locking as Hanna closed it.

Turning, I quickly bunched the covers of my bed, placing one of the pillows under the blankets. It would fool anyone at a cursory glance that I remained sleeping in the bed.

I opened the door and slipped through. The balcony had one set of steps leading down into a garden – *the* garden, the same one I had visited from the Den, though now I was on the opposite end.

Making my way through the gardens, I felt weary, but contented. As I rounded the path past the statue of la Grulla, I saw him there at the same moment he saw me: the Principe Regente.

He had divested himself of his shirt for some reason, though the night was not warm. His chest was muscled, his arms well-toned. He sat in the grass, his legs crossed, a burning cigarillo in his hand. He flicked it, again and again, making the sparks jump across the dew-laden blades.

He squinted at me. His words slurred, but his eyes didn't leave mine. "Night-maiden," he said, and it almost sounded like he was singing the words. "Like a splash of la Grulla's light in human form . . ."

Not knowing what to say, I stood there.

"You're not just a dream, are you?" His voice was almost pleading.

I laughed. "No, I'm not."

"Sometimes they seem so very real." He sighed, and flicked more sparks from his cigarillo.

I don't know what made me do it, but I went to him and kneeled in the grass; cold dew seeped through to my skin. I reached out a hand.

He squinted again, trying to focus on my face through the haze born of whatever coursed through his system. Then he grasped my fingers with his free hand, and raised them to his lips. The kiss was soft, barely a brushing of skin against skin, but the warmth of his breath made me shiver.

"Very well," he murmured, pressing my fingers to his cheek. It felt flushed, as if he nursed a fever. "I believe you now."

"What are you doing out here?" He did not look well, but what could I do? I couldn't fetch anyone without giving away my own forbidden nighttime wandering.

"I'm searching." All of a sudden, he leaned backwards, falling onto his back. He still held my hand, and I found myself pulled down alongside him. The cold damp grass was at once awful and pleasant, and my metrónomo pulsed with astonishment: I was lying on the ground with the Príncipe Regente. Above us, la Grulla shone intermittently through a cloud, giving the dark veil a silver haze.

"Isn't it incredible," the Prince said softly. "To think that out there in the Unknown, Old Earth still circles its ruined sun?"

I turned my head sideways so I could see his face. He was drugged, I reminded myself. People under the influence often speculated on such things – there were types of weed-grass that opened the mind to possibilities. Normally, when they recovered from its effects, such musings were far from their mind. I'd seen it often enough among the mecenas, who would become verbose and eloquent, but woke in the morning with sore heads and sharp tempers. My mother had used many types of drugs, too, taking whatever was available at the time. Sometimes they made her sleepy and stupid. Other times, she would become violent, lashing out with her fists and hurting anyone in range, even, at times, herself.

"Yes," I said, running through the stars and planets we couldn't see now: los Amantes, Nuevo Saturno, Constanza. "But there is nothing left there. It's a haunted planet, is it not?"

"No." The Prince shook his head. "No, *we* are the haunted ones."

He appeared to fall into a doze, and after several minutes it was clear he would not wake. I pulled away from his grip and left him there.

***

The next morning, I rose before la Grulla did. I was walking from the bed to the window and back again. My ankle felt much better, for all that I had tested it last night; and so did the rest of me. I had closed the door to the terrace, but tested it again and again, to make sure the card held.

When Hanna brought my breakfast, she beamed. "There is colour in your cheeks!"

I didn't want her to become suspicious about what might have caused this sudden change, so I put the tray to one side and smiled widely. "I feel better. I'm almost certain my ankle will be healed soon." Perhaps then I would be allowed to go home, I added silently.

But Hanna sat on the side of the bed and clasped my hands in hers. "Child." Her eyes were filled with sadness. "My daughter is no older than you. I see her whenever I look at you."

I wondered at the cause of her worry. "Has she ever been injured?"

Hanna shook her head. "No. But it makes me wonder at the world, that a girl so slight as you, so pure, can end up serving as a Daughter of the White Pavilion."

I pulled my hands back suddenly. "You can go," I told her.

She looked at me in puzzlement. "Child? What have I said?"

"What I am," my voice rang cold and distant, like the toll of a clock, "is no concern of yours."

Hanna stood and dusted her apron, her face creased in a frown. "I don't understand."

No, I thought. *You don't.*

I refused to look at her, and after another moment of silence, she finally left, closing the door quietly.

My stomach roiled. My head pounded. Some small voice told me I was being foolish, that Hanna had not intended to insult me; and yet it seemed that everywhere I turned, people were making assumptions and judgements they had no right to make.

The knot in my stomach seemed to expand. It reached out tiny black threads around my heart and squeezed. The pressure built until it was almost painful, a white-hot ache, and I reached for the nearest thing I could reach – the breakfast tray. Plates clattered and clanged as I hurled it. A bowl of sweet-smelling berries splattered over the coverlet like blood. A pot of sugar whirled through the air, tiny white grains sifting silently. For a moment, I was mesmerised by the sight of those grains. They looked so much like the snow in the globe my grandmother had given me.

And then the walls began to shake.

I heard the noise first, building up from the floor, like a great drum being pounded somewhere deep inside the earth. It ran through the walls and shook the globe-light fittings in the ceiling. One of them burst, spraying silver shards over the room. I ducked my head, clutching at the bed, which wobbled underneath me.

The door burst open, and someone rushed at me. I was aware only of firm arms locking around my waist, and then suddenly I was on the wooden floor, with Miguel's large body above me.

All at once, the shaking subsided. Other sounds replaced the deep rumbling: shouts, crashes, and somewhere, a bell ringing.

Miguel pulled back. "Are you all right, Imre?"

I nodded, then winced as my ankle disagreed. I had wrenched the muscles as we fell. Miguel lifted me swiftly onto the bed. "What on earth was that?"

But the big man was already back at the door, where he barked at a passing guardia. "Fetch Doctor Oren. Tell him to come at once," he growled.

"I've been called to the headquarters –," he squawked. "I can't disobey."

"Doctor Oren," Miguel insisted. "Tell him to come to this room immediately."

"What should it matter?" the tomato-faced guardsman burst out. "She's only a whore!"

Miguel's eyes flashed, and he grabbed the collar of the young man's shirt.

"Miguel," I said softly, and then, when he didn't turn around, more loudly. "Miguel. Please. He follows his orders. He has done nothing wrong."

Miguel still did not release him. "At *once*, guardia!" he barked.

"Sargento," the guard stuttered.

"You don't need to defend him," Miguel said darkly, turning to look over me.

I sat up, straightening my shoulders and meeting his eyes. He seemed surprised that I held his gaze, and slowly, the anger faded from his expression. He loosened his grip on the young man's shirt. The guardia, gasping for breath, shot me a poisoned glance; my defence of him hadn't won any good will in that quarter.

Miguel let go of the guardia's shirt. "Get out of my sight," he said through gritted teeth.

The young man scuttled out of the room.

Chapter Sixteen

The shaking had subsided, but at every noise I jumped, thinking it would start up again.

Oren was not pleased to be called. "There are a thousand injuries all over the Citadel," he grouched, but his words were directed at Miguel, not me. "Hers is not so serious."

"I was told to guard her. She is my responsibility," Miguel replied stoically.

Oren muttered, but he confirmed that my ankle had been strained, though not badly. "You will live," he told me.

"Was anyone badly injured?" I asked him.

"A man was killed," he said brusquely. "There are broken hands and wrists. A wall fell in one of the halls, and a roof has collapsed in the garages. I suspect a few autocarriages have been lost."

My heart twinged. "How could this happen?"

"There are rumours," he replied shortly, but before he could say anything more, Hanna appeared in the door behind him.

"The Principe Regente requested you," she said. "It appears – *Señor* –"

"A thousand curses," spat Oren. Without a second glance, he gathered his black bag, and hurried out after her.

Limited as I was by my window, I couldn't see what was going on in the rest of the Citadel, only the black smoke pouring from some fire, giving off a harsh, acrid scent. More alarms sounded, and one building halfway down a central street had collapsed, leaving a cloud of dust in the air that took hours to settle.

I felt relatively safe, but wondered if this was simply because of the distance it put between me and the action. For the first time, I felt almost glad to be sequestered.

Miguel came in to check on me not just once, but three times.

"You should go and see to your wife," I told him, but he shook his head.

"I can't leave my post. If I did, she would have my head, even if Senor Grath did not flay me alive."

"Are you worried for her?"

"Yes." He let out a breath. "But Risella is capable of looking out for herself. 'Never challenge a woman's will. It is stronger than iron and twice as unyielding.' "

This was from the Sacred Text. La Oráculo had spoken it to the Seven who followed la Relojero, just before they had boarded la Grulla, to fly across the Unknown, as Aurelia had stood up and asked to be counted. Miguel was truly full of surprises. "You know la Oráculo's Speech? Have you read the *Words of the Oracle?*"

"Only that one line, and two more," he admitted. "And those I learned from a friend. I do not . . . I don't read well."

A pang of sorrow lanced through my heart. "Is there a reason?"

"My father died when I was young." Miguel leaned on his spear. "And I went to work. My schooling was in repairing water pumps, not words and texts."

How similar our lives were, if he but knew it! "But the original Sacred Text is right here," I said. "In the Great Library. Haven't you ever wanted to read them?"

Miguel shook his head with an ashamed look. "I worked so I could raise my younger brother and sisters. It didn't leave much time for school. I never learned to read at all."

My mind churned. "You still owe me a walk," I reminded him.

His expression relaxed a little. "Tomorrow there is to be some great audience with the heralds. Most of the Citadel staff will be otherwise engaged. It might allow us some leeway."

I didn't want to cause trouble, but at the same time, I was sure Miguel could handle any that might come his way . . .

***

The following morning, I hobbled to the window. The damage to the Ciudad was noticeable, but people, hundreds and hundreds of them, were out in the streets: cleaning up the detritus, shoring up broken foundations, repairing windows and cracked pipelines. There were some automata with them, holding things that would have been too heavy for a human to lift, and a few servitors ferrying crumbled brick back and forth to the refuse hatches in the outer streets, where the grinders would reduce it to dust and the converters would make it into reusable material.

But soon I noticed a trend. A mob was gathering in the Plaza de Lagríma. The noise of their shouting reached my window, though I was too distant to make out the words.

After I had eaten a substantial breakfast, (which pleased Hanna greatly, and also steadied my nerves) and Hanna had left, she and I once again at peace, the big man cracked open the door.

"Your wife?" I asked him.

"Risella is perfectly well," Miguel assured me. "The most damage was caused to our commode, which spilled sewage into the street." He wrinkled his nose. "She was not well pleased."

I could imagine.

"Still, we escaped the worst of it. A man and his wife down the street have a son missing." Sadness tinged his voice. "The boy works at the Reservoir, and was out in a punt cleaning the winch mechanisms when the quake hit. They haven't found him yet."

I felt a sickness in my stomach, the knot clenching tightly. Did I ever live without this knot? "How horrible," I said, inadequate as these words were.

Miguel nodded. "It seems the people have stormed the Citadel. They know the Brotherhood's heralds are here, and they want to be admitted to the audience."

As well they should. They deserve to be heard, and, since meeting with our unstable Prince and his unkind Chief Adviser, not to mention the strange, unfathomable secrets I'd overheard being discussed by noblemen, I didn't know if any of our rulers could be trusted to make it known to the heralds exactly what the common people faced.

But Miguel was obviously thinking in practical terms. "If you want to go to the Library," he said. "There won't be a better chance."

He motioned for me to come to him. I did so, hobbling a little, but feeling much stronger than I had in the past few turnings. When I was finally outside in the hallway and the reality of it sank in, I breathed in and out past a flutter of excitement. I had fastened my new half-veil, and the anonymity gave me confidence.

We walked in silence to the end of the hallway, and there Miguel paused to make sure the way was clear. He looked down at me with a smile. "I promised, did I not?" he said, with a sweep of his hand.

Indeed, he had been entirely correct. There was no one to be seen in the connecting corridor, or in any of the rooms on either side. At the end of it, Miguel showed me a small lift-car beyond a caged door. There were two cars inside, side-by-side, and we stepped into the one on the left. It was a cramped fit, and the caged sides showed a dizzying view up and down the shaft.

"These are the servant's lifts," Miguel said. "If you need to get somewhere in haste, you're much better off picking these routes. Those who use these ways move much more quickly – and they don't ask questions."

He was right about this, as well; we passed five maids and footmen in the opposite car on our way down. They barely spared us a glance.

We went down for what seemed like a long way. The air chilled and there were fewer lanterns. "How far down are we?"

"The Library is below the ground floor," my guide said. "In fact, the only rooms lower than this are the prison cells. Did you not know this?"

I shook my head, and Miguel stepped ahead of me to open a solid-looking wooden door. This led into a passageway of stone, the ceiling curved and lower than was comfortable. Globe-lights were mounted on the walls, but the light they gave was intermittent, and deep shadows fell in the spaces between.

We were deep underground, but though I could smell cold earth and stone, the air was dry. We passed an intersecting passage, and I glanced down. There was a door at the end, bound with iron hinges. Obviously, there were many more rooms and passages to be found under the foundations of the Citadel.

"This way." Miguel pointed ahead. I left the side passage and followed him to a low archway in which was set a gate made of iron curlicues.

"This is a back entrance," Miguel informed me. "It's not guarded like the main one is." The door opened, and he peered inside, then looked over his shoulder at me. "Come on." He beckoned, before he vanished into the darkness.

***

The Library was bigger than I ever imagined, sprawling across the entire footprint of the Citadel, rambling through nooks and alcoves, all lined with shelves. These were crammed with books of all shapes, sizes, and conditions, as well as curling, creased papers and even ancient yellowed scrolls. Every book in Tierra Mejór must have been packed into this place.

We had emerged amid the shelves. Dust was thick in the air, but about a hundred paces ahead, I spotted a circular desk, which must have covered the main entrance. There was a man there – maybe two men, but I couldn't see them clearly, and they didn't look in our direction.

"Which way should we go?" I whispered.

He shrugged. "I've never been down here."

I would have been happy just to wander the shelves at random, but I was very aware of time, or lack thereof. Still, I couldn't help trailing a finger over the spines of the books nearest me, luxuriating in the worn cloth and paper that had been held by so many different hands over the years. How Tomas would love to see this place!

At that moment, there was a great noise, a resounding *thump*, and a shudder that came from beneath the floor. It shook my very bones, and I turned to Miguel to ask what could possibly be happening – was this another quake, and the Citadel about to collapse on our very heads? – but then I began to slide across the floor!

No, I realised half a heartbeat later; it wasn't me that was moving, but the shelf at my side. And all the shelves beyond. They were switching places, some moving forwards, some backwards . . . all shuddering and shaking. Oh! My confused mind made sense of this at last.

The shelves were built in concentric rings of varying widths and heights. Each ring slid, clockwise or counterclockwise, around the central desk. When the gaps in the shelves aligned, I caught a glimpse of the men behind the counter, only to have them hidden once more when the movement finally stopped.

A few papers fluttered free of their place, settling at my feet.

Amazed, I gaped at Miguel, who shrugged to say he knew nothing about this.

"Well," I whispered. "Even if I *had* known where to look, I certainly don't now!"

"Well, my Lady," Miguel returned. "This was your idea."

But I wasn't going to give up so easily. I wasn't really sure why it was so important, except for the niggling notion that Miguel had saved my life, and he was my one true ally – perhaps, even a friend – in this place, and I wanted to repay him. Teaching him to read would be a valuable exchange, at least in my mind. And so, resolute, I began to walk again.

I reached the end of a row of shelves, and found myself face-to-face with an automaton.

I had never seen one up close before. To be sure, he was a sight! Unlike the sentinela, with their blank, eyeless faces, and stiff limbs, his built was deliberately humanised. His face was sculpted from platinum, his eyes, two pinpricks of green light, looked out from deep sockets, beyond which some inner servos whirred. He wore a long brown robe, but it fit him awkwardly, and was caught in the joint of one elbow.

He was holding a lantern and several thick books, and saw me at the same instant I saw him. He looked surprised, then immediately lowered his eyes. "I'm sorry, my Lady." His voice had the rough edges and strange cadence of a music box. "I didn't expect to find anyone here."

It took me a moment to regain my equilibrium, during which I continued to stare. Would he think me rude? Did he truly think at all?

"Feval," I said.

His eyes blinked, uncomprehending. "Yes, my Lady?"

"Do you not remember me?" I prodded.

"Of course, my Lady."

Miguel shook his head. "This is not the automaton who piloted our autocarriage, Imre. They share one body, and one mind – their thoughts are loaded into a central crystal, located deep within the Tierra Mejór's core, which powers them also. Every now and then, their programming can be updated through the interface stations. There is one in the Citadel, and several more scattered across the Tiers and the Wheel."

I should have known it, of course, by the two working eyes. Still, the automata at the Pavilion did not share this face.

"Older models," Miguel explained, when I told him. "Probably cobbled together from parts of servitors and other automata. The only truly high-functioning automata are kept here in the Citadel."

"Then what is the name of this one?"

"Name?" Miguel blinked. "Feval was named by the guardia, as he's forever coming and going. But they don't all have names, you know."

"The Librarians call me Divon." The automaton tilted its head to one side in a very human gesture. "Normally, no one comes back this far into the stacks, except the Librarians. Are you looking for something in particular?"

"Yes!" Snapping out of my trance, I looking over my shoulder at Miguel. "Where is the Sacred Text kept?"

The automaton's eyes did not widen. He did not smile. But a slight shift in the tone of his voice suggested he would have smiled if he could. "Oh! I can show you. Do you have your permit?"

My blank look must have given me away instantly. "I think – I lost it."

But the automaton only glanced towards the desk, and when he confirmed no one was watching, he said: "Please, follow me."

He tucked his books under his arm, and, holding the lantern high, led us around the edge of the shelves and into the next curving aisle.

"So very few people ask to see the Texts now," said Divon. "There are permits that must be signed by secretaries and officials, and I think most people don't bother. So, the Librarians do not keep the Texts on show. But I prefer it that way."

"You prefer?" I asked him. "Do you have preferences?"

"I am not designed to experience emotions," the automaton said, "but there are often circumstances in which I find pleasure. Visiting the *Sacred Text* is one of them."

He spoke as if referring to an old friend, and I had to struggle to keep from laughing. They were just books, after all! Still, when we reached a point about halfway along this aisle, and he pointed the way into a narrow alcove in the wall, which would stay fixed even when the shelves moved. In here, I felt a sense of . . . quietness is the best word I can think of to describe it. As if a thick cloak had been draped over this area, and no sound from outside was carried within.

At the end of this alcove was a door, only just higher than my head. The automaton pushed it open with his elbow, and behind me, Miguel had to duck to pass through.

Beyond was a small room. The floor was cement, the walls – bare brick. The cold drenched me like ice water, but again, the air was dry. Against the far wall was a modest wooden plinth. Upon it was a large book, open, displaying tea-coloured paper. The brittle edges had started to curl and crack, but if the book was truly five hundred years old, it was incredibly well-preserved.

I stepped closer, breathing the smell of dust and a sweeter scent – perhaps the glue, or ink?

"The pages were treated with oil," the automaton said. "It has helped them last the ages, but you, as a human, should still handle it with care. The secretions from your skin will erode the paper."

I wasn't sure I actually wanted to handle this precious tome, but now that I was here, how could I shy away? And so, I reached out a finger and gently traced the paper. It felt soft beneath my touch, as if covered with the finest hairs. My fingers tingled.

. . .and the words from la Oráculo's mouth rang true in her ears. And though la Relojero turned away, and went to her home, and tried to block them from her mind, she dreamed that night of a voice, coming from the darkness.

"Why do you turn your face from me, child?" he asked.

"I am afraid," la Relojero said. "I do not know how I am to do this."

"You fear what you do not know. Trust that the Pattern will guide you."

La Relojero felt a gentle breath of warmth waft over her. She felt the safety and security of great hands holding her weight, and she knew that the voice spoke truly.

"Are you still afraid?" asked the voice.

"Yes," replied la Relojero.

It seemed to her that the voice smiled, and it was a kindly smile. "That is well, for that is human. But to do what you must, even when you are afraid, that is true divinity."

And so, la Relojero rose from her bed and lit her candle-lamp, and she began to fit the smallest of the cogs and gears together that would become the Tierra Mejór . . .

I turned from the open page to the next.

It was written in Español, as all important works were, but the text wasn't neat or orderly. In some places, it looked like it had been written by different hands, and the colours of the ink varied from black to blue and red, green, sepia, and a light orange. At times, it was decorated with curlicues, embossed, surrounded by intricate designs of spokes and wheels; a few flickerings of gold leaf or silver paint marked one or two passages, and a brilliant illumination done in vivid gouache illustrated one tract. There were smaller drawings in the margins: cogs and gears, ratchets and keys and springs and bolts and pistons. The makings of the Tierra Mejór.

The small room fell silent. Miguel and the automaton were behind me, looking over each of my shoulders. "It's beautiful," I said at last. "More beautiful than I thought it would be."

"It is," agreed Miguel. "I never imagined anything like this."

I turned to Divon. "Do you come here often?"

"I do," he said. "I find I like to be alone with the book. There is something about it which attracts me. I cannot say exactly what . . ."

"Have you read the whole Text?" I asked him.

"Several times," he admitted. "Many passages I've reread even more often."

I didn't have to ask him why. The book drew me in, even now, urging me to read it, to make sense of its pages. I carefully turned to the final few leaves, where I found several detailed drawings of the Inner Workings, and many technical labels and lists. "Do you understand all of it?"

Divon shook his head. "No. At least . . . not in that sense. But sometimes, I'm sure I can see . . . a pattern, a purpose . . ."

The drawings leaped in and out of focus before my eyes. I knew what the automaton meant. There was something here, something that could be understood, if one could somehow grasp just a fraction of it . . .

Miguel cleared his throat, bringing me back to the moment. We had been here a long time, longer than I'd intended, and we should be getting back before someone realised we were gone.

"Well," I said to him. "What do you now think of learning to read?"

Miguel was silent for a moment, then said: "I think, if I were able to read something so grand, it would certainly be worth it."

The automaton reached for one of the tomes under his arm, nearly dropping the rest. "This is a simple text. Some Old Earth poetry. It's a good place to start with letters and language."

I took the book. "Thank you, Divon."

He nodded, seeming pleased. "May I ask you, however, why you wanted to know my name?"

I laughed, for even I wasn't sure why it was important. "All living things deserve a name."

Slowly, he shook his head, his eyes blinking rapidly. "I am not a living thing," he said. "Merely, an automaton. A unit, only part of a whole, as all artificials are. An individual name makes little sense." He turned, revealing a slot on the back of his neck, where I supposed the crystals that controlled him must fit. Sorrow washed through me, and I wasn't sure why I should feel it. He *was* only a machine, just like a rotor-tram; designed for a function. Even his experience of pleasure was nothing more than a surety that his inner workings ran smoothly.

But then, wasn't that the case for the human experience of pleasure?

"My name is Imre," I supplied in return. Even if he already knew it, had received the information from the crystal core, I wanted to introduce myself personally. "May I come back here some time?"

Divon nodded. "I spend most of my turnings sorting books among the shelves here. I'd be glad if you happened to come by."

Miguel cleared his throat once more, and I caught a flicker of annoyance in his gaze. I humoured him to take my elbow and lead me back through the low door; once we were outside the alcove, Divon reached for a lever with a rounded handgrip that stuck up from the floor and pulled it, making the outer ring of shelves slide left, and allowing us a clear passage to the door, through which we'd arrived.

"It's the safest way to come and go," he said, "without the Librarians' knowledge."

Chapter Seventeen

It was a silent journey back up through the floors, except for the clanking of the lift-car. I looked at the book Divon had given me. It was called *Gilgamesh*. I'd never seen it before. The language, Inglés, was one I was familiar with – our own tongue was made up of a mixture of this and Español. This, however, seemed to be an archaic form. To Divon, of course, it probably *was* simple. In any case, it would do.

I handed it to Miguel, whose large hands fitted awkwardly around the clothbound cover. "At least it is fairly thin," he said dubiously, breaking the silence.

"A thin book does not entail meagre content," I told him, a favourite saying of my abuela.

The lift-car hissed to a stop at the end of the hallway where we'd first entered it. As the floor slid into view, I noticed figures at the far end. It was too late. One of them, seeing the movement, turned; and I recognised him in that instant. It was the Prince.

He looked at once vastly different and entirely the same: he wore a blue shirt this time, with a braided gold belt, and a dark blue sigil embroidered on the breast, brown trousers, and black boots that shone so brightly I could see the reflection of the globe-lights in them.

He was surrounded by three others, a man and two women. I saw with distaste that the man was Senor Grath. The others were unfamiliar, dressed in fine clothes – one of the women in trousers and a silk shirt, the other in a long blue dress with puffed shoulders. They were deeply engaged in their conversation, so even while the first man fixed his gaze on us – on me – they noticed nothing.

I waited for him to speak out, just as I had the other night in the garden, but instead he turned his eyes towards the others, and led them onwards.

Miguel turned to me. His face was almost ashen. "I shouldn't have taken you out of your room."

"I would have taken the blame," I said, but he shook his head.

"Never. Now, come, we must go back."

"Surely –" I protested, as the lift door clanked open. "Surely we could go and watch?"

Miguel at once began to refuse.

I'd been prepared for this. "Aren't you even curious?" I cut him off. He paused for a moment, then sighed. Tucking the book under his arm, we followed the group at a distance.

***

While Miguel and I had been skulking about in the hidden depths of the Library, the audience had been gathering in a great hall, the Cámara de Justice, which we reached by crossing a bridge and following an open walkway. We entered on one of the higher levels; the great room stretched high, through three floors of the Citadel, and was ringed with galleries. All of these, and the floor below, were crowded with people. The public were not normally allowed to enter the Citadel, and for some, it was probably the first time during their lifetimes that they had been inside. I had been only once before, to witness the Principe's return from the Estate.

But even though their presence had been allowed, this time, it wasn't wholly trusted. There were many Sentinela ranged along the walls, long revolver-rifles in their hands, and even two clockwork guns mounted above the doors. Security was paramount.

At the head of the hall was a dais, and here the Prince lounged in a cushioned chair. Next to him was Senor Grath, and several other advisers were arranged behind them. Sitting in a wooden chair with a stiff back was la Boca.

He wore a robe of pure black, so dark you couldn't see the shadows. It was like looking into a man-sized hole in the air. His head was completely covered by a hood, with only two diamond-shaped holes for his eyes. Colour was a sign of vanity and indulgence, which the Brotherhood eschewed; so was the indulgence of eating, hence the lack of a gap for his mouth, and the pleasure of scent, hence the absence of a nose-hole. I had often wondered how Tomas would look when his time of initiation was done and he, too, lost his thick, curly brown hair, and etched the black tattoo on his neck. Among the crowd, there were several heralds in their dull robes, but their hoods were drawn up. I couldn't tell one from another.

Miguel was a solid presence at my back, pressed close by the bodies around us, and unable to move further from the door than a step or two. I couldn't make out anyone's face – at least, not until a man turned slightly sideways, and I was sure – *almost* sure – that I saw a jagged scar running across his lips.

I pressed forward, trying to get a closer look, for I was puzzled that I had seen this man in so many places, but the crowd held me back; and I couldn't be certain I'd seen him at all.

"Children of the Seven, we are gathered here this day," Senor Grath's voice rang out over the hubbub, "to welcome the High Priest, la Boca, the Mouth of the Pattern, to the Cuidad mas Grande. It has been a decade since a member of the heralds has left the Pendulum . . ."

Here, la Boca stood abruptly, and Senor Grath, taken aback, faltered in his introduction.

"It has been twelve years," la Boca said gravelly, muffled not at all by the heavy material in front of his mouth, "since we have needed to leave the Iglesia."

The chamber, which had been quietening gradually, fell at once completely silent. La Boca's eyes were hard as he raked the crowd, a strange expression in them, one close to an accusation.

"We have trusted that in our absence, the Cuidad was being governed as befits our Greatest City. We have assumed that the people have heeded the guidance of the Pattern. We have presumed" – here, he gathered himself – "*too much!*"

His shout rang off the high ceiling, reverberating through the hall. The crowd, stunned, stared back at him.

I quailed. Miguel, just behind me, stiffened.

"The Brotherhood has withdrawn to work on our projects of faith and devotion," he went on in a quiet, even tone, all the more menacing now we had witnessed the fury it hid beneath the surface. "We trusted the judgement of our magnificent Reina. She has faced great challenges, this we know, and her health is not what once it was; but she has yet to name her son as her true heir. Prince Regent he remains, holding the seat for the Principe Verdadero, who will become King when she passes into the Beyond. Still, we swore our fealty to him, our *regent prince.*"

He turned his head to behold the Prince, who was still taking his ease on his throne. His hand was to his mouth, fingers straight against his lips, and his eyes did not quite meet the herald's. It was hard to tell if he was even listening, and this only incensed the herald.

"And where is our Queen?" la Boca spread his skinny arms wide; the diaphanous sleeves fell back, revealing fragile, pale skin, laced with blue veins. "Where is she? Appearing but once a year, at the Fiesta, to wave to her people from above! How do we know she is still whole and hale, of body, of mind?"

The crowd gave a low, discontented murmur of agreement.

"But when we heard of this latest outrage," la Boca continued, "this utter *blasphemy* against the Pattern, we could no longer ignore what was happening in this, our beautiful city. I was torn from my studies and research and forced to come here to see for myself. And what did I discover?"

We waited for his answer.

"A city full of vice and sinners," he growled softly. "A broken city, where the machines that once kept it running so smoothly are now falling apart. Why is this?"

Again, we waited.

"You have debased yourselves. Your greed and avarice has spread too far. You are, all of you, commit blasphemy where you stand, speak, eat. You have allowed the Agents of Chaos to walk among you unchecked. You are led by your Prince, who is barely worth the title. He keeps a harem in his Citadel! And one of you," his eyes searched the crowd, "one of you, a Daughter of the Pavilion, that depraved and horrid house of whores, has befouled the *Dance of a Thousand Steps.*"

I gasped.

Me. His eyes were searching for me. I shrank back against Miguel, my heart thumping in my chest, the pain in my gut flaring in white-hot agony. And it seemed as if, at that impossible moment, the la Boca's eyes found me. Through the crowd, across the space, through time; it was as if he knew where I was standing all along, and now looked straight into my soul.

"She missed a step," he said, so softly, "and fell. When has this ever happened, in five hundred years? Is it any wonder that the Pattern no longer speaks to us?"

Behind me, Miguel's stiff stance changed subtly. He drew in a breath, and I didn't dare turn to see the revulsion that must surely be in his eyes. I reached into my pocket, and there I felt the feather, sad and tattered; I hung on tightly against the raging current of fear that threatened to drag me under. Was it true? Had I caused the Pattern to be disrupted? Had I – I shivered, a vibration of horror – had I caused the floods, the broken servitors, the quake?

And then, someone stepped forward. A woman dressed in a blue robe. She was not tall. In fact, her figure beneath the diaphanous robe was slightly dumpy, her dancer's figure lost to old age despite her strict adherence to our plain diet. Her make-up caked on her wrinkled skin, a shade too white for her spotted skin, her eyes too sunken to be rimmed with such dark kohl. Senora R. nevertheless had a certain presence about her, and as she faced la Boca, she did not quail.

"I beg your pardon," she said, without sounding at all apologetic, "but while you seek to pin the blame for this upon the Daughters, who spend every turning in service of the Pattern, you must know that these disasters have been occurring since before the Festival of Time." She turned and looked at the crowd, and though she could barely see over the heads of the majority, her determined expression and fire-lit eyes were as convincing as the la Boca's hidden face.

"Ah," retorted la Boca. "But what errors might have been corrected had the Dance been performed correctly?"

But Senora R. would not be cowed. "Our Daughters are trained to serve the Pattern. Aurelia will speak through them, just as She may speak through any of us. If it comes about that a Dancer falls, then, for the sake of Faith, that is as it is. To question this is to question the Pattern."

The argument might have continued – and it looked as if the spectators were about to join in – had not the Prince stood up from his throne. He swayed a little, certainly intoxicated, but la Boca did not turn to face him.

"People," said the Prince. "This is all very interesting."

From behind him, Senor Grath gripped the Prince's shoulder, and whispered something into his ear. The Prince shook him off.

"But I think this debate is entirely senseless." He pointed at the crowd. His words slurred, and a foolish grin spread across his face. "These arguments go around and around like the hands of Reloj de pie. And just like that Clock, they will continue to spin. Tierra Mejór will continue to spin, the Tiers to gyrate, the Wheel to turn, and la Grulla circle every *night* and *month* and *year*–" He punctuated each of these words with shake of his forefinger. "– and we'll just go on and on, in the same manner, forever."

Now Senor Grath looked desperate. He was tugging at the Prince forcibly, trying to get him to sit down. But the Prince only listed drunkenly, stumbling a little as he stepped to one side.

"Don't you see how pointless this all is?" His beautifully set voice wavered. "How useless we all are? Don't any of you see it?"

The crowd, murmuring in shock and confusion, turned to one another for explanation; there was none to be had. Finally, Senor Grath stepped forward. "The Principe Regente has slept ill last night," he barked, as if the audience was full of disobedient children; though surely that description would more aptly fit the swaying man at his side. "He will retire." And so saying, he all but dragged the Prince from the dais, through a door at the bottom of the steps, and out of sight.

La Boca's dark eyes glinted in triumph. "There, you see," he said in a quiet voice that might have been sorrowful if it wasn't filled with mockery. " 'If a leader cannot lead as befits a leader, cut him free.' Those words as spoken by la Oráculo, as our Law, were never more apt than at this present moment. I ask you," he again searched the crowd, "I ask you all. To whom do you turn when your leader has fallen? Towards the Pattern, towards the word spoken by la Oráculo, as recorded in the Texto Sagrado. 'Turn to the Pattern, in your time of greatest darkness, and it will bring you hope.' "

He lapsed into silence, a deep, voluminous one that filled the entire hall. And then one of the hooded Brothers began to speak the Prayer of the Seven:

> When I was lost in silence, I sought the Pattern,
> In words of the greatest joy, the Pattern replied.

His brethren joined him, their voices chanting in unison.

> With an open heart and open eyes the Pattern will lead us.

The people around them joined, and like ripples in the lake, the parabra spread outwards.

> We love and we are loved in turn,
> We seek to follow the right path and eschew the evil of Chaos.
> Thus we will live and serve the Pattern.

It was too much. I turned and slipped through the door. I couldn't tell if Miguel followed, and I did not care. By that stage, all I wanted was to get back to my room, where I would now gladly stay for the rest of my numbered days.

***

I refused to eat when Hanna brought me food, and she fretted and worried and threatened to have Doctor Oren come; how could I tell her that it wasn't even due of my penchant for plain food, or my worry about my dancer's physique. I simply could not bring myself to choke down a morsel of the fare, rich or otherwise. The knot in my stomach felt like a stone.

Miguel's presence was a reassuring one, but I couldn't help but worry as footsteps approached, sometimes belonging to a person alone, sometimes to several, and low voices talked outside my door. Often, Miguel's growl would turn them aside at once, but there were times when I heard the violence of a scuffle, followed by the chilling sound of a revolver-pistol being cocked.

During those next two turnings, I wondered if I should, or could, end my life. If I was really to blame for what was happening to the City, if I had killed several people and ruined many lives through my actions. Why, how had I missed that step? I replayed it over and over in my mind, the moment of pain, the fall . . . but nothing could change what was done. The Clock, as always, ticked forwards; never backwards.

Miguel, I suppose, saved me from my demons. He came into the room, and I saw at last how tired he looked, his large face sprouting a shadowy beard, and his eyes red-rimmed. "Have you even slept?" I exclaimed.

He shook his head. "Senor Grath has tried to relieve me several times, but I don't trust those sentinela. I can't trust a thing that does not bleed with the protection of something that does."

I looked away, ashamed of my thoughts of suicide. "But you can't do this. Sooner or later, you must sleep."

He nodded. "There are guardia I trust. A man named Hendrich will be taking over for me in a few hours."

I looked at him carefully. I wanted to tell him that I wasn't worth protecting, but I said nothing. Still, as tears formed in my eyes, I think he read my thoughts. "Do you have no one in this world to call a parent?" he asked me.

I shook my head, miserably. "My father is dead. My mother would never claim the title."

"Then you must use your imagination, and pretend you have someone who cares for you."

I couldn't help but smile through my tears at what he implied. "But you are only my guard because the Prince ordered it. And I've only the need for you because it seems I have somehow caused the world to break."

"If I did not care to accept those orders, I could have passed them to someone else," he said. "I have many delegates. I am rather highly-placed in the chain of command." His eyes sparkled as he said this, and a sob escaped me, but it was tinged with happiness.

How had I managed to come across this wonderful man? How had I managed to make him care for me? I was nothing special!

"In the meantime, perhaps you can make good upon your promise."

I had forgotten, in the hours that had passed, about the book we had retrieved from the Library. He produced it now from a pocket in the front of his black shirt, and it looked very small in his big hands.

Gilgamesh. It was written in verse form, like poetry or prayer. There was a short introduction, that told me this was one of the oldest recorded texts that had been rescued by the Seven – even when Old Earth had been young, this story had been old, written in some language now long lost, along with the other secrets the Seven had left behind. I traced the words; the language was archaic, but not indecipherable. There was a certain rhythm to it that told me whomsoever had written this down had understood that language could be beautiful.

Teaching Miguel was easy. We traced letters on the coverlet with our fingers until Hanna arrived and produced a pen and a piece of tissue that had been wrapped around some medicinal herbs she had been carrying. We covered the sticky paper with blue-black scrawls until Miguel could write the whole alphabet. As stubborn as he had been that words were not for him, he was just as strong-willed when it came to learning them; he would not rest until he'd mastered these symbols.

"You'll be writing poetry soon enough," I said.

"Poetry?" Miguel coughed haughtily. "I think not."

I didn't remind him that the *Words of the Oracle* were the greatest poem of all, and he had quoted me that line from la Oráculo's Speech with such reverence he must see the beauty in the words. I stowed that lecture for another turning.

Miguel leaped up a few times to check the door. Twice more there was a heated discussion that I couldn't quite hear, and didn't want to. Miguel didn't elaborate when he returned, but by the time his replacement arrived, he had read the first few lines of the text.

> "He who has seen everything, I will make known to the lands.
> I will teach about him who experienced all things, . . .alike,
> Anu granted him the totality of knowledge of all.
> He saw the Secret, discovered the Hidden,
> he brought information of (the time) before the Flood."

I was amazed. The words struck a deep chord in me, and I turned them over and over in my mind. What was this strange tale? Why hadn't I heard it before? Why had it been kept, buried in the Library? Were there other Old Earth texts I knew nothing about?

Miguel, for his part, seemed to relish the words as well. By the time Hendrich arrived, he had successfully rewritten them twice on the scrap of paper, looking very pleased with himself.

Chapter Eighteen

Hendrich was a quiet man with a solemn face. He did not look me directly in the eye, and was rather thin, but there was a strength to him that I would have greatly admired had he ever attended an evening dance in the Room of Roses. Despite his quietness, he seemed concerned for me, and asked if there was anything I needed.

"A good night of sleep," was all I said.

Though he wasn't as reassuring as Miguel, I found I liked him, and that is why I felt bad about deceiving him.

When night had fallen, I slipped out of bed and placed my pillow under the bedcovers, scrunching the covers convincingly. Then I wrapped Xith's scarf around my shoulders and slipped through the balcony door, into the waning light of la Grulla.

I headed along my now well-remembered path to the door in the wall, and out into the streets. The City felt different, in a thousand subtle ways. It was as if the very air was charged with the anxiety of the people.

Only one rotor-tram ran, and it was packed full. Everyone looked tired and wary. They elbowed one another and glared angrily as they jostled for space. The tram itself ran badly, slowing down and speeding up intermittently. I had to stand, and it was hard to keep from falling into the group of men and women wearing the guild-belts of the Agriculture Centre who stood behind me.

"The yield will be very poor indeed," one of them said.

"I've done all I can to get the new mixture ready," responded a woman's terse voice. "There are higher levels of acid, this time. If anything can work, this will."

"What if it doesn't?" spoke a man to her left.

"What do you mean – if it *doesn't*? I've done everything –"

"We have to face the possibility," he said. "Despite our best efforts, a lot of the moth-meat we're being shipped is spoiled. Not to mention the fruit from the orchards, which is affected by blight. We've lost half the apples already, and much of the rice. If this continues, we won't have enough to supply –"

"Hush! Where do you think we are?"

"I know exactly where we are," he shot back coldly. "And unlike you, I don't believe in hiding from the truth. The people should know, so they can prepare."

"Prepare? How are they going to do that? There is nothing to prepare!"

Their argument had drawn attention, and those around us were starting to mutter. I noticed one familiar face; the pale man with the black hat. His clothes – were they the same ones he'd worn when I'd seen him last? – still looked odd, stiff, and brand-new.

"You would do well," he rumbled, "to trust in the Pattern."

The woman turned to him. "The Pattern?" she said scornfully. "Since when has the Pattern ever stepped down through the Unknown to right the wrongs of the world?"

"The Pattern," the man countered, "works through those who are open to it."

This bought a fresh wave of argument from the rest of the agriculturalists, and some outcries from other passengers.

I shouldered my way off the tram at the next stop, not wanting to be caught in any altercation, and walked the rest of the way down the Calle del Corazón.

When I kneeled in the Templo next to Tomas, I spoke softly, directing my words to la Relojero.

"La Relojero, hear my parabra," I whispered. "I am a humble servant. Call to me and I will obey. Speak to me and I will listen. I direct my actions in kindness and strength and the way of the Pattern in service to you. I am but a piece of the machinery you have created."

Tomas did not look at me, did not touch me, and did not speak. We kneeled, side-by-side, in silence. And though I waited to feel the calmness that usually descended on me when I prayed here in the Temple, there was no comfort in this visit, not this time.

***

La Reloj de pie was chiming eleven by the time I returned to the Citadel. I was cold in only my shift and Xith's scarf; as such, I hurried, desperate to get back to my room.

I had just shut the door and lowered the latch when a low voice said, "So I see you're still being a naughty girl."

I whirled and found Bethery standing in the shadows, a cigarillo burning in her fingers. I clutched a hand to my heart. "What are you doing here?"

"Nice to see you too, sugar," she drawled with a sardonic grin. "Come now! Aren't you going to say something?"

"What would you like me to say?" I *was* pleased to see her; I wanted her to wrap me in her arms and kiss me soundly with those perfect lips. I wanted her fingers between my legs. I could smell her scent from here – dusky perfume, smoke, and something deeper, a mysterious smell of trees and grass and summer fruit.

She stubbed her cigarillo against the stone wall behind her and flicked the butt carelessly into the shadows. She took a step forwards and leaned into me. "Kiss me. Say: 'kiss me.' "

"Kiss me," I repeated obediently, and she obliged. Her tongue was slick against mine, her teeth nipping my lower lip. I pushed myself closer, breathing her in, tasting her, desperately.

"I've missed you, sugar," she said at last, pulling away.

"Is that why you came?" I asked, a little breathless.

Her fingers traced my face, trailing over my metrónomo, running across my bruised lip, pinching my chin. "Of course. Didn't you miss me?"

"Yes," I admitted.

"I knew if you'd lived, you would have made your way back to your Brotherhood-lover eventually."

"And if I hadn't lived?" I tested her.

"If you hadn't lived, I would have been very, very sad." The mockery was there, but it didn't extend to her eyes.

"There is half a hundred women in the Den," I said. "What makes me so special?"

"What makes you so special?" She raised her eyebrows. "Oh, sugar. The answer is in the hatred you earned from Xith and Haretta, and the desire that showed in the other's faces when they knew I had claimed you. It is in that very dart-spider bite. Can't you see? You make everyone fall in love with you. Of course, they will despise you for it."

"What –" I tried to grasp what she meant. "Do you mean the dart-spider was . . . planted?"

She shrugged. "I'm not one for speculation. Either it was or it wasn't. It makes no difference what *I* think. What do *you* think?"

"I – I hadn't thought of it like that." My mind raced. The dart-spider had been in Xith's shawl. She had lent it to me, an uncharacteristic gesture indeed, given her earlier attitude.

"Of course you haven't. Sweet little Imre, the innocent Daughter of the Pavilion." She removed her hand, leaving me cold.

"I must go back," I said. "If I'm missed, my guard might be punished for it."

She nodded. There were no further words as we made our way through the garden, but we held hands until the last moment before we parted, her to continue on to the terrace outside the Den, me to climb the steps to my balcony.

So preoccupied was I with thoughts of Bethery, I didn't see him at first. Not, at least, until he turned to face me.

The Prince.

Under la Grulla's waning light, I noticed how handsome he was. He truly was beautiful, even in this state, with his hair ragged and his cheeks flushed.

"I hoped I would see you here."

"You were waiting for me?" And here I thought he could not possibly remember meeting me, but his presence here proved otherwise.

"I was," he said. "Come with me."

He held out his hand, as I considered his offer. How deep under the blanket of drugs was he this time? Enough to harm me? I'd seen terrible things done under the influence of white-powder. Yet, I sensed no malice in him, no anger. I put my hand in his and let him lead me.

Through the garden we went, to a back entrance. It was propped open, similar to my balcony door, and I smiled at the strangeness of having found a kindred wandering spirit in the Principe Regente of Tierra Mejór.

We climbed some stairs and crossed a walkway, then took a small lift-car. Soon we arrived in a suite of rooms so luxurious, they could only have belonged to him.

The walls were hung with heavy drapes, the floor carpeted in lush rugs. The bed was simply enormous – all my sisters and I could have fit in it at once! But the Prince did not lead me there. Instead, he took me to a small sitting room, off to one side, and there we sat in silence for a long moment on one of the couches.

"Why did you look for me?" I asked him at last.

"I think . . ." He looked at me with reddened eyes. "I'm not sure. There is something about you. Do you feel it, too?"

I wasn't sure that I did – or that I didn't. So, I kept my mouth shut.

"I feel as if you are meant to make something change. That someone *needs* to. Does that make any sense – any sense at all?"

I nodded, but I said nothing, in case the words I chose were the wrong ones.

"Tell me about yourself," he said, and there was pleading in his eyes.

"What can I tell you?" I looked away. "There is not much about my life that would be interesting to a Prince."

He stood up, abruptly, and kicked at the small coffee table in front of the couch. It clattered over, landing at an angle against the wall. Frightened, I drew away.

In the next instant, the Prince's expression turned sorrowful. He sank back down, lowering his head into his hands. "Forgive me." This time I heard true regret in his voice. "Please. Sometimes, I simply can't contain it."

"I know," I said softly, for I did. Violence of feeling, expressing itself in outbursts in which furniture was often destroyed, was not so foreign to me, after all!

The Prince shifted in his seat, embracing me suddenly. The full length of him pressed against me, even the erectness of his manhood against my thigh. I was at first startled; but this was washed away, all too quickly, by something much warmer and less controllable.

Together, we sank down until we lay on the couch. His breath wafted hot against my neck, but his intention, it seemed, was merely to spoon me, clasping me to his chest like a lifeline.

I must confess, I did not mind being held so.

Chapter Nineteen

I woke wrapped in the Prince's arms, his breath warm on my neck. I was warm and comfortable here, but I had an urgent requirement for the toilet, so I pulled away as gently as I could. It felt wrong to be moving around his opulent apartment without him present, but I couldn't help lingering over the beautifully carved wooden furniture, the paintings on the walls of streetscapes and parks. My eyes fell at last on a small wooden box sitting on a table near the door I suspected led to the bathroom; my need forgotten, I picked it up and opened the lid.

Inside was a small pile of white powder. It looked much like the powder we used in the Pavilion to prevent perspiration – and also like another type of powder I'd seen at times in my mother's room.

Horror and sadness rushed through me. Not at the fact that he used such a thing – I could see why. There was a pain in him, and it was deep, and this allowed him release. This was not unusual. Most street vendors would tell you the white-powder was harmless, just an enhancer for mood and an aid to enjoyment. I knew better – I had seen violence come from those under its influence – but I had also noticed that those who bought it were those who were unhappy. People who were already content had no real use for it. How I wished he didn't feel he needed it.

Lying in the left hand corner, half-buried in the pile, was the dried form of a tiny little moth, its wings the same shade as the powder. I knew, of course, that this was where the powder came from – the wings of tiny moths, but I had never seen one before. I had often wondered who was the first to discover the use of their scales, and how it came about. I reached a curious finger towards the little body, but at that moment there was a knock at the door, bringing me back to my senses. I shut the lid hastily and turned to see Senor Grath.

He did not look pleased as he entered, his eyes quickly moving between me and the Prince as he woke and groaned.

"My Liege," said Senor Grath stiffly. "You are to attend a Conclave this morning. Shall I help you dress?"

The Prince closed his eyes tightly and raked his fingers through his hair. "What's wrong with what I'm wearing?"

Senor Grath pursed his lips. He refused to look at me, instead focusing his dark eyes on the Principe Regente. "You look as if you've spent the night in the garden."

I took a step towards the door, hoping I could slip away unnoticed. If Miguel had checked my room, he would be worried not to find me there.

"Wait," said the Prince suddenly, and I halted, upset to be remembered. "Come with me."

"My – my Prince?" I managed.

"Call me Thaniel. If I must waste my morning stuck in a dusty chamber, then at least you are far more pleasing to look at than those dour old men."

"My Liege," protested Grath. "The Conclave is not the place –"

"Oh, don't make it sound so enticing!" the Prince scolded his adviser, before turning to me and whispering in a voice that would still be perfectly audible to Senor Grath. "Honestly, he thrives on them, these affairs of state. As if loafing around in a roomful of gruff, musty-smelling guildsmen and -women is so vital. I couldn't imagine anything I'd rather do less."

He actually sounded as if it caused him pain. In his corner, Grath shook his head in disgust, but Thaniel brightened instantly. He took my hand and pulled me up from the bed, almost dancing across the floor. I laughed and patted my hair. "Shouldn't I change my dress?" I asked him.

"Certainly not!" he exclaimed. "You look divine."

He said it as though he meant it, and for that moment, I believed it. We ran, like naughty children, through the hallways. Behind us, Grath followed at a sedate pace, a scowl on his face; the Prince took great delight in shutting the lift door before he reached us. He laughed and leaned back against the mirrored wall, his head lolling to one side as his half-lidded eyes shifted out of focus. "Sometimes," he slurred, "I think the lift-car is going to just keep going. Down, and down, and down. Right into the middle of the Spindle. Into the machine of Tierra Mejór. Maybe even beyond."

"Beyond?" I questioned him. "What is beyond?"

"The Core. Have you ever wondered what it is like, inside? If the Key still sits in the winding lock, where la Relojero placed it?" He sighed, sweeping a hand to indicate the lift-car, and beyond this, the world.

"The Core is forbidden," I reminded him, then quoted a passage from the *Sacred Text*. " 'Like the heavens beyond the Needle, the Inner Workings of this world are not to be tampered with. Stay your curiosity, for there are some things that are not for you to know as yet.' "

Thaniel glanced at me, then wrinkled his nose, as if I'd just spoiled his fun. "At the very least, I like to think it is something more exciting than this."

The doors slid open, revealing a wide room with tiered chairs; the room I had seen from the outside that night when I wandered through the gardens.

There were more men and women in here, now. Several of them carried notepads and pens, others thick, heavy books of law. They all turned to look at me as I entered, trailing behind Thaniel.

The chairs sloped down on all sides towards the centre, where there was a long table, around which were several more chairs. The Queen took up one of these at the head of the table, looking serene, in a green velvet dress, her hands folded neatly in her lap. A man in a very fine suit sat next to her, his dark skin gleaming softly. In his hand was a long staff, adorned on top with a crystal the size of his fist. I knew him as the Chancellor. His face was lined with age, and his eyes were pale blue and stared blindly into the room. Seven other men and women were gathered around him. Six, for the number of guilds; the Poet, the Architect, the Smith, the Physician, the Tinker, the Gardener. Aurelia had no representative in this room. The final seat was occupied by the herald. He who spoke for the Iglesia, and would be Tomas's master, which put paid to any exuberance I felt.

He fixed the Prince with a glance that was positively incensed. "You are late yet again."

"Then you shouldn't be surprised, should you, my dearest Benefine?" the Prince returned, pulling me by the hand. The eyes of all the councillors settled on me, and I wished at once I hadn't agreed to come. I was wanted by the Brotherhood, after all; and these people would not be as willing to defend me as Senora R.

"The Conclave is not a public affair." The man with the staff sniffed. "Who is this?"

"This is Imre," said the Prince. "Isn't she the most beautiful creature you've ever seen?"

"This is an outrage," one man murmured. "She shouldn't be allowed in here."

"Why not?" asked the Prince. "Why don't we ask La Reina?"

He turned and bowed. "Mother, dearest. What do you think of Imre's presence?"

La Reina – I had never been so close to her. I felt I should kneel, but the Prince held my elbow too tightly. I could only bow my head as I waited for her to scold her son for bringing a Dancer into the Conclave.

She inclined her head wordlessly.

"See?" the Prince said. He drew me with him as he sat in a chair by La Reina's side. To my mortification, he plopped me down onto his lap, slinging an arm around my waist. "Even Mother is charmed. Now, why don't we get this started, so we can all go back to more important things?"

At this, the man with the staff stood, and rapped it on the floor. "As Chancellor, leader of the Council, I call this Conclave to order. By the Pattern, and by the Law, as was given to us by la Oráculo."

There was a pause as the doors inched open, disgorging a flurried Grath. The Chancellor fixed him with an icy glare, which he returned threefold, stiffly taking his place behind the Prince.

The others looked put out, annoyed, and even angry. If I could have, I would have shrunk myself to the size of a pea, but as it was, I was forced to sit and endure my humiliation while he and Senor Grath descended to the level of the table and sat there.

The business of state began.

Never before had I pondered on how Tierra Mejór was governed. Seeing it now, I could only say that it was a wonder anything ever happened at all. Everything was done so ponderously, and with such decorum and deference; everything had to be recorded by the secretary, and voted on, by a show of hands.

First was the issue of rebuilding some of the vital systems and businesses that had been destroyed by the quake. Several of the council members wanted work to begin immediately, but first, costings for the repairs had to be presented in a report, then itemised and prioritised; the treasury records consulted, to see if funds were available, and then, the funds itemised and prioritised. Everything was checked and double-checked against ledgers and books.

I came to know their names, then. Chancellor Dahrn and Councillor Horoth, Guildsman Ollander, head of the Guild of Architects, and Secretary Allius, whose almond-shaped eyes kept flicking to mine; Commander of the Vigilar, Fedren, was one of the more outspoken members. Lyndra, one of the few women, wore the Guild-belt of Ante the Artisan as a representative for the education of young children who had not yet been apprenticed, was quieter, speaking only when she had something vital to add. Vice Chancellor Mardrey sat in a wheeled chair to one side. I had seen him before, during my time as a Dancer. He was noticeable on the streets, for there were not many born on Tierra Mejór with his kind of disability. The herald was Benefine, and he was the spokesman for the Iglesia. As such, he did not wear the black robe, but a simple one of roughly-woven brown fabric.

I could see why the Prince was so bored. I would have fallen asleep too, had it not been for the fact that the chairs were inordinately uncomfortable. Every now and then, as different people bought forth their issues, the chairs clicked and clacked through the room, to put the speaker in line with the front of the table. The other chairs moved out of their way, joltingly arranging themselves in new positions. It was disconcerting and at times dizzying.

The Prince, for his part, spent most of the time gazing up at me. I couldn't work out his expression, but it cost me nothing to endure it, so I did.

Halfway through, the door to the chamber opened, and everyone froze in place. It was probably my imagination, but a cold breeze seemed to sweep the room; I turned in my seat to see the tall, black-shrouded figure. Though all heralds looked the same, this could only be la Boca.

"I was not informed of this meeting," he said.

I sank further into Thaniel's lap, hoping he would not notice me, and knowing I hoped in vain. His eyes brushed over me harshly, leaving me feeling like I'd been scoured by sand in the wind.

"I suppose the presence of a whore is more important than that of the Mouth of the Pattern."

"Not at all, not at all!" cried Benefine immediately, standing and brushing down his robes. "It is only that it was an inconsequential meeting, and we did not wish to trouble you."

"Then, if you don't mind, I will sit in on this minor meeting," he intoned, taking a seat at the rear of the room. As the chairs spun, sometimes I found myself sitting opposite him, his gaze fixed unerringly on me.

Finally, the interminable meeting ended, and the Prince was whisked away to a luncheon. Left to my own devices, I wandered the halls, finding my way back to my room more by accident than design.

Chapter Twenty

Thus did the pattern of my life change once more.

At odd intervals, the Principe Regente would send a servant to my room. Once or twice he sent Grath himself, with the task of bringing me upstairs that he might have my company while he talked, moodily and dreamily, about things I did not understand, and some which I did.

Inevitably, he would have me sit by him, and once or twice he fell asleep in my lap. I, then, would drift into my own sleep, to wake when he had business to attend to; la Boca, it seemed, was a demanding guest. I wasn't required to attend any more of the Conclaves, and I supposed this was due to la Boca's objection, so during those times, I was allowed back to my room.

I spent the time teaching Miguel to read further and further into the *Epic of Gilgamesh*. Once or twice he would stumble, but his pronunciation got better, his words more fluid.

"I suppose I sound like a child in a classroom," he would sigh.

I could only shrug. "I would not know."

Miguel seemed puzzled. "But you must have gone to school."

I shook my head, bowing it so he could not see the blush on my cheeks. I did not want to lie to him, but I wished I could tell him some story of a happy childhood, such as Ketra's, or Vahn's. "I was born on the Third Tier. School was a luxury I had no time for."

"Then how," he put the book down, marking the place with his finger, "did you learn to read?"

"My abuela," I told him. "Until she died, I spent as much time with her as I could. She would teach me to read from packets and jar labels once she'd run out of printed books."

As I finished this sentence, I looked up, and jumped near out of my skin to see Senor Grath in the doorway. Miguel and I shared a nervous glance, wondering if he would scold us, but he simply nodded towards me. "The Prince requests your presence."

I stood up, brushing my hands through my hair. I had come to look forward to my time with the Prince. If nothing else, his unpredictability made my life seem less boring.

***

Despite the insistence of his many servants, the Prince liked to bathe on his own. It was during these times that I was generally by myself in the suite, and I would take the time to pick up one of the books I would find discarded on the floor, or dropped, forgotten and dusty, behind a vase on a sideboard.

It was during one of these times that Grath arrived. He obviously had something to tell the Prince, and, finding him occupied, sighed impatiently.

"He won't be long," I told him, though, to be sure, the Prince had been known to take an hour or more – nobody would ever question his profligacy with water, so why not?

"I see you're making yourself comfortable," Grath said in answer.

"I would much rather have a room of my own," I grumped, but I wasn't in the mood to fight.

"I suppose you would. Why not?" he said, then he narrowed his eyes at the cover of my chosen book. " 'The Law as it Applies to the Children'?"

As boring and dry as the book was, I had learned a few things from its pages. Firstly, that it was possible for a tenant to bring his landlord to trial if he felt his rent had been misused, and secondly, that a Red House whore could never testify against her master. There were also passages about the Law as it related to the Royal Family. A King or Queen, for example, had to name their heir before they could take over the throne. This was to give them time to observe which of their children was most deserving, for every monarch in our history had had more than one, and it wasn't always the firstborn who was most suitable. It was expected for royalty to lead by example, and children were strongly encouraged, to make sure Tierra Mejór's population flourished.

Likewise, la Oráculo told us in his book, 'let us not copy the ways of the past. Too many flawed leaders have taken the thrones of the countries of Old Earth. The Pattern will guide the hand and heart of Tierra Mejór's ruler, and through communion, they will know the name of their successor.'

It said nothing of the Law regarding what would happen if a King or Queen were barren, but I knew, from my abuela's books, that King Tolemy had been set aside by la Boca, three hundred years past. His replacement had been chosen by the Brotherhood, in keeping with the Pattern.

Thaniel, I realised, was the only Principe – or Principessa – that I knew of who was an only child. He was the only choice for la Reina to make, but he must still be named by her – or, if she thought him unsuitable, turn the decision over to the Brotherhood.

What use this knowledge would be, I had no idea, but I was sure Tomas would remind me that all knowledge was worth having.

"That is a book written by a fool," Grath huffed, plainly incredulous. "Granting rights and freedoms to those who, in all reality, will never face a fair trial to use them."

"Does that mean they shouldn't have them?" My tone matched his. "Perhaps, one day, the vigilar will walk the streets of Third Tier and actually enforce these laws."

"What would you know of the Third Tier?" he said scathingly. "Beyond, that is, slumming with your Pavilion sisters? Generalo Vanse arranges the patrols of his vigilar through their streets on a quarter-hour rotation."

I covered my mouth, for a snort of laughter threatened to burst free. "You're right. vigilar often go to such places, but the people who need their protection won't deal with anyone dressed in a uniform." In truth, they would likely jump from a roof to avoid the sight of an armed man of the law. It would be a better fate than what faced them when the Red House owners caught up with them. "As to how I know, if I told you I grew up in the Eastside on the Third Tier, I doubt it could make your opinion of me any worse."

He looked at me for a long time. "You think of me as a dupe, don't you?"

"I think of you as a man who thinks people have more opportunities than they actually do. You were born into circumstances that allowed you choices many do not get. You are probably the most powerful man in Tierra Mejór. How can you pass judgement on those of us who must not, for the sake of survival, count even on our next meal?"

"Pattern damn you!" Grath turned and slapped a hand against the doorframe. I could almost feel Miguel stiffen outside the front door; if it were anyone else in here with me, he probably would have barged in to see if I was alright. I wished he would, if only to save me from having to speak to this man any further. "You foolish girl! This is no game!"

"I'm not toying with you," I said, wary of showing him how he scared me.

"But you're not giving me the information I need, either, which is just as bad," Grath growled. "This is not the way I operate, girl. The Principe Regente is my charge. You cannot possibly understand the responsibility I hold."

There was a long moment of silence. I stared at my hands, rather than at him, for I didn't want to see the anguish I'd heard in his tone. My doubts about him wavered, and I almost considered telling him what he wanted to know. But then another voice in the back of my mind warned me that if he planned to do away with me, then this was exactly what he would be aiming to do – unbalance me.

No. Once I had done this, I would have my answers, one way or the other. And to do that, all I needed was to get into the Red House.

"No," I said slowly. "I don't understand that – any of that. How can I? You've said it yourself, I'm nothing but a dirty gutter-whore."

The words struck him. I was surprised, and a little pleased, to see him speechless, if only for a heartbeat.

Suddenly, he snapped his fingers. "Get a shawl. Or something to cover your head."

"What?" I questioned him, slightly alarmed. "Why?"

He strode across the room and picked up Xith's scarf, which hung on the back of a chair; I had never returned it to her. "This. Here." He dropped it at my feet. "Put it on. Your hair will give us away, if anyone should spy you."

I pulled it over my dress, looking at him sideways, but he was filled with a sudden fervour, stubbing out his cigarillo on the doorjamb and pocketing the remains. He wrenched open the door and spoke quickly and quietly to Miguel. I twisted my hair and tucked it into the collar of the dress, hoping it would do for whatever he had in mind.

"Please, tell me where we're going," I said, ashamed of the tremor in my voice.

"Just hurry up. Stay close by my side and keep your head down," he ordered.

I looked at Miguel as I passed him, pleadingly. He smiled reassuringly and nodded, but it didn't ease my mind all that much. Miguel trusted the Senor, but then, Grath had no reason to despise Miguel. Or to want him dead.

Grath led the way at a rapid pace, first down one corridor, then another. Here there were more of the small servant lifts; he opened the door to one of them and ushered me in.

The space was confined. I pressed back against the cage bars, trying to avoid being poked by the hilt of his sword; I hadn't realised how large Grath actually was. He wasn't built like Miguel, but underneath his plain grey shirt, he was clearly well-defined, in the careless way men of tall stature are, who have spent their lives working too hard to focus on the shape of their body. I wondered how he would compare to his Prince in terms of physique, then had to shake off a wash of confusion as to why I would even consider such a thing.

I turned away, but the clinging scent of cigarillo smoke still wove about my senses.

We rose through the floors in complete silence, passing a few cages on the way. I was glad others could see us this time, for it meant he couldn't try to harm me, not then. Once the lift clattered to a stop, another wave of nervousness crested, but that was soon allayed. Grath moved too briskly. I imagined a man intending dire consequences would not be so cavalier.

Soon, we were in a small room with a concrete floor. It was stiflingly hot in here, and there were no windows, so I couldn't tell exactly where we were. Almost certainly somewhere on one of the top floors of the Citadel; we'd come up a long way.

In the centre was a spiralling metal staircase, and shelves and racks around us filled with all kinds of tools and parts – hammers, cogs, oil cans, spanners . . . Besides the lift egress, there was one other door in the room, and it was crossed with a heavy bar, locked in place with chains. Many hissing, gurgling pipes protruded from the walls, but more alarming than that was a noise that seemed to come from above; a resounding, repetitive thud.

Boom. Boom. Boom.

I looked at Grath in puzzlement, but he didn't waste time on explanations. He crossed the room in three strides, to a shelf, where there were portable globe-lanterns. He retrieved one and nodded at the staircase. "Come on," he said impatiently, and I followed, curiosity overriding my fear.

The metal stairs shuddered under my feet with the incessant vibrations I climbed after Grath, through to the next floor, and here the clamour got so loud, I almost clapped my hands over my ears. Grath flicked on the globe-lantern, and light spilled into the darkness. Here there were great cogs and gears, some bigger than a bed, some so small and delicate, they could have powered a pocket watch. The whole room was one giant machine, full of a million different working parts. Pistons pumped and steam hissed, belts whirred and chains clanked, catches popped and levers lifted and dropped. At the very heart, sweeping back and forth, was a great pendulum. The tip gleamed silver, and it was attached by a long spoke to workings in the ceiling.

The smell of hot oil was overpowering, the noise – incredible!

But what that Grath paused to let me gawp. No, he kept climbing that staircase, which spiralled up through the centre of the working parts. I hurried after him, terrified of falling outside the sphere of his lantern-light and having to fumble my way in the dark.

It took us a good three minutes. At times, I felt we were simply circling the same section of staircase as rods swayed and the pendulum swung back and forth, back and forth, first over my head, then past my shoulders, knees, feet, until finally a square of light unfurled overhead. The staircase passed through it, and into another chamber. Though the stairs continued upwards, Grath stepped off onto the floor of this room.

There was more machinery here, but much of the space was taken up by three upright gears. The largest was as tall as a single-story building. The others, set behind it, were smaller, and smaller again. As the smallest turned, the larger one did so more slowly, and the largest slower still.

The noise was loudest here.

BOOM. BOOM. BOOM . . .

I would have had to shout to be heard. As it was, I could barely hear my own footsteps. Next to the gears was a window, a long, upright slit. This was where the light was filtering from, and I was shocked to realise it was daylight; I was looking out at the sky.

Pressing myself to the glass, I finally knew where I was.

"Reloj de pie," I murmured under my breath. I was standing behind her great clock face, and below me, spread out in ever-widening circles, was the Cuidad mas Grande.

The Greatest City.

I could see the White Pavilion, rising like a sculpture of ice from the green gardens. I could see the Calle del Corazón, and the bustling crowds. I could see the ruined buildings, and a stream of black smoke that rose from some still-smouldering fire.

I turned to find Grath close behind me. "It's beautiful," I said, but my heart ached for the damaged city. He seemed to hear me, though I hadn't thought he would.

"This," his deep voice wound its way over the noise, "is what you needed to see."

I turned to the gears. Beyond a gap in the wall beside me, the edges of the huge hands of the clock ticked, marking the time of our turnings, of our lives, resonating with my metrónomo, beating in time with my heart. How wonderful were the rhythms that made up our time on this earth!

Tentatively, I reached out to touch the edge of the largest gear. Just before my fingers made contact, I was yanked backwards; firm hands had clamped on my shoulders, wrenching me away. The clasp of a wristwatch dug into my collarbone. I stumbled and tripped, falling against a solid form – Grath. I looked up into his face, my own twisted in anger, and saw fury in his eyes. "What do you think you're doing?" he shouted. He didn't let go of me. "You stupid fool of a girl!"

"Let go!" I spat in return, pushing against his chest, beating his hands. He was far too strong! I drew my arms in to my chest and pulled myself downwards, breaking his grip. I spun, kicking out with my good foot, and catching him in the shin.

"Damn!" he cursed, his balance lost. He would have fallen but for the wall behind him.

Regaining my footing, though my bad ankle twinged, I raised my fists – such as they were! – and looked him square in the eye, ignoring as best I could the stairway behind me. If I made a dash for it, I wanted him to be unprepared.

And then, suddenly, all the ire drained from him. The corners of his lips pulled back, and he was laughing. He looked, suddenly, years younger.

"I've heard stories of Old Earth beasts called tigers. Their fur was covered with stripes, which hid them in the shadows of trees. From here, they would pounce on their unsuspecting prey, and they had very sharp teeth." He was mocking me, but it was gentle, almost friendly. "Who taught you that?"

"My instructor," I said, a little rueful that I'd hurt him, but still wary. "Maestra Tinir said it was just as important to learn to fight as to learn to dance."

"Indeed." He smirked. "She taught you one of those subjects well, at least."

The joke, aimed at my fall, was not missed, and added fresh fuel to the knot in my stomach.

"But I don't suppose her lessons extended to keeping your fingers out of working machinery?" He pushed away from the wall, motioning towards the gears.

I stared at him blankly, then shook my head. "We have servitors in the Pavilion, but only a few still work. Even the kitchens are operated by hand now."

He nodded slowly. "I see. Well, here is a new lesson for you, one I hope you'll take to heart; don't touch anything you don't understand. The Guild of Smiths would have your head if you damaged something, even if you didn't lose a hand in the process."

I nodded slowly, feeling the fool he judged me as. "Then why did you bring me here?" I challenged him, folding my arms to show him I meant to keep my hands to myself.

All at once, silence rang out.

It was an incredible interruption, once that stole my breath away. The resounding thud simply *stopped*, and the quietness was like a solid thing; it can have only lasted a fraction of a second, but in that time, the world seemed to stand still.

I turned, and saw the gears of the clock skip. Fractionally, each of them flicked backwards; first the smallest, then the middle, then the largest.

I gasped, and my metrónomo missed a beat in sympathy. Then the pendulum in the room below swung once more, a cloud of steam puffing up through the railings of the staircase, and the gears began to move just as they had before.

Boom. Boom. Boom.

I turned to Grath, my lips forming a question. He didn't look surprised; instead, he seemed profoundly saddened.

"Yes, this is what I wanted to show you, Imre. Do you understand, now?"

I nodded slowly. I did understand – at least one part of it. But – "Why?"

"I don't know," Grath said. "The finest técnico's in the Guild have been working on the problem for months, but they've yet to find a way to fix it. The cause, it seems, goes much deeper than even their expertise can ascertain."

"How often is this happening?"

"In the beginning – years ago, perhaps decades – it was only once a year. Then once a quarter. Then once a month. Not so much of a problem, and easy enough to ignore, to assume that it would right itself. But soon, it happened twice in one month. Then three times. Now, by the calculations we have, it is happening twice every turning."

"But . . ." Despite the heat of the room, I felt suddenly cold. "But what does this mean?" I went on, desperate for an explanation, for more information. "Surely it's not so bad. Tierra Mejór will continue to spin. La Grulla will light our days. The dawn regimen hasn't changed. The differences must be subtle. We will just have to adapt. Perhaps we can even build another . . ."

His eyes were dark and serious. "Reloj de pie tells us the time, the day, the season. If it loses even a fraction of a second, then we have lost seconds of every turning. Or perhaps even minutes. The dawn regimen has been occurring slightly later each turning. You haven't noticed it yet." He pointed towards my left temple with a vague gesture. "But your metrónomo will mark it, never doubt. The beats will fall behind, and with the cumulative differences, in less than five years, you will no longer be in sync with the Reloj."

He took a deep breath.

"The inner workings of Reloj de pie lie deep in the core of Tierra Mejór. We don't know exactly how they function, only that everything works in unity. That is the way Tierra Mejór was built by la Relojero."

I had known this too, of course. It was a fact, such as the grey-green of the sky, that one could easily take for granted.

"It is linked to the Tether, from which the Pendulum swings. If la Reloj de pie is losing time, then the Pendulum is swinging more and more slowly. What happens when it stops altogether? The forces that keep us anchored to the surface of Tierra Mejór require that we remain in motion.

"Who know what effect this would have on the Wheel, on the crops in the grain-harvestries? On the reservoirs and the crystal cells that control the remaining automata. Already the servitors and the rotor-trams are failing. The more complex machines like artificials are almost a thing of the past; most of them dead and gathering dust, unable to be repaired or charged. Just look at what's happened on the Lower Tiers – none of the reservoirs process the water as they once did, leaving people to make up for their shortfallings. But none of this would be quite so frightening if it wasn't for the recent disasters."

I glanced through the window at the city. The black smoke. The noticeable gaps where buildings had once stood, and the piles of rubble. "There must be something we can do."

"What would you suggest? Hm?"

"We're resourceful," I protested. "We can do *something*."

"The truth is, we don't even know where to start. We've spent so long obeying the Words of the Oracle, curbing our curiosity and expecting that things will be revealed in due time. Do you know aught of the expeditions to the stars?"

I shook my head dumbly.

"It would have been before your time, and they were very secret, in any case. There was an experiment done during the time of Queen Zabria, where gas-filled balloons were sent up into the skies to monitor air pressure in the outer reaches of the atmosphere. The heralds learned of it, and had them shot down and destroyed, and the knowledge they'd gathered suppressed. However, some records survived and were found in the Library, about fifteen years ago. The King authorised a pair of Tinkers to modify an airship to fly to the limits of the atmosphere. They made it airtight and pressurised it with the appropriate oxygen levels. They calculated the energy they'd need for the crystals that powered their repulsing fields. In theory, it should have worked. But a plague of mechanical malfunctions put them on the wrong course. They crashed into the Pendulum."

I covered my mouth with my hand.

"La Boca was incensed. He assured us that he would not tolerate any more experiments, and for a time, the King agreed. Too many had questioned the explosion in the sky, and had been frightened by it.

"But he was a stubborn man, and I must admit I did nothing to sway his inquisitiveness. Another ship went up a year later. I worked on this one personally, and I was as certain as the rest of them that they would make it through the atmosphere and be able to chart what lies beyond, bringing us back vital information about the stars and perhaps other habitable planets." He paused, the sorrowful look in his eyes indicating this memory was painful. "They made it out, but they lost propulsion. We can't be certain why. We'd measured the field of the Core, and there was no reason for them to have lost power – not for another day's journey. In fact, it should have been weeks before they were out of range entirely. Still, it failed, and the ship drifted off into the Unknown." The corners of his mouth pinched. "The communication crystals continued to respond for a week, but they had no supplies of food or water to last them longer than that."

A lump formed in my own throat at the thought. "Was that – was that perhaps a punishment from the Pattern for disobeying the words of the Oracle?"

Grath let out a bark of harsh laughter. "Come," he said to me, whirling back to the staircase. Clearly, this was to be my only answer.

He jogged up the first few steps, then waited for me. Slowly, numbly, I followed.

At the top of the stairs waied one final room, much smaller, with a low ceiling; it fitted just beneath the dome-shaped cap of the Clocktower. While I'd always supposed the roof was tiled, I saw now it was made of some kind of thick glass strengthened by brass bands. Daylight poured in from all sides, illuminating a chair, a desk, and several shelves and benches, all covered with loose pieces of paper; and a raised circular dais, surrounded by a brass railing, on which was a singular device. Not a powered machine, however, but an elegant tubular thing made of brass, mounted on a tripod.

Grath unbuckled his sword, pulling the sheath from his belt and setting it aside. The reason for this was soon clear, for he stepped onto the dais, and put his eye to one end of the tube. He adjusted some small knobs and a larger wheel, making fractional alterations to the angle of the tube. Then he looked over his shoulder at me.

Reluctantly, I joined him. The dais must have been insulated, for the thudding from below receded. There was barely room for the two of us to stand side-by-side, and although the railing pushed us into close proximity, the urgency of the matter had allayed my misgivings. I wanted to see what it was that he thought could possibly prove the things he'd told me.

I put my eye to the end of the tube. There was a small hole covered by glass. As I squinted, a plethora of confusing shapes swam into focus, the sort one sees after walking into a dark room after being out in the light of la Grulla on a day of few clouds; but as I lowered my head, I saw, incredibly, the night sky, sprinkled with stars and planets, a hundred thousand times closer and clearer than I had ever before.

I gasped and pulled away. But even as I peered out at the sky, I knew it must be some kind of trick. The sky was still grey. The stars were hidden – not even Los Amantes, the Lovers, brightest of them all, were visible.

"What you are seeing is beyond the air of Tierra Mejór. The telescope," Grath indicated the brass instrument, "magnifies the Unknown, pierces a hole through the layers of daylight. You're seeing the stars as they always are, unhidden by the light of la Grulla."

My curiosity overtook me. I tried to tamp it down, knowing that la Oráculo frowned upon such wild desire to know, but Grath had evidently felt the same burning need for answers, or he would not have built this device. "I've always wondered why it was that la Relojero set Tierra Mejór so far away from Old Earth. Why not build it closer? Why take the risk of travelling so far?"

"The Texto Sagrado tells us that it was to keep us safe," Grath replied.

"You've read the *Sacred Text*?"

A slight smile twitched his lips. "You sound surprised. In any case, yes, I think that was part of it. La Oráculo spoke the words of the Pattern, and the Pattern wanted us protected. Circling Old Earth at a close orbit would leave us in danger from a desperate, dying world. They might have built a machine to reach Tierra Mejór, and tore it apart. Or worse, tried to destroy it altogether, on purpose. Remember, they rejected la Relojero and the words of la Oráculo because they did not believe in the Pattern. The fools."

Yet, why did I think this too si mple? "But you say that's only part of it."

"Indeed. The other reasons are more complex. Large bodies orbiting in space create gravitational fields. I would hypothesise that Tierra Mejór is not made to withstand those kind of stresses – it would break apart, or be pulled into orbit around one of the planets, which, over time, would pull it down to its surface, burning us up in its atmosphere. Then there is the issue of radiation. Tierra Mejór creates its own atmosphere, a protective envelope of gases that are emitted form and stabilised by the Needle. But it's a thin shield compared to the one on Old Earth. If we were too close to a star – for instance, Old Sol, or a larger planet, we would be subjected to immense radiation. It would kill us. If the Pattern did guide la Relojero, it did so with great forethought. Here, our closest stars are thousands of lightspans away. In many ways, we are safe."

"But not completely," I said, reading his tone.

"Look again."

I did. At the very edge of my view, floated a jagged-edged silver shape. Even as I watched, it moved fractionally across the faces of those stars. "La Grulla?"

I felt him nod as I drank in the beautiful form of the Crane arching high overhead. She was as beautiful and elegant as I'd always imagined, her wings spread wide, her body long and slender.

"I have been charting her movements for years," Grath said, and I pulled away from the sight reluctantly to see him jump down from the dais and spread his arms to indicate the countless sheets of paper scrawled with diagrams, calculations, charts. "Plotting her relationship to the stars, to Old Earth, and to Tierra Mejór. This," he pointed to the tube, "is not the greatest instrument of its kind, for I made it myself, modelling it after the great Scope in Iglesia. But I've checked and double-checked my facts and figures, then passed them on to the various guilds – carefully, so that no one Guild has ever received the full scope of my research at once – and had them confirm everything.

"Tierra Mejór is slowing. There is no doubt in my mind now."

I clutched a hand to my chest, but it was my stomach that clenched painfully. No! "La Relojero created Tierra Mejór to last eternally," I whispered in denial. "It's our home."

"La Relojero was not a god – she was a clockmaker. Tierra Mejór is just a machine made up of many working parts. Like any clockwork toy, it will eventually wind down. Perhaps she thought the Children of the Seven would die out before it happened, or perhaps she just didn't think that far ahead at all – but I doubt it. Even if we disregarded the fact that she worked, every turning, with the essence of time and its passage; well before she made Tierra Mejór, she looked out into the Unknown. She would not have ignored the future."

I began to laugh.

It was a hopeless, desperate laugh, but there was true amusement in it as well. When Grath looked surprised, I could only laugh harder.

"They have been blaming me," I managed to splutter. "They say because I ruined the dance, I caused this. But it's been happening for years. Since before I was even born!"

Grath did not laugh. He came back towards me and leaned with folded arms against the circular railing. His gaze was level as he regarded me from below. "This is what is at stake, Imre. *This* is my responsibility."

And at last, I finally understood.

Chapter Twenty-One

I had thought the world had been shaken, in those turnings after my fall; it was nothing compared to this. I returned to my chamber, which looked exactly the same, down to the bloodstain bird on the floor; to Miguel, who was just as staid as ever; to the bed, which I had just begun to think of as *mine* – but none of it fitted into my perceptions as they had before.

How could they?

The world is slowing.

Tierra Mejór, so solid and firm under our feet – how could something so huge, so permanent, so vital – how could it fail us? Why?

I raised a hand to my forehead, feeling the steady ticking of my metrónomo. It had always marked the precise time, down to the second. It hadn't missed a beat in five years. But if what Grath said was true, soon I – and all my sisters – would be minutes ahead of Tierra Mejór's time. What would that mean for the Dances? And what about other clocks, wristwatches, machines tied to Tierra Mejór's Core?

I didn't sleep well that night, and fell into a doze in the early morning, failing to wake even when Adina brought in my breakfast. I finally roused myself at close to lunchtime. Struggling to tear my thoughts from what Grath had shown me, I went out into the garden.

It was not easy to sneak through the door. Had it been Miguel or Hendrich, I would have had no chance, but they had gone with Senor Grath, running some errand in preparation for tonight.

The Prince, I saw as I crossed the sitting room, was dozing, murmuring in his dreams.

I opened the door to the suite, and discovered our only guard was a rusted, ticking sentinela. He raised his spear in warning, but I wasn't afraid of him. I'd come to learn that the sentinela were designed to be hostile to people unauthorised to enter a space, not those already passing outwards.

I jogged along the corridor. I'd taken pains to cover my hair with Xith's beautiful scarf, but still, I doubted most of the servants and staff of the Citadel would recognise me. It was only the heralds whom I feared – well, them and Senor Grath.

Having made my way to my old room, I found everything as I had left it. Even my feather, and Miguel's hacer julepe cards were still on the table.

The terrace door had not been locked. No one had discovered the playing card still wedged in the latch.

In all honesty, the idea of going outside frightened me a little, in case someone was lying in wait, but it was a stupid fear, and one I was determined to conquer. I certainly wasn't going to let it dictate my movements.

Evening was approaching, and the garden was full of the pleasant scents of a long, warm turning. Late bees buzzed past my ears, on their way home to the honey-mills, and a few butterflies flittered past, their blue or brown wings glinting in the fading sunlight.

Though my path wandered wide, I was drawn, as ever, to the statue of la Grulla. Her wings were tinged with the purple of the sky, and blossom fallen from a tree rested on her head like a crown.

I kneeled here and prayed.

I believe in the Pattern. I believe in the word, the first parabra, which was sent to la Relojero in a time of need. She heeded the will of the Pattern and began her great work. Tierra Mejór was born from her hands. All that we are, we owe to her. But why, then, did she leave us to this terrible fate? How could she have overlooked her children's needs?

Spent, I opened my eyes and stood up, plucking the crown of petals from la Grulla's head. I tore them to pieces and threw them in the air, letting them rain down like confetti. My hands were stained with their pale blue juices.

How was I supposed to go on as if nothing was happening? As if I knew nothing? How were we supposed to live our lives, with this shadow hanging over us, an end drawing ever closer? It was a joke, a cruel joke.

"What is a joke?" asked a voice from behind me.

I whirled to find the Prince – Thaniel. He must have followed me!

Thankfully, Senor Grath wasn't on his heels. I was almost positive, now, that the Senor wasn't behind the plot to have me removed – not after what he had shown me in the Clocktower – but that didn't mean I liked him any more than I had.

"I'm –" I shook my head. "I didn't realise I'd spoken aloud. I thought I was alone."

"Crane-girl." The Prince smiled. He sat on the stone bench, pulling his knees up to his chest, and I couldn't help but wonder how young he seemed at times, like a boy who'd never been taught the rules. "I didn't mean to intrude, but I knew you'd be here."

He seemed, at least, to be quite sober, and for this I was glad. He didn't frighten me so much in this form.

He shifted, and motioned towards the empty space between the bench and the statue. "Dance for me?"

I laughed again. "I'm out of practice. It's been turnings, and I'm not even warmed up."

The truth was, the idea of Dancing again scared me. What if I couldn't do it any longer? What if my ankle gave way? What if I simply couldn't find the rhythm at all?

What then?

"I won't force you. But I'd like to see it." There was open honesty in his face, and my heart thawed. On the surface, I was full of mixed-up feelings and fears, thanks to Grath's speech last turning. What was the point in dancing at all? What could it possibly accomplish, or change? But deep down, at the core of my being, I longed for it, for the beat and sway and step of it, I truly did.

And so, I chose a dance that fit my mood. The Dance of the Rock.

One, two, step. One two, sway. Raise my hands – and down. Raise – and down. Sway, step, sway. Turn. Sway.

The rhythm of this dance was off, deliberately so. It was counted on five beats, then three, then nine, seven, four. The steps varied, slowly speeding up, until the Dancer performed them at such a rapid pace, they would seem to be falling over themselves. I had always been good at it, my movements swift and sure, even as they grew more and more rushed; but others, Yui for one, had always had trouble. She had cracked her head on the stone floor of the practice room once, after tripping on her own feet. I'd held her as she cried that night, and told her, even as she sobbed that she no longer wanted to be a Dancer, that the Pattern had chosen her. The next morning, Maestra Tinir had made her do it again. And again. She got marginally better, but never as good as me.

I whirled and kicked and stomped and stepped. The dance represented the slow building of sediments, year after year; it represented the way a rock could be worn by wind and rain, and the way it could tumble down a slope, faster and faster, faster and faster; until at last, I reached the first beat again, where rock served as solid and dependable protection and shelter. One two step . . .

By this time, I breathed hard, and was scarcely able to believe I had done it, the entire dance, without my ankle hurting. Exhilarated, I wanted to run it through again, but the Prince was clapping. "Magnificent," he said, his face alight with joy, with the glory of the dance, just as it should be.

"You are beautiful when you dance," he went on. "Is that why you do it?"

"I don't dance for myself." I took a seat on the bench with a respectable distance between us. "None of us do. The Daughters dance for the Pattern."

"I think the Pattern dances with you."

I ducked my head. It was possibly the nicest compliment I'd ever received. Suddenly, he leaped up, and held out his hand.

"Come with me?"

I wasn't sure it was a good idea to go anywhere else – I was pretty sure I should just go back to his suite and wait for Senor Grath, but Thaniel's eyes pleaded with me, and after giving myself another moment to find an excuse, I took his hand.

His face lit up as I did so. He walked quickly, almost running, and again I felt about him that boyishness as we dashed down the paths. Leaves slapped at our faces and caught our clothes, but heedlessly we rushed on. The sky grew much darker by the time we arrived at what I guess was our destination.

The trees here were taller, the grass a darker shade of green. Less flowers, too, and larger green leafy plants that I think are called ferns. The air felt cool and damp, and I could hear the water running. When we emerged into a small grove, I saw it came from a waterfall, cascading over rocks and running in a small rivulet away through the moss-covered trees.

Ahead was a small bridge over the gully, and on the other side, a fence of horizontal bronze bars. They stretched up high, taller than the tops of the trees, and as far as I could see in either direction.

We crossed the bridge. There was a gate set in the bars, and Thaniel lifted a latch and pushed it open. He stepped through, and beckoned for me to follow.

Inside, there were more tall trees, ferns, and moss-covered rocks. The scent of loam and dampness was strong, but it was a nice smell, one that reminded me of things I couldn't quite remember . . .

"What is this place?" I asked Thaniel.

He turned. "This," he spread his hand expansively, "is my favourite place in the whole of Tierra Mejór. Come on!"

He jogged on ahead, moving with ease down the narrow paths. I raced after him, trying to keep pace, but more than once I failed. "Wait!" I called, laughing. "I don't want to be lost here!"

"You can't get lost!" his voice came back from up ahead. "All the paths lead to the centre."

Seconds later, I found him. We were in a wide clearing paved with bricks. Now that I could see the sky, I realised the fence I had seen joined with a roof made of the same gold bars. The whole thing was a giant cage.

"Is this –" I began, but Thaniel held a finger to his lips. I walked to his side, still breathless from the dance and our dash; his forehead was damp with perspiration, but we were both invigorated. We paused, waiting.

And then there was a flutter of movement at the corner of my vision, just a blur of red. Another, just above it, in green, and another to my right. They were like bright jewels, these birds – nothing like their clunky, mechanical cousins, the carrier pigeons that flew laboriously through the sky. They seemed attracted to Thaniel and me, flitting closer and closer; with tuneful songs, they called others, until there were a dozen, two dozen, whirling around us.

"Hold out your arms." Thaniel demonstrated, lifting his arms out to the sides, palms up towards the sky. The birds flocked to him, perching on his sleeves, his palms, his head. They sang; there was no unity to their song, no rhythm, but that didn't seem to matter. The harmony was more beautiful than any I'd heard played by the greatest musicians in the Room of Roses in the Pavilion.

I lifted my arms as well, and the birds fluttered around me like a miniature whirlwind of beaks and wings. I lifted my eyes upwards, living fully in that moment, unwilling to ground my thoughts by remembering that the world went on outside this place.

"They like you," said the Prince.

"What are they?" I asked him, almost shouting over the noise of their calls, of their wings.

"Diamond finches," he replied. "There are so very few of them left, and none in the wild."

"Is that why they're kept caged?"

"The bars are wide enough for them to fly free, but not wide enough for a street-fox to get in. The birds are sensible creatures. They know the city is no place for them, and even if they do venture out, they always return."

He made his way to the side of the clearing, where there was a wooden box attached to a tree trunk. He opened it and scooped out a handful of grains and seeds. The birds pecked at it elegantly.

Finally, I asked him the question I always seemed to be asking. "Why?"

He shrugged. "I don't know. Do I need a reason?"

"There is a reason for everything. No one does anything without purpose."

"Don't they?" He raised an eyebrow. With a red bird perched on his head, pulling at a strand of his hair, he should have looked ridiculous. Instead, he looked as if he was exactly where he was meant to be. "Well, then," he said with a wry smile. "Perhaps my reason is this: I am the Principe Regente. I'm about to inherit this entire world, every part of which is slowly failing. That should suffice, don't you think?"

He had successfully brought me back to reality. "Then you know, too. Who else knows about this? Does everyone? Of all the people in the Cuidad mas Grande, is it only me who was kept in the dark?"

His shoulders slumped. The birds, as if sensing the change in mood, settled and quietened. "Grath has kept me updated on his little hobby for years. But truthfully, it's only recently that his calculations had really had any bearing. Do you think you're the only one who doesn't know? It's not something we can spread about widely among the population. Imagine the panic."

"But don't the people deserve to know what's happening to their world?"

"Is it a matter of them being deserving?" He shrugged. "I don't know the answer to that. Maybe. Maybe not. If you were told you had a terminal illness – chain-pox, or some tumour – would you want to know, or would you rather live out your turnings in blissful ignorance, enjoying life as you otherwise would?"

I knew the answer to this, but still, it didn't sit right with me.

"It's not up to me, in any case," he went on. "I'm under a mandate from the Brotherhood to say nothing. Grath went to them with his research several years ago. They lobbied to have him imprisoned."

I gaped. "But he's the Adviser – *your* adviser."

"He's not above the law. None of us are. The heavens are the province of the heralds, and not to be interfered with by mere laymen." There was a mocking note to his voice, and suddenly I understood the Prince better than I ever had. I knew why he took the drugs, and would drink himself into a stupor. I understood the weight on his shoulders – a greater weight even than Grath's, this burden of leadership to a people who loved and trusted him, but to whom he must lie, and the utter inability to share it. Thaniel fixed me with a hard look. "I promised them his silence. But if any word of this were to trickle free, they wouldn't hesitate to punish any of us, Imre."

"I will say nothing," I said solemnly, and he nodded.

***

The decision had been made – I'm not sure by whom – that I was to be moved from my current room. "It's too dangerous to keep you here any longer," Miguel told me.

"Dangerous?" I repeated, incredulous. "I don't see how it can be any more dangerous now than before."

"Just be ready at lunchtime. We'll cover the business with the meal."

I was getting used to having decisions being forced on me, but I still didn't like it.

At least, it wasn't like I had many belongings to pack. Just my feather, and the pack of playing cards, and Xith's patterned shawl. Seeing it made me think of Bethery, and I folded it away into the middle of my spare dress so I didn't have to look at it.

Miguel sat in the corner chair while I gathered everything and bundled it together with a corded belt. When I was done, I suggested we read some, and he brightened instantly at the prospect.

The poem continued in the same vein. We learned more of Gilgamesh, in the broken lines and inferred words:

> He who has seen all kinds of wisdom,
> and knows the mysteries and has seen what is hidden,
> he bringeth news dating farther back than the deluge;
> He has travelled far-distant roads,
> and become weary
> and now he has written on a memorial tablet all the other things
> the wall of Uruk-supuru
> He spoke a charm which does not leave him
> the god who from distant days

Miguel read well, and I found myself falling deep into thought. These words, so very old, predated the *Sacred Text*; they were possibly the oldest story humans had ever recorded. It was like looking back through a tunnel – or through Grath's telescope, through a hole not in the atmosphere, but through time – and seeing where we had come from.

"Do you ever think about what life was like on Old Earth?"

The question burst unexpectedly from my mouth, but Miguel frowned, his large features creased in concentration. "I can't say that I do. Those times are passed, are they not? We left Old Earth behind when we came to Tierra Mejór."

I didn't challenge him further on it. Miguel's view of the world was narrow, and simple, but certainly not wrong. In fact, I envied him that simplicity, that acceptance.

"You do, though," the burly guardia said. "Tell me what you think."

I put the book down on my lap. "I think that there were many, many different people. That the lands spread as far as the eye could see, all with those strange, foreign names: Aegypt, Cathay, Amerik, Australis, España. You could walk for a year and not reach the edge of the land, and when you did, you'd find the ocean, blue water as far as the eye can see. I think there was food we never even dreamed of. And rain that came when it wanted to, not when the heralds deemed fit."

"It sounds like hell," Miguel said gruffly.

"It sounds . . . different," I argued gently. "There have to be other things, too, things we can't even imagine."

"Then what is the point?" he teased me.

I picked up the book and shook it for emphasis. "*This* is the point. It's where we came from . . . it's who we were."

"But we're not who we *were* anymore. We're who we *are*."

I gave up. It was not like talking to Thaniel, who truly wondered about these things. Miguel's imagination centred around what he knew, not what he could dream of.

Hendrich arrived later. "I've been told we're to go down the balcony entrance," he said. Another guardia had been posted outside the door, so that it wouldn't be obvious that the room was suddenly without need of guarding. Miguel was to accompany us; of this I was glad.

I took my meagre belongings, tucking them into my pocket and draping Xith's shawl around my shoulders. The air was fresh in the garden. Energy surged through me, and I skipped my way down the steps, making Miguel and Hendrich laugh. I was careful not to pull my ankle, but it felt good to move again.

We took a stone path along the side of the building, turning at one corner, then another, until we arrived at a bridge. Made of metal and paved with cobbles, standing on tall pylons of lacey ironwork, it crossed into a deep expanse of water. Not a reservoir, but an ornamental eddy-lake. The water, deep blue in colour, swirled in a clockwise fashion, gentle streams cascading over rocks, leaping up occasionally to mist the air with fine, warm spray.

It led to a small octagonal garden house, rotating slowly on a grey metal pedestal.

This was the most beautiful building I'd ever seen. The walls were real wood, polished, with the grain of the timber showing through. Diamond-shaped windows were set into each wall, and the door, at the front, was painted green. Sitting beside it were several tools – large forks, a shovel, and smaller trowels.

"This – this is where I'm to stay?"

Hendrich nodded and opened the door. "The Prince felt it might be the most suitable accommodation. It is used by his gardeners, and you can easily be explained as an apprentice horticulturalist, come to study the flowers and plants."

Inside, as the floor moved with that gentle slowness under my feet, I ran my fingers over the walls, delighting in the ringed pattern. It must have cost a fortune for all this wood. We stood in a small entry room, set about with sofas and a circular rug with the tree pattern. An arched door ahead of me lead into a small octagonal room at the centre of the garden house. From this there were doors opening into the other rooms: a bathing room, a sitting room, a bedroom, and a small kitchen. Globe-lights turned themselves on as I passed, illuminating each new discovery with a soft white light. I paused in the main room and spun around, first one way with the motion of the house, then the other, against it: I was hardly able to believe it. The whole place was positively enchanting.

"You must thank the Prince for me," I said to Hendrich.

He nodded. "Your gratitude will be conveyed."

"No need," came a voice. I had missed a back door, leading out from the kitchen. Thaniel came in through it, his face alight. "Your delight radiates through the very walls."

"Thank you." I inclined my head. "My Prince."

He nodded thoughtfully. "Now, in the interest of maintaining our deception, you will have to do a little gardening. I hope you won't mind."

"I – I don't know much about gardening," I said.

"What is there to know?" he replied. "Pull out the things that grow where they shouldn't, and let grow the things that are good."

"I suppose so," I said. "But won't people think it's odd, a girl suddenly living in the garden, wearing a dress such as this?"

"That is why I've placed clothes in the wardrobe for you. All measured to your size."

I gaped at him. "Why?" I whispered at last. "Why are you doing this for me?"

He gave a thin smile, his gaze somewhere in the distance. "Do I not owe you a thousand times over, for allowing me to bring you here?"

I shook my head. "No, my Prince."

His attention snapped back to me. "Tonight," he said. "You will walk in the garden with me. Will you do that?"

I nodded.

***

I spent the afternoon sitting on a bench by the back door, in the company of bees and gnats and a few stray white-moths. Miguel and

Hendrich had been charged with guarding the perimeter, since two guards were likely to better cover the distance, but there was less need for it, as no one knew I was here. I felt pleasantly relaxed and happy; all I needed for my contentment was a book. And so, I convinced Miguel to sit beside me, and we continued the *Epic of Gilgamesh.*

As we turned one page, there was a sound like thunder. It came not from overhead, where the Pendulum sung in its wide arc, describing the limits of the few distant clouds, but from under our feet, somewhere deep in the workings of Tierra Mejór.

I dropped the book and clutched at Miguel, but this quake was nowhere near so horrific as the first, and subsided after only a minute.

When no further rumblings ensued, it was easily forgotten.

As evening fell, I returned to the bedroom, where I tried to decide which dress to wear. Miguel was no help at all, and Hendrich couldn't even seem to look at me directly. I almost stamped my foot in the end, but at that moment, there was a knock at the door, startling my guards. They hurried away, hands twitching over the butts of their revolver-pistols, only to return with Adina and one of the other maids – Paje.

"I knew it," Adina breathed when she saw me. "I knew it was you. They said you'd gone from the Citadel. I didn't believe it!" She curtseyed quickly. "My Lady."

When I rolled my eyes, she grinned. "But you are! A guildswoman can't be called anything else."

"I'm no guildswoman," I reminded her. "I'm only pretending."

"I beg your pardon, my Lady," she said cheekily, and I batted her softly on the arm.

Together, she and Paje helped me choose a dress, from one of the few simple creations in the wardrobe. Adina offered to do my hair, but I told her to leave it. It felt nice, brushing against my neck and cheeks as the breeze blew in through the open window.

When at last I deemed myself ready, I left the house and walked to the statue of la Grulla. There I sat on the grass, glorying in the wind of her wingbeats. If I looked up, I could just see the real Crane moving into view overhead. Her silver light coated my surroundings.

By the time I heard his footsteps, I had lulled myself into a pleasant daze. "I wasn't sure you would come," I said without turning around. I didn't say, *I wasn't sure you wouldn't drink yourself into oblivion and forget our meeting,* but I thought it nonetheless.

He settled onto the grass beside me, stretching his long legs out in front of him. "I'm here." He angled his body so he could reach across and flick a strand of my hair away from my face. "You look beautiful."

"It's a lovely dress," I said.

He shook his head. "Not the dress. It's only fabric and stitching. A veil, like a . . . a cloud across the face of la Grulla. If you took it off –" His hand moved lower, a gentle finger slipping beneath the neckline, shifting it towards my shoulder. "What's underneath would shine twice as brightly."

A delicious shiver ran through me. I wondered if he would take me here, lying on the grass, and knew I wouldn't mind if he did. "But you're a Prince."

He sighed. "A Regent Prince. Until I can be named by the Queen, as Principe Verdararo, I'll never be King; I'm nothing but a placeholder."

"And I – a failed Dancer," I told him. "In fact, it seems I'm the ruination of Tierra Mejór!"

He didn't speak for a long time. When at last he opened his mouth, he said: "Do you know what it is you did, Imre? When you fell?"

I had many answers to this, too many to count! But it seemed he had his own, for he held up a hand to forestall me.

"I'm not speaking about the Pattern, or la Grulla, or Aurelia. I'm not talking about you ruining the harvest of coming year or whatever else it is that's supposed to happen because a creeper-fish farts in the reservoir, or a fork falls on the floor the wrong way up on the first hour of the Tenth Month. I'm talking about what you *did*."

"I didn't –" I began, but he shook his shaggy head. It was a moment before he spoke again.

"It would be hard to imagine," he said slowly. "For one such as you. You have given your life to the Pavilion, devoted yourself to it by your own choice. Everything you want is there before you. I can see it in you, the way you love it. But just suppose your life was given away, without your consent, to a cause you could not love. Suppose that by circumstance of your birth you had no choice in what you would become. Suppose that every part of your life was planned, every action scheduled, every moment marked down by pen. When to rise. What to eat. Where to go, what to wear, how to speak. Tell me how you would feel."

"I would be . . . I would not like it, my lord."

"No. Tell me how you would *feel*."

I hesitated, and I tried then, to truly imagine it. "I would feel trapped, my Prince. I would feel a captive. I would . . . I would be bored."

"Ah!" he sighed with satisfaction. I had pleased him. It rocked me then, his need for drink and drugs. His need to blot out all and everything as much as he could, to filter it through a screen; he was powerless to enact change on his own.

"Imre. The turning you fell, you broke the Pattern. You destroyed the order. You changed things."

"I –" I plucked at the grass, but he gripped my chin in his fingers and gently but firmly turned me to look at him.

"That is why I brought you here. Why I want you to stay . . ." Here he paused, took a shuddering breath – "If you leave here, leave me, everything goes back to the way it was."

Chapter Twenty-Two

In the morning, I woke in time for the dawn regimen.

I slipped out of bed as la Reloj de pie chimed the first of its seven peals, and sat on the floor. One – I raised my hands. Two – I came to my knees. Three – I rocked back onto the balls of my feet. Four – finally, I rose to standing. Five – I raised my arms. Six – I lowered them. Seven.

"By all that is the Pattern," I murmured my parabra, "I have not been good. I am jealous and fearful. But I promise to serve you well, on this day and all others. I promise to put the life of my Prince above my own, for he is greater in the Pattern than I."

Feeling more clear-headed than I had in a long time, I dressed in a pair of trousers, a shirt, and a vest. I found a large, floppy-brimmed hat, and when I bound up my hair, it kept it in place, though not neatly. I didn't care.

Determined, I opened the window in the kitchen to let in the sun, and began to sing.

> One day my love turned me away,
> And nary a word said he,
> As he cast my heart upon the floor,
> And trod it to a million pieces . . .

"That's a cheerful song to wake too," Miguel said, appearing outside the window.

I unburied my head from a cupboard. I had found the kitchen laden with stores of jars, cans, and tins, a bowl of fresh fruit upon the bench, and a chiller-box containing milk, cheese, and cream.

"Don't stand out there," I told him. "Have you had breakfast?"

"I left before my wife woke this morn," he admitted. "I took over from Hendrich at four chimes."

I had never really cooked anything before, but all these good things could only taste better when mixed together, so I turned on the stove and, when I judged it warm enough, placed a pot on top, filled it with milk and oats, then added a sample of every piece of fruit I could find, some apple preserves, and a few spices I'd never even heard of. It smelled so good, I ate several spoonfuls right out of the pot, burning my mouth.

"Leave some for me," Miguel said, and his stomach gave a loud growl, making us laugh.

The meal was good, and all the better for being created by my own hands. "Perhaps Thaniel should have disguised me among the Citadel cooks!"

Miguel shook his head. "I can't see you hidden away in a dark, dingy kitchen. Though this . . . whatever it is . . . is quite wonderful."

"If I could find the ingredients," I mused, "I could perhaps even make some of my favourite coffee biscuits. Oh, how I would love just one!"

After this, I washed the dishes in the sink, then stepped out into the gardens. I wasn't sure where to start, or *what* exactly I was going to do, so for a few minutes I just wandered, with Miguel trailing a few steps behind. I found a path I hadn't been down before, lined with red bricks, which led me to a small patch of sweet-smelling herbs. I rubbed my fingers over them, revelling in the scent. In the midst of the patch was a small tree. It looked familiar, and I tried to think where I had seen it before – not in the Pavilion gardens, no, but – of course. "It's a Sacred Tree," I murmured.

"How do you know that?" Miguel asked.

There had been a drawing of it in the book Laisa had lent me, *The Cultivated Tree and its Uses*. But it looked much smaller than the picture, slightly stunted. The bark was tinged with grey, and the few leaves were speckled with yellow.

"It's a hardy tree, very adaptable, but it would do better with more light. It shouldn't be hidden here, with its roots covered so thickly."

Miguel pinched some of the surrounding foliage between his fingers. "I suppose you could trim these branches back?"

I didn't want to harm anything. "It would be better to move the tree itself."

Miguel raised his eyes to the heavens. "How are you going to manage that?"

I was already heading back to the garden house, and fetching the tools from outside the door. Digging was easy, I found, and fun; though I didn't have Miguel's strength, I refused to let him help me. Plunging the spade deep into the earth and turning the soil over made my muscles, unused for turnings, sting in a good way. Soon I'd cleared enough soil to lift the little tree free – for this, I did need Miguel. The tree itself didn't weigh much, but the clumps of earth attached to the roots did, and I knew enough from reading *Cultivated Trees* to know to keep the roots in as much of the plant's birth-soil as possible.

"Where should we plant it?" Miguel asked. I thought for a moment, then pointed the way, marching ahead while Miguel struggled behind, dropping clods of dirt on his boots. When we reached the right place, I found an area populated mostly by prickly purple leaves that I deemed to be weeds, and dug them out. The little tree looked perfectly happy, basking in the sun, and the sprinklers chose that moment to turn on, shooting arcing rainbows into the air, as if to prove I'd made the right choice.

I glanced across at the terrace, and the empty terracotta pot below a small, high window, and hoped that when the tree finally grew, Bethery would enjoy it.

***

I was standing there, looking at the water playing across the leaves, with filthy hands and dirt streaks on my cheeks, my hair curling down from underneath my hat, when Senor Grath found me.

His eyes raked me up and down, and with a familiar twist of his lips, he let me know what he thought about my morning's activities. "If you're done playing gardener, the Principe Regente requests your presence at the Conclave this afternoon."

***

Again, I did not know what was going on outside the walls of the Citadel, but things were changing, and rapidly. A new fear had arisen among the men and women of the Cuidad mas Grande. Men in green-ribboned hats walked the streets after dark, they said, and they would slit the throat of anyone they caught, whispering the words, 'It is the will of the Pattern'.

They painted more of their messages of doom on the walls of shops and businesses, from the First Tier down to the Fourth. A vigilar had caught one at work, and shot him on sight in a fit of what could only be thought of as piety; it was only afterwards that he realised it was a woman.

The man had been imprisoned, pending trial, until la Boca heard of it. "Set him free," he commanded, and no one protested. "The man acted in Faith. He has done no wrong."

In the basement of the building I once knew, men and women took off their green-banded hats and grieved.

It was nothing to me, not yet. I had not attended a Conclave since the first one, and I suspected strongly that the Prince had not, either; somehow, he had argued his way out of this duty, and possibly it was my embarrassing presence that had allowed him to do so.

It seemed, however, he couldn't dodge it forever; and so, once more, here we were.

At least, this time, I had the chance to dress myself more appropriately.

And this time, when la Boca's eyes settled on me, I was more prepared. It helped that the Prince decided he would sit by my side, in one of the upper chairs, instead of at the table – though this drew frowns from the other attendees, and what I thought was a mocking glare from behind the mask of la Boca. I did not try to shrink, but simply focused my attention below, on the table, and the beautiful figure of La Reina. How she sat so still, so silently, I would never know; for all my dancer's training at remaining poised and attentive, I couldn't help but fidget in my seat.

"We must discuss the tremors." This was the first thing Darhn said as the Council was seated. "They have grown worse. I have had numerous reports of failed machinery, especially in the third and fourth tiers. If this continues, it will seriously affect production of cloth, processing of grain, and even moth-meat."

The Prince did not release me. Instead, his fingers played over my shoulder, inching their way just a hair's breadth beneath my collar. It made me shiver.

"Not to mention the impact on the Treasury," said Allius. "I don't need to remind you of the dire figures we've come up against in the vaults of the banks and the Exchange. People are simply not seeing that they have any finances leftover to spend on luxuries."

His gaze slid over me, and left me with a slimy feeling. His meaning was clear. He considered me one of those 'luxuries'.

I wriggled, trying to turn away so the Prince would stop fondling me, but he placed a heavy hand on my knee. Through the silk dress, I could feel the smooth, solid grip, and an unwanted flush of excitement rushed through me. If the Prince intended to torture me, he was doing it very well.

"We should stimulate the market." By this stage, I had lost track of who was talking, and didn't much care; I could see why the Prince was so bored in these meetings. It seemed to be an excuse to sit around and talk, rather than take action. "While our Brotherhood friends are here, we might apply to them for an increase in wages –"

"To what end?" la Boca's voice was cold. "Will people work harder? Will they earn their privileges? I think not. Look at the level of crime in the lower tiers: smuggling, black markets, illegal trade in white-powder and other, less pure drugs. Robbery, rape, rioting. Will this decrease if we start handing out gold coins? I think not. It will encourage idle behaviour."

"It is a means to an end –" began one of the women.

La Boca waved his spindly hand. "I see no point in this discussion. I will never agree."

"Then we need to distribute the wealth more evenly among the people," came a soft voice, a younger man, Guildsman Ollander of the Architects. "Allow the lower tiers to visit the upper, come to the Pavilion, sample the pleasures. Give them something to strive for, an incentive to work harder."

"How?" The word burst out before I'd had a chance to stop it. I clapped a hand to my mouth, but I'd startled everyone in the room, not least, myself. For a heartrending moment, silence reigned.

"Forgive me," I said, appalled and wishing I could run from the room.

"Well." Dahrn clutched his crystal staff tightly. "Our Prince has decided that a Dancer may sit in a Conclave. If the Dancer decides to speak, she should at least finish her sentence. So. What have you to say, girl?"

"There is no work." My heart raced, the knot aching jaggedly with every beat. Nonetheless, I pushed my way free of the Prince's grasp, and stood. My stature did not put me on the same level as the rest, but at least I didn't feel so much the Prince's pet. "The machinery is so broken on the lower levels, it is almost unusable. There are no servitors left down there, and certainly no automata. Without someone to fix the machinery, they can do nothing but fight one another for scraps, or turn to the crimes you mentioned."

"Then what," said Benefine, his voice a warning growl, "do you suggest?"

"The people need work. And we need the people to work. Perhaps the money from the treasury," here I glanced at Allius, who met my gaze with a wrinkled expression, as if my words were painful, "may be used to allow them to open shops, or businesses."

"What nonsense is this?" the herald broke in. "Give the people money to create businesses for which we have no need? Why do we not simply spill the coin of the treasury from the Pendulum and have it mingle with the rain?" He underscored this with a sharp bark of laughter.

"I think it would give people a purpose," I said, but was quickly cut off by Benefine.

"And how long do you think it would be before every last one of the citizens of Lower Tiers were clamouring for more, and refusing to do the less tasteful work in the reservoirs, and we are all left without clean water? Or the Ruedans demurring to grow our crops, or work in the harvestries, or the moth refineries? Once these factories ran on their own, but no longer.

We need a workforce to maintain them. Prince, my Liege, I think you should feed your pet less white-powder."

"He is right," a man with long black hair spoke up from the back. His chair clicked and clacked as it moved through the others to take on a central position. "The real problem here is that there are too many people. The Lower Tiers are overcrowded. Perhaps we should think about implementing a permit system for children, such as we have on the Wheel?"

I bowed my head. I knew I shouldn't have spoken, but these comments made me glad I did, if only to defy the pompous, self-righteous man in his black robe. "Get her out of here," cried Benefine, and a guardsman appeared, ready to take my arm. "She is done here."

It was only Ollander who half-stood, looking as if he was about to raise his voice in protest. His chair turned in response, but as he sat back down, it whirred back into place. His eyes, though, followed me as I was led from the room.

***

Foolish though my words sounded, even to my own ears – giving people money from the treasury, with free rein to spend it on business ventures that might fail – or more likely, on the more immediate pleasures of goldwine and white-powder – they must have touched Guildsman Ollander, for he sent me a message. By a carrier-pigeon, no less.

I had only ever received one pigeon in my life prior to this, and it had been from Senora R., confirming that I was to come to an audition at an appointed time, and if I performed well, I would be offered a place at the Pavilion.

I had huddled in a corner of the night-café, listening to the lewd shouts of drunks, and hoping Vallencino won't find me, for he was a man whose taste often ran to younger girls – too young. I was heartsick and missing my very best friend in the world, who had escaped this hellhole a year earlier.

How I longed to keep that metal bird forever, just to hear it repeat those delicious words. 'Provisionally, you will be offered a place at the Pavilion.'

This pigeon arrived in the morning, ticking slightly as it set down on the windowsill.

"Greetings, Imre," it spoke through its rust-stained beak. "In two days, at noon, I walk the wall tops. I hope you will find the time to join me."

At first, I thought it must be some kind of joke, but in the end, I decided I would test it; I wanted to see the man again, for he had intrigued me, with his soft-spoken ways.

Miguel was not happy that I was going to leave my garden house, but I reminded him that I was not a prisoner, and he grudgingly agreed.

A path wound along the wall tops, where guardia marched and kept watch, and, occasionally, let off a shot of their revolver-pistols to scare away curious children. There were many, it seemed, peering up with their faces blackened by the soot and dirt of the lower tiers. What drew them to the Citadel, I knew not; surely it wasn't any notion that they could breach the thick walls. Perhaps, like white-moths to a flame, they simply couldn't resist the sight, even should it burn them.

Each time I heard a report, it made me jump.

I found Ollander at one corner, where the levels of the path changed and one had to step down to continue onwards. He was twisting something in his fingers and he smiled when he saw me.

"I wondered if you would come," he said.

I looked over my shoulder at Miguel, but Ollander seemed to have expected the presence of the big man. "Why did you ask me here?" I asked bluntly.

"You intrigue me," he said, and I knew it was almost true. Out here, in the sunshine, he was quite handsome. My gaze drifted down to his trousers, and I couldn't help wondering what kind of body he hid beneath those clothes. He continued to flip the thing between his fingers, and I saw it was a gold coin. Suddenly he flicked it, quite deliberately, over the wall. It traced a golden arc, down, down into the bushes below. Several small figures lunged for it, scuffling until one came up victorious, and fled into the streets, crowing loudly.

"Why did you do that?" I asked him. And then, thinking of what must draw those scrawny urchins, I followed with an answer to my own question. "You do this often."

"Indeed I do." He smiled. "The children know it, and come, hoping I'll be here. I have an autocarriage, did you know that? One of my very own. A few years ago, I had the idea that when I rode in it, through the streets on my way to a meeting, or luncheon, or some other petty, time-wasting party, I would toss coins from the window, or sometimes food. People knew to look for it, after a while. One day, while I was driving, a mob of men and even a few women set upon it. The windows were smashed, the driver – an automaton – dragged free and broken into parts, to be sold, I suppose, in the back alleyways for many more coins. The carriage itself was overturned and left lying on its roof. Such was the strength of their anger!"

I almost gasped, picturing it in my mind. "Were you hurt?"

"A fair bit. I was confined to a bed for a turning. Broken ankle, cracked ribs, blood pooling in my lungs." He smiled wryly. "When I was able to stand, I was left with this." He lifted his trouser leg to show an ankle twisted to one side, permanently. This was the cause of his limp.

"I'm sorry," I murmured.

He shrugged. "I didn't tell you this in order to gain your pity." He sighed, stepping away from the crenulations at the edge of the wall. "Those people, the ones who attacked me, had come to see I had coin. Indeed, I had twenty-one gold coins on me that day. They wanted it, or needed it, and so they decided to take it. If I had travelled those roads several times in a turning, I would have probably thrown away four or five times as much as I had on me that day, but their immediate needs outweighed the thought of the future. Just as a child cannot conceive of its own death. And so we are, as humans. This is what we do to Tierra Mejór, every day we live upon it. We call ourselves the Children of the Seven, and so we are; children, who take what we need from this world, understanding nothing of how it works, or how to care for it. And like my purse, its resources are not bottomless. It is already failing."

"No one knows how to repair the machines," I said. "That knowledge was lost."

"Indeed, it was. But has anyone ever tried to look for it? Has anyone ever studied the way it works, been down into the depths, uncovered the Core of our home? We claim it can't be fixed, but maybe we're just afraid to take the responsibility of fixing it ourselves."

"It's fine to muse on those things." I don't know what it was about this man that brought forth such bluntness in me. "But you've forgotten that we're forbidden to go into the Inner Workings."

"Forbidden? Perhaps. But what is really stopping us, Imre? A few words in a book? Think beyond that. Think of what we might uncover! The secrets of the Unknown could be lying in wait, beneath our very feet, at that!"

His enthusiasm was infectious. "How can you know where to start?"

A slow smile spread across his face. "The knowledge of all the world lies under the Citadel. In the Library."

We parted soon after that.

"I hope you will allow me to call on you," he said. "It has been a very interesting talk."

"You may, of course." I grinned, with genuine delight. "The Principe has me staying in the garden house, and you must come, please, at any time. I'll be glad to see you."

Chapter Twenty-Three

Talking to Ollander had introduced me to more ways of thinking, more incredible insights; truly, I had never questioned so much about our existence on this wondrous place we called Tierra Mejór. After our talk, we met once more, this time by accident in the gardens, and he invited me to take a drive with him.

Considering my first time in an autocarriage, I wasn't too keen to repeat the experience, but talking with him had certainly inspired me. I did not want to let another opportunity to pass me by.

We took a ground floor corridor lined with stone and cement, and smelling of hot oil and rubber. This was soon explained when I saw, through barred glassless windows in the wall, a cavernous room in which sat row upon row of autocarriages. They gleamed in the darkness. I couldn't even imagine the wealth that would be required for such a fleet, but, when we stepped through an open door, I saw that some of them had not been moved for a very long time. Their rubber tires were flat, and though some had been covered with dust-sheets, others were shrouded with cobwebs.

The bay had two large doors at the far end, with our autocarriage waiting for us just inside. It was green, with an open top. Feval – it was Feval, I knew, for he had only one working eye – was there, already behind the wheel, and I smiled at his one-eyed glance, while Ollander opened the passenger door for me. I took care not to crush my dress as I sat.

Feval cranked the engine by repeatedly pulling a lever beside the steering wheel. Ollander took the seat behind me, leaning over the back of the front seat so we could still converse. "Let's go, then!" he said, and we were moving.

And then we were out on the streets. Feval sped up, and I pushed back against a twinge of nervousness. It *was* rather enjoyable, coasting along like this, especially when I wasn't hidden in the backseat but rather at the very front, watching the street race by and feeling the wind pluck gently at my hair. People were turning to watch us go by, eliciting a secret thrill. They thought I was a noblewoman, of course, when, in reality, I far less entitled to this magnificent show than they were.

"Enjoying yourself, Imre?" asked Ollander, cheerfully.

I nodded, surprised that I actually was. "It is almost exhilarating."

"One of the few remaining autocarriages that functions well," Ollander said. "It is a great shame. Some machines I will be very sad to lose."

"You are certain there is no way to fix them?"

Ollander pinched his lips. "Oh, I am certain there is, but it is one we cannot see yet. That is why I'm about to propose an expedition."

"An expedition?" I repeated. "To where?"

"To the source of our issues," he said. "Into the Core of Tierra Mejór."

My heart did something strange at these words. It wasn't so much a flip as a wrench, as if something terrible, fearful, and wondrous had been announced. "Into the Core. When we spoke the last time, I thought you were just speculating."

"During the quake," Ollander's voice rose, in concert with his excitement, "a young boy was washed into a reservoir well."

Remembering the story Miguel had told me of his neighbour's child, I felt a stab of sorrow. "I heard of that. Did he survive?"

"His injuries were extensive, but that is beside the point. The point being – water."

I looked at him sideways.

"The water is pumped from the reservoirs," he said, "which reside below the surface of the First Tier. It flows through the necessary channels, carrying sewage and waste, from the First Tier, down to the second. Then the third. By the time it reaches the fourth, it is a filthy, stinking miasma. Here, it runs from the gutters back in through inlets, the reservoir-wells, where it cools the heat of Tierra Mejór's heart for a time, before it evaporates, leaving behind the undesirable parts; it rises, through a series of grilles and ducts, into the atmosphere, allowing clean water to fall as rain. The rescuers waded into the well, for a crack had formed in the bottom of it, and the water had drained out. Inside, they found passages and gantryways. I strongly suspect that these are accesses to the inner workings of the Spindle."

I shook my head. "But surely – the heat –"

"I'm certain there is a way in, Imre. Why else would the gantries be there? La Relojero must have built them, in order to reach the Core and wind the key, when she created Tierra Mejór. And this is where our answers will lie."

"It sounds unbelievable," I said, dubiously.

"You of all people I must convince to believe me, Imre. You are the one person I can hope to sway to my side in support of this mission."

I realised, then, why he had asked me on this trip. It wasn't just an enjoyable outing, but a chance to talk me into supporting his adventure. "I'm a Dancer, Ollander! Not a politician. The Council will not listen to me."

"Ah, but they would!" he exclaimed. "Can't you see? As an outsider, your voice is heard. You make them sit up and take notice, even if what you say is preposterous! What do you say? Will you do it?"

I had to admit, the idea was so incredible that it might just work. "It would be dangerous," I told him. "For the men and women who undertook such a venture, I mean."

"I've been thinking of that." He nodded. "I thought we could send automata in first, but I doubt the Council will agree to the possible wastage of our last few units. Personally, I think it would be worth the sacrifice."

I looked sideways at Feval. "I've come to think of them as more than machines."

Ollander snorted. "They are only bits and pieces of metal and crystal. They can forget who we are with a tap of a controller wand, their memory crystals wiped, returned to newborn status."

"They remember us," I insisted. "You do, don't you, Feval?"

The automaton had steered us around a corner onto the Avenida de las Estralles. I had never travelled the whole length of this road, for I'd usually gone along the Calle del Corazón towards the Citadel.

"Yes, of course, my Lady," he intoned. "How did you find the *Epic of Gilgamesh?*"

I was puzzled for a moment, until I realised he was also recalling Divon's memories. "It is truly wonderful."

"Divon did think it would appeal to you."

"Just the idea of it," I gushed. "It's so old! It speaks of another time – another planet – but it feels so familiar."

"It is the history of humankind," Feval said. "One is bound to feel a connection."

"But it's more than that, isn't it? It's your history, too."

He didn't turn from the road. "An automaton does not have a history," he said sadly.

"By the Pattern, you *do*," I said vehemently. "Your history is ours."

"That means little to a creature built of gears and springs. We were made in the image of humans, to serve humans, and even now we are failing in that respect. I," he finished, "am failing."

A moment passed as two children, out wandering late at night, waved to us from the footpath. I longed to wave back, but I was almost certain a Lady of the Citadel would not do such a thing; we whipped past, and the buildings to the left of us dropped away, revealing scrubby, dry grass and a few wind-twisted bushes.

"Slow down," I told Feval.

"My lady?"

"Slow down," I insisted, and his feet danced on the pedals, slowing the carriage. The Avenida de las Estralles led straight to the outer edge of the city, whereupon we were to take one of the adjoining roads to reach the Exchange. But instead, I pointed ahead. "Keep going that way."

"Imre, what in the Great Unknown are you doing?" Ollander enquired.

Something creaked and clicked inside Feval. "I have been directed to –"

"Just go ahead." I assured him. "It will only take a minute."

We drove for less than a few seconds before we crested a rise at the end of the Avenida, where it joined the Camino de Borde, the Edge Road, which circled the Cuidad. We were on top of a high cliff, giving us an unbroken view of the wide expanse of sky above and below.

Feval slowed the carriage to a stop. There was no one else here, just a breadth of scrubby grass growing through patches of metal.

"I've never seen it before," I confessed. "But I've imagined it."

"How does it compare to your imagination?" Ollander asked.

"It surpasses my wildest dreams." I pushed open my door and stepped out. My shoes clanged on the metal plates, and Feval, turning off the engine, watched me walk to the edge. I turned back to Ollander. "Come on."

"We will miss our appointed time for return," Feval reminded us.

"I don't care. Both of you. Come here."

Reluctantly, Ollander obeyed. Feval did too, if slower, creaking his way out of the car. I gripped his elbow and walked him closer to the edge, until we were standing at the point where the rusted metal crumbled away into the abyss. It was a good few hundred arm spans to the tier below, and looking straight ahead, one could see only a fraction of the Wheel, and then, nothingness. Nothingness. Silver sky faded to green and grey as the Viento Cósmico whipped the clouds into sharp-edged shapes. Beyond, the palest notions of the stars, winked like beckoning fingers.

"This is very unsafe," Feval said.

"That's the thrill of it, though, isn't it?" I let go of his arm, to raise both of mine. The Viento Cósmico buffeted me, hard enough to knock me over if I didn't lean into it. It tugged at my skirt and pulled at my perfectly arranged hair.

Ollander seemed to warm to the interruption now that he was out here, standing by my side. He leaned in close, pointing out into the ether. "Can you see it?"

"The Wheel?" I squinted through the clouds at the distant arc of grey metal, spinning slowly.

He nodded. "It takes half a day for a shuttle-train to cross the Spokes to reach it. And even further than that, at the border where the air turns to vacuum, there is the Pendulum. Isn't it incredible? That everything works as it should, the Pattern is followed, and this small piece of existence is ours."

I looked sideways at Feval. How much of this conversation could he actually comprehend? His bad eye blinked on and off, on and off, like a twinkling star, muted by the bright sun.

"And beyond that . . ." I went on. "The Unknown."

"That has always puzzled me," Feval spoke at last. "It is called the Unknown, because we don't know what it contains. But it does contain something, whether we can fathom it, or not."

I smiled. He did understand.

"Humans," he went on, "know who they are and where they came from. You are a Daughter of the Seven Companions. And you, Senor Ollander, are a Councilman, and a guildsman. You were given the title by your superiors, who, in essence, created you. But who created me?"

A silence reigned between Ollander and me, for we had no answer.

"That is what I mean. I don't know who I am. Am I a Son if I don't know my mother's name? Was she a woman, or a Goddess? Oftentimes, I regard my very self as the Unknown." Feval looked out across the void once more. "I would rather call it Space, as the Old Earthers did. I suppose the term was abandoned as it implies a vacuum. But I think it suggests that there is room for things to be, which we cannot name as yet, but will discover in the future."

"You are not alone in your wonderings," Ollander said. "We might know where we came from, but humans cannot have existed on Tierra Mejór without intervention. We owe our traits to the Seven Companions, but we know some outside influence must have given them the power to provide enough genetic diversity that we could survive. That secret, alone with so many others, has been lost."

We stood there for another few minutes before I sighed and suggested we complete our undertaking. I didn't think the salt in the air would be doing much for his inner workings, but when we climbed back into the autocarriage, Feval said, "Thank you, Imre, for telling me to stop here. If I might borrow a human expression, it has 'opened my eyes'."

"You are more human than many of the humans I know," I told him honestly.

***

Thus it was that I found myself once more in the Conclave, standing before the unfriendly eyes of the Council. This is what I said:

"I think there are two options. One is that we do nothing. The other is that we try, with everything we have, to fix what is wrong with our world."

"The flaws have been caused by excess and misuse of freedom and justice," cried the herald. "You, for one, are to blame! How dare you stand here and demand that lives be risked to fix this?"

In the end, it was la Boca who showed himself our ally.

His eyes glinting from behind his dark cowl, he rose. "What better way to prove a theory wrong than to test it? So, you want to risk your life, Ollander," he said, in the slow voice as rich as honey. "I say, it is yours to risk. Take any man you can convince to follow you into this place. See what you will find."

Benefine, however, spoke up against him. "The *Sacred Text* warns us against this. 'Do not enter the Core. The Inner Workings of this world –'"

La Boca fixed him with stare so long and cold that the herald began to shift uncomfortably in his chair. "That passage is a warning, yes," he said at last. "We have all read this. We all know it by heart. But we are not tampering. We are merely observing, are we not?"

Ollander nodded. "We will do nothing until it's cleared in the Conclave."

In the corner of my vision, Grath, his hands tapping a nervous rhythm against the armrests, tried to keep himself from bursting out with something. I had a feeling I knew what it was: he was remembering the failures of the modified airships, and the disasters that had befallen them, as if by the hand of the Pattern. The constant, ineluctable opposition by the Iglesia.

I looked around the room. There must be others in here who knew of those experiments; yet, no one raised an objection. Perhaps that had something to do with the secrecy of the missions, but the more likely explaination was that there was no solution being offered beside ours. We were all of us desperate.

"I like the idea," Thaniel said. His eyes were glassy, and he had seemed barely aware when I told him Ollender had asked me to speak. Did he even know what he was agreeing to? Did it matter?

The chamber was quiet for many long minutes before, finally, the Chancellor raised his staff and pounded the bottom against the floor. "We are in accord."

News of the expedition spread quickly through the Cuidad; it was all anyone could talk about. I kept myself out of the way, tending to my garden, not wishing to answer the questions that flew my way when I met servants in the hallways.

On the day of the expedition, I was bundled into an autocarriage, along with Thaniel. Grath would be riding separately with Ollander.

The doors were held open for us, and we climbed into the car; first the Prince, then me. Feval was at the wheel, a grim-faced guardia beside him. I settled into my seat, with Thaniel only a span from me.

If I had thought the Principe Regente to have been made robust, careless, or invincible by his station, I was soon proved wrong. The Prince of Tierra Mejór got terribly motion-sick.

He clutched the velour-lined seat with both hands, and his face turned almost green. He refused to look through the window as we made our way through the streets, a winding train of autocarriage and men on foot. The procession drew attention, and people came out of their doors to watch us pass, whispering and pointing. There was fear in their gazes, as well as wonder; this was a different type of spectacle from the Dance, to be sure.

"I'm not made for travel," Thaniel moaned. "I'd be well enough if I never left the Citadel."

I couldn't but feel for him.

As we turned a corner, several thuds resounded on the roof. I ducked, and Thaniel blanched; the carriage slowed, then sped up once more.

"What was that?" I called.

"Tomatoes," Feval answered flatly. "Perhaps a potato along with them."

Though the concept was amusing, the message was a serious one: 'we do not want this.' It meant that public sentiment was divided, and that the Brotherhood had many supporters.

"Idiots," Thaniel murmured.

I agreed with him, but I could see the other side of it. The people were afraid, and rightly so, of interfering with the things they didn't understand. They were afraid the Brotherhood were right. They were afraid their Prince, and their Queen, would make this choice for them.

We stopped, once, twice, three times, at the lock gates, waiting for all the vehicles to cross over the bridges. From the First Tier to the Third, this did not take long, but the crossing to the Fourth and largest was close to two hours, since the gates had to be timed with the movement of the Tether as it completed its revolution, slicing out through a gap between the high metal walls. By the time we'd passed through, the novelty had worn off, and the Prince's head drooped. I think if he hadn't been feeling ill, he would have slept. I might have, too. But, finally, we made it.

I had never been down to the Fourth Tier.

And what I saw through the windows would never make me want to return.

The streets winding their way between buildings that were little more than sheds made of patched timber and canvas, were narrow, and filled with filth. Older buildings stood there, larger warehouses and factories that had survived as long as Tierra Mejór had. Laundry hanging from glassless windows told us they were inhabited, but they were not meant as houses. The broken gears protruding from their sides, reaching down into dark chasms in the streets, and rusted pipes that spilled steam and putrid water into the overflowing gutters, were all that remained to show that the waste treatment plants and water filtration systems had once functioned with much greater efficiency.

Garbage blew in the slight breeze – there were no street-sweeping servitors here – and there was moisture in the air, tiny cold beads of water that coated the autocarriage. The light faded until everything seemed dark and murky, underscored by a pervading stench of raw sewage. The people who watched us here were ragged and dirty. They peered from the shadows like drain-rats, with small, beady eyes, withdrawing only when the guardia waved their revolver-pistols.

We arrived at the reservoir well.

It was a simple archway, leading into the wall between the Fourth Tier and the Third. Blackness lay within, for no one would think to venture inside. The smell was incredible, and I didn't envy Ollander or his team at all.

I saw them, as we emerged from the autocarriage. They gathered around the opening, fitting leather masks with protruding metal vents to their faces, and goggles, and rubber-coated boots over their shoes, dividing provisions and tools among themselves. There were nine of them. Five would go in, and four would wait to help collate whatever would be found.

A canvas awning had been set-up, to provide cover from the constant drizzle. Beneath, were several tables and folding chairs, as well as water and food and first-aid supplies.

The Prince looked better as he stepped free of the carriage, looking around at the squalor with sombre interest. "So," he said. "This is what it looks like."

"Have you never been to the Fourth Tier?" I asked. How had he not? He was our Prince, after all.

"Did you not hear me earlier? I hate to travel." He sighed. "Other noblemen and women talk of coming here. To hunt street-foxes – it's said to be lucky to shoot one. To minister to the poor – the Brotherhood occasionally organises a mission, to dole out soup for the huddled masses.

I suppose, to them, it's a game, an experience; something so wonderfully *other*. Some of them even make a game of it, bedding the locals."

I looked around at the misery about me, and wondered aloud, "Why did la Relojero create such a place for people to live in? If she cared for us, why create any divisions between the Tiers at all?"

Thaniel was not listening to me, busy scuffing mud from the side of his boot.

Senor Grath, too, was less than enthralled, particularly when he reached for a cigarillo and had one of Ollander's men quickly snatch it from his mouth.

"Forgive me, senor." The man bowed. "The gases are flammable."

"Pattern damn you," Grath cursed, flinging his matchbook into the sludge.

We were passed cotton cloths soaked with scented oil, which we were to tie over our noses and mouths, to help with the smell. As time neared for the expedition to depart, I grew increasingly excited. If only I was going with them! How incredible it would be, to delve into the depths of the very earth beneath our feet, to see what lay within!

Finally, the Prince moved to stand on a crumbling step, far enough away from the entrance that he could comfortably speak without his mask.

"I suppose –" His voice sounded thin without the acoustic qualities of the hall. "– I'm to make some sort of grand speech to be recorded in some great book, so all of Tierra Mejór can hear me praising these efforts. I could go on about what a heroic endeavour this is, and how brave the venturers who have volunteered for this quest of discovery; about how they will return with all the answers we need to repair our crumbling infrastructure."

Around me, swelled the dire mutterings, not least from the brave venturers themselves; and rightly so. They were risking their lives, after all, and they deserved at the very least some pomp and grandeur for their send-off.

"But the truth," the Prince's voice dropped lower still, "is that I have no words."

Silence fell for a few moments.

"May the Pattern guide you," he said at last, then stepped down from his perch.

Someone began to clap, and intermittent, halting applause followed. Ollander's men turned, and one by one, vanished into the darkness.

The wait began.

The idea was that this first expedition would last three hours. That would allow an hour and fifteen minutes to journey as far as they could, then half an hour to work, record, and study what they saw. Another hour and fifteen minutes to return.

We sat on the folding chairs under the awning, to one side of the tunnel, our masks clasped to our noses. Soon bored, Thaniel jumped up to pace, and when that wore thin, pick up the pieces of broken concrete and toss them against the tier wall.

The people came, as I'd known they would. After the initial shock wore off, they crept closer and closer towards the ring of guardia around us. A man with terribly sunken eyes reached out a hand to touch the shiny paintwork of one of the autocarriages. The guardia nearest snapped into action, drawing his revolver-pistol. "Halt! You're not to touch the property of the royal family!"

The man cowered, his hands over his head. But he didn't back away, just continued to stare, until a woman rushed forward and grabbed him by the shoulder. "Rubius!" she hissed. "You fool! Come!" To the guardia, who watched her warily, she said, "He's not right in the head. He's had too much of the white-powder. You must, please, forgive him."

The guardia looked unconvinced, and the woman tugged again on the man's arm. He shook her off absently – was he her husband? Brother? – and reached again for the autocarriage. "Used to work on the likes of these," he mumbled. "See, Marinta? That's what I told you."

"Stand away," the guardia warned them.

Rubius turned his blank-eyed stare on the guardia, a small line of saliva dribbling from the side of his mouth. For a moment, the pair of them stood there, neither making a move, and then Rubius turned away, allowing the woman to lead him off.

"Beauties," he murmured.

After this, it began to grow cold. The shadow of the Wheel lengthened, creating a deeper gloominess on the Fourth Tier. Thaniel slept in his chair, fitfully. Here, la Grulla's light was so diluted that the world was almost permanently in night. Still, overhead, I could see the slow passing of the Pendulum, the Tether stretching tight, the twisted cables as wide as a building. This close, it made a noise, a ponderous *whooshing* as it progressed through the murky clouds.

Near the mouth of the tunnel, Senor Grath conversed in low voices with Ollander's team. It took me a while before I registered that the tone of their conversations was becoming more urgent.

" . . .allow for unexpected delays . . ."

" . . .three emergency carrier pigeons were sent in their packs . . ."

"– not dispatched –"

" . . .could be interfering, meaning the pigeons cannot fly . . ."

I made my way closer, and confirmed that it was now almost an hour past the time the venturers were supposed to return. Two of Ollander's men, both wearing guildsman's rings, offered to go in after them.

"We've no idea what lies within." Senor Grath shot back, stark and emphatic. "Or what might have caused their delay. I don't like sending more valuable men into danger."

" . . .valuable?" one of them said. "What of the men inside there? Ollander is Guildmaster of Architecture himself!"

"Which makes you the senior-most guildsman in his absence, Carneth," Grath responded grimly. "If you're lost, who is left?"

Another fifteen minutes passed in this manner, as the sky dimmed. Apprehension had settled over the group, and the people of the Fourth Tier sensed it. They drew as close as they dared, gauging us like predators scenting ailing prey.

"We can't simply wait here all night," Grath spoke. "The Principe Regente must return to the Citadel. We're long overdue."

"We will stay, then," said Carneth, but his face showed that he didn't expect good news. "Senor Grath, I beg you. Give us leave to enter, and at least render assistance if any are still alive."

No one was paying attention to me, so I edged closer to the mouth of the tunnel. Frigid air blew from it like cold breath, mixed with the smell of hot oil and metal. There were sounds, deep, unintelligible sounds, clattering like chains and the puffing of steam, and . . . was that a voice?

" . . .here . . . here . . ."

"Help!"

I gasped, almost falling, as something burst from the darkness. A hand grabbed my arm, and I saw at once a hulking monster with blackened skin and glowing eyes, and Ollander, his face darkened with soot and oil, his hair plastered to his head with sweat, his goggles slipping from his eyes, his mask gone. In this split second that I realised it was Ollander, holding the arm of one of his men, I was already slipping my arm underneath his, taking his weight. How my shoulders bore him, I do not know, save that I got strength from somewhere, and used it to help him limp from the tunnel, into the arms of Carneth. The wounded man he had been carrying in turn dropped to the cobbled ground like a stone.

His skin was gone, from the top of his head, down the left side of his face, his arm, and his outer thigh. Blood and tissue showed, red and glistening; as his head flopped to one side, I could see the flesh had been stripped from his eyelids, half his nose, and his lips. His teeth, uncovered, showed in a wide grin. His eye was a white orb, held in place only by its inner workings. Bone poked through the exposed muscles in his cheek.

I screamed, scrambling away from him, only to smack straight into Grath. His hard, flat chest effectively blocked my escape, but I clutched his shirt like an anchor, burying my face in his shoulder to block out the grisly sight.

To my surprise, Grath put one strong arm around me, and guided me away.

The next I knew, I was in the backseat of our autocarriage, the Prince at my side. He looked as if he had lost his lunch *and* dinner.

Chapter Twenty-Four

It wasn't until the following day that we learned what had happened. An emergency meeting of the Conclave had been called, and it was attended by all; serious faces lined the chairs, the only exception being the herald, Benefine, who looked self-righteous.

"Did I not say this effort was ill-advised?" These were the first words out of his mouth, as soon as Darhn had called the Conclave to order.

"There will be time enough for your recriminations," Darhn said. "First, I ask that Guildsman Ollander of the Architects tell his tale, for he has been allowed to speak for only as long as Doctor Oren deems fit."

Ollander did not stand. It didn't look like he could. He was wrapped in bandages, most of which were stained with a red so deep it was almost black. Next to him sat Doctor Oren.

I had known Ollander as a man of words and deep thought. Now, he hunched a little in his chair, his eyes fixed on his own bandaged hands, and his face rigid with pain.

"The mission was a failure," he said at last.

"As we knew it would be," Benefine interjected. There were hisses and glares to silence him. La Boca himself settled back in his chair, exuding an aura of faint glee.

"We walked the length of the reservoir well," Ollander began again. "It was a long, dark passageway, and we were glad for our globe-lanterns. Soon, we felt heat, as of an engine. A noise, a throbbing, filled our ears. It spurred us onwards.

"Soon, a light washed over the floor. It grew hot, so hot! It prickled the skin, and made it hard to breathe. Some of my companions began to complain. "Do not remove your masks," I told them. "You might be killed instantly by gases or vapours we know nothing about."

"Finally, the tunnel ended, and we found ourselves in a large reservoir. It was – oh! – a hundred spans across, and shaped like a coiling spring. Above us were grates, leading into various channels and outlets. One of my men confirmed that these would funnel the water from the reservoir when it reached its capacity, pumping it around the inner Core, where it would stay in circulation, cooling it for a time before it evaporated into the atmosphere to resume the cycle . . . I could just imagine what this place must look like, after a rainfall; when all those tons of water rushed through the tunnel we'd just walked down, cascading into this space!

"There were stairs. They spiralled up around the walls of the reservoir and were covered with greenish slime. We climbed them, carefully, for they had become slippery. When we reached the top, we found a gangway, too rusted to be safe. Instead, we went through one of the grates, crawling on our hands and knees through one of those channels we had seen from below.

"It was a long time before we emerged, and in that time, the deep, deep throbbing continued. None of us could hear the others speak. It was hard to concentrate, with such a noise in our ears! Still, we reached an outlet, and by that time, the metal beneath our hands was so hot, it charred our skin.

"Anyone who wishes to turn back," I told them. "Go now!"

"But none of them heard me over the noise. That's how loud it was! I gestured, and finally, one of our men – Jobruth – did turn back. I didn't blame him, nor did any of the others. He has –" Here, Ollander stopped, a sob wracking his body. "He had a wife and daughter.

"The rest of us dropped from the lip of the duct, onto a metal ledge. How to describe it!"

He paused again, his eyes still fixed firmly on his hands. Then, suddenly, he looked up, his expression one of incandescent wonder.

"It was grand. The biggest machine I could ever hope to see. The scope of it!" He shook his head. "Let any man who doubts the existence of the Pattern look upon this work of la Relojero, this fantastic Core of Tierra Mejór, and they will never doubt again.

"Most of it, we could not see, for the bright light and the heat scored our eyes, even with protective goggles. But what we could see –" He raised one arm, the other, obviously, being too sore, then lowered it, unable to speculate on the size. "Cogs and gears. Mighty pistons, as big as houses. Pipes the size of this room, through which the water is pumped, and oil, and who knows what else? I admit, I had an idea of the design and makings of the Core, but to see it in person, I know I will never understand it all.

"We walked along that ledge, writing down a few measurements, gauging the angles as best we could, scribbling notes. But as we went on, I think we all knew it; finally, we stopped. We shared a moment then, all of us, knowing that we had come here to map and chart this place." He took a deep breath. "Knowing, all of us, that it was impossible."

The entire chamber was silent, as a wave of despair washed over me. *Impossible.* It had been our hope, perhaps our only one; where, now, would we turn for help?

"I motioned to the others that we would turn back. That was when Middi slipped. I think one of his boots had melted, and stuck to the metal ledge. As he pulled free, he toppled over the side. If he screamed, we didn't hear it. We searched the depths for him; all I could see was bright, flaring orange light, and the dark shapes of cogs and gears.

"The others were visibly distraught, but I refused to let them stop. We were halfway back to the outlet through which we'd crawled in when the thudding missed a beat.

"It was like a skipped heartbeat. For a moment, there was silence for much too long, and then it returned – erratically. And too loud.

"A pipe burst above our head with a terrible *pop*, and steam spewed out. I ducked, but it caught Hob and Cedra full in their faces. They didn't stand a chance, and went over the edge. I tried to grab Cedra's hand, but she flailed, slipping free. I had to let her go, lest I go over with her.

"I was yelling, then, at Bodrun and Faily. "Get out! Get out!" Not that they could hear me. The thudding was terribly irregular by then, and the gears below crunched and screeched as they jammed. There was a terrible clunk of something ripping free from its moorings, and the ledge shook as if the Pattern herself was rattling it like a toy, then . . . everything went dark.

"I thought I was blind. I found some niche in the wall and clung to it, wedging my hand tight, and waiting. I thought I would die. I thought the others already were dead. It wasn't until I felt a hand on my arm that I realised at least one of them was alive, and that I wasn't blind – the fires below had merely darkened, and they were now brightening again.

"It was Verta who was leading me. She tugged me onwards when I stopped to cough as if my lungs would burst. I did not remove my mask, but I could feel some thick gas filling the air. It was so hard to breathe! She pushed me, head-first, into the outlet, even as a rain of molten embers descended from above. They caught in her hair. She beat at them, but they dripped down her face. She fell backwards while I reached to pull her through.

"Instead, I gazed into the vastness of that black space. And I saw it, now that the fires dimmed: huge, and hulking, a giant sphere – who knows how big? In that vast space, I couldn't even guess – and around it, crackling energy, like lightning.

"It was charred black. Covered in scores. Fragments were missing, from the edges and the sides, and even as I watched, a sprinkling of dust fell from the base, turning molten as it sifted through the electrical currents. It dripped into the workings below, and there was another screech as the cogs tried desperately to continue turning while the stuff dribbled and cooled like icing on a cake.

"The keyhole. I must tell you about the keyhole." Again, Ollander paused. His eyes were fixed straight ahead, but he wasn't seeing what was before him, no; he was seeing the key. I sat forwards in my chair, clutching the back of the seat in front of me, and I wasn't alone. My posture was mirrored by others all around the room. Only two seemed unaffected: Herald Benefine, and La Reina. He sat very still in his fathomless robe; she, looking slightly downwards, her expression unchanging, might as well have been wearing a mask.

"It was large – the length of my forearm, from fingertips to elbow. It was set halfway up the sphere, and rimmed by a ridge of metal. It could have been reached, once, by means of one of the gangways, but no longer. There were remaining struts to show where such a bridge had been, but no structure remained."

"And the key," spoke Chancellor Darhn, unable to contain himself, and voicing the question every person in the room ached to ask. "What of the key?"

Guildsman Ollander breathed out, long and slow. He tilted his head, putting his thumb to one temple, his fingers to the other, pinching his eyebrows together. "The key was gone."

"Gone," Darhn repeated. His dark hand gripped the crystal staff; his milky eyes stared sightlessly. All around the chamber, we whispered this word: *gone.*

"Such was the heat," Ollander continued, "that it might well have melted, or turned to ash. It may lie even now among the molten slag in those dark depths of the Core. I tried to see, but the fires were glowing much brighter now. I knew my window of opportunity was fast closing.

"The throbbing was settling, now, becoming rhythmical once more, and the heat near unbearable. I could not hope to accomplish anything more. As I pulled myself along that metal tunnel, I could feel my hands burning." He held up his white-mittened hands as evidence. "It wasn't until I was halfway along that I found Jedrun, lying there. A burst of steam had come along the tunnel, scalding him. He told me to leave him, but I wouldn't. I'm told I got him out of the tunnel, at least, before he died."

He looked at each of us bleakly.

"We lost any notes we had taken," he said. "But they wouldn't have done any good. The Core is burning up. The key is gone."

We were silent for several long minutes before Benefine stood. "I think I won't be the only one to agree that this information does not leave this room."

One after another, the guildsmen and women blinked as if coming out of a trance.

***

I did not hear from Ollander again, not for a very long time.

We were a shocked, horrified, scared people who left that Conclave. But something else happened once Guildsman Ollander had stepped through the doors, led by Doctor Oren; chatter broke out, exclamations, disbelieving snorts. Almost immediately, the atmosphere changed from one of enthralment to one of disbelief.

"Surely the key cannot melt," I heard.

"There must be a way to retrieve it."

"Or fashion another – we could have the best smiths design one –"

And then, even louder: "It might all be lies. How do we know what really happened in those tunnels? Ollander might simply be covering up some ridiculous accident, in which the men and women under his authority were killed foolishly, and he does not want to accept the blame."

And I confess, even I doubted. The key could not be gone. La Relojero had made it, after all. She had made this whole world. The key must keep Tierra Mejór wound and working.

And so life continued. Though I spent my days indulging myself in the gardens, by night, I was often called to the Prince's chambers. There I would sleep, or talk with him about anything or nothing, and I'd even managed to become comfortable.

One morning, I stirred early, hearing the seven chimes of la Reloj de pie. I slipped out of the Prince's arms, we had fallen asleep on the couch again, and went to the window to look out over the Cuidad. It was a bright day, one of the few when the murky clouds seemed further away and the air was clear and crisp.

I jumped when I noticed the Prince behind me.

"I didn't mean to startle you," he said. "You look so beautiful, standing here, surveying the Cuidad as if it were made for you."

I lowered my head shyly. "I'm no Princess." I held out my arms, displaying the sleeves of my Horticulturalist's tunic; though clean, for Adina would wash my clothes every day, it was wrinkled, since I had slept in it last night.

"Oh." The Prince's eyes lit up. "There are clothes for you in the bedroom. I had them made specially." He pointed towards his bedroom. "I was going to have them moved to your garden house, but you might as well look now."

I couldn't help myself. I dashed into his bedroom and saw that three wheeled racks of clothes stood beside the bed. Hanging from them were at least a dozen dresses, made of silk and velvet and fine cotton. There were pairs of shoes to match, and shawls hanging from hooks. There were also pairs of trousers, shirts, and boots. On a small cart next to the racks were several pots of make-up, and a large mirror.

"This is too much," I protested, swamped with blossoming guilt. How Ketra would love these dresses! How Rehina's eyes would shine! All of a sudden, I wanted my sisters there with me, to exclaim over the fabrics and necklines. "It can't just be for me."

The Prince didn't seem to understand. "If you don't like them, I'll have others brought."

"No, no!" I laughed. "Please – they're absolutely beautiful!" I took one from its hanger and held it in front of me. It looked to be the perfect fit. "But – how did you know?"

The Prince shrugged. "Oh, that was Grath's doing. He had them ordered and made to measure."

I tried to keep my surprise hidden. "These dresses, though, aren't made for working in."

"No indeed," he replied. "They're made for gatherings such as the ball being held tonight."

"Ball?" I repeated, shocked.

"You will come, won't you?" he pleaded, looking very childlike. "It's a gathering for the noblemen and women to see the visiting members of the Brotherhood. Since they don't believe in frivolity, it will be a dry and boring affair. But with you by my side, I won't feel so claustrophobic."

Flabbergasted, I tried to imagine it – a Citadel ball. It wasn't as if Daughters of the Pavilion had never been invited to one. In fact, many mecenas took an escort, if they were so inclined. But never had I dreamed I'd be one of them. "How can I –?"

"You will be a visiting horticultural guildswoman from Rueda," he said. "You can wear a half-veil across your temple to hide your metrónomo. They're quite in fashion is Rueda. No one will notice you're not supposed to be there."

Still, I hesitated.

"Are you so afraid?" he challenged me. "Come now. Where is that girl who wanders the gardens at night, alone?"

I wanted to tell him that I didn't really want to go, but it wasn't true; I longed for it. And how could I refuse, after he'd given me these gifts? I nodded at last, and the grin that spread across his face made me glad of my decision.

Chapter Twenty-Five

In the end, I picked out a green gown with pale blue silk, patterned with spiral designs. Adina brushed my hair until it fairly floated, then chose a small, beaded piece of gauzy material for my half-veil and pinned it with tiny jewelled pins. Paje helped me into the dress, and I allowed her to, for I didn't want to risk damaging the beautiful garment. Together they painted my face, and polished my nails, and only after all this was done did they let me to turn and face the mirror.

I didn't recognise myself.

I'd never looked so refined. I touched my cheek, just to make sure I was real, but Adina batted my hand away. "You don't want to be smudging your make-up."

Together, they walked behind me, lifting the hem of my dress. I could have done it myself, but apparently, this was another thing that wasn't done by ladies. We walked along the stone path, then through a side door, up some steps, and into a lift; we crossed a bridge, Adina, as usual, chattering the whole way.

"I've never seen one of those heralds attend a ball. Truly, they look as if they'd suck the life from any party! I wonder what they look like, beneath those robes? Paje, do you think they're covered with scars, like Groni says? I think it more likely they're just horribly ugly."

I would have laughed, but my heart beat in the vicinity of my throat, and my metrónomo pulsed rapidly beneath the half-veil as we entered a lift similar to the one I'd been in on my first night. As a Sentinel pulled the doors shut and the lift whooshed up, I was at once terrified and excited, but then – then I heard the music.

And I was neither.

There was a harp, and a flute, and a soft low drum keeping time. Oh, it was exquisite, that sound; so long had it been since I'd heard such sweet, melodic notes. The sentinel did not open the door fast enough, and I pushed it aside. My feet seemed to move of their own accord, and I was hurrying ahead of my maids as I exited the lift and found myself in the great hall I had been in at the audience with the heralds. I had seen it from above, then, but now I was looking up into the cavernous space, and it was twice as astonishing. The pillars and arches were picked out with delicate gold leaf. The floor was tiled in red and blue, geometric interlocking patterns that resembled the delicate inner workings of a clock. Everything was placed precisely, mathematically designed to be pleasing to the eye and spirit.

And the people! There were so many! They were all dressed in finery – men and women, and even some children, the youngest darting about, laughing, and those approaching adulthood standing very stiffly, with serious expressions on their faces as they tried to emulate their elders.

They gathered in groups, music twisting and twining through them like a living thing, women wandering slowly around the perimeter, exclaiming over the fashions, men sitting on couches or propping up walls, sipping cups of espiritu. Maids and manservants darted here and there, mopping up spills, fixing skewed headdresses and straightening jackets. Servitors roamed about, too, their trays laden with platters of fruit, cheese, moth-meat cubes, dry crackers, and ale.

It was nothing like the Room of Roses, even on the busiest of nights.

I looked over my shoulder at my maids. Adina looked ready to swoon, Paje – disinterested and slightly frightened. "You will stay with me, won't you?" I asked them.

While Adina nodded eagerly, Paje looked less certain. "Perk up," Adina hissed at her. "I don't want to be sent away because *you're* busy looking like you swallowed a lemon."

I suppose I should have been daunted by the throngs; especially when, as I moved away from the doors, they began to notice me. The ladies whispered behind their hands. The men appraised me from head to toe. It was very much like my introduction to the Den. But I found I was able to meet their looks with a haughty expression of my own, and was secretly thrilled when a few of them couldn't match it, and looked aside.

Even though I was an outsider here, unlike in the Den, nobody else knew it.

Snagging a few peppered crackers from a nearest servitor, I passed one to Adina, who nibbled on it rapturously. Paje refused to take hers, so Adina ate that one too. "You're supposed to allow us to feed you, my lady," she whispered to me. "Not the other way 'round! People will stare!"

I waved a hand. People were already staring, and I wanted her to enjoy herself – she was the closest thing I had to a friend within my field of vision. To prove it, I snatched two fluted glasses of clear sparkling liquid from another servitor and passed one to her to share with Paje. It tasted like berries and sugar, and the bubbles danced over my tongue. It settled warmly in my stomach, and I took another sip. If it was goldwine, it was the best I'd ever tasted. "Shall we go and find something to do?" I asked Adina. She nodded, and, giggling like children, we made our way through the crowd.

I saw snatches of faces that were familiar. Men, mostly, who had probably come to the Pavilion as mecenas. Their eyes passed over me enquiringly, but I could tell they couldn't place who I was. It gave me all the more confidence.

I was stopped halfway across the great room by a woman with pale white hair, piled high on her head. She had two young girls in tow, who looked so similar they must have been relations, if not daughters. "Excuse me," she said. "I simply must ask you where you got that dress. I've never seen one like it."

There was a deep intelligence under her outward demeanour of lightheartedness. I suspected it was best not to engage her in conversation, and motioned towards the far side of the room.

"Oh, I had it made specially," I answered airily.

"It's quite stunning, especially on you. Was it quite expensive?"

I couldn't deny that it was, so I improvised quickly. "It was, but my stipend as a horticulturalist covered it nicely."

She raised an eyebrow, and I realised I'd given her too much information.

"You're from Rueda?" she asked.

"Yes –"

"How coincidental! My name is Liliath. I am a worker at the moth refinery. My daughter, my niece, and I have just travelled down ourselves. We're here for a turning or so – on a visit to the Library, to research the growing techniques for a new variety of moth. You must meet us, we'll have a meal together some time!" Behind her, the two girls nodded eagerly. I could feel their admiration – they truly thought I was a guildswoman, but a beautiful, exotic specimen, the likes of which they'd never seen.

I did the only thing I could. "Forgive me, I've no time. Someone is waiting!"

I slipped away before she could protest, and, ducking through another knot of people, found myself near the musicians. They had set-up to one side of the hall, seated or standing as their instruments allowed; and again, I saw a few familiar faces among them. The harpist's name was Pherie; she had played brilliantly at the Pavilion. Her long fingers danced across the strings as if she and the music were one. The flautist was a man name Pielo, I'd spoken to him once or twice after a long night of Dancing; his first love was theoretical mathematics, but he had never been accepted as an apprentice.

Instead, he applied everything he knew about equations to his music, and the results were as close to perfection as I'd ever heard. There was also a cellist providing the bassline, and a drummer playing a wide, oval-shaped drum. Together, they sounded worthy of the Pattern Itself.

With the goldwine feeding a fire in my heart, I made the first steps of the Dance of Joy. Adina laughed when I took her hands and pulled her into the dance. "My lady! I don't know the steps!" But it didn't matter at all. I directed her, backwards, forwards, turn and spin – we whirled as the music washed over us, and people turned to watch. The tune ended at precisely the right moment, and we came apart. I bowed to her, and she did the same to me, both of us unable to contain our laughter. As if a great weight had been lifted from my shoulders, I felt, for now at least, as if nothing was wrong with the world, and I was exactly where I was supposed to be. Here, dancing, joyful.

There was a smattering of applause before the musicians moved onto the next song, and I pulled Adina into the Dance of Slow Delight. She followed me willingly. Her own movements were shaky, and Maestra Tinir would have had a fit if she saw her footwork, but there was more to Dancing than that. I could tell Adina felt it as she stepped around me, placing her feet, gripping my shoulder with one hand and my waist with the other. And, when I next looked up, I saw others had joined us, performing ordinary dances that were imperfect but joyous.

How long did we stay there, my maid and I, dancing among those people? I can't be sure, except that my feet had started to hurt, and there was a twinge in my ankle. It might have been an hour, or only a few minutes, before I whirled around Adina and found myself face-to-face with Senor Grath.

His face was twisted in fury.

Shocked, I missed a step, treading on his boots. I had to grab at his shoulder to keep myself upright, and my half-veil slipped. With deft fingers, he tugged it back in place, but his glare was positively murderous.

"What," he muttered through gritted teeth, "in the name of the Pattern, are you *thinking*?"

"I –" I was breathless and confused and a little frightened, and the goldwine was making my head continue to spin now that I'd stopped dancing. "The Prince told me to come. He said it would be all right – as long as I disguised myself –"

"And you *listened* to him?" Grath spat, incredulous. He leaned down close to my ear. "Why? Because you wanted to cavort here in front of a crowd?"

"No, because –"

"I don't need to hear your reasons. Don't you know how stupid and dangerous this is? By all the Unknown, girl! You're a Daughter of the Pavilion. You don't belong here."

That was the final straw. "How do you know where I belong?" I pulled out of his grasp. "It's not among the Daughters, because I can't dance. It's not in the back alleys or the night-cafés of the Third Tier, because even my whore of a mother didn't want me. And it's not among the women of the Den, who hated me almost as much as you do. Maybe I don't belong anywhere, in which case, I might as well be here as somewhere else!"

"Quiet!" he hissed. I hadn't spoken loudly, and, in any case, those around us were too involved in their merrymaking to pay much attention to the Prince's Chief Adviser's exchange with a Ruedan horticultural guildswoman, but he looked about warily nevertheless.

"Oh, don't be stupid, no one cares! Can't you see that? It was a mistake, or a blunder, or . . . I don't know! Why don't you go and find your precious Principe Regente and leave me to my life?"

He continued to glare at me, and for one moment I thought he might pick me up over his shoulder and carry me out of the hall. But instead, he folded his lips into a thin line, turned on his heel, and marched away.

I had stood there for a moment, breathing heavily and watching after him, when Adina came up behind me. "My lady? Is everything well?"

I turned to her determinedly. "Yes. But I could use another glass of goldwine – would you mind?"

She didn't, and with the heat of the drink burning in my heart, I felt the ever-present knot in my stomach loosen, until I could barely feel it at all. The room seemed soft and bathed in a golden light. It was only the effects of the alcohol, but still, I relished the feeling.

Adina's cheeks were flushed, and she looked terribly pretty. I had seen more than one of the men turn to look at her as she danced with me – noblemen and servants alike. "Do you have a sweetheart, Adina?" I asked her, as we leaned against one another, trying to right our whirling heads.

"No," she said. "Though Fillin, the little rat, has more than once tried to bed me. He crawls into my pallet, thinking I'll be happy to find him there."

"Is he handsome?" I asked teasingly.

"Oh, by the Pattern, no! He has a face like a . . . a boiled potato."

We giggled, and she pushed her nose up with her thumb, which made us giggle even more. And it was then, as I was half-bent over with laughter and drink that I saw them moving through the crowd, like black clouds; the heralds.

Their clothes were so black that among all the colour, they looked doubly odd. They seemed to time their steps together, so while they moved apart, they were still in unison – a strange version of a Dance. People stopped moving and drew back, as if afraid to be touched by them, and, though the music played on, everyone stopped speaking.

A semicircle formed, and I found myself near the front. Adina had vanished, and though I looked for her blindly, I couldn't see either her or Paje. Next to me was the woman who had asked me about my dress earlier, and her two daughters, if daughters they were.

"I hate to see them here," she whispered to me quietly. "They should just go back to the Iglesia and leave us be."

Shocked, I edged away, hoping no one would think I welcomed her comments. I certainly didn't want to draw the attention of the heralds.

Abruptly, the music stopped, and at last, I saw the Principe Regente. He sat on his throne, as he had during the audience that time I'd watched from above, but tonight, he slouched further, leaning on the arm of the great chair, a flask of goldwine in hand. His blue shirt embroidered with gold, and paired with rich brown trousers looked regal, perfect for a man who ruled an entire world. But he was deeper under the influence than I'd seen him yet. His face shifted into a wide smile as the heralds neared, and he raised the flask jauntily.

"Greetings, my fine friends! I see . . . you're dressed for the occasion!"

I put a hand to my mouth, partly in astonishment, and partly to contain my amusement. How he dared to show such insolence, I don't know; was it only the wine talking?

The heralds – there were seven of them – had reached the front of the hall, and as one, they bowed. At the corner of my vision, I caught sight of Senor Grath striding towards the throne, probably trying to get there before the Prince further insulted his guests.

"We are honoured to be invited to this event," one of them intoned. Which was it? Beneath those black robes, they were all the same.

"Of course you are." The Prince bobbed his head sagely. "Everyone is always honoured! Well, I say it's time to stop honouring. We've done enough of that. Perhaps it is time for dancing? Will you not dance with us, my *honoured* guests?"

We all of us in the hall held our collective breath. The Prince was wavering from side to side where he sat, but his stare was fixed on the foremost of the heralds. There was more here than drunken idiocy; the Prince was challenging them.

Why? What could he hope to gain? My neighbour might not believe it, but if you asked me, no one held more power in Tierra Mejór than the heralds. They monitored the stars, and calculated the alignments of the planets, and the movements of the workings deep inside our Core. They used this knowledge to govern the weather, which grew the crops, and made certain the Cuidad mas Grande did not burn or freeze. To anger them seemed insane.

But then, perhaps he was, after all.

The la Boca stepped forward. "We thank you for your kind offer, my Prince. However, we came here for one reason only. Will not La Reina make an appearance?"

The Prince paused for a moment, then took another swig from his flask. "My mother," he slurred, "will come if she's able."

"All we ask is a sighting of her," the la Boca said. "We understand she is ill, but we would be happy to know she is still well enough to greet her guests, who have travelled such a long way."

Senor Grath had reached the dais, and he bent to whisper into the Prince's ear. The Prince nodded and waved him away with splayed fingers. "Very well. She will come, but only for a minute. Doctor Oren tells me she isn't well enough to move from her bed, but for you, she will make an effort."

"It's all we ask." The la Boca bowed his head with false humility as Grath slipped away through a side door, leaving behind silence reigning over the hall.

It wasn't often that anyone got a glimpse of La Reina, and when we did, it was fleeting; once a year, at la Festival de Tiempo, we saw her, high above, on her balcony. And this year, her sighting had been marred by my mishap. So, I, too, looked about excitedly, as the minutes ticked by; the la Boca, however, seemed quite content to wait.

It was five minutes before the largest door at the side of the hall opened, and in she came, leaning on the arm of Senor Grath. From this close, I could see how pale her skin was – so white, it was almost translucent. Her hair, pale gold streaked with silver, was pinned neatly above her ears. The long train of her green dress spread across the floor as she walked, rippling like wavelets in a tranquil pond. Something about the way she moved didn't seem quite *right*, however, as if she thought she was about to fall over. We all knew she'd been ill – that was the reason the Prince had been bought back from the Ruedan Estate, and named as Regent, in case she did not recover; if things had gotten any worse, she would have named him at a public audience as Principe Verderaro, so that he could take over should the unthinkable occur. But she didn't look sick, at least, not in the physical sense, which made me wonder if perhaps it was her mind that was ill. That would account for her strangely vacant expression, her halting steps, and most certainly her absence.

"My Queen." La Boca bowed deeply. "Thank you, most kindly, for agreeing to come."

La Reina inclined her head.

"Please accept my solicitations. I regret that your illness removes you from our company, especially the fine gatherings such as this."

La Reina's expression did not change.

"I would like to offer the services of Brother Allyn," he went on. "He is the best and foremost physician of the Iglesia."

Beside her, Grath took one step away. His left hand wrapped around his right wrist, and he fiddled with his wristwatch. La Reina gave a slight shake of the head. Her eyes did not move, giving the impression of a marionette being pulled by the strings.

La Boca, clearly disturbed by this lack of response, took a step forwards. "I assure you," he reached out a hand as if to touch her arm, "he will attend you far better than any healer you have in the Cuidad. He has the blessing of the Pattern –"

But La Reina shied away from his advance. She bowed her head, her golden curls falling, lopsidedly, around her neck. Senor Grath steadied her, then fixed la Boca, who still held out his hand, with one of his frostiest glares. "My Lady is tired. I will take her back to her rooms."

La Boca was left standing in the middle of the empty floor, watching as the doors slammed shut.

I couldn't say I felt at all sorry for him.

"Well," the Prince said. "Now that you've interrupted my mother's convalescence, perhaps you'll indulge me." He paused here, a drunken grin spreading across his face. "A dance. Just one."

"My Prince," la Boca replied, "we do not dance."

"Ah, but you must! Everyone dances. With all your calculations and charts, all your knowledge of movement and geometries – you must know how to dance!"

"My Prince," la Boca began, but just then, the Prince lurch up from his throne. He almost fell as he descended the steps to the floor, but once there, he looked up into the unveiled eyes of la Boca unflinchingly. La Boca was a good deal taller than he, but that didn't seem to daunt the drunken man. "Dance!" he growled.

We froze. I don't think any one of us doubted that he was insane at that moment.

"Perhaps you need to be shown how," the Prince went on, his eyes sweeping the crowd. "You," he said. His eyes were fixed on me. I searched them imploringly, thinking this must surely be a mistake, that there must be some plan or reason I wasn't privy to.

"It is true. This girl can dance," said Liliath, from beside me. To this day, I do not know whether or not she intended to do it, or had simply drunk too much goldwine; in any case, she pushed me in the back, and I stumbled forward. Those few steps put me in front of everyone; the entire hall turned to me. I froze. To retreat wouldn't help my cause – they had all seen me, and if I acted like a rabbit scurrying to hide, that would only draw more attention. My metrónomo throbbed.

The Prince broke his icy stare-down with la Boca and motioned towards me. "Yes! Indeed, beautiful woman! Dance. Show the heralds what they're missing!"

I didn't move. I just looked at him, wondering what he could possibly be thinking, or if he was thinking at all.

"Dance!" said the Prince again, and this time his voice was steady, deep, and sure. This wasn't a request, it was a command.

Keeping my attention on the Prince, on his beautiful blue shirt that matched his eyes, I stepped further into the open. Then I let my lids slip closed, and began to dance.

I wasn't sure which Dance to choose. Usually, the right one came to me as needed, as if Aurelia had whispered a suggestion in my ear. But what could possibly be the right one for this occasion? A dance demanded by a Prince, to prove some obscure point to men who didn't believe in dancing? A dance with no music, with hundreds of eyes weighing down on me? I didn't think there was one.

So, I began to make it up.

I stepped and turned, then leaped high. I whirled and kicked and turned again. My beautiful dress swayed around me, matching the sinuous gyrations of my body. The slippers I wore did not give me a solid grip on the marble floor, but that added momentum as I spun, faster and faster, raising my arms above my head; I heard the gasps of the crowd, but still, I didn't open my eyes.

I tumbled out of the spin, rolling to the floor, then pushing back up, stretching high; I arched my weight from one foot to the other, then spun again, and again . . .

This is the Dance, a beautiful voice echoed inside my head, singing a song so perfect and clear, no instrument of the earth could replicate it. *This is what it means to Dance, querido.*

"Stop this." The growl seemed to come from a great distance away, but I didn't heed it. And then, suddenly, firm, large hands gripped my shoulders. Cruel fingers dug into my collarbone, and I was flung to the floor, landing hard on my knees, my bad ankle wrenching. Though my eyes snapped open, all I saw were bright stars flashing across my vision. "I told you," the cold voice snapped, "to stop this blasphemy."

I raised my head and saw the la Boca towering over me. His eyes glittered through the slitted eyeholes in his robe, and his long, thin, pale hands were exposed, like claws.

"Is it not enough," his voice rung in the silence, "that you refuse to allow us to meet with La Reina? Is it not enough that the Cuidad is filled with sinners and criminals? You must flout our laws before our very eyes?"

I ducked my head, looking at the floor. Please, by the Pattern, I prayed. Do not let him recognise me as the falling Dancer.

"A Pattern-damned Pavilion Whore," the growl in la Boca's voice turned it into some ancient machine's, hungry, malicious. "The very one I have sought. See how, even now, she sullies the dance, imbuing the Pattern with Chaos."

His eyes passed over the silent crowd. At his feet, I dared not move.

"Give her to me, and you might atone, in part, for your errors."

No one in the room moved, and neither did I. La Boca's cowl filled my vision, the two points of his eyes boring into me. He moved an arm, and the diaphanous sleeve of his robe billowed. A pale, claw-like hand extended towards me.

Mesmerised by fear, all thoughts paralysed by the wonder I had just experienced, followed so closely by terror, I would have let him pull me to my feet, let him take me wherever he chose.

Two booted feet stepped into my line of sight, blocking my view. There was the sound of metal ringing on leather, and it was only then that I realised the man was Grath. An involuntary surge of anger made my fingers tingle and the knot in my stomach churn. I hadn't asked him to defend me!

"This woman is under the protection of the Principe Regente," he said in a tone as sharp and hard as the blade in his hand. "If she chooses not to go with you, then here she stays."

La Boca's robes rustled. He must have looked across at the Prince. "It is clear to me now that there is nothing able to be salvaged here."

He kicked out at me, and I tried to scuttle aside, but the heavy boot connected with my hip, sending me skidding a few paces across the floor. I barely felt it, for the Pattern still sung in my ears.

The last I saw of him as I lay there on the floor was la Boca and his retinue making their way back through the hall.

All I could feel was relief.

Chapter Twenty-Six

I felt a man's hands on me, strong hands, lifting me up. At first I was relieved, but then I realised it was Senor Grath, and jerked myself out of his grasp.

"I don't need help from you."

He ignored me, half-lifting, half-supporting me to a sofa near the wall, in a quiet, secluded alcove, then pressed a cup into my hands. I drank thirstily – it was pure, cold water, and welcome indeed.

"Please don't stare at me," I said, embarrassed, as I lowered the cup. "I know I look a perfect mess."

He took the cup wordlessly and refilled it.

"I've proven the worst of myself to you this night, haven't I?" I said as he pushed the second cup into my hands.

Senor Grath shrugged. "You are a creature of habits. They are no worse than my Liege's. In fact, they are probably not quite so bad."

I lowered my head over the cup. "I wish he would tire of me." I sighed, unable to stop the words now they were flowing from my mouth. "I wish it was as you said, that he would put me aside. I like him; I like to talk with him. But I don't want any more of this." I waved a hand jerkily.

To my surprise, Grath did not laugh. Instead, a look of possessiveness crossed his face, which I thought at the time was directed at the Prince in a paternal, protective manner. "Tierra Mejór could do worse than you for a Queen," he murmured.

I laughed, holding the cup high, spreading my arms, displaying my ripped dress. "Really?"

"Really," Grath said, and of course, I didn't believe him for one moment.

I think the tiredness, and the lingering effects of the goldwine, had made me irascible. Grath had always been so cryptic, and now I wanted to push him. I wanted to make him angry. "He would lock me up in the Den, after he was done with me. I'd be out of the way for good."

Grath had been about to walk away, but instead, he turned back to face me. "The Oak Door is not locked," he pointed out. "Women can come and go as they please. They choose not to, for what is out there for them that is better than this?"

The Oak Door is not locked. I almost laughed, for the idea that I had crept through that tiny window, sneaking through the gardens, for no reason at all, was ludicrous.

"Did you think them his harem?" Grath continued. "They might like to think they were all worthy of his attentions, but the simple truth is, they are women who have run into trouble with violent husbands, unwanted pregnancies, and parents so poor they would be sold into near-slavery, or worse. They are women brought here by the vigilar, women the kindhearted guardia have encountered in taverns and Red Houses. The Prince allows them to stay."

I felt a flush of embarrassment, for what I had believed, and what I should have known, had I only asked the right questions.

Adina arrived, then, carrying another glass of water, Paje at her shoulder, looking pale and frightened. Grath, seeing them, made his escape.

"I'm fine, I'm fine," I told my maids. "Truly."

Across the room, there was a cry for the music to start again, and start it did, though less energetic than before; conversation resumed, and the incident was, if not forgotten, at least finished.

Doctor Oren arrived to give me a cursory glance. Though he looked grave and advised me not to move for an hour or so, he told me no real damage had been done. Then he gave me another glass of goldwine. "Since you'll have a terrible headache in the morning anyway, you might as well keep the pain at bay for now."

I was only too glad to, as the ball rolled on its merry way.

People started to drift away at about midnight. Sooner than I'd thought possible, the great hall was empty, except for myself and Adina. "I don't know how I'm going to get you back to your house," she fretted. She had been crying, I saw, and felt bad for having her night ruined like this. "I can't carry you."

"I'll be fine to walk," I told her, and when I stood up, I realised this was true. My legs felt like they were made of clouds. I laughed. "I think I need my bed."

But even as I straightened, I heard footsteps, and turned to see one other person who had not left the room. Striding across the floor – now littered with dropped food and spilled wine the Servitors buzzed about trying to clean it up – was the Prince.

He did not look any more sober.

"My night-dancer!" he cried. "You performed brilliantly."

"Oh, did I?" I asked frostily. Adina stiffened at my side, obviously appalled at my directness. "Thank you for inviting me, my Prince. It was a pleasure."

"Oh, don't be like that," he said carelessly. "It was a joke. Harmless fun."

"It was humiliation," I informed him. "Not just for me, but for everyone who witnessed it. Except you – *your* humiliation is all your own."

He moved quickly, grabbing my wrist. His hands were strong, and Adina gasped as he tugged me effortlessly out of her grip. "You are dismissed, servant."

Adina – Pattern bless her – didn't move until he raised his hand. After that, I would have screamed at her to get out of here, to get away, had she not scurried towards the door of her own accord. Then he shook me, rather violently, so that my head whipped back and forth. A sudden pain lanced through my brain, and I thought I might vomit. It would have served him right, but it seemed my body would not cooperate even in this small rebellion.

His hands moved to my hips, now, pushing me back. I felt one of the tables behind me as I bumped it with the backs of my knees. Beneath his trousers, he stirred against me. My breath caught in my throat. "What do you want, my Prince?"

"You are a Daughter of the White Pavilion." He ran a hand up my body, resting it on my breast, squeezing it roughly. My nipple hardened against his palm, and, against my volition, hot desire rushed through me. "You must know what I want."

"I know very little, my Prince." I gasped as he pinched my nipple, the bolt of sudden pain making me arch back against him. He transferred his hand to my hair, dragging my head back and setting his mouth against my bared throat.

"No," he murmured. "You're lying. How many mecenas have you Danced for?"

"Seven," I replied in a choked voice. "Seven in total."

"Seven. Well. Grath is right. You *are* a whore. An expensive one, but just . . . just a whore."

I won't cry, I told myself. *I won't give him that pleasure.* Where was the man I had seen in the gardens? The introspective, thoughtful, enlightened man? How could he change so drastically from one to the other?

He rose, pushing me down across the table and lifting my skirt. My cheek was pressed hard against the wood. All I could see was a red stain of spilled wine, but feel . . . Oh yes, I could feel. I could feel his hand on my thigh, gripping me, stroking my skin, drawing aside my underwear.

And then his touch softened. "Do you want this?" he breathed in my ear.

I nodded. "Yes." Oh, how I wanted it!

All at once, I fell into him, and he into me.

He moved inside me with long, slow strokes. It felt, at first, uncomfortable; and then quite suddenly, perfectly wonderful. Tears trickled from beneath my closed eyelids, for this was the part of the dance I had longed to experience. It was so different from being with a woman, so foreign. So right.

It grew slowly, like a tiny flower, and then all at once, it burst into bloom. Warmth, the shock of pleasure, spilled through me; I let out a gasp, and the Prince gave a small laugh as he let himself finish.

He let go of me, and I struggled to catch my breath, to pull my dress down and right myself.

"What is this?"

The Prince's sudden interjection stopped me. I followed his narrowed eyes to a spot of dark red on my skirts. I looked at it, uncomprehending for a moment. I suppose I had forgotten, in my rush of pleasure, exactly what this was.

The Prince flicked his gaze up to meet mine. "You are – you were –"

"It was my first time," I told him. "It is normal –"

"You told me – *seven* –" He did not look pleased, or curious. He looked aghast, and I wondered what I had done wrong.

"I have Danced for seven different mecenas," I said. "The Dance of the Rock, the Harvest, the Warm-season, and the Cold-season, three times. I've passed my initiation, but I'm not yet eighteen. I've never danced a Dance to its conclusion. Not with a man."

"No." He pressed a hand to his forehead, his fingers at his temples, covering his eyes. "No!"

And then he was gone.

Adina found me tugging my beautiful dress back into place. There were tears in her eyes as she helped me straighten my skirts. "Oh, my Lady, your beautiful dress . . ."

"It doesn't matter." I wiped her cheeks. "Please don't cry."

"Did he – are you hurt?"

I nodded. "A little, but –" I made her look at me as she threatened to launch into fresh sobs. "But," I said firmly, "it is not a bad kind of hurt. Adina, I am a Dancer. This is my purpose."

***

I felt strange all the next day. The ache between my thighs reminded me with every movement exactly what had happened at the Ball, which made me both glad and sad at once.

For his part, the Principe Regente seemed either to remember nothing at all, or to pretend as much. When he called me to his suite that evening, he was drunk, as ever; he asked me what my favourite types of flowers were, and speculated on how some varieties differed from others.

He drifted to sleep on one of the couches, sprawling on his stomach like a child.

***

I made my way to the commode, and wondered if I could somehow slip out of the gardens without him noticing, to make my way to the Temple of the Seven. I wondered, too, if Tomas had completed his initiation, and graduated from novice to herald. He may have, and if so, I wouldn't find him waiting for me, despite his promise. Even if he did not, even if he knew how desparately I longed to see him, would he welcome my visit?

Consumed by these dark thoughts, I did not at first notice anything amiss as I returned to the sitting room.

There was a man there. He was bent over the chair in which the Prince slumped; just a dark shape in the dark room, and there was something in his hand. With a swift, decisive movement, he brought the object down. But at the last moment, the door, which I had left open just a fraction, made a quiet noise as it swung under my touch; but it was loud enough to startle him. He whirled, and I saw what he had in his hand – a knife.

I gasped, stepping backwards. My shoulder struck the door, and I cried out in shock rather than pain; blindly, I thought perhaps there was another man behind me. The door slammed shut.

The figure rushed at me. He held his knife high; his face was covered in black paint. His eyes glinted coldly as he brought the blade towards me, aiming, I think, to slice my neck.

I ducked. It was instinct more than anything, but my dancer's reflexes served me well. The blade whistled over my head and stuck into the wood of the doorframe, rattling the glass panes. The man wasted a moment trying to pull it free, and I dove at his legs, pushing him off-balance. His weight was greater than mine, but I had struck at his weak point, and he tumbled to the floor with a heavy thump.

There was a shout from outside the door. Hendrich had heard me yell, and burst into the room with his revolver-pistol drawn. He didn't flick the switch for the globe-light, his training telling him it would take too long for his eyes to adjust. Instead, he crossed the room in two steps, pushed the barrel of the pistol against the man's painted temple, and pulled the trigger.

Blood spurted, spraying over my skirt like rain. Something else came with it, small pieces that once would have been inside the man's body. Horror coiled in my gut, a serpent wrapping itself around the hard knot in my stomach.

I wasn't aware that I was making a sound until moments later, when the ringing of the revolver shot left my ears. It was a long, low whimper of fear and disgust. I had never heard such a sad noise in my life, and instantly told myself to shut up.

Only then was I aware of Hendrich's voice. "Imre? Imre, are you injured at all?"

Numbly, I shook my head, and the next thing I knew, he was carrying me down the hall, into the bathing room, turning on the taps, stripping off my dress, and placing me under warm sprays.

I couldn't feel it. All I was aware of was my bloody shift crumpled on the floor.

There was a lot of commotion in the Prince's suite following this. Hendrich had closed the door when he left, but even over the hissing of the water, I could hear them talking.

" . . .nothing but a hired assassin," someone said.

"But how on earth would he have gotten past the guardia? . . .a serious breach of security."

"Through the balcony door. It is a weak point in the room . . ."

And then, a voice I knew too well. Senor Grath had arrived. He strode across the room, assumingly to look down at where the body still lay. "This man is known to the vigilar," he growled. "I've seen his likeness in the papers. He's a petty criminal. A thug-for-hire. He could not have entered the Citadel without the inside help – a bribe, most likely."

"But why . . .?" Hendrich protested.

"Why indeed?" Senor Grath replied. "Where is the girl?"

The door opened, then, and I flinched, startled.

The water had covered me, washing the blood from my skin through the drain. I shivered under Grath's disdainful glance, but at that moment, I didn't care whether he thought me a common whore. I couldn't think at all.

Predator-quick, he snatched up my bloodied shift and left.

When finally Hanna arrived, she bought Adina, and together they coaxed me out. "Let me look at you." Hanna cast a critical eye over my body. I was shivering, despite the hot water, now rising as steam from my skin.

The bandage around my ankle had come loose and trailed on the floor, heavy and sodden. Where it had lain, there was a strip of pale skin, but otherwise no sign of the injury. The bite-mark in the crook of my arm had faded to a small red weal, no bigger than a coin.

"You seem in relatively good shape," she said cheerfully.

Adina's mind was on more practical matters. "Where shall we put her?"

"Oh, into bed is the best place." Hanna removed her cardigan and wrapped it around me. The difference in size between us was such that it covered me quite modestly.

"I don't want to sleep in the Prince's bed," I protested as they steered me into the bedroom. They were the first words out of my mouth since I'd screamed, and I was surprised that my voice still worked.

"Well," Hanna said. "I doubt very much he'll object."

It made a certain sense, but when I caught a glimpse through the door of the sitting room of the bloodstain that spread across the floorboards and seeped into the edge of a beautiful blue-and-white rug, and the crumpled body which had yet to be removed, I nearly slid to the floor as my knees lost all their strength.

It didn't help that all eyes turned to me, namely those of the three members of the vigilar, and Hendrich, and the Prince, he at his customary dishevelled and confused.

Then there was Senor Grath.

" . . .how do you suppose the man entered?" he was saying.

Hendrich looked pale. "I didn't hear anything until Imre screamed. Nobody went past me, of that I'm sure."

Grath turned to me, still with a hard slant to his features. "Did you wake? Did you hear a noise at all?"

I nodded. "I was . . . seeing to my needs."

"And he came after you?"

"Yes." I shivered as I saw again that blade arcing towards my face. But I recounted what little there was anyway, as cogently I knew how.

"So you screamed *after* you pushed him?" Senor Grath raised a sceptical eyebrow, making me wonder if he was aware, somehow, of my previous nighttime escapes from the Citadel.

I swallowed, straightening. My hair dripped over my shoulders as Hanna's cardigan clung to me damply. This was the second time he'd seen me soaked – not that it could have made any difference to his opinion of me, and that gave me courage. I drew back my shoulders and met his glare with one of my own. "I don't know," I said firmly. "I was kind of shocked."

He tilted his chin back and nodded towards Hanna.

"She's right, in any case," he growled. "The safest place for you is here in the Prince's suite, at least for now. The man must have come in through the window –" here he looked at me as if daring me to confirm this, but I held my tongue – "which means he'd scaled the walls. How he managed that, I don't know. We'll post vigilar down below and on the nearby bridges. Provided whoever sent this man did not hear the commotion – and I suspect he or she would be keeping a careful distance – they may assume that the murder succeeded."

"M-murder?" I bleated.

The Prince had still said nothing. He stared blankly ahead, leaving me to wonder if he even comprehended the danger.

"Moving the Prince would be inadvisable," Senor Grath concluded. "We want to make sure no one immediately knows the attempt on his life failed. At least for the moment. We will keep this as quiet as we can. You will stay in this room until I say otherwise. Do you understand?"

Did he know? Was he just guessing? Or was he simply trying to make me uneasy? I nodded. "I understand."

And then, Hanna put me into the bed and pulled the covers up to my chin. The Prince they set-up on the sofa, since he refused to leave me alone in the suite.

Chapter Twenty-Seven

They moved the corpse while I slept. I'm not sure how they got it out, but when I woke, morning light was streaming through the window.

I was just struggling up from the remnants of sleep when I heard the footsteps coming down the hallway. Someone spoke, and Miguel rumbled back, and this had me sitting upright. How Miguel had heard about what had happened I did not know, but he did, and he had insisted on changing his post to guard the Prince's suite, and that was enough.

The first voice returned, and there was no mistaking that tone. Senor Grath, my personal ray of sunshine.

A moment later, he walked into the Prince's room, without so much as a knock.

"Get up, if you please." His gaze flickered over me, the surprise registering in his face at the change in my appearance since last he'd visited. However, clean and groomed as I was, I still didn't seem to meet his standards, as evidenced by his wrinkled brow.

"Now?" I said, trying to remain composed. I had displayed far too much weakness in front of this man last night, but the truth was, I did not want to face anything this turning except sleep. "I have no clothes here . . ."

It was true. Everything I had was still back in my cottage, save for Xith's scarf.

"Now, you foolish girl," he barked harshly.

My heart froze, and the knot in my stomach clenched painfully. My composure vanished and I stared at him desperately. He was going to send me away, I just knew it.

Yet, where would I go? I had no place at the Pavilion, of this I had no doubt. Even if I could still somehow dance, with my ankle as it was, la Boca's words against me would ensure no mecenas ever chose me.

The man clicked his fingers impatiently. "I'm sure I don't care if you're primped and made up. Rise. My Liege is waiting."

Fear suffused my very bones. Rise I did and found that, after all, Hanna or Adina had left me a dress and some clean undergarments folded on a chair. I pulled them on quickly and went into the sitting room. The floor had been cleaned thoroughly, but still, a faint dark patch overlapped the rug, in the shape of a bird with its wings outstretched.

For once, the Prince was sitting straight in his chair, but though his eyes were bleary, it seemed as if he'd had a restless night rather than an indulgent one. He was freshly shaven, his shoulder-length hair bound at his nape, and his clothing neat and clean. He was, in this state, quite unbearably handsome. How my sisters would envy this moment!

Still, this was very different to the times I had spent in his presence before, sitting beside him, talking, or not, as the occasion required, or trailing behind him to the Conclaves. Never had he looked so regal and princely. Now, I was aware that he was truly the ruler of Tierra Mejór, in all but name. I kneeled on the floor.

"Stand," he commanded. I did so, feeling awkward. This setting, this room, this closeness made him seem so much less like an ordinary man.

I tried to smooth my hair surreptitiously, but I had the feeling the only one who noticed was Senor Grath, standing in the corner with his arms crossed over his chest like a stern chaperone.

"I must apologise –" And the Prince lapsed into silence, which lasted perhaps a full minute.

"My Prince?" I said, when it became clear he wasn't going to continue. "I'm afraid I don't know what you would have to apologise for."

His gaze snapped back to me, as if he'd forgotten where he was. I was beginning to wonder if he had quite ruined his mind with drink and smoke.

He waved a hand. "Cease, please, calling me 'Prince'. I've had all I can take of 'Prince' this and 'Prince' that from that Pattern-bedamned walking black hole and his retinue. It will be Thaniel, or nothing."

I put a hand to my mouth. The giggle I stifled was half-hysterical, but he noticed my amusement, and a glint of appreciation showed in his eyes.

"What happened last night – you saved my life. But you were nearly killed. And I can't help but feel responsible. After all, it was my decision that brought you here in the first place."

I shook my head. "If the man had killed you . . . I could not let that happen."

Thaniel looked surprised at my response. Then he nodded slowly. "It is not the first time my life has been threatened. But I suspect it's the first time you've ever faced death."

I raised my shoulders in a helpless gesture. "You don't owe me any thanks. Any one of the sisters would have done the same. Any one of your loyal subjects."

"No," Thaniel replied slowly and softly. "You are not just a subject, Imre. You're not simply a Daughter of the Pavilion. I can't tell what it is, but there is more to you than . . ." he made a sweeping motion with his hand, indicating my whole body. Since I had spent the last four years of my life preparing my body for service to Aurelia, I wasn't sure whether this was truly a compliment, but still, I knew what he meant.

"There are more than just me who recognise it." Thaniel stopped pacing, as his eyes flashed. Suddenly his true self was revealed to me in full; a man driven with purpose, with an inner fire that burned turning and night. A man with a heart capable of great kindness and love, if only he would allow himself to feel them; it was my experience that men who hid such things from the world also hid them from themselves. But such motives were many and varied. What was the Prince's?

"That is the key, I'm certain of it," he said. "They have wanted me to turn you over to them from the moment they arrived. In fact, la Boca has insisted on it during every Conclave.When I refused, he began to seek support of the Councillors. I begin to wonder if he seeks to set them against me."

I tried to work out why he was speaking to me of this. Were these real fears, or simply a paranoid delusion? Those who used enough of the white-powder could often suffer from such notions. Usually, they were baseless.

"La Boca, surely, has your best interests at heart," I spoke quietly. Unspoken were the words: *if you wanted to hand me over, to satisfy the heralds, I could not stop you – nor blame you.*

"La Boca has only one interest at heart," the Prince said. Suddenly, he stopped pacing and motioned to me. "Come!"

Grath stepped forward from the shadows. "My Prince. You should not leave your rooms. It's not safe."

Thaniel gave him a look that could only be described as scathing. "You would order *me*, Senor?"

"Not at all," Grath returned. "This is, purely and simply, my *advice*."

Thaniel gave a humourless smile. "She needs to see, Grath." He gestured at the bloodstain on the floor. "Has she not earned it?"

Grath's lips thinned into a line, but he went and conferred quickly with the guardia at the door, then motioned for us to follow him.

In the hallway, we collected Miguel, who, it seemed, refused to be moved from his new post. He trailed behind us as we stepped into the lift-car.

We rode down until we reached a long corridor, and here we moved to a second lift-car, a larger, less opulent version. Down we went, again, and down, through more and more levels of the Citadel, until I was sure we would end up belowground.

And, when we at last drew to a stop, it seemed that was indeed the case. The air was cold, the same kind of chill of cold metal that filled the Library. We were perhaps on the same level, or even below it.

We stepped into the darkened passageway. A single globe-light hung from the ceiling.

Grath led the way, now, down the passage. At the end was a door, made of thick oak, bound with iron. I had seen this door before, or one very like it; in my dream of Prince Thaniel, and again, when Miguel and I had made our illicit trip out of the Library using the way Divon had shown us.

Grath turned a key in the lock. Some complicated mechanism turned within the door before it swung open, releasing a blast of frigid air.

Inside the room beyond, it was cold. Not just the cold of being far below the earth, where damp soil insulated and dispersed any warmth from Tierra Mejór's core, but deliberately cold, artificially cold. There were vents in the walls, which blew this icy breeze over us, making my breath steam. Ice inched its way along the metal walls, creating beautiful, intricate, perfect patterns.

In the very centre were three large cases, the size of beds, covered with glass canopies. I did not want to think of them as coffins, but this was precisely what they resembled.

The glow that came from the first and second casket was muted, covered by a thin layer of frost. The third was completely dark, its glass covering cracked from corner to corner.

Intrigued, I stepped closer, peering through the nearest glass at the shape within.

It was a woman.

She lay on her back, her face pale and weathered and so sunken, it seemed the only substance she was made from were bones. Her body was naked, her breasts exposed, nipples pinched and white. The thatch of hair between her legs was silver, matching the hair spread beneath her resting head. Her arms were at her sides, fingers long and thin. Her eyes were closed, and she was utterly still, her hair just a short crown of curls.

I turned to the Prince and found his face grim, his eyes sad.

"What is this?" I asked him.

"These chambers have been here, below the Citadel, probably since it was first built. It was Grath who discovered how they worked."

"It's a simple principle," Grath spoke up gruffly, coming to stand at my side, so that he, too, could look into the casket. "The body temperature is lowered by increments until the heart and brain stop, without actually freezing the tissues. I had no idea that it would work, but when La Reina fell ill, it was our best and only chance. I'm still not certain if she will ever be revived."

"She's not –" I began.

"Dying?" The Prince said the word too easily, and I could tell it wasn't through lack of compassion, but rather, because it was something that had been on his thoughts too often. "But of course. She's been dying for years."

I touched my fingers to the cold metal casing, more to keep myself upright than anything else. La Reina, dying? How was this possible? Had I not seen her at the Dance? At the Conclave? Was this some preposterous, elaborate ruse at my expense?

"How?" I asked at last.

"Pneumonia," Thaniel answered, his voice still carrying that matter-of-fact tone. "She weakened over the years that followed, and the sickness refused to abate. Oren could no longer drain the fluid from her lungs."

I stared at La Reina. It was a fate too terrible to contemplate.

"But I have seen her. At the Festival de Tiemp. And at the ball. She looked . . ."

I had been about to say that she looked well enough, but that was far from the truth. Had I not thought she looked *wrong?*

At a gesture from the Prince, Senor Grath moved to a cabinet by the door. It was as wide as a human, and the reason for this I soon saw. When he opened it, he revealed the last thing I had been expecting: an automaton.

It looked different from Feval. It didn't have a blank, metallic head, but instead a realistic human face, surrounded by golden curls, and wore a dress – a long blue gown, inset with velvet.

Grath flicked a switch on the back of the machine, and it whirred slowly to life. He drew up his right sleeve, revealing his watch, and with his left hand, he twisted the dials this way and that. The crystal face began to glow a soft blue.

The automaton moved an arm. All of a sudden, it was a metal being no more, but rather, a woman, wearing a green gown, her blond hair tinged with silver, her face tilted slightly towards the ceiling, an expression of cool hauteur across her fine features. I switched my gaze between the woman in the cupboard and her twin beneath the frosted canopy behind me.

Before me stood the Queen. In fact, compared to the lifeless, wrinkled, grey version in the coffin-like case, I could more readily believe that this trick version of her was the real one.

I dropped to my knees, bowing my head.

"Stand up," said Grath, with a hint of amusement in his voice. "This is not the Queen."

I stood, still unable to contain my wonder. The automaton stepped stiffly forward from the cupboard, then took a step to the left and to the right.

I reached out to touch her, then pulled my hand back just in time. Even if she was just an artificial, I didn't dare.

"Did you make this?" I asked Grath.

He nodded. "Though not without much research and countless failures. The face and hands are made from rubber, carefully sculpted and painted to resemble flesh. The hair is actually la Reina's." He gestured towards the casket with a rueful expression. "The smith who worked on it is a genius."

"And you control her using that device on your wrist." I should have known it for what it was, but the controlling wands I'd seen used on the artificials in the Pavilion were much larger and bulkier devices. Grath must have created this mechanism himself.

"It was a desperate effort when it became clear my Lady wasn't going to get any better. She was insensible when she was awake, and unconscious for the rest of the time. She was never going to be able to name Thaniel as Principe Verderaro. We had to ensure it still looked like she was healthy, or the heralds would have seized the throne."

"But that can't work forever? Eventually, they're going to find out."

"We were hoping for a cure. Or something. Just a glimmer – enough time for her to make her announcement, to name the Prince as her rightful heir, as the Law requires. But we dare not risk waking her, lest all chance be lost."

"You can't make the automaton speak?" I asked.

Grath shook his head. "That's beyond my capabilities. Not that I haven't tried. I've rigged up moving jaw-pieces and even tried to manipulate the automaton's vocal processors. But nothing looks or sounds even remotely convincing."

I looked at the realistic imitation of a woman they had made in the automaton. It was true, that the thing was lifelike enough to fool the people at a distance, but it would not stand up to close scrutiny. And without the Queen's voice, it could not do the duty of naming Thaniel as true Principe Verderaro.

Chapter Twenty-Eight

Chancellor Darhn met us as we made our way back to the Prince's suite, tapping his way with his staff. He never had a servant with him, as an aid, curiously adept at finding his way through the Citadel. I looked at him sideways, wondering, desperately, how many people knew the truth about the Queen. Would they admit it if they did? This whole thing was beyond the Law, and it made our whole world a lie.

Darhn looked drawn and worried, and he and Grath fell to discussing increases in security measures and stepping up the hunt for La Rebelde. "In all likelihood," Darhn said in a low voice that told me he thought this should have been taken care of long ago, "he thinks if he can murder the Prince before he is named, he will have won."

"Then he's as crazy as we suspected," Grath countered. "If the Prince is murdered, the system will not fall apart. Anarchy will not rule the streets. Does he not realise that the Brotherhood will be the ones to take up the reins? It is everything la Boca hopes for!"

"We must make plans to get my Liege off the Spindle," Grath said finally. "He must go to the Estate, and the sooner the better."

As I left them and made my way back to my little garden house, guarded by an alert and jumpy Miguel, who kept his hand firmly on his revolver-pistol, my thoughts were whirling over their conversation.

Someone wanted the Prince dead.

Was it, perhaps, not la Rebelde at all? Was there another member of the Council who would benefit from his death? Was it – and this was the thought that chilled me the most, for it made the most sense – was it the Brotherhood themselves?

I weighed the supporting evidence in my mind.

La Boca had pinned the blame for the failures in the Cuidad squarely on my shoulders, for falling during the *Dance of a Thousand Steps*. He had wanted me to be given over to the Brotherhood – for punishment, most likely, for what else could he hope to achieve? Nothing I could do could make things right, after all.

But I was under the protection of the Prince.

Did he want me enough that he would murder the Principe Regente, to remove that obstacle?

Miguel, unaware of my racing thoughts, let me into the garden house and took up his post outside the door.

But I did not sleep that night.

Instead, a slow-dawning realisation was settling upon my shoulders. If I was to blame for this attack on the Prince, I should be removed from the equation. It wasn't just his life, after all; if my mistake truly had something to do with the failures that had plagued Tierra Mejór, it was for the best if I gave myself up to la Boca, and let him do what he wished. If he could not seize me himself, I would have to do it for him.

But first, I had to make sure the Prince was safe; if he was not, nothing I did would account for anything.

My mind was made up. I needed to go to *The Nightingale's Song.*

***

I did not know what was said to the people of the Cuidad about the attack. Later, I would learn that nothing was said at all; if anyone was looking for reports of the Prince's death, they must have been frustrated, for while there were no rumours to say he had died, there were none to say he lived, either. The people were used to silences from the Citadel, since, as far as they knew, the Prince was often indisposed, the cause of this indisposition ferociously speculated on, but never confirmed.

The Conclave met without him. La Boca, of course, questioned his absence, but the explanation was the same; the Prince was indisposed. The defence would not hold up for long under his probing, but for now it sufficed. Meanwhile, the Prince kept to his rooms, and even I was not called to visit.

Preparations for my venture took all of the following day. Hardest of all was pretending that I was up to nothing unusual. I puttered in the garden, and cooked Miguel another meal, and read with him, and chattered inanely with Adina – who, of course, had heard nothing about the attempt on the Prince's life, for which I was glad; but all the while, my mind raced ahead in time, plotting on my coming escape.

I searched my wardrobe for my plainest clothes, and thanked Grath's thoughtfulness in giving me a Guild-belt to complete my disguise. These I hid under the sheets of my bed.

As evening began to fall, I told Miguel that I was tired, and would be having an early night. I think I looked the part – drained and worried – for he didn't so much as bat an eyelash.

When I reached my bedroom, I sat for a moment on the soft bed and wondered if I could not just go to sleep, and pretend none of this was happening. But in the end, did I really have a choice?

I couldn't spend the rest of my life in this garden, pretending to be a guildswoman. Sooner or later, the Prince would have to answer to the Law; if his mother did not recover, he would never become heir, and what would happen to me?

And what of the tremors and quakes, the blights on the crops, the spread of this incurable illness, the slow decline of the machines all over Tierra Mejór? If I was to blame, if there was some way to fix this, I had to take it.

***

I waited until deep evening, when la Grulla was but a pale shade of herself on the horizon. Then I slipped from under the covers, when I had lain fully dressed in my guildswoman's disguise, my hair wrapped under Xith's scarf. For the sake of superstitious luck, I had my feather in my pocket, and the hacer julepe cards. I'm not sure why I felt I should take them, except that, while everything else in the garden house was supposed to be mine, these were the only things that I felt truly were.

I went to the kitchen and looked through the window. All I could see was the water of the swirling eddy-lake, so I eased up the casement as quietly as I could, then folded myself through the small space, grateful for my dancer's body.

Dropping to the wooden boards of the bridge, I turned to slide the window closed.

Getting past Miguel was much harder, but again, my dancer's training served me well. I swung myself over the edge of the bridge's railing, and there placed my feet on the angled joining struts. I edged my way across, from one to the next – it took time, for as they crossed one another, their distance from the bridge varied, and I had to test each foothold before I could trust it.

I peered over the edge only once, to see Miguel standing steadfastly at my door, his arms crossed, staring into the darkening night.

A pang of guilt washed over me – he was doing such a job protecting me, and yet here I was, sneaking into the heart of danger! – but I refused to let myself dwell on it. I'd already come this far.

I knew my way to the side gate by heart now. Slipping through it was easy. Beyond that, it was a little harder, for I had to get my bearings once more.

Thankfully, my disguise this time was perfect. A horticulturalist guildswoman had every right to walk the streets at any time of day or night, and would not look any more out of place on the Third Tier as the First. My tan trousers, a loose mauve shirt, and brown leather boots attracted no attention as I walked past the Citadel and into the side streets.

Here, I was a little lost. I did my best to remember the way, but things changed hour by hour on these lower-levelled streets, let alone after four years away! I could have used the more well-known lock gate, the one on the Calle del Corazón, but there was far too much of a risk of running into people I didn't want to see.

Finally, I found the first lock gate, in a back alley, and began to descend, first one tier, then a second. As I left the shadow of the Citadel behind, the streets acquired a tinge of familiarity.

Rows of closely packed shops offering a range of herbs and drugs, ceramic smoke pipes, and other dubious-looking artefacts. Several shopkeepers called out to me, but I kept walking, my head purposefully down, knowing well that to meet anyone's eyes would invite the vendors to try and sell me something – "for a very good price."

After several corners, I began to feel like someone was following me.

It was small things, at first: a series of footsteps that seemed to match mine, a glimpse of a shadow behind me as I turned down yet another narrow street. I knew better than to think it was probably nothing. Around here, it would be more likely to have a pickpocket or two shadowing you than not. I dared not stop, so I took a different route, ducking through a small marketplace, then down a back alley so narrow, I could barely squeeze my shoulders through. After this, I was almost certain they'd lost me in the crowd.

Down here, the Third Tier streets had transformed somewhat over the years, but the differences were subtle. A grocery had changed hands and the sign had been painted over very badly, but it still sold the same flyspecked fruit and dusty beer bottles. A two-story tavern had been pulled down and replaced by a hatter's, but the shop next door still sold reconditioned furniture. Metal piston-tram lines were set into the cobbled road, but no trams ran down them; a few handcarts and pedal-pushers used the tracks instead, whizzing by at insane speeds, their passengers and luggage almost overbalancing them. Piles of discarded rubbish were left wherever they happened to fall, and in one alcove, I even noticed an old automaton, its innards stripped and its body cavity laid bare, looking eerily like a dismembered corpse. I hoped Feval never saw it. And there was an old playground the neighbourhood youngsters frequented, not to frolic among the rusty swings, but to exchange illicit substances and indulge in their effects.

Another three minutes of walking, and I stood before a narrow building with a rusted sign that read *The Nightingale's Song*. The ground floor was a cramped little night-café, with several tables set out on the footpath. Music came from within, a resounding drumbeat and guitar underneath a woman singing *Lost Child*. The sound was cheap and tawdry, the rhythm all wrong, and the voice thin and reedy.

> Lost child, lost child, where have you gone?
> Lost child, lost child, I miss you so . . .
> I had hoped never to see this place again.

I lost a moment, standing there, listening to the mournful tune. It was as if I'd stepped into the past, to a time when I knew I would have to go back in, sooner or later; to a time when I shivered in this very spot, aching from bruises, tired of lifting and carrying and running errands for Vallencino, and afraid that everything I had done would not be enough for him today, that it would not save me from another beating, and more bruises.

A hand settled on my arm, and I gave a sudden, involuntary yelp. Whirling, I grabbed my assailant's arm, twisting it as hard as I could. I heard a satisfying gasp of pain, and raised my knee to kick the man's belly –

– to find myself looking up at the last person I would have expected.

"Senor Grath!" I breathed.

He looked down at me, one eyebrow raised. "Would you release my arm?"

I let go of him, quickly.

"What are you doing here?" I hissed. Already our confrontation had attracted the attention of a patron walking out of the café. This was the last thing I needed!

"Following you, you stupid girl," he said. "And the question should be mine to ask of *you*!"

I straightened my back and lifted my shoulders, then remembered I was supposed to be an apprentice Horticulturalist, not a Daughter of the Pavilion. I couldn't look haughty or proud; I should look like I was here to find a good time, and this man – my father, or an overzealous uncle – had decided to interfere.

"I am here to get information," I told him. "That's all."

"Information?" He spread his arms, effectively blocking my way. "Girl, what kind of information can you get in a place like this?"

There was nothing for it. He would never let me past if I didn't tell him. "I can find out who tried to kill the Prince. But you have to let me go. People will recognise you, and I can't have you revealing me before I get inside."

He reached out, and I shied away, sure he was about to drag me by the ear back to the Citadel. Instead, he pulled the scarf from my head and wrapped it around his own. It looked odd – but certainly no stranger than some of the other fashions in this district.

"I'm coming in with you."

"No, you're not," I growled. "You will ruin everything! You're the one who chased after me. You're putting the Prince in danger, just by being here!"

"The Prince will be leaving in two days for the Estate," Grath said. "He'll be much more easily guarded there. This venture of yours is foolish and useless."

"Somehow, I think you place too much faith in your guardia and vigilar." I wanted nothing more than for the Prince to be safe – but I couldn't allow myself to believe it, not after looking into the eyes of the man who had died trying to kill me.

"You don't trust me, girl; well, I don't trust you, either. Show me you're doing this in the interests of the Prince."

I looked around helplessly. There were too many people, and they were starting to look our way. If I didn't go inside now, it would be too late.

Grasping Grath's hand, I pulled him through the door behind me. In actual fact, I might just use him to my advantage.

"If you insist on being here," I threw over my shoulder. "Then you'll be the one to speak. Ask for Marlin."

Inside, the night-café was filled with cigarillo smoke. Vallencino, the owner, seemed to be turning a much better business these turnings, for the tables were almost full, and so were the chairs along the bar. A small crowd clustered in front of a low stage that had been erected to one side – that was new, and so was the woman standing on it, clutching a small ampliphone. Her voice truly was dreadful.

Lost child, lost child, when will you come home?

The accompaniment wasn't produced by real instruments, but by echoing speakers, and it was scratchy and badly recorded. The patrons didn't seem to mind, possibly because the singer, her sloppily-tinted dark hair falling across her pale face and painted lips, opted for only a beaded strap across her breasts and a pair of thigh-length black leather tights. Despite her large bosom, I could count her ribs.

I let Grath lead us past the tables to the bar, and order two glasses of beer – the cheapest brand. I would have chosen ale, myself, but I couldn't protest now.

The bartender leaned across the counter as he pushed our glasses towards us. He was a burly man with a stain on his collar and a voice that sounded like gravel when he asked, "What are you and the lovely young lady up to this evening?"

"We're here to see Marlin." Grath pulled aside one of the chairs and taking a seat, just as I'd told him to.

The barman looked quizzical. "I've not seen you here before."

"Not for many years, no," Grath said. "Was a time, though, I was here once a turning for Marlin."

The barman grunted, removing the towel from his shoulder to wipe a spill from the counter. "What you say your name were, again?"

"Not that it's any of your business." Grath picked up his beer and took a long – and, given the quality of the brew, impressive – draught.

The bartender chuckled and looked up, his feigned disinterest turning to amusement at this response, which proved Grath was not an imposter. No guildsman would reveal his name in a night-café, certainly not after requesting admittance to a Red House. "It's not, at that. Very well. I'll see if Henny will go up and enquire. You just enjoy your beer, Senor, Senorita." With a salute, he moved on.

"I assume he's going to get this Henny fellow, and not the manager," Grath said quietly as his eyes followed the bartender through a door behind the counter.

"You passed inspection," I assured him, taking my own seat, then an experimental sip of my beer. It might as well have been dishwater. "You could have ordered us something nicer."

Grath had finished his glass, but he didn't look any more impressed than I was. "Indeed, I'll go for some goldwine next time."

"Goldwine?" I laughed. "In a place like this?"

It was strange, being in this place with him. Striping away the layers of the formality of the Citadel, and removing the haze of dislike from his eyes, he was relaxed and almost approachable. I wondered if he'd ever been in a night-café before, and if so, which one; had he bedded many women? I couldn't imagine him doing so – he'd made his feelings on women evident on that first night in the autocarriage – but then, only a few turnings ago, I couldn't picture him consenting to be here with me at all.

"What are you thinking?" he asked me suddenly.

"Nothing," I said cautiously, letting my gaze wander across the other patrons. One of the men, sitting by himself at a table in the corner, seemed to have been looking at us; there was something familiar about him, but as I peered closer, his gaze was firmly on his drink. It might have been my imagination.

"I can tell you're lying. Your eyebrows furrow when you're deep in thought," he went on. "You're one of those people whose feelings are written across their faces for the world to see."

"I am?" I bristled. "Well, I suppose you're an expert on the matter . . ."

"Actually, I am." He sighed, turning the empty glass between his fingers. "Given my Liege's disposition, reading volatile emotions is rather in my job description. For instance, I can see now that I've irked you with my observations."

I turned aside to hide my face. "Then you'll know I'd rather you didn't analyse me, especially not now."

"My apologies," Grath muttered, but he certainly didn't *sound* apologetic. "You know this area well, then."

I tilted my head back. "A little."

"You spent some time on the Third Tier as a child?"

"What would it matter if I did?" I challenged him.

"Pattern damn you, woman." He huffed. "It's like talking to a thistle!"

"Then do forebear!" I responded. "No one –"

It was then, thankfully, a small boy appeared behind us, sparing the need for further conversation. "You're to come up," he said. He had very fine features, almost feminine, and his hair was long and badly cut. He had a smudge of dirt on one cheek, and for an instant, I felt like I was looking in a mirror back through time; this youngster was me, ten years past.

"Henny?" I asked, and his head jerked up, as if startled that I had known his name, let alone used it. He nodded warily, then, motioning, turned and scurried ahead of us, across the crowded floor to a door painted with the symbol of the crescent moon.

Aurelia's symbol.

Henny took a key that hung around his neck and fitted it into the lock. The door slid aside, revealing a staircase. They had dressed it up a little since I'd last been here; the cold stone walls were covered with red drapes, though they'd been hung unevenly, and tied haphazardly with gold tassels.

At the top of the stairs we reached a foyer, which again had changed since my last viewing. Several terracotta pots filled with sickly-looking plants sat in each corner, corroding the air with a stink of mildew. The carpet was buckled, patterned with stains, and the one window hid behind a thick curtain. There were three doors, one in each of the remaining walls.

On a divan in the centre sat Marlin.

Her figure had become even softer since last I'd seen her. She was wearing a jade-green silk robe, which fell open around her copious bosom, and was tied at the waist with a gold sash that almost vanished into the folds of her stomach. Her half-lidded eyes were rimmed with gold paint that settled into her wrinkled skin, and kohl that was smudged as if she had applied it last turning.

Henny stepped to one side, so the woman could look at us.

"So," said Marlin, "You're here for a lesson, are you?"

"No." Heat crept into my voice.

"My apprentice enjoys watching," Grath said blandly.

She blinked slowly, once, twice. "Pretty young thing like her?"

"Would you believe that," Grath replied. "And I'll pay double the price."

Marlin's sleepy eyes settled on me. Then, slowly, she nodded and waved Henny away. Giving us one final glance, the boy vanished back down the stairs.

"Double, then." She heaved herself up from the divan with a painful groan. "What's your pleasure?" She pointed to one of the doors. "Sensuality?" she asked. "Excess?" Another door. "Completion?" This final one made her grin as she looked at Grath, her lip paint cracking ghoulishly. She had lost another tooth, I couldn't help but notice.

"Privacy, for a start," Grath said at once.

She nodded with a disappointed sigh, then made her slow way towards the first door. This room contained only a wide bed covered with a gauzy curtain. The globe-lights were dim, but I could still make out the marks on the walls, the chipped paint, the rotten gap in the floorboards. Marlin heaved herself onto the bed, which groaned much as she had earlier, and her robe parted a little, revealing most of one wrinkled breast. I turned away, revolted, but Grath, to his credit, did not flinch; I wondered, with a silent laugh, if he was actually enjoying the sights.

"So." She nodded at Grath. "Are you going to stand there all night?"

She undid the sash, and everything it contained spilled free. Grath let slip a small huffing breath then, as he took a step back towards the door. I shook my head. I was surprised he'd made it this far; his staid demeanour was something I saw all too often among untried mecenas.

"Mother." I crossed the room in three steps to tug the robe back into place. My fingers brushed her skin – hot and slightly damp with sweat. "You certainly haven't changed."

She sighed and turned over, reaching for a stand beside the bed, where there was a small powder box. She pinched some of the white-powder inside and sniffed it noisily, then replaced the lid and resettled herself on the cushions. Her body rippled with her movements. "And neither have you, Birdie."

"My name isn't Birdie any longer!" I burst out, then, clenching my fists at my sides as I stood over her. She rolled her eyes.

"You can dress a pig in silk," she said scathingly. "It's a pig underneath, still and always. Didn't I tell you that?"

"Yes," I whispered. Tears pricked my eyes. How did she manage to do this to me every time? "You did. Over and over."

"And wasn't I right?" She smriked. "You thought you could Dance the Crane. But you couldn't even finish the Steps."

I closed my eyes for a moment, savouring the brief haven of darkness, where I couldn't see her leering face. But I couldn't block her voice from my ears.

"Oh, child," she said as I looked at her again. "Forgive me. My meaning is that you'll always be my little Birdie, at least to me."

Her eyes flickered to Grath. "But I see you're growing up, at last. I suppose you've been removed from the Pavilion for your blunder, seeing as you're wearing an apprentice's rags. Or is this one of your mecenas? Charm him into giving you a place at his grand house, did you?"

She hadn't heard, obviously, that I had been taken to the Citadel. I had assumed it would be the talk of the City, just as my scandalous ruination of the *Dance of a Thousand Steps* had been. My Mother, the Queen of Gossip, would have heard it if such a rumour there was; Marlin trafficked in information just as well as her other trade.

But then, perhaps I was overestimating my own importance. The passage of time had probably bought all sorts of other dramas to the forefront.

I turned away, only to find myself face-to-face with Grath. What was that expression he wore? Disgust? Triumph? He'd just been proved right, after all – my protestations to the opposite notwithstanding, the girl he despised as a whore was the next best thing: the daughter of a Red House woman. One who was prepared to reveal herself in front of her daughter. Could he understand now why I hadn't wanted to tell him the identity of my contact?

Mother cackled. "You could do worse, Birdie. After your embarrassment, you could be walking the streets, since you think working honestly for your own coin, as I do, so distasteful. Does he have a wife?" She squinted up at Grath. "They say the wives of nobles often like having another woman about to satisfy their husband's needs. It leaves them more time for parties and goldwine, rather than popping out babe after babe."

I shuddered. Mother knew nothing of the relationship between a mecenas and a Dancer. She was not a replacement for a wife, but rather a spiritual companion, a way for the man to connect with the Pattern. Women were not excluded, and the wives could, if they chose, join the Dance. No man would ever take a Dancer into his household without the permission of his wife, and it would be against everything we were taught to subvert that arrangement. But while it was an honoured position, every Dancer always dreamed of having a mecenas chose her, and her alone, to be his companion or wife. That was what we all whispered about at night in our dormitories, what we hoped for every time we went out into the Room of Roses. We were only human, and we were selfish.

"Ma'am," said Grath. "I'm *not* a mecenas. In fact, the reason for our business here is something entirely other."

"Is it really?" The powder was making her voice thick, as her eyes drooped lower and lower. "What *possible* business could possibly bring such a fine guildsman to a Red House?"

I winced. "Mother, this is Senor Grath."

She looked at me as if to check for a lie written somewhere upon my person. She, of all people, knew the name, and didn't expect me to be in the company of someone so high and mighty.

Grath put a hand on my shoulder, and even though his touching me made me uneasy, I was grateful for his steady, solid grip – and surprised that it came. "We are here because we need to know the name of the person who hired the one who entered the Golden Citadel two nights ago with murderous intent."

Her eyes went wide. "This is a joke?"

"Not in the slightest." Grath kept his voice clipped and formal, and I could tell this was having an effect on Mother. She straightened a little, and pulled her silk robe around herself. "The one hired is well-known. He goes by the name of Chette. Do you know him?"

At the sound of the name, Mother gave a little squeak and covered her mouth.

"You do, then?" Grath prompted.

Her eyes, small and beady beneath the folds of flesh, darted left and right.

"Mother," I said. "It's very important that you tell us."

"Chette?" she squeaked at last. "Someone hired Chette . . . to break into the *Citadel*?"

"They did. And he carried a knife, which he intended to use."

She closed her eyes – they turned into pools of rippling gold paint – then fumbled blindly for the powder box, dropping the lid from senseless fingers. She sniffed another pinch, then, wiping her nose with a chubby hand, said in a husky voice, "Tell me who he was targeting."

"No need for that," Grath said.

Marlin's eyes snapped open. "You come to me for information, you better be prepared to pay for it."

"I've told you I'll pay you twice," Grath said.

"Money pays for my *time*. But *information* costs an equivalent price – an exchange, if you will. Birdie knows this, don't you, Birdie?"

I met her gaze and nodded.

"Who was it?" she continued. "The Prince? La Reina?"

Grath considered this. "He came to kill Imre."

There was a long pause before she burst into laughter. Her bosom heaved and her gown slipped to one side. "This *is* a joke." Mother spluttered. "You've come to toy with me, little Birdie!"

"I assure you, ma'am, this is no joke," Grath said. "Imre has been residing at the Citadel since her injury. The other night, she was attacked in her bed. We are here to discover who hired Chette to do this job, and why."

"Why don't you just ask Chette himself?" she challenged.

I shivered. "He's dead."

"Chette? Surely not. He's one of the best. The best of the best . . ." Her voice was trailing off. The powder was working its magic on her, slowing her reflexes, her heartbeat. "Who killed him?"

"I thought you said this was an exchange," Grath growled. "I've given you one piece of information. Now, your turn: who could have hired Chette?"

Mother's head was falling closer and closer to her chest. I could almost see the fog of powder clouding her mind, drawing her down into sleep. "Hired Chette? Many people. Many, many people. Why, I only saw him, when was it, three or four turnings past? Aye, that was Chette, skulking in the shadows down below." She indicated the floor, which I assumed meant the night-café. "I was down there for a pick-me-up of spice-ale. A customer paid handsomely that night. I called to him, but he was in a right hurry – when I asked where he was off to, he told me there were business to be had at the White Pavilion! White Pavilion, I tell you – he was joking, I was sure, for they'd never let a man like Chette through those doors, not without enough solid coin to make up for his ratty appearance and odour. Asked him, I did, but did he answer? Not a word. That's Chette for you."

"Do you have any idea who might have engaged his services?" I could tell Grath was starting to think this was a waste of time, but I knew if I asked the right questions, we would get something.

Marlin chuckled. A small bead of saliva had gathered on her lip and was trembling as she spoke. "Sweet Unknown, Birdie-pie! All's I know's that Chette was good. "You c'n pinch the fingernails from a woman's hand while she scratched 'er behind," I says to him once. But you know what? He wouldn' broke into the Citadel for a cheap price. That I can tell you straight-up."

It wasn't much, but the more I thought about it, the more important it seemed. "Someone would have had to pay him a lot?"

"And in gold. I doubt he would've done it fer his normal fee." She nodded sagely, and the spit rolled down from her mouth, across her chin.

"And what was his normal fee?"

"Why, yer 'spec me ter know such things, Birdie!" We were losing her now. She was sinking lower and lower into a stupor, and soon she'd be incomprehensible. I wanted to leave before that happened. "Yer think I'd hire 'im? Ter cut up my ungrateful little bitch of a girl, thinks she's too good, larks off with the prissy girlies at the Pav – pavel – lilion, as if she's some Pattern-bedamned *nobility* . . ."

I came closer. Steeling myself, I drew her robe closed as best I could, and replaced the lid on the powder box. Then I leaned in closer, trying not to breathe the cloying scent of her perfume mixed with perspiration. "Gold coins?" I asked her quietly.

"Two gold coins fer a hit," she murmured as her head lolled to the side, smearing gold make-up on the pillows. "Pattern knows, business bein' wha' it is, he wouldn' roll outer bed fer less . . ."

I nodded and turned for the door.

"We can't leave her alone like this," Grath sounded genuinely concerned, making me cast one more glance at the pathetic woman on the bed. Asleep, she looked far smaller, and older, and less intimidating.

"She needs to sleep it off," I told him.

Grath shook his head. With two strides, he crossed the room and, bending, placed two silver coins on top of the powder box. Only after he'd done this did he follow me down the stairs. I charged ahead, resolution giving me speed, but Grath held back when we squeezed past Henny to slip him another silver coin. "Get someone up there to tend her," he said in a voice I guessed I wasn't supposed to hear.

I marched across the room, ignoring the bartender, who called out to ask if all was well. A man held the door open for me, and as I brushed past him, I caught sight – or *imagined* I caught sight – of a dark, jagged scar across his lip. I half-turned, but whoever he has been, he was gone.

I was too much in a hurry to pause, in any case; the door swung shut behind me.

It was only once we were out of that place, in the cool night air, that I stopped to wait. Even though the breeze was tinged with unsavoury smells,

I finally felt I could breathe again. Grath kept a formal distance between us, for which I was grateful, but just as I'd expected, he had questions.

"Why didn't you tell me the contact was your mother?"

I put my head down and started walking back in the direction we'd come.

"Imre." His long legs easily kept pace with me. When I didn't respond, he tried again. "Imre!"

I whirled to face him. "There you have it," I spat. "Everything you need to justify your beliefs about me."

We stood under one of the few street-globes that wasn't smashed. It stuttered on and off, casting intermittent shadows across the pavement. A few white-moths buzzed around it, confused, battering their wings and bodies against the warm crystal, then falling dazed through the darkness as the light vanished once more.

"What is *wrong* with you, girl?" Anger tinged his tone. "Do you think this is about *you?*"

"No." Tears choked me. "That's why I did this. The *only* reason I did this, because believe me, this wasn't pleasant. But I did it for him. For your precious Prince, to try and keep him safe while you're so busy with your brass instruments and papers and predictions of doom!"

"I –" He brought himself short. "And I would never place my love of science above the safety of anyone. Including you." Another beat passed, then he said: "A telescope."

"What?" I stared at him.

"It's called a telescope. The brass tube in the Tower Room."

My glare lasted a moment longer, in which I clenched my fists and teeth and tried to find something to say. Did he think I *cared* what the thing was called? Did he honestly think I cared about any of it – his charts and prognostications – his sureties that we were all going to perish in some cataclysmic finale? I turned on my heel and marched on up the street, my heels crunching on the bodies of white-moths that had burned to a crisp.

It was then that I heard a scuffle behind me. I thought it was Grath, who in trying to catch up to me had tripped on a paving stone. I turned to find that he *had* fallen – but not through accident. A man was on top of him, holding a revolver-pistol to his head.

I started forward – though I'm not sure what I thought I could do – when another hoodlum stepped from the shadows. The muzzle of a revolver-pistol pointed at my heart, and I looked into a face shadowed by the brim of a hat with a green ribbon tied around it.

Chapter Twenty-Nine

Beneath *The Nightingale's Song,* there was a basement. It could only be reached by going outside and in through a door in the side alley, which is why it was rarely used. I had snuck in here often as a child, to hide in the discarded, smelly old sacks. Anything was better than facing mother, or Vallencino.

Here, we were taken. I should say, I was taken. Grath was dragged, bound hand and foot, and gagged, since he had raised a ruckus when the thugs had applied the first bindings. Luckily for them, in this neighbourhood, a man cursing and spitting while another pummelled him into silence caused little alarm.

I found myself plopped onto a hard, wooden chair, while the man who had apprehended me sat opposite, his gun resting on his knees. His face was still shadowed by the brim of his hat, but I was more concerned about Grath, whose breath was coming raggedly through the gag. I hoped he wasn't badly injured, but the boots did make a few solid thuds when they connected with his body.

"Well?" the man said. His face was curiously delicate. His hair was a dishevelled, sandy mop. He wore a black velvet waistcoat and mismatched shoes, and was only a little taller than I was. If not for the scar, I would think he was younger than me, but that mark lent his face a curious age. "I hear you've been asking about Chette. Tell me. What have you found?"

I was surprised that he knew our business, though I suppose I shouldn't have been. On the Third Tier, the walls had ears, and those ears had ears.

"Nothing," I said instantly.

The boy stroked his gun, as if it were a tame street-fox. "You'd be wise to take us seriously, child."

I looked around. The space hadn't changed much since I was last here, some ten odd years ago. It even smelled the same, thought evidently someone had made an effort to tidy up, putting several rows of chairs and benches, and a few bottles of something the colour of dark red grapes on the otherwise empty shelves. A dull, cracked globe-light hung from the ceiling, casting two more men into shadows, from which they watched this exchange very closely.

If I remembered my Third Tier protocol, it was best to assume your enemies knew more than they thought they did. If not, you could act pleasantly surprised, and give them what they needed; you were likely to get off much more lightly if they got more from you than they expected they would.

"A man broke into the Citadel," I said. "And tried to kill the Principe Regente."

"This we know. We also know that man was Chette. What I would like an answer to," the man with the revolver-pistol said, and he finally tilted his head back, exposing his face, "is why, in all the forms of the Pattern, were you sent to ask questions about it in the Third Tier?"

He looked familiar, but it was a moment before it clicked into place. The man with the scarred lip. I had seen him before, in the Room of Roses at the Pavilion – he had winked at me, across the crowded room.

"I am familiar with the territory," I managed after a pause.

"You were born here, were you not, Birdie?"

I ducked my head, and he chuckled, removing his hat at last. I realised then what I hadn't before. He wasn't old enough to be called a man, and I'd only thought of him as such through some clever way he had of carrying himself. He was younger than me, barely a youth.

"I was," I conceded.

"Your mother works in the Red House above this very place," he went on.

I nodded.

"Your father stumbling home drunk one night fell over a lock gate and was lost in the darkness between the Tiers."

Again, I nodded.

"You've risen to Dance the Crane, and fallen, not just once, but twice."

I bowed my head. Was he determined to lay all my flaws out before me, like a woven tapestry of failure? How did he know all this about me to do so?

"None of this matters." My voice sounded thick. "It changes nothing. I came here because we need proof that the men who hired Chette were connected to the heralds. They want me, and the Prince stood in their way. But now that we've confirmed his identity, we've hit a dead end. There's nothing to link him to the heralds, not without knowing what he did with the money he was supposed to have been paid." I sat back in my chair. "Now, my turn. Why am I here? Why have you been watching me?"

The boy leaned forward, resting his arms on his knees, the gun threaded through the space between his elbows. "You are not the only person we have watched. We have a network of spies, and all reports find their way back to us. There is little that happens in the Cuidad that we don't know about."

I stared at him, waiting for him to reach his point.

"We have been working towards an endpoint, an ultimatum," he obliged. "One I will not divulge to you now. Suffice it to say that every person we work with must be trusted implicitly."

"What," I prompted him, "does this have to do with me?"

"I'm getting to that!" He grinned. "To do what we do, we have a need of money – untraceable funds that can't be linked to any particular person and are easily hidden. For this purpose, we have several benefactors. Most of these men and women choose to remain anonymous – understandably. Lately, however, I have begun to suspect one of these patrons – in fact, our most affluent one – is working not with us, but against us. As such, the truth of his identity becomes paramount."

I continued to look at him, asking my question silently.

"There aren't many places in the Cuidad that money can change hands without record. One of those places is –"

"The White Pavilion," I finished. "That is why you were there." At least that part had become clear. The mecenas who came to the Pavilion did not want records kept of their wins or losses. They wanted their indiscretions hidden from their wives, lovers, or disapproving families. And the Treasury certainly didn't care where the money came from, only that it existed, and would fill the coffers. I knew all this from the discussions held around the gaming tables, when the mecenas thought my sisters and I were too unintelligent, or too preoccupied, to pay them any mind.

The boy raised a finger to his scarred lip. "You recall me, then." He sounded like a proud father congratulating a son on catching his first street-fox.

"If you have been to the Pavilion, you can talk to your benefactor." I shrugged. "You don't need me."

"On the contrary." He sighed. "If the man is who I suspect he is, I cannot speak to him without revealing myself. That is something we can't risk, not yet. This is where you come in. He will never suspect a Daughter."

I should have felt something – horror, fear, denial. Yet suddenly, all I felt was incredibly tired. "It might have escaped your informants," I said, "but I'm not a Daughter any longer."

"No," said the boy. "But you are a dancer. And with your face hidden by a mask, and a pretty dress to disguise you, who will know the difference as you dance for him?"

I shook my head. "I won't do it."

The youth sat up straight, putting one hand, not so much threateningly as carefully, on the butt of his gun. He seemed to sense my thoughts. With a flick of his fingers, he motioned one of his fellows forward. The man stepped neatly in between me and Grath, and though the look on his face was not exactly menacing, it was determined. He would not move until the boy told him to.

"Just so we're clear: if you don't agree," said the boy. "We have no need for either of you. And if you happen to think you can run away – which I don't think you would, but I will play it safe, just in case – Senor Grath here will pay the price."

"You won't kill him," I said. "He's the Adviser to the Prince. You'll bring the wrath of every vigilar in the city down upon you."

He gave me a hard stare, one that told me, in no uncertain terms, that he was not afraid to risk it. He would do this, and more, to achieve his goals. I shivered. He had me, and he knew it. His first option was unimaginable, and his second, just as unthinkable. Return to the Citadel without Grath, and very little would stand between Thaniel and the heralds. Which made my own wall of protection slender at best.

"He will remain here, as our guest, in assurance. You do not want to go back to the Citadel without him, surely? After all, how long will the Prince last, without his Adviser?"

"Why should I trust you?" I burst out. "You Green-bands – you are lawless! You have no reason to keep Grath alive, even if I do what you ask. I have no intention of helping la Rebelde spread his messages of hatred and doom – surely it only fuels your cause to have the Prince die."

The boy smiled simply. "And leave the throne open to la Boca? Let me just say, in the instance of keeping the Prince alive, our interests are very much in line."

***

The Green-bands gathered in one corner, talking in low tones, and I turned my attention to Grath.

He was lying on his side behind my chair. His eyes were closed, and there was a bruise on his left cheek, and a cut above his lip, which was trickling blood. His shirt was torn, but otherwise, he looked intact. I suppose I should be grateful it wasn't worse, but for some strange reason, I felt angry that he'd been hurt so.

I kneeled down to remove his gag. "Don't shout," I told him as I worked at the knot. "They'll just put it back on again if you do, and it won't help."

He nodded, a jerking motion. When I took the fabric away, he spat. "It tastes like old socks."

I suspected he was more disgusted at his position than the taste.

"Hie!" came a shout, followed by a loud *clang!* The door to the basement burst open, admitting another Green-band, trailed by a disoriented-looking automaton. "Found this about to get dismantled by some hoodlums upstairs."

"Feval!" I hadn't known it was possible for me to be more astonished at what could happen this night – but I was. It turned quickly to anger, however, as I glared at Grath. "You bought *Feval?*"

Grath had the sense to look ashamed. "Neither Miguel nor Hendrich would let me go alone. And I had to leave them to guard the Prince. I promised to send him back if there was any trouble. When I saw you on the corner, I told him to stay concealed behind a garbage can. I suppose he tried to follow us when he saw we were in trouble."

"What were you *thinking?*" I almost shouted. "You're lucky he wasn't stripped for parts!"

"This is your automaton?" the boy asked.

"He is the property of the Citadel," Grath said, threateningly.

Clearly our captor agreed, as he gave a snicker that was the first entirely suitable gesture for a boy his age to make. "We have no intention of dismantling him, I assure you."

With a gesture of his hand, two of the men came forwards, standing on either side. One of them reached behind Feval's back, and I shot up from my chair to stop him, but the second man blocked my way. I couldn't see exactly what was done, but Favel's arms fell limp at his sides, clanking against his metal body.

"Feval?" I cried

"I am well," the automaton said. "It is only a temporary adjustment. My arms can be reenabled when required."

I was sobbing. How much more of this could I take? Dart-spiders and knives, subterfuge, kidnapping, and now espionage among my own sisters? What had my life become?

But oh, how my heart ached. How I had longed to go back to my home! To collect my belongings; find my snow glass. To see Ketra, and Yui, and the rest of my sisters again, and maybe, just maybe, never have to leave again.

Grath would be pleased about that.

But would I?

I had been gone for more than a month, now. It was a long time; and throughout it, I had found myself in places I did not want to be . . . and places I did. I had loved, and been loved. I had a friend in Adina, in Hanna. I still needed to teach Miguel how "gh" together made the sound of "f", and play hacer julepe with him, until I was good enough to win. For the Pattern's sake, I had slept with the Prince's head upon my lap! Could I ever go back to being just Imre, Daughter of the Pavilion?

"Untie him," I begged the boy. "Please."

The boy hesitated a moment, then shook his head. "I'm afraid I can't risk it."

I took this to mean that Grath was probably better trained and more powerful than any of the Green-bands. They didn't trust that four of them could hold their own against him. I filed this away; it was useful information.

"Imre," Grath said gently, his voice surprisingly warm. "If you do this, you will be doing it for your Prince."

My Prince.

The words jarred me. I hadn't really thought about it – about him, not properly, not ever. What was he to me now? Not just some distant figure seen on the Citadel steps on the turning of the Fiesta de la Tiempo. He was a real person, with skin and bone and blood, just like me.

"I know," Grath continued, and it felt as if we were the only people in the room. "He is not exactly what you would expect. Or want. In a leader, or a man. But you must also know how deeply he feels things. You've seen that, haven't you?"

I had. Oh, I had seen it. In the garden, lying on the grass under the moon, his bare skin damp with dew. In the great cage, with the birds flittering around like a colourful whirlwind. Beneath the fog of drugs and alcohol, I'd seen the man Grath described, who felt everything too deeply, and didn't know how to block it out. "Yes," I managed at last, in a very small voice.

And I knew I had to do what was asked of me.

Chapter Thirty

I was tired, so dreadfully tired; yet I was not allowed to sleep. The Green-bands were set on achieving what needed to be done the following night. I was in no position to argue. I learned their names, from their quiet conversation – Jornel was the man who had captured Feval. Davique was a small man, quiet as a mouse, who wore round, gold-edged spectacles. Nathuin moved restlessly, even when he was sitting down, and was so tall, he had to fold himself to fit in any of the mismatched chairs. There were others who weren't here – Alen, Minitah, Parde, and Foester.

"If you had only told us where you were going," Grath growled, once. He subsided back into silence following this, but I knew what he meant – *someone would be out looking for us, if only they knew where we were.*

As I sat there, beside Grath, who seemed to have fallen into a doze, in which I hoped his pain was lessened, the men worked. They came and went through the door, bringing baskets and taking packages. Low, murmured exchanges were had, most of them unintelligible.

I drifted in and out of sleep, such as it was, snatching pieces here and there on a pile of rough sacking. I dreamed of Thaniel, and woke in a panic, wondering if all was well at the Citadel. The only thing that calmed me was the thought that Miguel was still there, looking after him. And wondering where we were. He must be beside himself . . .

Favel's head-rotors whirred a few times as he surveyed the basement, once or twice fixing his one good eye on me. "Are you well, my Lady?" he asked.

"I am fine, Feval," I assured him, though this was far from true.

The men, for their part, were intrigued by the automaton. It seemed he was better kept than most they had seen, and once or twice I tensed as they fiddled with his blinking eye socket or his lifeless fingers.

They gave us a few handfuls of dried raisins to eat, at what I guessed was midday.

"What if they demand my name?" I asked the boy, who had slipped in and out several times.

"Give them that of one of your sisters," he said. "No one will know the difference."

He made it sound simple. In some ways, it was. Our masks hid our identities on the floor, and we rarely paid much attention to one another when we were dancing or entertaining.

"How will I know this man?" I asked.

"Even I do not know what he looks like," he admitted. "But he plays at hacer julepe. He keeps money in rotation on the table, and when I play, I use a trick of the cards that ensures I win. I pick up his losses as well as my winnings. You will need to find a man who loses more than he wins, or loses a suspicious amount; a man who tells the automaton to keep anything he has won in rotation."

Still, I had the feeling it would be anything but easy.

"You will need to wash," the boy decided at last. He took me into one corner, where a rusted, dirty sink spat a stream of muddied water.

"My clothes," I said, when I'd finished rinsing the dust and grime from my face and hands. "They'll give me away, if nothing else does."

But it seemed they'd thought of this, too; a few minutes later, a man entered, carrying something long and shimmering in a garment bag.

The dress within was so beautiful, I could only imagine they had somehow brought it from the Pavilion itself. It was low-cut, flowing, made of pale blue and scattered with tiny silver beads.

I stripped off my guildswoman's garb gratefully, dropping it to the floor. The dress, at least, was far more to my taste. It was only as I pulled it on that I realised every man in the room was staring at me, and none more so than Grath, who had woken especially for this. I asked for pins, and was given these, too, another one of the unexpected supplies they seemed to be hoarding and dispatching through this underground space. The men watched me, spellbound, as I brushed them through my hair, releasing the worst of the tangles made by spending a night on hessian sacks. With practiced fingers, I twisted my locks into a large curl, and pinned them in a loop on top of my head, exposing my metrónomo. For disguise's sake, I wove Xith's beautiful scarf over the top, hiding most of my hair's unmistakable golden shine.

The finishing touch were pale blue shoes, almost exactly the right size – and very much the sort of thing Ketra would have worn, and I wondered, again, how long the Green-bands had been planning this – or if they'd somehow known, all along, that it would be me.

When I was done, the boy looked me over with a critical eye, then nodded, his mouth pressed into a thin line. "You're clear on what you need to do?"

"Yes," I said with considerably more composure than I felt, smoothing my silky skirt.

He took another package from a bench. I removed the layer of brown paper and found an exquisite mask; blue feathers across the brow, angled eyes surrounded by glitter, and a delicate design trailing across the cheeks. I held it loosely in one hand. How easily I would have slipped it on, once, and sashayed into the Room of Roses, confident in what I would do that night! Now, I would be returning – no longer a virgin, speculating on her first dance – no longer a Daughter at all, but a spy for la Rebelde.

He gave me a long black coat then, to put on over my dress, and, with a gesture of solemnity, untied the green ribbon from his hat. Then led me outside, and up the steps to the street level. The wind was cold, and I shivered, even beneath the coat.

"We will be taking the backways," he said. "Walk quickly and don't turn back for any reason."

I followed him. Some paths were familiar, others new to me. The boy seemed to know his way better than I had as a child; skillfully, he avoided the busier streets, and the gatherings on the quieter ones. We reached a lock gate that I had never known was there, and as we counted seconds on a crumbling step while the curved metal wall rotated past with a sound like constant quiet thunder, before it was in place and we could cross to the higher steps, I asked the boy his name.

He gave his by now familiar grin. "You can call me Jark."

"That isn't your real name," I pointed out.

His only answer was to cock his head. I think I knew, then, impossible as it might seem, that he was la Rebelde himself.

Once on the Second Tier, we did not have far to go before we reached the Calle del Corazón. Here, Jark took off his band-less hat and bowed to me. "I have the greatest respect for you, Lady Imre, and will be waiting here until you return."

Chapter Thirty-One

I stood to one side of the Calle del Corazón, the brilliance of the Pavilion's white walls showing through the tall trees to my left. Last night I had looked up at a building that had once been my home, and now I did the same thing. A tangy mixture of regret and sadness filled me.

It was always busy, even in these earlier hours of the night. There were autocarriages, and several pedal-cycles, drawn up in the curving driveway. A few distinct groups were gathered on the steps, all dressed in their respective finery.

The tall double doors, I noticed, were now attended by sentinela. When had that been arranged? Was there something to guard against, where there was not before? Perhaps Senora R. had put them there for show. I hoped that was the case.

I did not cross the driveway. That would have been too obvious. Instead, I headed left, and ducked through the dark shapes of the trees. There, I could just make out the Templo. It was tempting to duck my head inside, just for a quick moment – but I dared not. To be discovered there, before I'd even begun my mission, would be unthinkable.

I turned instead to the walls of the white building, revelling in their gentle, radiating coolness as I walked beside them.

It wasn't long before I found my secret door, and jumped up easily onto the small balcony. I pushed aside the vines to enter.

The familiar scents and sounds and temperature washed over me, but I couldn't pause to indulge my senses. I pulled on my mask and settled it firmly in place. Then I crossed the room and tiptoed into the hallway outside. From here it was the work of moments to reach the Room of Roses.

It looked so exactly like it had the night I'd peeked in, after spraining my ankle all those turnings ago. The floors were tiled with ochre and rust-coloured tiles, perfectly smooth. Marble pillars rose on either side, lavishly decorated with vines and fluted flowers; these revolved slowly at different rates with the gears and cogs far below the Pavilion, and were in turn connected to the workings that moved the rooms above.

The chairs and alcoves were hewn of polished wood and lined with velour. In the high ceiling, a domed skylight let in streams of light to glitter through the graceful chandeliers. But for the first time, I noticed how the paintwork was chipped, and in some places mismatched where it had been hastily touched up, and some of the globe-crystals in the chandeliers were dark, and the velour on the chairs was slightly worn, or stained. Had this room always had this aura of slight shabbiness?

"Are you hiding, my pretty?"

I jumped, but quickly hid my startlement with a knowing, seductive smile. Turning, I found myself facing a young mecenas wearing a beautiful grey suit, perfectly-tailored. He was handsome. If I was among my sisters now, we would probably have fought over who approached him first. "Merely enjoying the view, senor."

He smiled, and there was a greasy quality to it that ruined the effect of his dashing looks. He reached out a finger and traced it over my cheek. "Perhaps I can point out a few of the more noticeable landmarks?"

"Oh, I'm simply here to wander and . . ." Here I batted my lashes, amazed at how easy it was to fall back into my training as a Daughter. "See what catches my eye."

"A pleasant idea," he said. "I admit, I could use something to take my mind from my work."

"You do not find pleasure in work?" I queried, edging past him into the room.

"I work at the Treasury. I was in charge," he said, in a voice that told me I should be impressed, "with loading the turnings' costings on board an airship, ready to be transported to the Pendulum, and one of the deposit boxes had jammed tight. I had to get a locksmith in to cut it, and let me tell you, la Boca does not like delays in the shipment of funds. It interferes with the Pattern."

I nodded as if I was as interested as he was, though he was only telling me this to make himself sound important. I supposed it was a good tactic. If I had never left the Pavilion, and I was not here in disguise, I would have been happy to flirt with him in a proper way. As it was, though, I had to play the part.

"Were you in terrible trouble?" I gasped, fluttering my lashes.

"Oh no," he laughed. "They know me quite well, and trust me implicitly. However, it just goes to show, these things –" he waved a hand at the room, where several of the automata were busy counting cards and credit chips, and I winced for them, bearing the brunt of the man's stupidity "– are really just useless pieces of junk in the end."

"Well, I can assure you, there is no limit to the pleasure you can experience within these walls." I giggled, doing a perfect impression of Ketra when she'd made a misstep in practice. "Your mind will be well and truly diverted. But you'll have to excuse me one moment. Please, find me later, and I'll explain in more detail."

I ducked past him with a final, teasing smile.

Having always entered from the corridors and various stairways, I'd never quite experienced the full effect of this space before now. And it was grand! The arched entranceway opened into a massive, vaulted ceiling. The floor spread out on either side, paved with red and cream stone, intricately fitted together to create a beautiful pattern that was divine. The gaming tables were set in seemingly random locations, but if one followed the pattern on the floor, one could see that they were strategically placed according to their stakes and appeal to the mecenas, while allowing enough room for servitors and Dancers to pass by.

The Dancers, of course, breezed around the room like golden petals blown on the Viento Cósmico. I looked for faces beneath their gauzy veils and curled hair, but they moved too quickly; a flash of red lips, fluttering blue eyes, or a perfectly placed beauty spot was all I saw.

Would they even recognise me if they knew I was here? I could easily imagine them forgetting me; it really felt as if I had been away for ages.

I took a tall flute of goldwine from a passing servitor, to give my hands something to do, and sipped it as I made my slow way through the tables. The heady drink warmed me pleasantly and helped wash away my misgivings as I passed men and women playing at jacks and poker, rolling dice across tables marked with squares, and spinning wheels while trying to predict where a ball might land. I could feel what the mecenas must feel here, the reason they returned time and again, even when their losses were so great. The Pattern reigned, woven into the very fabric of the place; if one could just discern it, it would make one very rich indeed.

The Dancers, my sisters, flocked to the gamblers. One man cried out in victory as the dice he rolled found the right numbers; he clutched a nearby Dancer's hand, and she laughed and pulled him from his chair, into a Dance of Victory.

And then, suddenly, someone gripped my arm.

I nearly spilled my drink, but saw almost immediately that it was Carla. She looked wide-eyed, almost frightened, and my overjoyed greeting turned to ashes in my mouth. She tugged me urgently into a corner. I tried to indicate that I must stay here, but she would not listen, and only when we were shielded from view by a curtain, did she speak.

"What are you doing here?" she demanded.

Struck by her tone, I let my eyebrows furrow. "I – Carla, I'm so glad –"

"Don't you know what people are saying? And then – to come here! Dressed like –" Waving a hand, she indicated my fine dress, my delicate slippers, my hair so carefully looped over my metrónomo. "Like one of *us*!"

"I'm here because I need to be." I searched her eyes for the kind woman, only two years older than I, who had pressed her head to mine and told me I would dance beautifully as la Grulla. The only one of all my sisters, I think, who could recognise me underneath any mask.

"What need can you have here, with us?" she snarled. "If Maestra Tinir finds out –"

I cut her off. I didn't know where this was coming from, but I didn't want to hear any more. "Carla, please. You must help me."

"*Help* you? How can I help you? I should have already turned you in!"

I stared at her blankly. "Carla, what are you saying?"

"You truly don't know, do you?" She rubbed a hand across her forehead, displacing her sheer veil. A dark curl sprang free as her lips trembled. "Oh, Imre. They want to take you to the Pendulum. They came here searching, turnings ago, after you'd just left. When Maestra Tinir told them the Prince had taken a liking to you . . ."

I took her hands in mine, a reflexive gesture, but one she didn't pull away from. "Who?" I asked urgently.

"The heralds," she whispered, as if speaking their name would summon them.

At first I almost laughed. I had seen the hatred in la Boca's eyes, after all; but that had been across a crowded room, with none of them except Miguel knowing I was there. This, now; this was much closer to home.

My metrónomo throbbed.

"They broke her finger, Imre," Carla went on in the same whisper. "They said they would break her toes if she didn't tell them the truth."

My stomach roiled, and the knot in my heart clenched. "Did they hurt anyone else?"

She shook her head. "But if she hadn't told them, I fear they would have killed one of us."

I staggered a little, feeling for the wall.

"They said they needed to ensure proper punishment was taken. That it was the only way to ensure the continuation of the Pattern. The only way Tierra Mejór would ever be righted."

"You don't believe that, do you?" I croaked.

"The Brotherhood are our guides," she answered. "Why would they lie?"

"You haven't turned me in, though," I reminded her. "You have me here – warning me – instead."

She nodded. "You are my sister, Imre. Nothing will change that. But truthfully, I don't know what to believe. And people are dying."

I wished I could embrace her, as I would have in the past. But I knew I could not. "I'm sorry. I'm so sorry." I couldn't tell her it wasn't true. Because, how could I be sure?

And beyond that, what did it mean for me? Only that I couldn't ever come back, not for good. The heralds would kill them all just to get at me.

"You need to leave," she said. "I will help you get out, through one of the side doors . . ."

I shook my head. "I can't. I have to do something first."

She pulled her hands away, wiping frantically at the tears in her eyes. "No."

"Please," I said. "Just pretend you didn't see me. Tell me; is there a man here, who has opened a line of credit, paid, but not collected?"

She stared at me a moment. "What do you need to know this for?"

"Carla!" I implored. "It is very, very important!"

"There is a man," she said, very slowly. "He plays hacer julepe. He only arrived a few days ago, and he looks very . . . odd. He played seven rounds, and won seven gold coins, which he had one of the automata keep in circulation at the table rather than cashing out. Yui told me he likes the Room of Rocks. He likes . . . rough play."

"Can you tell me his name?" I asked, but she shook her head.

"Yui said he refuses to give it, even when he takes an assignation. But he's here now."

"He is?" I peered around the curtain. "Can you show me?"

Carla straightened, pulling herself together, and pointed across the room. "That's him."

I followed her perfectly shaped nail. The man was the only one playing at his table, which was manned by a copper-coated automaton, and he looked familiar. It took me a moment before I placed his dark hair and awkward frame – I had seen him on the tram, coming down the Calle del Corazón to the Pavilion, twice, dressed in oddly stiff clothes, just as he was now. He had a furtive manner about him, as if he had something to hide.

I turned back to Carla. "Can you please try and keep the others away? Just for a little while?"

She hesitated before she nodded. "But I can't help you if anyone else sees you," she said, and reaching out, she tugged a loose tendril of my hair. "That shine!"

"It's all I ask. Go, now."

She nodded and slipped out from behind the curtain.

***

Taking a deep breath, I followed, heading for the hacer julepe table. As I went, I carefully undid my hair, letting it fall down my back. Then, carefully avoiding the gazes of the other mecenas and their wives, and certain that my sisters were all in other parts of the room, I slipped into the seat beside the awkward man.

He turned away from the game to look at me.

"What are the odds?" I asked him sweetly, resting my chin on my hand.

He seemed startled, but his eyes told me he'd caught my unsubtle insinuation. "If I like what I see," he said, in that strangely clipped voice, "they improve exponentially."

"How about we make things more interesting, then?" I rose from my stool and circling him, trailed a fingernail across the back of his neck. I looked down at the cards in his hands, and frantically tried to remember what Miguel had taught me about the game. Three sevens, a two, and an ace. Were those cards any good?

"I must say, I'm tired of betting with cold, hard coin," he said.

"If you win the next hand," I purred, "you might take a more sensual prize instead."

He smiled widely, showing gaps in his yellowed teeth, and releasing a cloud of noxious breath. "Very well."

He played skillfully. The automaton dealt him three bad cards, but I leaned down and whispered in his ear. "Switch only the Three of Spades."

He looked at me as if I was stupid. Of a surety, he would have switched out the other sevens as well, hoping to get cards of a higher value. But when the automaton dealt him the next card, it with another seven. Four straight – an undoubted win.

"Congratulations, senor," the automaton said. "Would you like me to inform the Concerje to pay you out before you leave? You did say this would be your last game."

He nodded. "Certainly. Tell them to get it all ready while I'm occupied. But leave the seven gold – that will be played for at a later date."

"Oh." I pouted. "Are you leaving?"

"I have business," he replied enigmatically. "It requires me to leave the Cuidad, at least for now. But I still have time for you, my beauty."

I took him by the hand. Careful not to let my eyes wander to see if anyone had noticed me, however badly I wanted to, I led him to one of the side stairways, to ensure we wouldn't be seen.

"Which room do you choose?" I asked him.

He inclined his head, indicating that we were to go higher, to the Blue Rooms, at the very top of the central tower. The ones reserved for special *mecenas*. I had never used these rooms, but I moved confidently, not wanting to betray myself.

Choosing a door at random, I guided the man through it, then snicked it closed behind us.

This was a harsh room.

The walls were solid, cold stone, cut jaggedly. This, in my imagination, was what a grotto would have looked like, back on Old Earth. The globe-light was dim, set to permanent twilight. Under our feet was an uneven surface of moulded plaster, painted to look like more rock, and in one corner, a pool moved in ripples, created by a breeze from a vent in the wall. The sound it made was a loud, unceasing *shhhh, shhhh, shhhh* . . . strangely comforting, but so very alien.

There was no bed here, not so much as a chair – no concession to luxury. The floor was painted with the seven symbols, one for each of the companions, one for each Guild: a tree for the Gardener, an anvil for the Smith, an open book for Ante the Poet, and so on.

He took a seat on the edge of a rock and watched me.

I took a deep breath. The smell of his sweat was strong in my nostrils. His eyes lit up lasciviously.

Sometimes, it takes a while to discover what a mecenas desires. Several dances might be tried, until the right one become clear, and the movements synchronise. But with this man, I knew instantly what he wanted.

When I reached him, I kneeled on the uneven floor, my head still bowed. I took a breath, then, in and out. Was this truly to be my first time servicing a mecenas? Here, in this room? None of my sisters had taken a *mecenas* to a Blue Room on their first time. And I was no longer a Daughter!

Would it be like it was with the Prince? Hurried, leaving me slightly sore? Of course, it was not for me to judge a man. 'The Dance celebrates unity, a unity beyond physicality, beyond emotion, beyond thought. The Dance is unity with the Pattern.' Maestra Tinir had drilled those words into our minds during training sessions. But try as I might, I could not equate this man's large, flabby body with the Principe Regente's smooth, soft planes.

"In the name of the Pattern," I said, "I offer my body. For Aurelia's glory, I will dance. What is your will?"

And, as I'd known he would, he chose. "The Dance of Death."

I turned, I stepped, I whirled. I raised my arms, making my body long, showing him my curves, seeing his desire strengthen. I pirouetted back to him. Step, step. The symbols on the floor marked my movements. My metrónomo kept the time. I took his hand, raising him from the rock, feeling him shudder.

"So," I whispered. "What is it you do?"

He groaned.

I reached for his belt and slipped it free, then tugged gently at his trousers, until his *pene* sprang free. As I slid them to the floor, I gently felt the pockets. Nothing inside them, nothing to give me a clue as to who he was.

I gritted my teeth. Most mecenas were bursting to chatter about the important work they did. I had learned this as I had danced for my earliest mecenas, after my initiation – seven of them, each eager to spill their woes and worries as I practiced my movements, teasing them to the edge of ultimate pleasure.

But this man was different. How could I possibly discover his identity if he did not talk? Until this moment, I had refused to believe I couldn't do this. Now, failure seemed very, very real.

I lifted his shirt free and undid the buttons, one by one. Then I let my hair trail his bare chest as I pushed it off his shoulders. And there it was. A black tattoo of a wheel at the base of his neck.

I had only a moment to focus on it before he pushed me away, so hard that I stumbled. "Do not touch me," he hissed.

Startled, I fell, stepping on the hem of my dress. I was unable to keep from crying out, but at this sound, I sensed – and saw – his desire stirring. He let a hand fall lazily to his crotch, stroking his pene with long, slow, familiar movements.

Even if I hadn't seen him on the tram coming to the Pavilion, I had known this wasn't his first time.

This is for the Prince. This is to protect and serve him, and thus, Tierra Majór.

"By the Pattern," I began my parabra. "As a man and woman fit together, so do the parts of the world. In all things is the Pattern, and the Pattern is all things."

But what happened next was the last thing I had expected. He kept his eyes fixed on me, narrowed and unkind, but not once did he move towards me. "Filthy woman," he muttered beneath his breath. "Your hands are tainted with the sin of chaos. You will not touch me."

He went on, murmuring in this way and stroking himself until, finally, he shuddered and gave a low moan of release. His seed spurted onto his pallid thighs.

Some mecenas wanted only to watch the Dance to its completion, when the Dancer was divested of all clothing, and that was enough. My seven mecenas, whom I had danced for, coaxing and teasing, had been some of these – but they had known, once I turned eighteen, that they could return, and lobby for my first time. They had been gauging me, evaluating me, deciding whether or not I was a worthy candidate with which to serve the unity of the Pattern.

I hadn't expected a man fully capable, seasoned, and willing to want nothing more than to look at me, fully clothed.

He stood, breathing hard, then wiped his sticky thighs with a corner of the bedspread, and tugged up his trousers.

"Did you enjoy yourself, senor?" I asked him.

He gave a snort, then turned and walked towards the door. "I will ensure you are paid the amount you earned," he said, and then he was gone.

Left alone, I finally started to tremble. I couldn't believe I had succeeded. Aurelia must have helped me this day.

Chapter Thirty-Two

I slipped out of the room and into the hallway. It was, at the moment, revolving clockwise, in order to match the movements of the Cold-season room and the Flame room, both of which, by the sounds emanating from behind their doors, were occupied.

Picking up my skirts, I ran, virtually tumbling down the stairs, my slippers skidding on the polished marble, until I reached the right floor. Oh, it had been so long, but even though everything had changed, this place remained the same. I made the familiar steps, putting my hand on the doorframe, tracing the well-known grooves beneath my fingers. I stepped through, and into the room that had once been mine.

It was no longer.

The beds were the same, their sizes varying; we constantly fought over who got the larger ones, and sometimes deals were made to swap. Lace shrouds covered some, and more curtains hung from the ceiling.

There was a girl in the far bed, but her face was to the window, and her shoulders rose and fell with the rhythms of sleep. The others were empty, neatly made up, as Maestra Tinir insisted.

I crept inside, careful not to wake the sleeper. Slowly I sank onto the bed I had called my own. It wasn't the largest, but I knew the curves of its mattresses and the creaks it made when one moved. If I lay down, now, and closed my eyes, would I wake in my life as it was before? I ran my hands over the covers – they were new, and they smelled of another girl's perfume.

I stood. It wasn't the same. Most of all, what struck me about the room was how *small* it seemed. I didn't fit here anymore.

Crouching beside the bed, I reached underneath. A small, hard shape filled my hand. I drew it out. My tiny figurine of the blue woman.

I slipped it under my dress, tucking it into my underwear.

A set of back stairs took me to a side door. From there, using the curtains as cover, I swept through the Room of Roses.

It all seemed to be going perfectly, running like clockwork. Already in my mind I was outside in the street, finding Jark, and blurting out the truth of what I'd just discovered. But as I turned to the hallway that led straight ahead, something caught my eye, and a sudden curiosity halted me.

Light spilled from the door, halfway down the adjoining hallway to my right.

The infirmary.

The door was ajar, only slightly, but enough to show me that someone occupied the bed where I had lain with my ankle bruised and swollen. Which of my sisters was it? Had someone else been injured? And – the worst thought of all – had it been because of me?

If the Brotherhood had threatened Senora R., had they tortured one of my sisters as proof of their intent?

It was foolish. I knew it even as I did it, and I know it more so now, but I could not help myself.

I went to the door, and peered around its edge.

There she lay, her straw-coloured hair fanned out around her face. But her skin, oh, her beautiful, porcelain skin, was shrunken and sagging. Her cheekbones looked about to cut it through like knives. Purple-blue veins showed on her forehead, spreading like the legs of a dart-spider around her metrónomo. Her eyes were closed, though the lids fluttered like the wings of rasp-wasps. Her hands, just as pale, just as thin, were folded on her chest, on top of her blanket.

"Ketra." All other thoughts forgotten, I went into the room and put my hand atop hers. Feeling for the warmth and life I had always sensed from her, that vivacity that had given me strength during my darkest hour as I lay in this same bed; I found nothing. She was cold, slightly damp with sweat.

"Oh, Ketra, no," I sobbed. I bent over her, hoping to urge some semblance of life back into her. Those eyelids fluttered open.

"Imre," she murmured.

"I'm here," I told her desperately. "Ketra, what happened?"

She smiled, opening raw cracks in her lips, but her eyes filled with tears. "I displeased Aurelia."

I caught her tears on my fingers. "No, no, no. Never. My sister, you served Aurelia with your very breath!"

"I took my first," she whispered. Her voice was dry and hoarse, and she licked her lips. There was a glass of water on the table beside the bed, and I tilted it over her mouth. She drank greedily, then pushed my hand away. "You should not be touching me. It passes through contact, I'm told."

I looked at her pale hands, pushing me without strength. "What passes?"

"The illness. He died, yesterday; the man who was my first."

I set the glass back on the table, my mind whirling. The illness I had heard of, it had all been occurring in the Lower Tiers. How could it have spread here, to the Second? To Ketra, of all people? "You mean to say your mecenas gave this to you?"

She nodded, tears spilling from her eyes. "But you, Imre, why have you come? I didn't expect to ever see you again." A ragged, wheezing cough interrupted her. "Do you know, when first I saw you, I had this futile thought that you were Aurelia, come to take me Beyond."

I clutched her hands, and tightly. I could not divulge my true mission to her. Instead, I bent and kissed her forehead, and felt her sigh with happiness. "Aurelia is pleased with you," I said.

"What are you doing here?"

I leaped up, whirling, and found myself facing the Concerje. He didn't look calm and friendly, as the man I had known. In fact, he looked slightly confused, and I realised too late that he had recognised me.

"I was just going outside for some air," I said, blithely, and watched his eyes widen with surprise. "Took a wrong turn," I continued, trying to regain my haughty tone. My best defence here was probably to stick to my story and hope I could bluff my way out of this. "I drank too much wine. But I feel much better now. I've a mecenas waiting . . ."

For a moment, it looked as if my ruse might work; but then his eyes drifted to my hair. For all Jark's work at disguising me, my damned hair had given me away once more. I had forgotten to cover it after leaving the Room of Rocks. It fluttered in time with the ache in my heart.

The Concerje grabbed my arm. He was a tall man, and his grip was vice-like. In his hand he held his dagger-knife, keeping it low. He was practiced at this; sometimes unruly mecenas had to be encouraged to leave.

"There is no point in trying to run," the Concerje said. "You will not get far."

"I promise you, this is all a mistake," I said desperately, but it was no use. "Please. Please. Let me go."

The Concerje glanced around, clearly no more willing to make a fuss than I was. Thankfully, all was quiet, save Ketra's laboured breathing that broke my heart anew. Was this to be that last I would see her?

"Come with me," he said firmly, pulling me from the room, and into a side passage. My feet skidded in my slippers as he stopped before a mechanised door, and I knew exactly what lay beyond.

Or at least, I'd heard the stories. The Pavilion often had visitors who became rowdy with drink and drugs. The pen ensured they could be contained until they had calmed down.

The Concerje put his finger to the small, coin-sized pad in the centre, and with a slow hum of gears, the door slid open.

Beyond was a set of steps leading downwards.

At the bottom was a wide bay, from which the gouts of steam escaped, accompanied by the grinding of gears. Indeed, as we stepped through, I was treated to the sight of the workings of the Pavilion. Beyond a railing that edged the floor, there were gears larger than those I'd seen in the the Reloj's tower. A massive boiler glowed with burning heat, and the smell of hot grease filled my nostrils. At the far end of the platform, against the soot-blackened wall, was a sectioned area, caged with steel bars. The Concerje opened a door at one end and ushered me inside.

"I'll inform Senora R.," he said, relatching it firmly. I'm not sure whether he thought this a reassurance or not, but given what Carla had told me, it wasn't. My heart pounded so loudly, I couldn't hear his footsteps as he moved up the steps.

***

How long I was there I can't be exactly sure. My hair stuck to my forehead with the heat and moisture of the machinery, and my ears rang and popped in time to the turning of the great wheels. After pacing the length a hundred times – seven steps across, two wide – my ankle had begun to ache in my high heels, and I'd sat on a sooty metal shelf at one end, hoping it wouldn't stain my borrowed dress. Not that it mattered.

I waited for Senora R. I knew, once she saw me, the game would be up. She might not recognise me – in all my time at the Pavilion, I'd seen her only twice – but she would see the metrónomo. She would know my identity. She would know that I was the one the heralds sought.

I wasn't frightened, though. In fact, I was almost relieved. Senora R. might be a frightening figure, but it was because of her that I was at the Pavilion at all. Without her influence, I would still be nothing but a scrawny Third Tier street-rat, probably plying the same trade as my mother. And she had spoken in my defence against la Boca with such fire and ferocity; she cared for me, for all her Daughters, more than my own mother had.

When she came at last, led by the very self-important-looking Concerje, she looked much as I remembered her, but older. Creases marked her face, and her eyes crinkled at the corners. She still had the aura of slightly faded beauty about her, though her Dancer's toned muscles had gone to flab, and she breathed heavily through her mouth. The weight of rings on her fingers seemed to drag her shoulders down. I stood and pressed myself against the bars of the cage, my eyes filling with tears.

"Oh, Daughter," she cooed, coming across to stand just inches from the bars. Was it my imagination, or was she unsteady on her feet? "How ill you look, caged so. How do you come to be here?"

"I'm so sorry," I replied, my voice hoarse. "It is a long story, and I can't tell you all of it. Please, I must get back to the Citadel. I have important information."

Her eyebrow rose, as she turned to the Concerje. He shrugged as if to say, *I know not what she speaks of.*

"You can tell me what brings you back here, girl," she said. "After disgracing us by ruining the *Dance of a Thousand Steps.* Did the Prince tire of you so quickly?"

I stared at her. Now that I looked, I could see that her eyes were unfocused, the unsteadiness I had seen clearly evident. I could almost smell the poppy-smoke on her breath. "Senora, please. You must listen to me. The Prince's life is in danger."

"What danger could there be for the Prince of Tierra Mejór?" A slight smile twisted her lips. "Hm? Broken fingers, perhaps. Or worse?"

The knot in my heart clenched tightly, and fear began to take root.

She paced away, stopping to stare at the wall, then placed a hand to her forehead. "I used to be beautiful, once," she sang softly. "More beautiful than you. Did you know that?"

I shook my head, though she wasn't looking at me. "Please," I begged her. "You have to let me go."

She turned back, lurched towards the bars of the cage, and pressed her face close. Behind her, a sudden rush of steam filled the air, and a burst of light cast her in shadow. "They will kill all of them, one by one, if I set you free," she whispered, her voice cracking.

I didn't need to ask. I knew she meant my sisters.

"I have to get to the Prince. I have to tell him. Please."

"What will you tell him? What can he possibly need to know? Oh, Daughter," she sighed. "You've caused so much trouble already. You fate is in the hands of the Pattern now."

"No – you *can't* –" I almost screamed, but another jet of steam drowned out my voice. Senora R. turned and shuffled back across the platform.

The Concerje hurried after her.

***

I slid back down onto the dirty shelf and drawing my knees up to my chest, tilted my head back against the bars of the cage, trying desperately to calm my raging fear. How could I get myself out of here? How could I get this message to Jark and his rebels? Forget that – what did it mean for the Prince, that a herald was funding the Green-bands?

I couldn't think.

I must have dozed for a little while. I woke when I heard a voice, and struggled to sit up. But when I saw the Concerje with a bright glint in his eyes, I was instantly wary. What reason did he have to come back to speak to me?

As he unfasted his belt, I realised he had no intention of speaking at all. "What are you doing?" I called to him. "Senora R. will never allow this!"

"Senora R. is no longer your mistress." He smirked, cowed not at all.

"Why don't you fetch her and ask?" I said defiantly. "Don't you know who I am?"

He shrugged. "I assume your name is not one that would mean anything to me. But that's la Boca's concern, not mine."

He crossed the room, and slipped a key into the lock, opening the door. I tensed, the knot in my stomach roiling.

"I'm the Prince's mistress!" I shouted, but he did not stop. He came for me, grabbing my arm. I tried to jerk free, but he was strong. Far too strong.

"See?" the Concerje said. "You knows you want it. Little hussy like you – you spend your life on your knees, begging for a good, hard ride. Don't you, my sweet?"

I tried to keep the distaste off my face. *Pretend he's a mecenas,* I told myself. There were plenty of men I would have chosen not to spend time around, had a choice been involved. As it was, he wasn't the worst of them, looks-wise; it was his manner that appalled me. I wondered whether he had a wife at all, and I suspected not. He probably visited Red Houses to relieve himself, not out of necessity, but desire. Not for him the pleasure of the act, the union, the Dance; he wanted to degrade the woman he shared it with, making it into something dirty, a perversion.

At least the door was no longer locked, but to get to it, I would have to get past him.

I gathered myself. Three steps was all it would take, if I could make them fast enough. I eyed the cage wall – Maestra Tinir had trained me well. I could, possibly, leap and grab it higher up, swinging my way out of his reach. I had nothing to lose, after all.

I jumped, and he lunged, having anticipated my bid for freedom, though not my exact movement. He grabbed me around the waist, but my own momentum put him off-balance, and he fell against the side of the cage, squashing me under him. He wasn't heavy – he was only a little taller than I am – but I felt a jarring shock as my head hit the bars.

"You little talon-cat," he hissed in my ear, his words rolling together. It had been a mistake to try and flee. It had only incensed his desire. I could feel him now, poking through his trousers, and he shifted a little – at first, I thought he was just getting comfortable, and then I felt the prick of something sharp and cold against my neck. The silver letter opener.

Sticky wetness dripped into my eye. Blood.

I took a deep breath, trying to steady myself, but the room spun. If only I could have gotten my arms underneath him, I might have rolled his weight into the cage. But he was stronger than me. I struggled, and he tightened his grip around my arms and chest, squeezing until I couldn't breathe. Bright spots danced before my eyes.

His own breath was heavy, with more than exertion. Heat radiated from his skin, aflush under the spell of desire. Despite my fear and disgust, a profound sadness washed over me. This was not the dance. The dance involved consent from both parties, no matter the reasons behind the agreement. This was a perversion on the deepest level. How many others had he done this to? Red House whores? Other young women? Men? Did he hold this blade to their necks while he took them?

To me, Feval, all the other automata, seemed far more human than this creature. He locked one strong arm around me, keeping the blade flush with my skin, and fumbled at his belt, unzipping his trousers. The rod of hot flesh pressed into my buttocks. He yanked up my skirts, cursing when he found my undergarments barring his way. He ripped those from me, and I felt a pang as the fine silk tore. Lifting me bodily, he thrust me into the cage wall. The cold metal cut into my skin in a crosshatch pattern, and, remembering all Maestra Tinir's instructions, I slipped my fingers through the grille for purchase. If I could rear backwards, I could knock him out, or at least break his nose – though it wouldn't stop him cutting my neck with that damned knife. But even if I survived that, how would I get out of here – even if I could get back through the door without a fingerprint, dozens of vigilar still swarmed the main room.

"You're going to wish you'd tried this years ago, sweetness," he whispered, and then he ran his tongue along my neck, from my collarbone to my earlobe, licking the blood oozing from the wound. I twisted away, revolted.

And then – then he slipped sideways with a curse. At first, all I was aware of was that his weight was gone and I could breathe. Then the cage started to vibrate under my fingers. A rumbling started in the floor below my feet, and I realised the Concerje had fallen to the floor, twisting his knee. He struggled to get back up, hampered by his own trousers, but the rumbling swelled until it felt like someone was pounding beneath the stone floor, trying to get through from the earth below. The cage swayed as if made of string, and dust rained down in sheets, clotting the air. Then there was a tremendous *crack*, and the very stones in the wall split apart. Two of them, high up near the ceiling, shook free, and I crouched with my hands over my head. The Concerje, hobbled by the pants around his ankles, couldn't shield himself so well. One stone fell with a sound like a melon splitting, onto his head. Blood spurted, mixed with something grey and fatty, and he dropped senseless to the floor, the silver blade skittering into the corner.

I stayed where I was as the rumbling subsided. There were a few quieter aftershocks, and then, finally, it faded to nothing. I raised my head.

"Go," I told myself, and I went.

With every step, I was afraid the tremors would start up again, but, apart from a few echoing *bangs*, there was an eerie silence. I reached the door, and pressed my hands against it, half-hoping the tremors had loosened it or broken the lock. No such luck. It was just as solid as before.

I turned to the other rooms in the hallway. They were small and cell-like, with no windows – of course, this was a highly secure area, and deep inside the building to boot. There were vents high up in the ceiling, letting in cold air as the fans churned out the dust, but they were barely a handspan wide.

Reluctantly, I returned to the metal door.

It was a touch-lock. I knew how they worked. A crystal pad sensed the markings on your finger. If they didn't match the memory inside, it wouldn't unlock. And stay locked it would, unless you had a controller wand to override it.

I didn't.

My heart shot up into my throat. I did *not* want to do this, not under any circumstance. But how else was I to get out of here? This plan had been foolish from the start; it had all hinged on no one guessing I wasn't who I said I was. I'd set these events in motion. Now I had to finish them.

I turned and plunged back through the dust-laden air. The Concerje was sprawled where he'd fallen. A good deal of blood was pooling around his scalp, and I knew this was a bad sign. Living blood gushed. The blood of the dead oozed in precisely this way.

I tried not to look at him as I turned him over. His face was pale, his jaw slack. His pene, flaccid now, flopped piteously. His eyes stared glassily at nothing, or at something beyond this realm. I knew even before I tried that I wouldn't be able to lift him.

"Oh, no," I moaned.

As if in encouragement, the discarded dagger gleamed through the slowly settling dust.

I picked it up, held the Concerje's hand in my spare palm. Then I pushed on the blade.

I had expected it to cut cleanly, but while the blade was sharp enough to have nicked the soft skin of my neck, it took considerable pressure to make an impact on a man's finger. At first I was almost certain it wouldn't be enough to cut through, but I pressed harder, and with a *pop*, it sliced through to the bone. Blood dripped lazily, still-warm, onto my hands. My stomach roiled and the knot clenched tighter.

It was harder to do than I thought; the sticky blood made it hard to hold the digit securely. In the end, I gripped it and yanked hard. The connecting tissue stretched wetly, and I sawed the blade through it. It came free in my hand.

"Got it," I said, disbelievingly. I stood, clutching the bloody letter opener and the finger, and dashed back down to the door. My hands shook as I pressed the finger to the small button, and it was hard to hold it still. For a long moment, I waited, almost certain it wouldn't work, but then came a solid *click* and the door swung free.

The hallway was empty. Even what I could see of the Room of Roses through the archway at the end seemed deserted. In the time it had taken me to cut off the Concerje's finger, most of the people had fled, and those who hadn't lay scattered on the floor, unmoving. Even the automata were gone, rescued, probably, by those quick-thinking enough to realise that an automata was just as valuable as their own lives.

Papers littered the floor and a few chairs were overturned, but apart from this, the only damage seemed to be to one of the huge stone pillars, which had crumbled at the top. A pile of rubble lay below it, covering two human-shaped bundles.

Two other figures were dashing towards one of the side doors, but they were in too much of a hurry to pay me any attention. I tried to do the same as I made my way across to the main exit.

I was almost out, almost free, when the doors burst open, and vigilar thundered in.

"Hold!" one of them called. He left his fellows, crossing the floor in a few quick strides. His eyes focused upon my metrónomo, and his eyebrows shot upwards; that was before he noticed the blood on my dress. "Are you injured, Daughter?"

I struggled for an answer, one that would sound believable, but instead I stood there gaping unintelligently. It aroused his suspicions enough, and he took me by the arm – and it was then that we simultaneously realised I was still clutching the concerje's severed finger.

The man frowned, as if he didn't quite comprehend what he was seeing, or thought it was fake. A beat of my metrónomo, and then – a man wearing a green-banded hat, crashed into him. The vigilar went flying, and so did his revolver-pistols; one, into a nearby pillar, with a resounding crack, the other, into the air, to land in the man's hand.

He smiled cockily, his lips split by a twisted scar. "Well, that worked out better than I thought! Come on, Imre. There's no time to be idle."

"I —" I squeaked.

"I would think I'd find more gratitude, for having just saved you." His eyes lighted on the finger, which I still clutched tightly. "What in all heavens have you got there?"

I wondered if I could run; probably not faster than he could pull the trigger on that gun. "I was trapped," I said helplessly. "I had to get free."

"You," he said after a moment, "seem like a girl after my own heart."

"You are la Rebelde," I breathed.

"Am I?"

"You are — aren't you?" I wasn't so sure now, whether he was, or was just a supporter.

He bowed then, which was neither a confirmation or denial, and held out his arm. When I looked at him warily, he sighed.

"Would you rather wait here for the other vigilar to return?"

I pulled my hair to cover my metrónomo, took his arm, and he removed the hat from his head and folded it into a pocket. We walked out of the Pavilion, looking like husband and wife, virtually unnoticed.

Chapter Thirty-Three

Outside, it was impossible to believe that the stars still shone in the sky. I could see distant clouds of smoke, and there were a few clusters of people at the bottom of the steps, but though some turned our way, and one of them called out, Jark and I paid them no heed as we slunk, quiet as street-foxes, back into the shadows. There, I took my companion's arm, and turned him to face me.

"Your man," I said, "is a herald."

He took a moment to digest this, but he didn't look shocked – certainly not as appalled as I had been to see the black tattoo, in any case.

"You're not surprised," I said.

"Let's just say I had a suspicion. Otherwise, why would I have sent you on this mission?"

Anger burned, a hot rock just below my heart. "You put my life in danger because you had an inkling?"

"Come now, Imre," he said, with a smile that seemed a little self-depre-cating. "You were already in danger."

I sighed and pushed my hair back behind my shoulders.

"Come," he said. "I'm eager to make sure everyone is safe at the headquarters."

His youth showed through once more. I let him lead the way, kicking off my shoes so I could move quieter and quicker. My feet, which used to be callused from walking these very streets, then from dancing, were growing soft. I felt the cold seeping in through my skin.

We arrived back at the Third Tier, and found *The Nightingale's Song* almost deserted, but, at least, still standing. A fire burned somewhere up the street, and I supposed people were helping contain it – or looting the shops nearby while everyone else was distracted.

Jark knocked at the door three times, then pushed it open. There were three men inside, and one woman, a green ribbon tied in her hair; each of them looked up with soot-streaked faces. How like the Conclave this was, this gathering of rebels; a mirror held up to those wealthy, privileged men and women I had seen in the Council Chamber – a gathering of the destitute, in an attempt to accomplish something for the people of Tierra Mejór.

My eyes sought only Grath, and then Feval, and when I found both, I breathed a sigh of relief.

Grath, still with his hands and legs bound, was propped up against the wall. His gaze landed on me, fixing with such fervour that I was a little taken aback. Had he actually been worried? Not just that I might endanger the Prince, or that the Prince might be upset that I was missing – but for me?

"The Avenida Bridge was lost," one of the men was saying. "Several food-carts with it, and at least seven people, possibly a child."

"I've seen at least three separate fires," another joined in. "Still, this did not seem to hit as badly as the first one. Perhaps we'll be lucky, and it will be the last."

"It won't," said Grath roughly.

Jark held up his hands. "Speculation can wait while we deal with facts. Imre has confirmed that the man we suspected is in fact a herald. He's been donating so heavily to our cause, and I, fool that I am, have been taking every last penny, and thanking him for it."

"So, what does this mean, exactly? Why would the Brotherhood be funding the Green-bands?" I didn't know if it was my place to ask, but ask I had to.

"There are only two possibilities. One is that he is a kind of rebel himself, or thinks he is. The other is that he is not, and is doing so for some as yet unfathomable reason."

"What do you do with the money you receive?" I asked.

"We feed our families," said Jark shortly. "Those who don't have the means to feed themselves. We pay-off the vigilar, to look the other way while we paint our slogans on the sides of factory walls. We buy clothing and shelter for people on the Fourth Tier; we offer them the chance and the assistance to move up to the Third, if they agree to spread our message. You would be surprised how many take up that offer."

I don't know why, but I felt slightly shamed at his answer. I'd never imagined that what the Green-bands were doing was so extensive – or so vital.

Another thought was dawning on me, however, a much darker one, all the more so for being realistic. "If the Brotherhood are knowingly donating to the Green-bands, it can only be for a nefarious purpose. After all, you are breaking every law they hold dear."

"This is true," said Jark, settling into a chair and cupping his chin with his fingers.

"So why would they encourage you to continue?" Warming to the topic, I found my thoughts spilling over. "The only reason can be that they want you to spread the unrest."

I looked sideways at him, and he sighed. "There are many twists and turns to that tale. Suffice it to say that the Principe Regente has only compounded his fate by refusing to take a wife or produce a child who might carry on the royal line. At its very heart, it's the simplest question ever asked; who stands to inherit the power, should the one who may rightfully claim it is removed?"

This question, I could answer. "I suppose it would be la Boca, at least until another heir is traced."

"They want," Grath spoke up from his corner, "to take the throne. To throw the Principe Regente to the street-foxes. They have more than enough reason to do so; he is hardly the good and levelheaded leader Tierra Mejór needs. Only one thing stands in their way – the belief of the people that La Reina will soon name him as Principe Verderaro."

"An assassin was sent after him." I picked up the thread of his argument, spinning it before the Green-bands. "Chette. Who was hired by a man who had dealings with the White Pavilion. Possibly the very same herald."

Jark assimilated all this with a ponderous expression. "If the Prince was killed while you were in his suite, Imre," he said slowly, "the blame might easily be pinned on you."

A sharp needle of ice stabbed my chest. No. Surely it couldn't. But . . .

Jark nodded, his hat slipping to one side. "The heralds have always controlled the balance of power. The weather, trade, wealth. All passes through the Pendulum. I suppose, until now, they have been happy to do so from a distance, as a silent shadow in the background. But something has changed."

"It could only be the tremors," I said.

"Most likely," Jark agreed. "Perhaps they see this as their chance to seize what they've always coveted."

Grath looked to me. "Feval knows better than any of us."

Feval inclined his head in a strangely dignified gesture. "I am tied to the workings of Tierra Mejór. Just as any machine is. I have felt the slow winding down, the oddities and irregularities, for a long time. Ask any automata remaining, and they will tell you the same, if they are still capable of speech. The sentinela will also know, and the servitors; the rotor-trams and shuttle-trains. We feel it as you feel your own heartbeats."

"Then why don't you tell them?" I burst out. "Just tell the Brotherhood. They're so powerful – perhaps there is something they can do to fix this! If they know it's not me, they'll have no reason –"

"Imre," Grath snapped. "I told you, in the tower, that my telescope was not the only one of its kind. It was modelled after another."

I tried to remember. "Oh. On the Pendulum."

Grath nodded slowly. "That is so. The Brotherhood knows of the slowing, or, at least, the heralds do. The Pendulum has felt its effects long before we have. The Thread which ties the weighted end to the Spindle has been slackening for years."

"In any case, it doesn't bode well for the Prince," spoke Jark. "I would advise getting him to Rueda, to his Estate, as soon as you can."

Grath nodded. "The arrangements have already been made. If you would be so kind as to release me –" this, with a sardonic lilt in his voice – "I will see if we cannot leave tonight, under the cover of the darkness and the chaos of the quake."

Jark nodded towards the men, who set about slitting the ropes on Grath's wrists and ankles.

"But there may be something else we're missing. Something about this doesn't quite fit," he said as Grath grunted at the pain of his returning circulation.

"What doesn't?"

"You, my Lady." Jark glanced at me. "The heralds want you, and badly. La Boca has been insisting that you are to be given over to the Brotherhood. If killing you, or getting you out of the way would truly right the wrongs of the world, they could have done so easily. There were times, after you fell at the Dance but before you were taken to the Citadel, that you were unguarded. There were times since then, as well. Why, in all of Tierra Majór, do they want you, so incredibly badly?"

And to this, I had no answer at all.

***

I'm not sure when I started to shake – some time very soon after this. It came upon me suddenly, and once it started, it would not stop, as if the quake had started some tremor deep inside that was now forcing its way out.

I had been talking, still, to Jark, but then my memory fades a little. I remember a blanket being placed around my shoulders, a few concerned words, and then myself repeating, over and over, that I was fine.

My next clear thought was that Grath was about to leave. "Don't. Please." I think it must have sounded pathetic, but at that moment I didn't care. I didn't want to be alone. I didn't want Grath going into danger.

"Imre, I must," Grath replied softly. I felt his hand on my shoulder, heavy, comforting. "We cannot risk sending a carrier-pigeon. It might be intercepted. As it is, Feval must stay here with the Green-bands – he is too much of a risk. Go with Jark – he will keep you safe."

I didn't want to be safe if he wasn't. I wanted to gather everyone who'd ever meant anything to me together – Tomas, Ketra, Carla, Feval, Thaniel, Miguel – and keep them somewhere, in some form of haven, while these frightening things went on without an effect on us.

"Imre?" He put his fingers under my chin to lift my face. "We will be with you before you know it."

I tried to manage a small smile, and I'm not sure if I succeeded, but at least he smiled back. The sight of that filled me with warmth. "Please," I said. "Be careful."

He was gone in the next instant.

What happened to Grath during his absence I will relate later. For my part, the events of the next few hours were unclear.

I washed the blood of the concerje from my skin and changed from my ruined dress back into my guildswoman's garb. I put my figurine in the pocket, alongside with my bent feather, and the pack of playing cards, then pinned up my hair and covered it tightly with Xith's scarf.

An autocarriage was found, I know not where. In the confusion on the streets, it was barely noticed. We walked a little way down the block, where it was hidden behind some scrubby bushes.

Feval, his arms reengaged with a few quick twists by one of the men, raised a clanking hand in farewell, and my heart ached to leave him behind.

Instead, Jark slid in behind the wheel, and cranked the engine. I braced my hands against the seat, wondering if I would ever get used to this. Then we were off, traversing the darkness.

We took some back way, up through another little-used lock gate to the Second Tier. Then, we went through a long dark tunnel. The streets sloped down, rather drastically, with many twists and turns. This was the residential area for those who could afford houses with land around them, rather than apartments in the crowded Eastside blocks. Some of them looked almost as grand as the Citadel, and if they weren't as big, they were still large enough for ten families to live inside.

"How can people look after such places?" I asked.

Jark waved a hand. "There is wealth to be flaunted, even in these times."

Slowly, as we descended, the buildings changed – large, boxy warehouses and factories hogged the landscape. Looming over them were the tall latticed pillars of cranes. Even the scents in the air were sharp and strange: spices, wood shavings, fertiliser.

On we went, winding our way to the West, passing a few rotor-trams hauling goods in large metal containers, and a few scattered pedestrians on their way home from late shifts, or on to early ones; most were not wearing Guild-belts, as they were of the Fourth Tier and could never hope to obtain that kind of rank. They were the lowest paid of workers, their provinces – the stinking sewerage pipes, or the hard days and nights hauling cargo at the docks. They glanced at our car with tired eyes, no doubt cursing us for being the spoiled rich people from the houses we'd just passed, their Guildmasters, or wealthy merchants.

We arrived at the shuttle-train station after another few minutes. It was a large building, open at both ends, so the trains could pass through into the cargo yards. I stared at the messy network of tracks and signal lights, as a huge black-and-yellow engine puffed its way slowly into the darkness.

It was noisy inside, despite the early hour, a chaotic scene as people fled the destruction, or hurried home to see what they still had left. A large board hung from the ceiling, listing departure times, but several of the labels made no sense at all, and the clock was frozen on seven chimes. I could make out at least three shuttle-trains, but the clouds of smoke pouring from their engines filled the space like heavy mist, turning them into hulking shapes. The platforms were linked by arching bridges, the figures of both passengers and workers scurrying over them.

I had no idea where we were supposed to go, but Jark seemed to know the way. He directed us towards a glassed-in counter that had a sign saying, "Tickets".

"You will have to buy your own," Jark told me. "It will look much less suspicious, since you are supposed to be a Ruedan returning home. I already have a pass, since I travel frequently."

I had never purchased a train ticket in my life, and I wasn't even sure how to.

Lacking his green-banded hat, Jark looked oddly inconspicuous, despite the scar across his mouth. It must have been quite a skill, to blend so easily in any crowd, to look as if one belonged, no matter the place. "I've sent a carrier-pigeon on ahead," he told me. "I have men on Rueda, as well. The man who will be meeting us is a vigilar, one we can trust implicitly. He knows who you are, and will ensure your safety in getting to the Estate."

I nodded and took a deep breath.

"You'll be buying tickets to South Gate," Jark assured me, as he pressed two silver coins into my hands. "That's all you need to ask for – two tickets to South Gate. You won't be the only one going there, surely. You'd better hurry, though, or we'll miss out on a seat."

I looked around, nervously, seeing no one I could recognise through the frantic swarm.

"They will come," Jark told me with a knowing look. "Believe me, that man, Grath? He will make it happen. Go on, now. I will wait here and keep an eye out for your companion."

The line at the ticket counter moved far too slowly, and I was worried that I looked conspicuous without any luggage. People jostled and pushed, several of them stealing my place in the line before I'd finally had enough, and shoved my own way forward with a few well-placed jabs of my elbows. By the time I reached the counter, I looked just as red-faced and grumpy as the others who'd spent long minutes being bumped and pushed, which I suppose fitted in with my disguise.

"Two tickets," I said to the man behind the desk, proffering my fare. "To South Gate."

The man glanced at me. "Reason for your visit?"

Caught off-guard, I furrowed my brow and gripped my Horticulturalist's belt. "For the sake of the Heavens," I snapped. "My apprentice and I need to return to our work."

He held up a hand defensively. "I'm required to ask. There are more instances of this illness, and those who have no urgent business on the Wheel are urged not to travel."

He cranked a lever on his machine, which spat out two tickets stamped with a time and date. "Platform Two. It says nine-twenty departure, but that's wrong – we've got an issue with the timers. Shuttle leaves seventeen minutes from now, sharp."

He handed me a few coins in change, and I turned away, tucking the tickets into my pocket.

"I knew I saw a familiar face!"

The voice startled me, and so did the sudden grip on my arm. I whirled, and found myself facing an older woman wearing grey garb and a horticulturalist Guild-belt. It took me a moment to place her, but then I saw two younger women approaching, holding pink ice creams that were running down the sticks. Of course. It was the Ruedan and her two daughters I had met at the ball. The one who had pushed me to dance.

My heart leaped into my throat, but it wasn't me she was looking at – rather, she embraced Jark and kissed his cheek, leaving behind a sticky red imprint of her lips. "How are you, Benoi?"

"Well, Liliath! Very well indeed!" Curiously, Jark's voice had changed, become lighter and less gruff. In fact, he sounded almost feminine. "You must meet my friends – on their way to South Gate, they are! This is Lady Arabel. And . . . this is her apprentice, Anders."

I turned, my heart pounding, to see the Prince and Miguel. It took me a moment to recognise Thaniel, for his hair had been cut, and dyed black. His clothes were old and worn. With his sunken eyes and drawn cheeks, his disguise would easily fool anyone who didn't know him.

I knew him. And so did la Boca.

It unnerved me, to see him guarded only by Miguel in such a public place. Not that I doubted Miguel – who had swept me into a large, comforting hug. "Imre, if they had *hurt* you, in any way . . ."

"I am fine," I assured him, but I hugged him back just as tightly. "Are there no vigilar to travel with us? No guardia?"

Miguel shook his head. "Senor Grath's orders. No one is to know."

"You will be coming, won't you?" I pressed him, desperately.

He shook his head again. "Senor Grath wouldn't allow it. We have to guard La Reina. And if what he said is even half the truth, you will be better off on your own."

I let him go, and saw that there were traces of tears in his eyes.

"Do I trust them?" he whispered, his gaze flicking to Jark. I knew whom he meant – the Green-bands. A bead of warmth flickered in my heart that he would trust my judgement on this.

"*I* do."

Miguel nodded. "Good enough for me. Please take care of yourself, Lady Arabel."

"I will."

I found myself still under Liliath's gaze. "Arabel," she murmured. "Of course – we met at the dance. I was quite certain you had broken your ankle."

I spread my arms. "As you can see, I'm well enough."

"Off to South Gate, as well?" she said. "You must travel with us, my dear. And who is this?"

"This –" I began, but Thaniel stepped forward, taking the woman's hand.

I had been worried that she might recognise him under his dyed hair and costume, but it seemed not. Of course, he was sober for once, which she'd probably never witnessed. Nor did she seem to think it odd that Thaniel was the same age as his Maestra – I had heard it was fairly common in Ruedan guilds, as they had fewer skilled hands to choose from.

"I'm so pleased to run into you both. Benoi's friends are always delightful company. Benoi, you must tell me how you met them." She glanced back at her two girls, laughing as they tried to keep their ice creams from dripping all over their dresses. "This is my daughter, Naia, and my niece, Aiva. They're apprentices in the moth refinery, along with me, though the Pattern knows they'll have forgotten how to sort a Green moth from a Grey by the time we return." She rolled her eyes. "But what do you say? We might as well fight for a seat together." She gestured towards an iron bridge, where a sign pointed towards Platform One.

"Our tickets are for Platform Two," I told her.

She glanced at the pieces of paper in my hands. "Oh, that's no matter. They never check."

As much as I didn't want to sit with her – she seemed far too gossipy for my current mood – I was relieved when Jark took charge, linking his arm with hers. "Of course! You must tell me about the latest fashions . . ."

Crossing the station was an experience in itself. Never had I seen so many people from so many different places at once! There were dark-skinned Ruedans, pale night-workers, servitors carrying bags and frantically whirring at their masters' heels, and even a few sentinela in their dark armour. Several women strolled about dressed as only Red House workers would, in gauzy fabrics that left little to the imagination, despite the chilly air, and Thaniel's eye was caught by each of these with far too much alacrity for my liking.

Platform One was across one of the arched bridges, so we got a good look at a shuttle-train from above, snaking into the distance, steam jetting from between its wheels and carriage roof vents. The front carriages were made up of freight cars, probably empty on their return trip to Rueda, and the passenger cars sat behind. Another shuttle-train was chugging at the opposite platform, passengers already boarding. There were two or three tracks running out along each of the four spokes to Rueda, so we would probably be travelling alongside this other train for most of the journey.

Our carriage was already mostly full by the time we arrived. We found our way to a car occupied mostly by youngsters, novice cargomen and women, Lilliath informed us, on their way back from training in the dockyards. "At least we won't be starved for entertainment on the journey."

That much was clear. The children were fractious, arguing and fighting, tearing up and down the two aisles, pulling on one another's hair. We managed to find six seats facing one another at the rear of the carriage, with a window on one side. Thaniel insisted I sit next to it. I had a feeling he wasn't doing this out of the kindness of his heart, but rather so he could have an excuse to sit opposite Naia and Aiva, leaving Liliath opposite me. He promptly pulled out a cigarillo and lit into it. I could feel his tension and hoped the giggling girls, who were now exchanging licks of their ice creams, would prove distracting enough. Jark took the seat in the aisle, which I suspected was deliberate, so he could keep an eye on what was happening along the length of the carriage.

"Whereabouts do you work in South Gate?" Liliath asked me. "I haven't seen you in any of my areas, have I?"

"We've only just recently moved there," I said, trying to think of all I knew of Rueda. Tomas had told me plenty when we were younger, having been friendly with a few Ruedans who regularly crossed over from the Wheel with their parents. *The Cultivated Tree and its Uses* helped as well, but the facts were abstract and distant. "We worked in the vegetable patches, near the Estate."

"Oh, that would explain it, then!" she said. "And your ability to dance. I've heard they hold a lot of parties. I suppose they must have the time for it." She laughed. "Not so in South Gate!"

"No indeed," I agreed.

"It seems we've got the worst of things, doesn't it? With all these failures. The vegetables will flourish, even without the irrigation channels; the orchards can be hand-watered, and they'll still produce passable fruit, even if much of it is small and spotted. But the white-moths will not be able to hatch without the warmth of the heat pipes, and the ceramic is cracking apart faster than we can repair it. I don't know how they expect us to cope. There will be a reduced shipment this time, and even fewer next."

"Are they still using ceramic? Why don't the Guild replace that outdated stuff with metal?" I asked her, and then backtracked. "Forgive me if that's a stupid question. I'm more used to growing carrots than moths."

Liliath nodded. "Oh, well, that's easy enough. Metal is too hot. It doesn't radiate heat in the same way. The moths burn themselves if they get too close. And besides, the pipes run through the walls of the moth-chambers. We can't very well remove them without replacing every cocoon tunnel."

"I see," I said, though I still didn't know exactly what she was talking about. I hadn't known moths were born in tunnels and farmed in bays, but I filed this away for future reference, and hoped Thaniel was paying attention.

The carriage gave a sudden jolt, and I clutched instinctively at the seat. Beside me, Thaniel grabbed at the wooden armrest, almost dropping his cigarillo. When he saw that I'd noticed his fidgeting, he looked apologetic. "I don't like travelling," he said in a plaintive voice.

"It's all right," Jark piped in soothingly. "The shuttle-trains are piloted automatically. Their speed is regulated by internal workings, linked to the Core so they will be timed to miss the passing of the Tether. There's nothing to fear."

Except, I wasn't sure I trusted the system anymore, so this wasn't much of a comfort; too much of it was breaking down and going wrong.

With a loud hiss, the brakes released. Steam billowed up past the window, and with a long whistle, the train pulled out. The platform slid by, slowly at first, then faster and faster. A few onlookers waved, but then they too were gone; we were out of the station and racing into the night.

We whizzed by the buildings and yards surrounded by high chain-link fences, then dove right under one of those huge cranes, the magnetic hook on the end of its cables swooping back and forth in the night breeze and the vacuum created by the passing shuttle-train. Then, we picked up speed again until everything was a blur of lights and distant jagged shapes against the low, silver-tinged clouds. Everything except la Grulla.

Liliath chattered on about this and that, trivial things, such as how the fashions in the Cuidad compared to those in the few outlets in Rueda. Occasionally she would turn to one of the girls and prompt them for their agreement, but for the most part I found myself nodding and smiling. It seemed to be all the response she required.

My gaze drifted to the window, and, despite the roiling feeling in my stomach created by the rocking motion, I found myself drifting towards sleep. Then, I realised the shuttle-train was rising.

No – not rising, of course, but travelling steadily upwards. We had crossed smoothly onto the moving section of track that would transfer us onto the Spoke.

It was a curious sensation, as if I was at once weightless and heavier, being pressed back into my seat at the same time every jolt threatened to send me floating into the air. I tried to keep the alarm off my face, given that I was supposed to have travelled along the arms before, but the knot in my stomach clenched tight.

Thaniel sucked energetically on his cigarillo, keeping his gaze firmly ahead so there was no chance of catching an accidental glimpse out the window. Wedged where I was, short of closing my eyes, I was stuck watching as the buildings turned on their sides and the ground rose up behind us. Surely, surely gravity would pull us back! But while the carriage rattled, adjusting to the new direction, it held to the tracks firmly.

As I looked down, I could see through the gap between the Third Tier and the Fourth, as I never had before, directly down into the massive inner workings where the Tether ran deep into the body of the Spindle. There were enormous gears down there, churning with the power of a great internal engine, but visible were only the faint glint of metal teeth, highlighted by a soft red glow, and a gathering of shadows. I had heard of the mechanics behind this from one of my mecenas; the Pendulum turned at a fraction of time faster than the Spindle itself, as did the Wheel. Every shuttle-train had to time its journey perfectly, to ensure the tracks were locked in the right position to both miss the Tether, and link with the track that led out along the Spoke. No shuttle-train could be longer than seven carriages, or the last carriages would not make it onto the arm before the tracks disconnected.

As with many things, knowing the theory of it, and seeing it in action, were entirely different matters.

I could only just see the connecting track by pressing my cheek to the window; it was a curved bridge, dipping down as it swooped over the Fourth Tier. Below the Fourth, the arms of the Wheel spun. Even as I watched, one passed by, and all that was left ahead of the sloping track was the murkiness of the sky. It seemed sure that we would plunge directly over the edge, but the shuttle-train did not slow.

A loud thump, and the carriage jerked, but none of the passengers batted an eyelid. It was markedly rougher than the first crossing, since the gap was proportionately larger, but the train had crossed successfully onto the Spoke.

I checked to see if the Prince was watching with the same fascination I was, but he steadfastly puffed on his cigarillo, ignoring everything else. I turned back to the window and saw another shuttle-train, running along one of the other tracks, travelling slightly faster than ours. There were people in the rear carriages, looking out at us just as we were at them. The children in our carriage scrambled to wave at our counterparts, and cheered when a few of the passengers waved back. Then it had pulled ahead, and we were alone in the night.

After this, the journey became a long wait for our destination. The children fell asleep one by one, then Naia, Aiva, and Liliath. Thaniel slumped sideways, his cigarillo burned to a stub. Finally, it was only Jark and I who were still awake.

"Benoi?" I asked him, raising an eyebrow.

"At times, it becomes necessary to adopt other identities," he said.

"That must be confusing," I prodded with a lighthearted laugh.

He shrugged. "Benoi is actually much easier to maintain. I'm not sure what the reason is; perhaps she was what I would have been, had I not chosen my path."

"Benoi is a woman." Now I was intrigued. I had thought of Jark as a male, but suddenly realised he could be either. Oh, I'd seen plenty of my sisters play at being men, for the pleasure of their mecenas, or their own. But the ease with which he maintained the mannerisms, the speech, the carriage of his body. That was infinitely harder to feign. "Tell me about the Green-bands?"

"What is there to tell?" He spread his arms, giving that enigmatic smile.

"Plenty, I suspect," I said. "I have always thought of you as the enemy. I daresay most of the population of the First Tier does as well, since you paint your slogans all over their property."

"We are not the enemy of anyone." He sighed. "But it doesn't surprise me to hear those words. In fact, I'm glad."

"Glad?" I repeated incredulously, but he was perfectly serious.

"We cause chaos where we can. It makes people think outside the Pattern."

"How can you disrupt the Pattern? It simply exists." I frowned. "In all things. Why do this?"

"What force in this world exists without opposition?" he shot back. "Dark exists because of light – and light because of dark. The Pattern does not exist without Chaos."

I mulled over it, approached it that way and this, but ultimately I understood it best when I didn't think on it too deeply. It's like telling a person not to think of a honey-pie. Inevitably, the first image that springs to mind is a honey-pie; a kind of reverse suggestion. And it had worked brilliantly.

Chapter Thirty-Four

Soon I drifted into a kind of waking dream, where I was sitting in a chair inside a large dome of glass, being rocked backwards and forwards gently.

I gasped when a piercing sound jerked me awake.

Liliath was rousing her charges, but by the look of alarm on her face, I could tell we hadn't arrived at our destination. Still, the shuttle-train was slowing, with many great jolting clanks. I turned to the window.

Far, far below glittered the pinprick lights of the Cuidad. The silver points of the stars shined closer, much larger than I'd ever seen them – los Amantes, the Lovers, the Yellow Planet, and the bright gaseous form of Constanza. But all that was eclipsed as I beheld the uneven shape of la Grulla, circling into view over what could only be the curving edge of the Wheel.

I was transfixed by her beauty. From the ground, she had always seemed a jagged shape; even through Grath's telescope, her true form was indiscernible. But here, where the atmosphere was thinner, I could marvel at the rounded shape of her belly, the outstretched wings, the graceful neck. She must be truly huge!

But her light was blinding. My eyes burned to look at her too long, and it was what she showed in her light that alarmed me. We had caught up to the other, faster shuttle-train. Except, it had slowed considerably, and copious amounts of steam hissed out from between its wheels.

And its front cargo carriages were twisting.

It took my mind a while to make sense of what I was seeing. The carriages had bunched together in a *wrong*, impossible way. Two were piled up against one another, their couplings snapped, their edges crumpled. Slowly, as the weight of the rest of the train compacted into these, they drifted into one another almost gracefully. Ripped metal sprang free, torn apart by its own momentum. And, as la Grulla moved overhead, stretching our shadows with her brilliant silver light, the passenger cars – lighter than the cargo carriages or the engine – rose up from the tracks as if lifted by the hand of the Unknown itself.

I could see them, those passengers. They were panicked, their hands and faces pressed to the glass. One of the rear doors sprang open and a man tried to jump. He tumbled free, but – by the Pattern – the distance by then was too far. I couldn't hear his scream, but it was there, ringing in my ears. Or perhaps it was my own as he hit the steel tracks and bounced, brokenly, before being swallowed up by the light of la Grulla.

The carriages continued to rise, pulling back on the cargo compartments. Then the couplings tore completely, and they drifted free, turning, twisting, up towards la Grulla. And then . . . then . . . they were gone.

I searched the brightness, even as it seared my eyes, looking for some sign of where they had gone. But it was too dazzling. Horror settled over me – even until now, I'd thought something must surely happen to save them. Whatever force had torn those carriages free was not powerful enough, and would drop them back onto the Spoke. But there was nothing. Nothing.

And then – there was something.

A dark line, slicing across the field of whiteness. At its end was a cone-shaped nodule, huge, but so distant that I could barely focus on it through the blinding light. The great Tether, swinging around as the Pendulum pulled the huge cable tight.

Its shadow fell briefly over that small, children's toy-perfect shapes of the floating carriages. Only the slightest of instances – and just enough to see with utmost clarity the Tether strike home. There should have been some sound, some indication of the dozens of lives ending in pain and terror. But the moment of impact was silent. The carriages, smashed apart, sparked with small flames, most quickly extinguished in the low-oxygen regions beyond the Spoke, a few left burning where material had struck the Tether. But the massive cable – as wide as a house – swung on, passing over our shuttle-train with a rumble like distant thunder. Miniscule pieces of metal rained down, one shattering a window further up the carriage with a noise like a pistol-shot.

Only then did I become aware of Naia's horrified yelps, and Aiva, holding onto her sister. Liliath, for her part, looked stunned, and Jark bolted from his seat, vanishing down the aisle, towards the door between the carriages – to do what, I had no idea. The children had woken, many of them in tears, others screaming. And Thaniel – as I live and breathe, I had never seen a person so horrified in my life.

His skin had turned a pale grey, and his eyes were filled with it: the knowledge that people had died, and he had been helpless. He clutched a cigarillo in one hand, unaware that the tip burned close to his fingers; the red flame touched his skin, and he jumped, cursing, then dropped it carelessly to the floor, where it smouldered and singed the carpet. He stood, leaning over me, and pressed himself to the window.

"There is still a driver in the engine," he said in a thick voice. "We have to stop."

But the shuttle-train did not stop. Our own engine thundered, the vibration of power shuddering through our carriage, rattling the windows and tipping luggage from the racks on the floor and the heads of some of the children.

The Prince turned to me. "Why aren't we stopping?"

As if I had the answers! "I don't know!" I cried, but then, suddenly, I did. The children were right to be afraid. "If something has gone wrong with the tracks – it could be us next."

He almost fell on top of me as the we picked up speed. "But we can't just abandon –"

"We can and will," Liliath said through gritted teeth. "Pattern be damned if the driver stops this train and risks our lives!"

The driver was evidently of the same mind. The train sped up, and again, faster and faster, until it was racing and we were pressed back into our seats. Thaniel sat down, his hands shaking. Slowly, the children quietened, and the light of la Grulla faded as she passed overhead and beyond the edge of the Spoke.

I looked up into the night sky, but all I could see were stars.

Jark returned, his face grim. "There was nothing to be done," he said curtly.

It was another hour before we arrived. It is impossible to remain afraid for that length of time, especially when there is no further cause for alarm – in fact, quite the opposite. It would have been a pleasant journey had we not witnessed the accident.

Still, when I saw the Wheel loom up before us, I'd never been so grateful to arrive anywhere.

The station was nothing like the one on the Spindle. It was open to the air, just one platform, a narrow strip of cement with a swaying sign that read "South Gate". A few people were gathered in clusters underneath the globe-lamps. They seemed worried, the engine driver and crew having likely warned them of the accident via emergency carrier-pigeon. The passengers poured off the shuttle-train, those with someone to greet embracing their relatives and friends, the people clinging desperately to each other, confessing in shaky, broken voices how terrified they were, they were never going to lay eyes on each other again.

My own legs were shaky as I managed to stand, picking up our belongings from the aisle, though I hardly cared if we left them behind at that moment. Liliath, however, seemed to have the most presence of mind. She chivvied her girls down the aisle, and turned back to make sure Thaniel and I followed. We made our way onto the platform without incident, where the seething crowd proved impossible to navigate.

"Were you meeting someone?" Liliath asked Jark.

He shook his head gravely. "I'm on my own for now."

Liliath smiled at us. "You must stop by, if you get the chance. We do love to receive visitors! Please, we are at Level 4, Unit 193B, Calle de las Luces."

I nodded and thanked her, sincerely doubting that we would ever see her again.

Jark turned to us. "Anders, Arabel – it was lovely to spend some time with you. But I see your guide, just over there."

He pointed to a man making his way towards us, dressed in the smart, black uniform of the vigilar, a revolver-pistol clipped to his belt. "This is Foester. You can trust him as you would trust me." Turning, he tilted an imaginary hat towards us. "I will be in touch soon. Stay safe."

Foester was a man with a very serious expression. I wondered how he had fallen in with Jark and his Green-bands. How many more were there, among the ranks of the vigilar and the guardia? Secretly working against the Brotherhood and the Council, stealing food, taking bribes, allowing disharmony for the cause of la Rebelde? Risking their lives if they were caught?

There was nothing about this man that marked him as a rebel. He nodded to both me and Thaniel, then motioned us ahead of him. With a lazy glance around, he then followed.

Positioned above the platform on tall poles were several ampliphones, and these crackled to life. "Seven-nine-five," came an artificial voice. "An incident has occurred involving shuttle-train Service Nineteen, due at Platform Seven, Nine Chimes. Please be advised. Cooperation and calm acceptance are valued. Return to your homes and workplaces. Do not linger in the streets. Hampering the investigation will not be tolerated."

Vigilar and sentinela were walking among the people, directing the laggards to move away. As the crowd thinned, moving towards a gate at the exit ramp, I scanned the people more closely. It certainly didn't seem like anyone was paying us any undue attention.

Chapter Thirty-Five

The Wheel was odd.

It wasn't just the shift in gravity, noticeable from the moment we descended the ramp into a paved street below the station. Our very steps felt lighter, for which I was grateful, but my hair lifted from beneath my scarf, drifting around my face, which was not practical or comfortable. I tucked it into the collar of my shirt, but still stray wisps rose free, tickling my nose.

It wasn't just the buildings, which were set out in lines instead of blocks, and all made of cement instead of stone and brick. They were cracked and chipped, and many of the windows were boarded over. Though the Wheel was rounded, the curve was much sharper than that of the Spindle, so the horizon seemed always to be just beyond the next rooftop. And it wasn't even that the air was thinner, making each breath a slight effort, or the strange hand-drawn carts pulled by large, boxy servitors – in even worse repair than the ones in the Pavilion, by the looks of things – and, in some cases, actual men.

It was the feeling. The coldness in the air as the wind blew ceaselessly – not an ordinary wind, but that of Cosmos, the Viento Cósmico, as it circled past the outer edges of the atmosphere. The profound loneliness that permeated every cobblestone, every breath of foreign air, something that spoke of the distance between here and the warm, beating heart of Tierra Mejór.

We took a carriage pulled by a servitor in exchange for several bronze coins dropped into a modified slit at the front of its square head. It ran along tracks that had once carried rotor-trams, but it appeared there were no running rotor-trams in this part of the Wheel, and hadn't been for some time.

The road we took wound through the streets, back and forth, rising slightly until we had left the squat, decrepit houses behind. We passed several workshops and warehouses, and through their open sides, I could see men and women at their jobs; bending over long planters full of greenery, plucking edible roots from the soil, loading them into crates; lifting the full boxes, carrying them or shifting them about on a few rickety carts. One thing struck me, and that was that everyone seemed to know their job, their place.

This, I knew, was the Pattern at work.

Why, then, did they look so miserable, so forlorn?

I was so tired by this stage, I did not think I would ever sleep again, but all the same, I wanted desperately to eat something, anything, and claim a warm bed. My mind conjured up delicious meals, but truthfully, even a slice of bread and some cheese would have been welcome. By then, the Estate and whatever amenities it offered seemed like an impossible dream.

Finally, the servitor slowed. The road ended in an arched gateway, the ironwork gates closed by an immense lock. We had reached a tall grey wall, an impenetrable barrier stretching up across the dim sky.

Beyond this were several tall, grey buildings with gabled roofs. If they looked drab, well, they were a Palace compared to local construction; there seemed to be gardens, by the glimpses of treetops above the wall. The lights in the upper rooms beckoned welcomingly.

Foester, however, was craning his neck. His serious face creased into a frown.

"Is something wrong?" I asked him as the servitor whirred to a stop.

"There should be guards," he said. "Along the wall top, and at the gate."

"Perhaps they've changed the rotation," I suggested, but Thaniel shook his head.

"They would never leave it unguarded."

Foester suddenly stiffened, then unclipped the pistol from his belt, alighting from the car. Telling us to stay where we were, he approached the gate cautiously, crouching down, and reaching out a hand through the bars to touch something on the ground beyond. Instantly, he drew it back, and stood.

"Quickly," he said sharply, over his shoulder. "We need to get out of here."

We stepped down from the servitor. I don't know about the Principe Regente, but my heart hammered in my chest, making me sick.

"Quickly," urged Foester. "Don't look beyond the gate."

I averted my gaze instinctively, but then, just as I had to watch the shuttle-train rising in its inexorable path of destruction, I turned to look over my shoulder.

I saw two bodies sprawled just beyond the gate, dressed in vigilar uniform. There was no blood, no wounds upon them, not, at least, that I could see. But that was all the more frightening.

They looked as if all the moisture had been drained from them, for I could see the face of one, and the hands of the other; bones protruded, the pale, nearly grey skin papery and thin. I covered my mouth with my hand, and then had to cover my nose as well, for a smell hit me.

A rotten, sweet smell. The smell of death.

I retched, deeply, painfully, for there was nothing in my stomach to vomit up. I was aware only of Foester hurrying us along the street, and Thaniel's breathing, harsh in my ear.

I had no reserves left, but somehow, I ran. We left behind the larger houses, passing back into the narrower streets. Past the ubiquitous unit blocks we raced. I took Thaniel's hand and pulled him with me, but he was far less fit than I, and I found him dragging me back. Foester stopped once or twice to wait impatiently. Finally, we ducked into an alcove, just off a busy lane where people hurried this way and that, unaware, as yet, that anything was deeply, terribly wrong.

There were questions, but even if we had breath and energy to ask them, they were pointless. None of us knew who had killed those men, nor how. One thing, however, was clear; if two vigilar lay dead in front of the Estate, and no one had moved them or collected the bodies, then no one else inside was alive.

In any case, that smell had consisted of more than two rotting bodies.

"The atmosphere would have made the decomposition much slower," Foester said at last. "I don't know how long it has been."

"Surely," I gasped, "someone must have noticed. A carrier-pigeon would have been sent. Councilmen would have noticed if their missives were not responded to."

Foester checked his pistol. "Unless it goes much further than this. Missives can be falsified, after all."

"A conspiracy?" Thaniel gasped for breath. "Is that what you're suggesting?"

Foester's grim expression was his only response. We needed no other.

"Then what do we do?" I asked him.

"We must return to Benoi," Foester said, and sore glad I was to for his decisiveness. "The plan must change. But at least my Liege is safe."

We moved out into the street, Foester walking more slowly now, the pistol concealed under the flap of his jacket. We blended in with the streams of workers, our dishevelled appearance not much different from theirs.

There were even a few vigilar passing by who nodded to Foester; I guessed he did not trust them, for he only nodded in return.

I realised I was still holding Thaniel's hand in a vice grip when he shook me off, reaching for a cigarillo; in need of my own form of comfort, I slipped my hand into my pocket, stroking the fronds of my white feather.

Thaniel's cigarillo refused to light. The reduced atmosphere made a spark slow to catch, and he stopped a moment to shield his match. The flame finally caught, but I had paused for a just a moment to watch him – a moment too long.

Foester was gone.

I looked over my shoulder. All I saw was the listless crowd of identical faces. Ahead – nothing.

"Where in the Pattern did he go?" Thaniel didn't sound concerned at all, even as my own panic was rising.

"Hurry," I told him, then took hold of his sleeve just in case I lost him too. We quickened our step, but Foester did not appear. I dragged Thaniel across the street, dodging a racing servitor, but there seemed no end to the sea of faces, and certainly no sign of our vigilar – or any other. We had passed out of the wider streets and into meaner, narrower ones. I wondered if we should go back, but if, perhaps, someone had captured him, that wouldn't be wise.

I was not in the mood to be wise. "We'll go back. Just a little way."

The Prince nodded his agreement, and we retraced our steps as best we could. To tell the truth, I was starting to think we'd come entirely the wrong way, when I glimpsed a knot of people up ahead.

We took small, cautious steps towards it. Some were chattering animatedly, some hurrying away. I pushed through them, and saw at last what had created the spectacle.

Foester.

He was lying on his side, his revolver-pistol, having dropped from his hand, sitting untouched on the road beside him. His skin was pale. And from his mouth protruded a small, curling green tendril, with a delicate leaf attached.

Horror washed through me, and I grabbed the Prince's sleeve, drawing him away just before the vigilar arrived.

"Move on," they called, waving their own guns. "Move on!"

My mind raced, ineffectual and panicky. I was alone with the Prince, and he was solely in my charge. I guessed the best thing to do would be to return to Jark. But how would I ever find him? I had no idea where he resided – he'd said that he'd contact us, and we'd made no alternative plan.

Fools that we were!

Still, I did have one address. Liliath's. What had she told me? Level 4, Unit 193B, Calle de las Luces. I thanked the Pattern for Maestra Tinir's discipline in training our memory!

After I explained my plan to Thaniel, and he raised no objection, we wandered along several blocks of those blank, featureless buildings, turning several corners, until we reached a street that felt as empty as it looked. Dust blew in spirals, lifted by an eddying breeze, and it was a relief when I found an empty servitor-cart.

I told it the address, dropping in the remaining coins I had from the ticket change, and soon we were on the right street. The unit was not hard to find. Each block was numbered with flaking white paint.

We disembarked at a set of steps leading up to a door. It was no warmer inside, but at least we were out of the neverending wind.

A short hallway ended in a shadowy staircase – apparently, there were no lifts. The walls were covered with peeling, yellowed paper. We climbed past many, many doors, painted a dull green, until we reached one that seemed no different than the others. This, I hoped, was Liliath's.

I checked to make sure my scarf was in place, still covering my metrónomo. Then I raised my hand and knocked at the door.

It was opened seconds later, by Naia. Her eyes lit up to see us, and unquestioningly, she ushered us inside.

It was a dull place, smelling of mildew, and there were patches on the walls where damp had seeped in around the narrow windows. The single globe-light spread only a murky yellow glow over the bare floorboards and shabby furniture. Something chattered in a corner, and Naia promptly wrenched a chair out of the way and stamped her foot. "Roaches!" She rolled her eyes. "We've been gone over a month, so we'll be finding them everywhere."

"Naia, have you –" This was Liliath, coming through one of the doors leading into, assumingly, a bedroom. Her eyes widened. "Oh! Arabel! I didn't expect you quite so soon!"

I smiled as best I could, choking down my exhaustion and fear. "It seems there's been a mix-up," I said. "Some . . . error in the system. The apartment we were supposed to stay in has been let to someone else, and our belongings – and money – misplaced. And since we were being transferred into this area anyway, we need to find a new place to stay. Can you . . . can you help us?"

I hoped my desperation didn't show in my eyes. I had no idea if what I said was even remotely plausible. If she questioned me further, I doubted my story would hold up.

"No," she said. "No, of course I don't mind if you stay! We have a spare bedroom, if you don't mind sharing it between you. And plenty of spare clothes, if you need them."

She bustled around, organising the girls, bringing fresh sheets and blankets from a cupboard, and all at once, I was a little overwhelmed. My own mother, after all, had never acted much like this woman, with such genuine compassion.

"It's no wonder," she said as she showed us through to the bedroom that would be ours. "The system is showing more and more errors. This was my brother's room, in fact. He was recently transferred across to the grain-harvestries, would you credit it? He'd worked all his life with the white-moths."

I couldn't care less about her brother by that stage. I was only relieved that my cover story made sense.

"Oh!" said Naia from behind us. "Are you being reassigned to the moth refinery, then?"

"Yes!" I answered, seizing on this support for our story.

"We were expecting replacements. In that case, you can stay with us for a while, can't they, mother?"

Liliath smiled widely. She could hear the plea in her daughter's voice, the longing for something different, something exotic. "Of course," she said. "For as long as you need."

After this, however, Liliath's briskness ensured that everyone kept their mind on a task. She directed me through to the bathing room, to "freshen up", and Thaniel through to the kitchen, to look through the cupboards and find something he thought might do for a late dinner.

With that, we fell into an easy rhythm. We didn't feel so much like guests as part of her family. Sitting down to dinner at a cracked linoleum table, we ate rice mixed with several varieties of mushrooms, the properties of which she listed extensively, while Naia rolled her eyes. "They will think we can talk about nothing else," she hissed to her sister when she thought I was distracted.

I felt sorry for them. I supposed the trip to the Spindle had been a treat, probably one that wasn't repeated too often. No wonder they had seemed aloof – they'd probably been far out of their depth among the glitter of that ballroom.

Our bed, when it came time to retire, was in a room to the side of the living area. It seemed Naia and Aiva shared a room, though this one was larger, and clearly spare. I was too tired to wonder why as I removed my belongings from my pocket: my feather, the playing cards, and my small figurine of Mary, the blue woman. I tucked them under one corner of the bed.

When Thaniel entered, I was laying some of the musty-smelling, but obviously clean, pillows on the floor to make my mattress.

"What are you doing?" he asked me, a blank look on his face.

"We can't very well share the bed," I answered.

He waved a hand to indicate the others. "They clearly have no issue with it." His eyes narrowed. "Or – is it you who dislikes the idea?"

"Not at all." I frowned. It was true – they had simply assumed we would share the bed. I wasn't against it, for the floor was cold, but I hadn't wanted to presume my Prince would be so amenable.

He was.

He took a step towards me, and I took a step back without thinking. He took another, and I found myself against the wall. The paper crinkled under my hands as I pressed them flat to the solid surface, and he gently tugged my hair free from my collar, running his fingers through it to straighten the tangles. Then he pressed his mouth to mine, gently at first, then demanding; his tongue sought to part my lips, and I let it, revelling in the slow, glorious strokes against my own. He was hard already, and my own desire surged to feel him against me. When he unbuttoned my shirt and pulled it, along with my undergarments, over my head, I craved his bare skin against mine.

"Imre." His breath tickled my ear. "Our first time, I should have been more careful. I ask you now –"

I guided him back towards me, and this was my answer.

Blindly, I loosened his own shirt and the belt that was wrapped around his narrow waist. Tugging down his trousers, I shivered from the heat radiating from his erection; he stepped free of the pile of fabric, tugging my brown pants down to my ankles. He turned me, then, and pushed himself into me from behind. I muffled my cry of pleasure, but only through long years of discipline and preparation; a small explosion of exquisite sensation building inside me. He drew himself out, then thrust back in, again, again, harder. My cheek pressed to the cold, damp wall, I closed my eyes and allowed myself to simply feel.

It did not last long, but I came as he shuddered, spending himself inside me, and it was glorious.

We caught our breath, and then, wordlessly, he picked up his discarded shirt and gently wiped the moisture from my thighs. The contrast between this sober Thaniel and the one who had used me so quickly and coarsely was too much to fathom.

I gathered the scattered pillows and returned them to the bed. I finished making it while he lit a cigarillo and stood at the window, looking out.

"We should have stopped the shuttle-train," he said, his voice cracking.

"I don't know that we could have helped." I focused on the way the sheets billowed as I lay them over the top of the mattress. "I don't know that anyone could have."

"We could have tried," he growled. "We should have tried."

"Come to bed," I told him. "You need to sleep."

His eyes, when he faced me, were bloodshot, full of grief and anger and despair. But he relented, and we climbed beneath the sheets, his body warmth pouring into mine. He wrapped an arm over my shoulders.

"You are much more divine when I'm sober," he whispered into the darkness.

Chapter Thirty-Six

I had kind of hoped it had all been a dream – all, that is, bar the feeling of Thaniel beside me, but as I woke, such wishes were soon stripped away, along with the remnants of night.

The Dawn Regimen rang out from the street – it appeared ampliphones, like those at the station, were fastened to the sides of the buildings, funnelling the chimes of Reloj de pie all the way from the Spindle. The parabra was foreign, however; instead of a silent chant, spoken to oneself, this message was piped through the phones, that all might hear.

"Wealth and comfort are promised you," said the bodiless voice. "So long as you are willing. Strive, and you will be rewarded. Obey, and you will be exalted. Work with all your heart, and true happiness will be yours."

On and on it went, extoling the virtues of obedience; I couldn't tell if the voice belonged to a man or a woman, or some automaton who had been recorded. The crackling speakers made the words disjointed, the message losing some of its intended gravity.

The sky outside the window in our small room was an odd shade of purple, as if it was close to evening, dotted with the faint outlines of stars. The noises filtered from the main area outside our door, so I roused my reluctant body and dressed in some fresh clothes from my bags. The Prince was still sleeping deeply, so I let him lie in and closed the door quictly behind me.

"Good morning, there!" said Liliath. She was standing behind the kitchen counter, stirring something in a pot. Aiva and Naia took up the sofa, a shared blanket wrapped around their shoulders, clutching mugs of steaming tea. "Would you like a mug?" Liliath asked, seeing my glance.

"Yes, please," I said, and she poured me a cup of something hot and spicy. It tasted horrible, like weakened espiritu, which, I suppose, is what it was; the final product might be distilled for turnings or years, but this was its initial stages. Nonetheless, it warmed me from the inside out.

"Moth tea," she said. Noting my expression, she chuckled. "Made from brown moths, not the white. An acquired taste, but it's very good for circulation, which you'll need when working in the cold and damp of the tunnels. I add plenty of ginger for heat, and it improves the taste a little."

I tried to take another polite sip, but in the end, I set it aside, hoping she wouldn't notice.

Breakfast was a kind of porridge, made with mushrooms. It tasted salty, an unusual choice for this time of day, but I was hungry enough to gobble it up.

"We are going in later this turning," Liliath informed me. "We were granted a morning to ourselves to recover, but work must go on. You will ride in with us, won't you? That is, provided your apprentice ever rouses himself."

I dithered. I had supposed we would spend this turning waiting for Jark, who I was growing worried for; but it would sound suspicious if we refused to attend the place that was allegedly paying our wages. It might be easiest to make an excuse to slip away once we were among a crowd.

In the end, I had to wake Thaniel. I leaned over him and shook his shoulders, and he started wildly, almost hitting me.

"It's me, it's me," I said, and he fell back on the pillows. "Bad dreams?"

He nodded.

"Well, we have to work out what we're going to do," I said.

He blinked, bleary-eyed. "Perhaps we should send a carrier-pigeon to Chancellor Darhn. Someone needs to know what's happened on the Estate."

I shook my head, despairingly. "We have no money for a carrier-pigeon, and we don't know for certain it won't be intercepted."

Thaniel huffed a sigh that would have sounded petulant if I didn't feel precisely the same. "Well, I don't like the idea that no one knows where we are – even less than I like the idea that *we* don't know where we are."

He gave me a strange look.

I swallowed. "We need to find Jark. He will know what to do." At least, I hoped so.

I left the Prince to get dressed in some of Liliath's brother's old clothes, and went to the bathing room to wash my hands and face. I tied a towel around my head to hide my metrónomo, for Naia and Aiva joined me, jostling one another for the privilege to stand beside me and share the pitted, misty mirror.

"Can you show me how you shape your eyebrows?" Naia asked me. "Please? I mean, if it's not too much trouble?"

I raised the eyebrows she was speaking of. It had been a long time since I'd been able to pluck them into their usual careful lines. Ketra had taught me how to shape them when I had arrived at the Pavilion, as a dishevelled thirteen-year-old with wild hair that had never been cut and bare feet. "Your brows are almost perfect," I told Naia, "You don't need to change them."

"They're not as perfect as yours," Aiva said, worshipfully. "You are so beautiful, you could be a Princess."

I laughed. The joke had depths beyond her intention, and I couldn't explain it to them, so I simply had to agree.

I spent the rest of the morning in the bathing room, using some twisted wire as a pair of tweezers. Both girls were thrilled with the results, even though their skin looked puffy, and danced about the sitting room as they showed Liliath.

"Anyone would think you're near nineteen," she said, but she was smiling.

"Liliath." I sat down on the sofa beside her. "We must get in contact with Benoi. It's rather urgent. Do you know where she lives?"

Liliath nodded. "Oh, of course! But it will have to wait until after the workday. We must be going, or we'll be late."

I wanted to protest – seeing Jark was much more important – but I dared not, lest I raise her suspicions. For all she knew, we had come here to work; and at the very least, we could earn our keep if we were paid.

***

The moth refinery was nine blocks away, too far to walk. We took a carriage pulled by a servitor in exchange for several bronze coins, which Liliath produced with great care. Not having ever earned any money of my own, I was coming to realise how hard it was to part with. But when I suggested that we take the servitor-carriage only halfway, Liliath waved me off. "There is a lot of work to be done. Tiring oneself out before one even arrives is not wise."

Carefully, I nodded, my hair covered with Xith's scarf once more, my hair looped over my metrónomo. Despite my doubts that anyone would think to look for us here, with Liliath, I still thought it much better to hide in plain sight than skulk in the shadows.

We passed more of the concrete buildings, and pedestrians who all looked like they had somewhere to be. Most Ruedans, like Tomas, were tall and thin thanks to the lessened gravity on the Wheel. Many shared a darker-hued skin that was not only caused by their genetic heritage, which was handed down by the Gardener, Nuru, who was Afrikan, but also the diminishing of veil that protected them from the airless Unknown. Out here, the healers said, it was so much thinner that the Wheel-dwellers were significantly more at risk of developing tumours and cases of blood-sickness.

In this district, there were no shops selling fabric or ribbons, no night-cafés, no restaurants. No children played on the street corners; even the youngest were running errands, carrying packs or crates, or riding two-wheeled motion-cycles laden with packages. Those boisterous adolescents we'd seen on the shuttle-train had vanished, replaced by these young people who looked far too responsible for their ages.

Still, I had seen children who had grown up too fast on the Third Tier. I'd been one of them, the dead-eyed kids roaming the streets, with purposeless lack of direction; those Eastsiders, destined to be nobody. These ones, at least, had a purpose, a reason for being.

Soon the carriage slowed. At the end of this road was a huge, dome-shaped building. It was surrounded by several smaller domes, like satellites, all made of the same semi-luminescent white material. It didn't look like stone or concrete, and as we got closer, I saw it was in fact some kind of polymer or resin, cut into thin sheets, and held together with steel braces.

We heard the commotion before we saw it; a mob was gathering itself outside the building, and, unlike those staid, placid workers we had seen on the way here, they were shouting and angry. Thaniel and I slowed our approach, and I caught the words " . . .tell us the truth!"

"Cannot keep this . . ."

" . . .demand justice! Someone is . . ."

In front of the crowd, near the doors, a vigilar stood. Behind him, several more nervous officers held their revolver-pistols at the ready, while their leader had his arms raised as if this futile gesture could somehow placate the people. "I understand!" he was saying. "I hear you! Please, remain calm!"

"Calm!" a woman shouted. "My *son* was on that shuttle-train!"

The throng erupted once more. Someone threw something, and it struck the vigilar in the face – a sliver of cement, sharp enough to slice open his cheek. He cursed loudly, and the officers behind him shifted uneasily. "Hold!" he barked at them before turning back to face the crowd. "Is this going to help?" he shouted. "I ask you! Is this going to help?"

There were mutterings, but the people quietened.

"I have no answers for you," the vigilar went on. "Not at this time. But let me assure you – *each* one of you – that there will be a thorough investigation. We will not let this happen again. I have received orders that all shuttle-trains are to travel at half-speed until further notice. The number of shipments and services will be reduced by one-third. It may cause inconvenience, but we must make do until we know more."

"I have a shipment of field mushrooms due in the Cuidad by tomorrow!" a man shouted. "How am I to get paid?"

The complaints came thick and fast then. The vigilar turned his back, and I could tell he was trying hard to hold this situation together, but with little hope – this was a problem with no solution. The people wouldn't be happy if the shuttle-trains stopped running and they weren't paid. Neither would they be placated if they *kept* running. The vigilar knew it, but his hands were tied.

A loud gong sounded through the ampliphones just as we pulled to a stop. "Citizens. The workday has resumed. Please ensure you are at your stations, ready to begin. Remember that your work serves the Pattern."

This message was a signal that obviously could not be ignored, for the crowd began to disperse, some making their way up the steps into the arched entrance of the dome-building, others drifting away down the street to their places of work.

As we stepped out of our conveyance, Naia looked as if she might burst into tears. "What's going to happen, Mother? Everyone is so upset."

"We will go on with our day," Liliath assured her. "Come, we need to hurry. Afternoon shift will start soon." She turned to us. "Do you know where you're to go?"

I shook my head. "All our papers were misplaced. Honestly, I've no idea where we're supposed to be."

"Then you must stay with me. I'll show you to Level 6 – which is most likely where you would have been assigned, in any case, since we've lost so many workers . . ."

"You've been too kind," I said, but she shook her head, looking over my shoulder at the disgruntled remnants of the crowd, an unreadable expression on her face.

We climbed the steps and passed through the door. Inside, the building was unlike anything I'd ever seen. The arched roof was like an upside-down bowl over our heads. The polymer plates reflected the light of huge globe-lanterns placed atop high pillars at regular intervals. It made the room so warm that water condensed on the curved walls, constantly running down and collecting in drains around the edges with a laryngitic gurgle.

The slitted grates clanked and clanged under our feet and let in glimpses of unfathomable darkness down below, which made me dizzy. The humidity, in its turn, contributed the sensation of being covered with a wet blanket. How did people work here?

But work they did. Men and women in overalls, their hands covered with gloves, bustled around, wheeling barrows full of brown, grey, and green moths, their wings still, their tiny bodies heaped atop one another. These were tipped onto long tables and benches, where they were brushed around and picked over by other workers, also gloved, deftly sorting them into barrels. The barrels were in turn rolled towards large conveyer belts, and vanished through holes in the walls, where I assumed they were loaded for transport.

The place was a hive of industry. I had never seen so many people united in a single purpose, but it was very clear to me then how alive the Pattern was here.

Liliath had gone on ahead with Naia and Aiva, who, it seemed, were employed in a different part of the refinery. She waved them goodbye, then motioned for us to catch up.

"I had no idea," Thaniel said to me in a low voice. "I never knew this was how it worked. All these people . . ."

I suppose he'd thought all the food he ate somehow magically prepared itself, and his cigarillos grew inside their paper rolls. Yet I couldn't blame him. I myself had never understood what a massive operation it was to supply Tierra Mejór with this, our only real source of protein.

"We need to move," I urged him.

"These people," hissed Thaniel. "I know nothing of them. How they work. What they do."

"Well, you can come back here any time you want!" I pulled at his arm. "You're the *Prince*. When this is all done, you can come for a tour."

"Do you truly think they'll ever let me come back?" He shook his head, but he walked alongside me as we picked our way between the tables. "They'd come up with some excuse to keep me locked inside those Citadel walls. Even if they did not, I'd never get this close. I spent half my childhood at the Estate, and I hardly ever went beyond its walls. They'd never let me see this –" he swept out an arm, "– as it truly is. They'd put on a show, and hide any unpleasantness."

Yet again, my Prince had managed to surprise me.

Liliath led us past some workers wheeling fine-mesh cages full of live moths, obviously in transit from some other tunnel or facility. They looked like churning masses of coloured smoke. Some of these workers wore masks, and I realised why when I saw one of the far tables, over which a cloud of mist seemed to hover – the powder from their wings. After all, it wasn't just the scales of the white-moths which could have an effect if inhaled. Some species grew scales which were plain dangerous. I led Thaniel a good distance away from them, but as we reached Liliath, she handed us a pair of masks from a hook on the wall. "It's best to keep them on, even if you think you're safe," she said, before we left the room through a back door.

We were in a stairwell, leading down.

It grew darker as we descended, and colder. The walls were still slick with moisture, though, chilling me to the bone. We passed a few doors, opening into tunnels or bays, and there was a heavy smell of loam. We spied a few workers, but they were all too busy to notice us.

After several flights, we finally arrived at Level 6, the high ceiling covered with pipes, pulleys, and wheels of ancient machines. Only some of them continued to work, a few mechanisms and pulleys whirring and whizzing. Most were dormant.

Above this was a grated ceiling, like the one we'd seen in the upper level, showing the shadows and shapes of workers moving in the bay above.

Floating all about us were small white-moths, which flittered and flickered through the gaps.

I finally saw what the purpose of the damp and the heat was. Condensation gathered on the gratings, dripping over the ancient machines, mixing with old oil that oozed from the myriad valves and spigots. If I remembered the facts I had read in *The Cultivated Tree and its Uses,* there were microbes and fungi that could dissolve refined oil, using it as sustenance, then excreting the matter somehow. Moths could subsist on most things so long as they were dissolved in water; it was the excretions of these life forms which they were ingesting.

It was a cycle of life, one so perfect that the Pattern could only have designed it itself.

Using nets on long poles, several workers were busy catching the moths in mid-flight. The creatures would flap and flutter their wings in panic, trying to get free, and in doing so, brush the scales from their wings.

The air was thick with the white dust. It fell like rain in parts of the room, like mist and drizzle in others. Some of it landed on the grated floor beneath our feet, vanishing into the darkness below, but a lot of it collected on a dozen or more tiered shelves the size of double beds.

The tiered trays rotated. While remaining flat, they sank to the floor, travelled along it, pushed by the arms of the large wheel, then moved up. At any one time, there were three or four trays on the floor, workers gathered around them, all wearing masks. They puttered around the beds, gathering the dust in small metal sieves, tapping it gently to separate any dirt or impurities, or the occasional body of a moth, either already dead, or, having lost too many of its scales to fly, would soon die. Once this was done, it was poured gently into small baskets, ready for transport.

Liliath handed me a set of sieves, and another to Thaniel, and indicated that we should do exactly what she did; walk around the trays as they rotated through, scoop the dust, and checking its consistency, place it gently into a basket. Once the basket was full, it was to be taken to the overseers, who would weigh it on their scales, and pour it into the appropriately marked barrels.

I held out my smallest sieve and scooped the white-powder gently, just as Liliath had shown me. I could feel how light it was, and it suddenly struck me how incredible it was that such a thing had such value – and power. I sifted through it, making sure there was no dirt or irregular-sized pieces, then took it to the overseer. He glanced at it but barely, quickly switching it from the scales to pour it into a barrel, then motioning me out of the way to allow the next worker to step up.

"Do none of these work?" the Prince asked Liliath as I returned. He was pointing upwards, at the ancient machines, some of their parts dangling idly.

"Once – once they did," she answered. "But no longer. Who knows what they were for? In any case, there's no need for them now. They serve another purpose."

I reflected on this. "How many other things on Tierra Mejór are running the way they were when la Relojero built them?"

Thaniel looked interested, too, but Liliath moved onwards, and no one answered. But I couldn't shake that notion. I had wondered, when I stood on the Fourth Tier, why la Relojero would have allowed people to live in such squalor. Perhaps she had never intended it at all.

After a while, the rhythm of the process settled into me, the purpose behind it. As my fingers grew numb with cold and the damp earth soiled my sleeves, the Pattern enveloped me. As my eyes adjusted to the darkness, I could see only those mounds of white-powder, tray upon tray of it, as they rotated down, and up, and down once more.

With this, my apprehensions faded away. I felt calm and safe, and almost content.

"Did you choose your Guild?" I asked Liliath, as we walked beside one another, sifting and gathering. "Was this always what you wanted?"

Liliath laughed. "Heavens, no. I dreamed of being a Scribe."

I gaped. Scribes were few, and theirs was regarded as a useless calling, fit only for the carrier-pigeon centres; and then, usually a person would train as a técnico, not singularly a wordsmith.

"I was good with words. I composed tales in my head, dreaming I would one day write them down, like Ante himself, and gain a place in the Great Library!" She shook her head. "Such delusions!"

"Do you remember those tales?" I asked her.

"Oh." She waved a dismissive hand. "No. Bits and pieces, perhaps. I realised that there was no point. My father was a Horticulturalist. I spent much time with him, making notes, studying plants and trees, but he fell ill, and I was left to support my brother and two sisters." Her eyes became distant. "I took up his work for a time, before landing here, in the moth refinery. It is not an easy life, but then, none is. I suppose your story is no more glamorous."

If only you knew, I thought. Instead, I seized upon the one part of it that was not a deception. "I love growing things," I said. "To see a plant thrive has always bought me joy."

"That is a sentiment I have not heard often." Liliath regarded me closely. I turned my head, disliking her scrutiny; I was not supposed to attract attention, and here I was, doing just that.

At one stage, Liliath left us. Her journey to the Spindle, and the Library, had been fruitful, she told me, and she was tinkering with something very important in a workshop located through a narrow, winding passage to one side of this great bay.

"Send an Overseer to find me if you need to," she said. "You won't be allowed into the laboratory, even with your guildswoman's status."

"What is it you are working on?" I asked.

"A new project, involving hybrids and extracts of plants and insects. But it's uninteresting. I won't bore you." She gave my shoulder a pat, which I found strikingly maternal, before she went.

The day passed into night, though down here you would not know it. The light did not change with the passing of la Grulla. Rather, we were told by the clanging of a gong through the ampliphone speakers that the turning was drawing to a close. By that time, I had fallen so deeply into the Pattern that I was startled by the loud sound. I had sifted fifty or sixty baskets, and my fingers were rubbed raw, my legs ached with cramp, and I was more physically tired than after one of Maestra Tinir's most gruelling classes. Despite my mask, the small irritations in my nose told me I had breathed in at least some of the dust.

How much did it take before one became addicted? How many of the workers were already, unknowingly, hooked?

As I climbed the steps, following Liliath who had returned to find us at the end of the workday, my ankle felt as if it was full of stones grating against one another. Thaniel looked similarly exhausted.

Liliath did not lead us directly home. Instead, we followed a flood of workers down the long street to an open-air market on a street called the Bulevar Principal. There were a few other stalls, selling clothes and jewellery, and even hiring out carrier pigeons, but it was the food vendors who did the most business at this time of day.

Here, men, women, and children gathered around various stalls, from which drifted the smells of cooked food; dried moth-meat, seasoned with spices, topped with nuts and mushrooms. No matter which vendor you went to, it was the same ingredients, in varying combinations.

"Is there nothing fresh?" I asked Liliath.

"You have been living upon the Spindle for too long," she laughed, as Naia and Aiva approached, carrying a tray of bowls of thick greyish stew, in which a few brown chunks floated. Naia looked sympathetic as she noticed my expression. "It's one of the best," she assured me.

I still had no coin to my name, but Liliath shook her head before I could say something; I resolved to pay her back double, when we had somehow worked out what we were going to do. Thaniel and I followed the small family to a series of tables and benches, set in a recess between two tall buildings. We found a seat, and I dipped my spoon into the broth.

It was certainly nothing like the food of the Citadel, but in the end, the taste was unimportant. I was hungry enough for two bowls, but I didn't dare ask for another; it seemed that, while no one had eaten their fill, the stalls were already closing up, sold out of their meagre rations.

Thaniel, however, simply picked at his meal. He looked nauseated, which worried me. "You should eat," I whispered to him as we walked back to Liliath's apartment. "You need strength."

He pulled a cigarillo from his pocket and lit it instead.

"Thaniel?" I questioned him.

"Did you ever think such a place could exist?" He turned his eyes on me, and they swam with sadness. "I feel as if my soul is being slowly pulled from my body."

He had been breathing the dust, I realised. His eyes were rimmed with red. But then, I could not blame him for it – after all, I suspected that I too, had been affected.

And I understood what he meant. Even if caused by the white-powder, it was still very much real, this feeling we were unable to put properly into words – such displacement, such unreality, such strangeness. Was it the work? The constant exposure to the dust of the white-moths? Our fear?

***

Once we were back at the apartment, I asked Liliath again about Benoi. She told me she would send Aiva along in the morning to summon her. "That way, it will not interfere with your workday."

I thanked her, not just for that, but for all she had done. She brushed it off, but I think, truly, I had found in her the mother I wished I had.

Chapter Thirty-Seven

The lozenges I took for my flow were also readily available on the Wheel. Liliath, without being asked, had given me a packet from a stash she kept in her bathroom.

We made love, Thaniel and I.

I could not think of him as the Principe Regente, not here; here, he was truly Thaniel, just a man. A handsome one, at that, but still just a man. I found pleasure in his body, and I know he found it in mine. Still, something about it was wrong. The act felt desperate, born of a need to feel close to someone, a desire to touch brought on by loneliness and fear of being even more alone.

In the morning, Aiva was dispatched to Benoi's house. She returned looking frustrated, and I suspected she was one of her favourite people, and she was disappointed to miss out on a visit.

"She's not at home. I knocked and knocked," she said. "But there was no answer."

Cold, all-pervading, filled my veins. Jark had said he would contact us – so why had he disappeared? Had something happened to him? Sinister thoughts prowled at the very edges of my mind. First, Foester. Now Jark.

Were we in danger?

Thaniel and I agreed, in a hurried and hushed conversation, that we would stay where we were, and hope that Jark contacted us soon. Once the decision was made, however, this was very easy to do. Neither of us wanted to leave the normalcy and relative safety of Liliath's little unit.

Over the next few turnings, the room in Liliath's house had become our own, and we filled it with sounds of our lovemaking. I came to know the stains on the damp, mildewed wallpaper, and would lie abed when I could, snatching a few minutes of extra drowsing time in the morning or evening, picking them out. There was one, I thought, that looked remarkably similar to the shape of Chette's bloodstain on the floor of Thaniel's suite; a bird in flight. No matter how I looked at it, all I could see was that dark mark on the floorboards and carpet. And yet, though this should unnerve me, I felt only a strange kind of lassitude, as if it had all happened a lifetime ago.

Sometimes, Thaniel and I would talk about subjects that were obscure and ideas that were half-formed.

"I have often wondered," he would say to me as he traced a finger across my metrónomo, "How time passed on Old Earth. The circling of the sun and moon . . . was a year as long as ours is? Were their months the same? Might we be older, or younger, when measured in their years?"

"I might be one hundred and seventy." I stretched provocatively. "Or only twelve!"

"Oh," he said with a wicked smile, his finger finding its way beneath the bodice of my gown. "No, not twelve. You are, most definitely, a woman."

We speculated about other things; whether or not humans had truly trained animals as pets, and allowed them into their homes; how their meat had tasted, fresh and raw and bloody, carved in great slabs from the sides of beasts bred only for the purpose of feeding humans, not kept, like our pigs and sheep, for their milk and wool and their hides when they died a natural death. What the sky was like, whether it was truly blue as the books told us, and why it would be so. What the sky had looked like after it had been torn open by the fire; and whether or not there was anything left of that impossible, alien world.

Sometimes I would sit alone in our room as Thaniel joined the others in the living room. The window faced inwards towards the centre of Tierra Mejór. On a day when the clouds were lighter, I could see the Spindle in all its glory; from the First Tier to the Fourth, and the workings between the Third and the Fourth, where the Tether swung. Twice every turning, the Pendulum would pass overhead, casting a sharp shadow that seemed to slice the muted daylight in two, or cast an even deeper one over the night.

I learned more about the moth refinery, and how it worked. The white-moths were no good for food. Their bodies were discarded, broken down into fertiliser and transported to the vegetable gardens. The other moths, which favoured the upper levels, where different types of fungus grew, were all harvested for their wings and bodies, and turned into protein cubes and espiritu. Nothing, I saw, was wasted.

We earned our wages, and they were paid to us by the overseers at the end of our first turning in the form of several bronze coins, which we lined up for and palmed gratefully. Never having held a coin of my own, it felt very strange, and oddly liberating. I tucked mine into my pocket along with my white feather, my playing cards, and the little Mary figurine. On the way home, I stopped at the market, letting the others go on ahead.

"I'm hoping to buy a new clip for my hair," I told them, a lie which was easily believed. My hair was always pinned up under Xith's scarf, hiding my metrónomo, though the girls often begged me to let them brush it free.

I did not buy a clip. Instead, I hired a carrier-pigeon, which I hid under the bed in our room, alongside my cards, the feather, and my figurine.

The rest of my coins I gave to Liliath, in return for board and food.

Thaniel spent his, too; he bought me perfume.

Sometime, in the past few days, my eighteenth birthday had passed. It had come up when I was talking to Liliath, who smiled and congratulated me, not knowing the true meaning of this milestone. Had I been in the Pavilion, a party would have been held. I would have taken my first mecenas that night, and danced the full dance of his choosing to its conclusion.

Here, an eighteenth birthday was just another day.

And so, the gift was a surprise, which Thaniel sprung on me one night while I was helping Aiva – or rather, she was helping me – prepare dinner. Aiva had taught me several techniques, such as frying rice in mushroom juices, and making a broth from almost nothing. Moth-meat, though we worked in the very place where it was farmed and made into the tiny, wrapped cubes we enjoyed on the Spindle, was far between. Most of it was shipped directly out, for sale in the Cuidad.

We ate at the food market when we could, but there was something to be said for our quiet meals, spent alone. I wondered if this was how Miguel and his wife and children ate, together, around the table – and if my own mother had ever dreamed of such a thing.

"Come." Thaniel took my hand to lead me from the kitchen and into our bedroom. There, he produced a small glass vial, and when he opened the lid, the thick, rich scent washed out.

In all truth, it reminded me of the cloying perfumes my mother wore – the scent redolent of close, dark rooms, full of smoke and the smell of sweat and rumpled bedclothes. But I did not show this to Thaniel. It had been so long since I had such a luxury, and I was stunned by his thoughtfulness. He seemed likewise rapt with my enthusiasm.

"It is made from violets. The seller told me it fades quickly, but it is a pretty scent."

He dabbed a bit on my neck and cheek, using his fingers, which I caught in my palm and raised to my nose, breathing deeply. The scent itself was crisp and clear, and should not be tarnished by my memories. This I told myself.

"Thank you." I reached up a hand and pulled him closer. His beard was starting to grow, and the rough hairs scratched my fingers. He clutched my hand, trapping it against his cheek. I took in a sharp breath, as his hands trailed up along my arm, cupping my breasts. He spun me around, wrapping his hands tightly around my belly, and pressing his lips to the side of my neck.

"What is it about you?" he said. "How do you stir such desire in me?"

I smiled. "Surely no more than any other woman."

He shook his head. "That is not true. There have been others, of course. There are thousands of other women in Tierra Mejór. But *you* . . . "

"Thaniel," I whispered. "You are a Prince."

"I could make you my Princess. When I am declared heir . . ."

I pulled away from him, turning to face him. "Do you think the people of Tierra Mejór would accept me as their Princess? A Dancer of the White Pavilion?"

"They should," he said.

"They won't," I reminded him gently.

"Today," he went on, "I walked through a market, on my own. I selected this bottle from the dozens of choices. I paid my coin. It made you happy, did it not?"

"It did," I said.

"Then imagine how it felt, for me, to buy something for a woman I care about. To provide her with some small thing. It's all I've ever wanted out of life, Imre, though I didn't realise it until now. To do such small things."

I sighed, and laughed, somehow at the same time. "You are the strangest of men."

And we fell together into the bed, only emerging an hour later, rumpled and sheepish, to find Liliath, Naia, and Aiva had finished their meal and covered ours to stay warm. They left us to eat, while they shared knowing, smug glances.

Chapter Thirty-Eight

Turnings passed, and we worked. We rose to the Dawn Regimen at seven chimes, piped through the ampliphones into the streets; we passed the day on Level 6, sifting our dust; we stopped at the food market, or we came home to a thin, bitter tea. Thaniel and I crawled into our bed, occasionally finding the desire to make love, but sometimes too tired and sore and lightheaded even for that.

Liliath's work was taxing on her, as well. Oftentimes she would not return home for the night, and when I saw her during one of our short breaks in the dome, she was red-eyed and drawn. Still, she managed to summon gentle banter to goad her two girls, or veiled words of praise for their work or a new hairstyle. It impressed me greatly, how strong she was.

On odd occasions, I saw the other men and women who lived in the apartment building. Mostly, they were complete families, a mother, father, and one or two children. Very rarely, there were two women who were partnered, or two men, but these couples were always childless. It seemed rare that any family had more than two offspring, which I supposed was because of the small lodgings, but Thaniel informed me that to have more than two, a couple had to apply for a permit. Population control was important on the Wheel.

"The men and women here are charged to carefully time their unions. If a person is found to violate this, they can be imprisoned or fined."

"That sounds incredibly harsh," I observed.

"It's only sensible," he replied with equanimity. "There is only a number of jobs to be done, and people to do them, on Rueda. The balance would be tipped by indiscriminate childbirth."

I mulled this over. We had always heeded la Oráculo's words, which told us that a woman's job was to bear children, the more, the better. What if such a precept was employed on the Spindle? Certainly, as an unwanted child, I would never have been born. And in this place, where there were no night-cafés, or Red Houses, it would be much easier to avoid the temptation of a liaison outside of marriage.

However, the couples I saw seemed content. They moved in perfect unison with one another, seeming to exist in happiness and comfort, of a type I had rarely seen in life. I envied them.

We waited for Jark.

"It's just like Benoi to disappear for days," Liliath told us comfortingly. "You shouldn't worry. She'll have some important business or other, and in the meantime, you're welcome to stay with us as long as you need."

And indeed, with every passing day, as we fell deeper into our new normal, his presence seemed less and less likely. It was almost as if, now that we were inside this new life, the other one had ceased to exist, along with Jark, the Green-bands, the heralds, and the entire Spindle. Here, in this dull, twilit place, such things as my little garden house were merely dreams.

The Wheel was not entirely without recreation and amusement, however.

"Tonight, a Fete will be held," the ampliphones informed us one morning. "Please gather in the Bulevar Principal at eight chimes."

Aiva and Naia were overjoyed, chattering and giggling with pure excitement. Even Liliath looked thrilled.

There was no time to go home and change after the workday. We were still covered with dirt when eight chimes rang out, and we made our way towards the Bulevar. I must admit, I was tired enough to want nothing more than my bed.

Strains of music floated towards us, tinkling bells, the jangle of a guitar, a soft drumbeat. The tune was muted and flattened, for it was played through the ampliphones, without a single instrument in sight, but, still, music it was. My soul longed to dance, but my ankle was sore; the longs days of standing and walking, bending and carrying had made me accustomed to the slight twinges that now seemed the norm.

However, when I saw the gathering, my metrónomo leaped beneath the skin of my forehead, and a yearning filled my heart. All my aches and pains were suddenly gone.

I think Naia must have seen it on my face, for she pulled me by the hand. All at once we were surrounded by people, the rhythm of their footsteps on the pavement echoing through my body like the aftershocks of a tremor.

Naia's movements were gentle and slow, and she went carefully with me. I followed her lead, stepping carefully, and soon I relaxed into the easy pattern of this simple music. I could not Dance, but I could join this modest, easy dance with small movements and gentle steps.

"Perfection is found in unity," announced the voice over the ampliphones. "Unity brings joy. Let us celebrate our contentment and our place on Tierra Mejór."

"To the Pattern!" cheered the crowd. "To the Gardener! To Nuru! To the Wheel!"

The music changed tempo, and the pairs made a circle across the street. I spied Liliath with one of the men from Level 4, laughing as he brushed a hand over her shoulder, and smiled. Beside me, Naia giggled. "It's been a long time since I've seen her enjoy the touch of a man," she whispered. "Since Ibban left, anyway."

"Your father?" I asked, and she nodded.

"She asked him to leave," she said sadly. "She knew he wasn't happy here. He was from the Spindle, and not used to working underground."

"What does he do?" I asked her.

"He is a plumber," she said proudly. "One of the best. He was here for nine years, trying to repair the sprinkler systems in the domes. In the end the Guild recalled him for more important work. The sprinklers are still broken."

"What of Aiva's father," I asked her. "What is his name?"

"Holthe," she replied promptly, but then her small face wrinkled as an unpleasant thought occurred to her. "And he'll be home soon. I hope you won't have to leave. Perhaps we can find you a place nearby?"

The dance began.

We clapped in time as a pair from each quadrant skipped their way into the centre, whirled around one another, and skipped back; then every second pair turned around each other, joining hands. In this way, we made our way around the circle and back again.

The tune was lively, the movements faster, but it was still a straightforward dance, one meant to honour the Pattern. In its simplicity, my exhaustion melted away as I drank in the true joy of the night.

At one point, I looked across to see Thaniel watching us.

"Do you love him?" Naia asked me. It was a naïve question, one I hated to hear, for it was often spoken by my sisters as we questioned one another about a mecenas to whom we were particularly attached. The question, from her lips, was so innocent, so beautiful, I couldn't fault her. But I couldn't answer her, either.

Did I love him? Thaniel, Principe Regente of Tierra Mejór? Was it possible?

My heart raced when I was with him. He spoke of things that haunted my mind. He had torn me from the Pavilion, and everything I had known, on a selfish whim; he had abandoned me, then, and forgotten me. He was careless, and stupid, and addicted to substances which made him other than what he was. He was lost, as lost as I was, and this tenuous connection vibrated between us like a plucked guitar string.

When we joined, it was blissful. We buried ourselves in one another, hiding from our demons and our fears. He made me feel wanted, and needed, and beautiful, as if he had waited all his life for this. But love? The true, undying love that was spoken of in books? I did not know how to measure it.

I felt some strange irony in this. I had learned the Dance of Love, all its steps, perfectly. But of all the Dances, this was the one we practiced least. 'The Dance of Love,' Maestra Tinir would always say, 'is not the dance for a Daughter. We learn it in memory and honour, that two human entities may work together as one unit for the purpose of the Pattern. If you find a man or woman to dance as your partner, in life and Beyond, then you will dance the Dance of Love. But a Daughter, a true Daughter, will love only one thing, and that is the Pattern itself.'

And so, for all my skills, for all that Maestra Tinir had taught me, for all that I had the knowledge to make a mecenas scream in ecstasy and still beg for more – though I'd never yet put it to use – the actual concept of love, such as Miguel spoke of with Risella, or such as I saw in those families of South Gate, was frightening. It meant giving up my place in the Pattern as I knew it. It meant I was no longer a Daughter of the Pavilion, not even in my heart.

Perhaps I was not even capable of it.

We broke away after this, Naia and I, to join the others at a table that had been laden with food. None of it was particularly enticing – the same dried biscuits and hard lumps of cheese that you could purchase from the food market, but someone had taken care to arrange them in concentric circles on the platters. Cups of spice-ale circulated, and even a few of watered goldwine. Thaniel secured three of these, which we shared, while Naia and Aiva quaffed the ale like seasoned patrons of a night-café.

Across the way, Liliath's man was holding a bite of a biscuit to her mouth, and kissing away the crumbs; we shared delighted glances.

As the next tune started up, Naia and Aiva ran giggling with a group of their friends into the crowd. How young they were! I had become accustomed to seeing them smudged with dirt and their eyes glazed with tiredness. In reality, they were only girls, barely older than I had been when I first arrived at the Pavilion.

Thaniel held out his hand, inviting me to dance. I took it.

This dance was done in pairs, and we circled, learning the steps as we went. Side, side, twirl; clapping our hands together, then turning away.

Conversation was almost impossible, and we were both breathing hard, but it was so much fun; the crowd grew as more couples joined, and soon we were pressed for space. It didn't matter. That was part of this dance, to be one moving part amid many. Step, step, turn, clap. My metrónomo marked the rhythm. Someone behind me knocked my shoulder, pushing me into the Prince's arms. I laughed as he caught and spun me, before we resumed. I looked up into his eyes and found them locked with mine.

Step, step, side . . .

And then completed my turn, only to find him gone.

Surprised, I missed a step, and someone crashed into me from behind. My ankle cramped, and if there had been room to stumble, I probably would have. Instead I was pushed upright by heedless arms. I pushed against them, trying to break through, to see where Thaniel had gone. I felt strange, almost panicked. A woman smiled at me, and a man flicked his gaze at my breasts, such as they were, beneath my work-stained shirt. I didn't recognise any of the faces.

"Excuse me." I wriggled between a couple, turning my head left and right. Still he was gone.

But someone else was looking my way. Not with the casual greeting of one of our neighbours, but with a directness that spoke of intention. It was just a glimpse, before a tall man stepped between us, blocking him from sight, but instinctively I ducked and turned away. Something about him, his deliberate steps cutting through the joyous dance, uncaring as he spoiled the pattern, chilled me to the bone. I saw – I thought I saw, just beneath the collar of his shirt, a small, black tattoo of a spoked wheel.

I dared not look back to see if he followed me. Perhaps I'd been mistaken, but if not, it was best to pretend I hadn't noticed him at all.

I ducked and wove, apologising as I stepped on a girl's toes, catching an elbow in the ribs, steadying myself on the shoulder of a stranger. Again, panic threatened, as if I would be forever trapped in this crowd, fighting to free myself, hopelessly lost.

"Imre!"

And then he was there, my Prince, a slightly bemused expression on his face and a cigarillo in his mouth. I plunged into his arms.

"What is it?" he asked me. "What's wrong?"

"A herald," I told him.

"Where?" his eyes narrowed as he surveyed the crowd.

"No," I grabbed his hair, pulling his face back to mine. "Don't look for him. Don't draw his attention."

He paled and I let go of him, aware that it was my painful grip that had convinced him of what I'd seen.

"We should go," I said, and he nodded.

We found Liliath by the table. Her man was nowhere to be seen, but she looked very content. "I'm afraid my ankle pains me," I told her. "We must go home."

Home. As if it was our place, as much as hers.

"Oh, child," she sighed. "I'm so sorry. Here, take the key. The girls and I will be along shortly."

I took the time to smile and wave to Naia and Aiva, hoping we wouldn't arouse suspicion as we left the Bulevar. Thankfully, a servitor waited around the corner, and I spent a few of my hard-earned bronze coins for it to get us there as quickly as possible. Every second of that ride, I turned to check over my shoulder, but the dark streets remained empty.

Perhaps I had imagined it after all, or at least, that's what I hoped.

Chapter Thirty-Nine

Back at the place that had become our home, I washed myself thoroughly and wrapped my hair in one of the rough towels. My ankle still ached, but not as badly as before. I felt drowsy, and that helped keep my fears at bay. I poured two cups of the moth-wing tea and took them into our room.

"This should restore –" I began, but my words were cut short when I saw Thaniel sitting on the bed, one hand held in front of his face, fingers splayed. He moved it slowly left, then right. He spied me between his fingers, and his face lit up with that vacant grin I knew too well.

His trousers were dusted with white-powder.

"You didn't," I said, angry and incredulous.

"My Princess," he moaned, moving his hand from side to side and laughing at whatever effect this had on his drug-afflicted vision. "Sometimes, I think you're made of stars."

"Where did you get the powder from?" I demanded. "Did you steal it from Level 6?" Oh, I hoped not. If we were caught thieving from our employers, it could only cause more trouble! We were trying not to attract attention, after all.

"It's all around us." Thaniel slurred. "They don't sell it freely, but everyone takes it, here. Didn't you notice?"

No. I hadn't noticed, of course. I'd thought nothing of the relaxed state of most of the workers. Naively, I'd thought their striving for perfection was due to a desire to serve the Pattern. Then I remembered the uproar when we had first arrived, over the ruination of the shuttle-train. How quickly their ire had faded. Did anyone even recall it, now?

I pushed the cup of tea at Thaniel. "Drink this. Hopefully it will wipe some of the cobwebs from your mind."

"I like the cobwebs," he said forlornly. "I've missed them."

I placed the cups on the floor and sank onto the bed next to him, shrugging off his touches and covering my face with my hands in despair.

I was alone.

***

Later that night, I awoke in darkness, as the front door opened and closed. I'd left our bedroom door slightly ajar, and now saw Liliath and the man she'd met at the fete. He pressed her against the wall of her bedroom, his fingers slipping underneath her skirt, pulling up her top. She gasped as he ran his lips over her collarbone, her head rolling back with ecstasy.

She pushed him away, and they moved from my line of sight, but I could still hear their quiet gasps and happy sighs.

I knew sleep wouldn't return that night.

I slipped out of bed and crouched down, fishing underneath. The carrier-pigeon was still where I'd left it.

It came to life in my hands, twitching its legs and flapping its wings experimentally.

"Grath," I whispered to it. "I don't know what to do. We are trapped here. A shuttle-train was sabotaged, and the Estate has been attacked. Now Jark is missing, and I'm frightened for Than – for Anders. I think I've seen someone who might be a danger to us. I've heard nothing from anyone, and I'm . . . Please, tell me what to do."

I paused, wondering how this would sound to him: a weak, trembling woman, pleading for help. But I had no other ideas, and I was scared.

"We are staying with a woman named Liliath, Level 4, Unit 193B, Calle de las Luces. I don't know who else to contact, and if they come for us, I can't protect him. I wish I was strong enough to sort this out on my own, but I'm not. I'm sorry."

I went to the window, and, cupping the metal bird in one hand, used the other to push it open. Then I tapped the pigeon again, and whispered, "Message for Senor Grath only. Fly to the Citadel." The bird fluttered its wings in response, and flew into the night.

I turned back to bed and slipped under the sheets next to Thaniel's prone form. In the room next door, Liliath was enjoying her man. The knot in my stomach was a tight, hard pain. I strove to recapture the joy I'd felt for our hostess earlier, but instead, I felt as if I missed someone whom I wasn't quite sure I'd ever met.

***

In the morning, Aiva and Naia had returned, having spent the night with their friends. They were pleased to see the man, whose name, I learned over breakfast, was Miron. He was an agreeable fellow, a little older than Liliath, but I could tell he would be good to her – and I could tell that she wanted, desperately, to give him the chance.

Work would start later today, we were informed by the voice over the ampliphones. To be sure, this suited Thaniel, who did not seem inclined to move from the bed. He clutched his head, responding only with a grunt when I told there was food to be had.

***

The announcement came later that evening, while we were at the food market. I had coaxed Thaniel out of bed only with a great deal of effort, and he was irritable and grumpy for it.

When the ampliphones crackled to life, everyone looked up, startled by the interruption; my spoon of rice paused halfway to my mouth, and beside me, Thaniel stiffened.

"We serve the Pattern," said the montone showing no hint of personality or inflection. "We honour the order of the world, and find joy in its movements. But there is an enemy among us. An enemy of the Pattern, one who seeks to bring us to chaos. Prince Thaniel has fled his throne, evading the rightful hand of justice, choosing instead to hide, like a drain-rat, along with his sullied concubine. He would abandon his people."

Every word was like a dagger to the knot in my heart, plunging deep and twisting. Fear rose in me, and it had a taste – copper, and the smell of my own terrified perspiration.

"You must watch for them, these Agents of Chaos. Be wary. They will not be far from where you sit. They are your enemy, and they must be brought to face the justice they deserve. If you notice an increase in the number of vigilar, or are stopped in the street, know that this is for your own protection. Answer any questions truthfully, and you will be serving the Pattern. Above all, do not believe the falsehoods that are told to you by these Agents of Chaos."

There the voice ended, and suddenly, movement and excited chatter resumed.

I had dropped my spoon. Several clumps of the glutinous rice had fallen on the table, but no one had noticed. They were too busy looking around, searching the faces of their neighbours to see if they might be the Prince, or his wicked concubine.

I glanced at Thaniel, and then, reluctantly, at Liliath. Her face was filled with a curious expression, and she leaned across the table to me. "I was sure

I'd seen something. In the halls, the other day. A dark man, who slipped into the shadows. What do you think?"

"I –" I brushed at the grains of rice on my shirt.

"It might have been them, might it not, Arabel?"

Her gaze was unwavering, her eyes locked on mine. She *knew*. Then why this question? Was it a warning? A hint? A joke?

I swallowed against the dryness in my mouth. "Yes. Perhaps."

Liliath nodded, satisfied, then said: "Come, we should be getting home."

Chapter Forty

The next morning, I asked Aiva if she could take me to where Benoi lived.

"Of course!" she said, happily. "We'll go after breakfast, since we have a few extra hours before we need to start."

"Perhaps we'll keep it a secret," I suggested. "Just you and I?"

She seemed delighted at the idea, and Liliath raised no suspicions when I told her we were taking a short walk. With Thaniel still abed, she had said nothing more about the announcement, but I remained uneasy.

In contrast to the dark anxieties playing through my mind, the day had a relaxed feel to it, with only a few starting work at the normal time. Children took to the streets, men and women walking alongside them arm-in-arm. I looked at them all differently, now, scanning them for signs of intoxication, and was mortified to find many; dilated pupils, slow reactions, and two women leaning against one another, laughing like naughty children as they drew some rude symbol on a wall.

Aiva rolled her eyes at the behaviour. "It's always like this," she whispered. "After a Fete."

"Do you mean – the white-powder?" I asked her, and she nodded.

"I only ever take a little," she confided in me. "And sometimes I just pretend. I don't like the way it turns my thoughts."

My heart ached with the knowledge, borne of my years living on the Third Tier, that she and her sister were exposed to as much of the drug as their elders. Aiva might only pretend to take it sometimes, but she still spent every day in a place filled with the stuff, and I didn't doubt that there were times when she had taken more than a little. Even if she and her sister hadn't worked in the refinery, breathing the dust inadvertently, children always were in an incredible hurry to grow up when it comes to the pursuit of forbidden pleasures.

Aiva led me down a side street, startling a ratty-looking house-cat that was chewing on some dropped scrap, and it wasn't long before we arrived at a blocky building almost identical to our own, then climbed the stairs almost to the top level. Aiva paused, however, on the topmost step, for the door was slightly ajar.

I, too, was puzzled. "This is her apartment?" I asked her, and she nodded.

I stepped past her, pushing the door open all the way. It was dark inside, and smelled of smoke and something else – like freshly-turned earth.

"Benoi?" Aiva's voice was too loud in these quiet rooms. I stepped forward, my eyes adjusting until I could make out a sparsely furnished space. There was a table, a sofa, and many unwashed plates – and a roach, I noticed with a gasp as it ran over my shoe – but not much else.

I crossed to the bedroom. The curtains were drawn over a small window, and the dull light that fell through it was murky. There was no bed, only a mattress on the floor. And here he was.

Sprawled on top of tangled sheets, which had bunched under his kicking feet, he lay. His face was angled away from us, and for this I was glad, for I was able to herd Aiva from the room.

Her hand to her mouth, she went.

I closed the door and went back to examine him.

A long white jacket fitted over his grey shirt and boots. A Tinker's Guild-belt marked his status. His cheek was pressed to the floor, his eyes open and glassy. His skin was pale, his veins engorged, stark, dark blue. But worst of all, sprouting from between his lips, a mirror to the twisting red scar that pinched the skin below his nose, was a small brown flower.

I reached out a finger, stroking the velvet petals. They quivered a little under my touch, so delicate they shivered under the tension running through my body. I gasped, and pulled away. The thing was real.

"Don't touch him," I whispered to myself. And then: "Don't breathe."

I turned and opened the door. Aiva stood there, her mouth open, shock twisting her features. "We should go."

"We need to tell someone," she protested. "We need to get help!"

"No," I said. "Go. Now."

She must have heard the dire urgency in my tone, for she followed me without further question. I marched her all the way back down to the alleyway. I looked, down the darkened street. Suddenly it seemed full of shadows and dark spaces.

"Aiva," I said when we were alone. "You can't tell anyone about what we saw."

"But –"

I cut her off. "Aiva, this is very, very important. Jark – Benoi – is not who you think she is. Do you know of the Green-bands?"

She looked at me in confusion. "Yes, I know of them, but Benoi –"

"It's the truth," I said. "For reasons I can't go into now, I can't tell you the whole story. But if people find out we were there, that we found him like that, it could be very dangerous for you and your family. And for me," I added. "Benoi is known as a criminal."

"But she's a good woman!" she said.

"She was," I corrected her. "She fought for the right things. But not everyone sees it that way. You know that Green-bands are imprisoned, or sentenced to hard labour. So are those who help them. No one will care that you didn't know who she really was. That is why you can't even tell Liliath. Do you understand?"

The look on her face broke my heart; when she nodded it broke a second time.

***

Thaniel was furious that I'd gone to Benoi's apartment without him.

"What are you *doing*?" He whirled on me as I came into the room, and I was shocked by his anger. "You should have asked me."

"While you were drooling into your pillow?" I shot at him. "I don't need to ask your permission for anything I do."

"I'm the Principe Regente!" The words were loud – too loud. They bought him back to himself, and he covered his mouth with his hand.

I turned to leave the room, too upset to confront him with the myriad truths that I longed to shout in return. That he would claim his title now, when it suited him, just like the spoiled brat he was – but not when he needed to act like the ruler of Tierra Mejór!

"Wait!" He slumped onto the bed, his shoulders hunched, his hair hanging lank over his face. "Just . . . wait. Talk to me. Please, Imre."

"What is there to talk about?" I asked him, more kindness in my voice than I felt. "Thaniel – Jark is dead."

His head snapped up. "What?"

"He was there, in the bedroom. He was – he had been poisoned."

"How do you know that?"

How to describe the horror of that small, innocent flower bursting from his mouth? "The illness, Thaniel. It's here. It may have been an accident. But, knowing who he was . . ."

Thaniel pressed a hand to his forehead. "No," he whispered. "We need to tell someone – one of the guildsmen, the vigilar. We can't just leave the . . . the body there."

"It could be *your* body lying there," I hissed back at him. "Is that what you want?"

"That man – he was just a boy! – how long is he going to lie there before someone finds him?"

"Hopefully a long time," I said, surprising myself with the callousness of this wish. "The longer it is before he's discovered, the more time it buys us to work out what to do."

"What can we do?" Thaniel said. "It this is the work of the Brotherhood, where can we hide?"

I leaned across and pressed a hand to his mouth, startling him into silence. "These people have been good to us," I said in a low voice. "Don't endanger them."

He looked contrite, but I doubted he felt it. At least, he now spoke in a quieter tone. "Jark was an activist, a gainsayer of the throne. He must have made enemies. Perhaps it was one of them."

It was a possibility, I had to admit. But something about the way this illness developed made my skin crawl. It did not seem random, like the influenza strains we dealt with in the cold months. It seemed somehow more calculated, and, though horrific in its end, surprisingly non-violent.

"You said the door was unlocked," Thaniel continued, warming to his theory. "In fact, it was open, didn't you say? He either left it unlocked himself, before the person entered, or it was someone he knew well enough to let inside. In which case, he would probably have closed the door behind them, don't you think? He was dead in the bedroom, after all, so it doesn't fit that he would have lain down there to die after greeting a visitor."

"What are you saying?"

"I don't know," he said. "But we can't be sure it was anything to do with us. After all, no one knows who we are."

I hoped he was right, but it was so damned hard for me to think. I felt as if my thoughts were dragging themselves through mud, becoming thick, sticky things that refused to fit together. I knew it was the effects of the white-powder, but try as I might, I could not think of a solution.

I had not spoken a true parabra in turnings.

Chapter Forty-One

As confused as we might be, one thing was clear, and that was that neither of us knew what to do. We were frightened, and it paralysed us. And so, we dumbly went through the motions.

This was our mistake.

Liliath, I think, knew something was awry, though, of course, we could not tell her nothing. When she asked me how my walk with Aiva had been, I told some lie about visiting the market, and Aiva picking a necklace at one of the bead sellers that she liked best. She nodded and laughed, but there was a strained quality to her mirth. "Just like her! She does love things that sparkle and shine!"

To put her mind on something else, I asked after Miron, and she told me she was meeting him after work. This, at least, set a genuine smile on her lips.

Aiva, however, became withdrawn and snapped once or twice at her sister, her mother, and me. Twice I found her crying when she thought she was alone. I left her to it, not knowing how to offer comfort; I began to suspect that she had harboured a girlish crush on the person she knew as Benoi. I felt for her.

"She was a good woman," she whispered to me, as I helped her wash the dishes after the meal a day later. Since the announcement, we had taken to eating at home, rather than at the food market; again, I was stymied, trying to work out whether this was deliberate on Liliath's part.

"That she was," I assured her. "She didn't deserve this fate."

"Sometimes, I just want to turn back the hands of la Reloj de pie," she hissed, scrubbing hard at a stubborn piece of food. "I want to go back in time and prevent things from happening."

I knew what she meant. "There are many times —"

But all of a sudden, Aiva's hands stilled. Her eyes rolled back in her head, and she slid, as if boneless, to the floor, hitting her head with a resounding thump on the cracked tiles.

"Aiva!" I cried out, and Naia came running. Close on her heels was Liliath, who covered her mouth with her hands, shrieking. It was Thaniel, surprisingly enough, who lifted the girl from the floor and placed her on the sofa, so gently, so reverently. Her eyelids fluttered, and she tried to sit up; he pushed her back down. "Rest," he told her, refusing to let her speak.

He sat by her side for an hour, which I suspected would have given her great pleasure at any other time. When she finally stirred, she looked much better, but her voice was very hoarse.

"What happened?" she asked of us, as we clustered around her, unable to answer.

"Shouldn't we send for a healer?" Thaniel asked, later.

It drew strange looks from Naia and her mother. "There are no healers on Rueda," Liliath said, shortly. "We must speak a parabra to the Pattern, and hope for a cure."

Aiva rallied the next morning, enough that she begged to be allowed to go into work, but Liliath's lips only pressed into a thin line. "You will stay here and rest," she said. "I don't want to hear that you've left the apartment."

Her gaze had become haunted.

Thaniel and I could do nothing except go back to the moth refinery, and work, pretending we were nothing more than we were. I can't say why I took my feather, my figurine, and my playing cards and put them in my pocket that day, except that I felt comforted when I had them close by.

I had made friends with several workers. One, a woman, was particularly kind to me. Her name was Elvin, and she was probably no older than me, but plump, with curling brown hair and rosy cheeks. She could have been a Dancer, such was her innocent beauty, but it would never be her lot. Instead, she worked fiercely, catching the white-moths with her net and sifting enough white-powder to surpass her quota regularly. It often bought her grim nods from the Overseer.

"He likes you," I said, as she passed me an empty basket one morning.

She blushed. "He likes workers who do their jobs well," she murmured.

"He likes your breasts," I corrected her. "And your smile. See the way he inclines his head when he looks at you? He does that for no other woman."

She pushed me gently, laughing. "You are mistaken," she said, then nodded towards Thaniel. "What about you and your man?"

Thaniel had been working much more slowly, and I would like to believe he was being methodical, but it was the opposite: his work was sloppy. Several times, the Overseer sent back his baskets, full of lumps of dirt and moth bodies, and told him he would take a cut in his pay. Thaniel did not protest, simply staring at him with glassy eyes; nor did he pick up his game.

Almost every night that turning, I had found him stretched out on the bed, white-powder caked around his nostrils. We talked rarely, and no longer speculated about Old Earth. Our lovemaking was growing less common. I missed how we had been, when we'd first arrived, even if our feelings had not been actual love, but I think I understood, at least in part, what was wrong – he had found, once more, some fearful truth he needed to hide from.

"What about him?" I sighed.

"He is handsome," she said. "I can tell there's something between you. Do you deny it?"

I shook my head. "There is . . . something," I admitted carefully. It was nice to talk to someone about it, even if I couldn't tell the whole truth. "But what it is, exactly, baffles me."

The moths went wild seconds before it happened. It was as if a switch had been flipped, and they whirled into a fury, their small hard bodies hitting us with much more force than usual. Then, a sudden shudder passed through the floor. At first I thought it was an aberration in the machinery, that a wheel had come loose or a belt had snapped, but the shaking continued; it was an all-too-familiar feeling now, to have the world tremble this way. I clutched at the person nearest me, a young man who looked terrified. Someone screamed, and there was a loud crash, but I couldn't see what had made either noise, for the moths blocked my vision.

An alarm rang out, a piercing klaxon, and I clapped my hands over my ears.

"Attention," came the emotionless voice through the ampliphones. "Move quickly towards the stairs and exit the refinery. Remain calm."

At the front of the bay, the Overseer waved his arms, directing everyone to set down their baskets and sieves. I saw Elvin, walking briskly past, motioning to me to hurry. Thaniel, I noticed, stood back, watching as the trays kept rotating past, their contents unharvested; with a frustrated groan, I went to him and took his arm, steering him after the others. We climbed up through the levels, only stopping when we had reached the steps outside.

We moved aside and made way for the other workers, hundreds of them, who streamed out, chattering excitedly. They were followed by others, and then more and more. They poured down the steps which we'd recently vacated, gathering in tight knots, some looking worried, some annoyed, some bewildered. None of them seemed to know quite what was expected of them.

I stood on my tiptoes, searching for Naia or Liliath, but I couldn't see either of them. Nor was there any obvious damage – this tremor must have been a minor one. Perhaps, as the shocks radiated out from the Spindle, they were dispersed, lessening in intensity.

The stream of people slowly died to a trickle, and a man appeared at the top of the steps, his thumbs hooked through his Guild-belt as he surveyed the crowd below.

Suddenly, the klaxon died, leaving empty silence in its wake. The guildsman at the top of the steps raised his hands. "I apologise for the interruption of our workday. I know this had never happened before, so you must know how serious this issue is."

"What's happened?" called someone, and others cheered to hear the question asked.

"That is yet to be determined," the man said. "I assure you, a full investigation will be conducted. For now, we will be closing the factory early. You will all need to go home."

"Home?" another shouted. "We're in the middle of sorting a shipment of green moths! They need to be frozen, or they'll spoil overnight."

"I assure you, I wouldn't be putting a shipment in jeopardy if it wasn't necessary," the man said. "Go home."

Angry mutterings swelled all around us. I shifted closer to Thaniel, tugging his arm. "I think we should get out of here."

"I agree," he said, and we made our way along the edge of the crowd as a few angry shouts rang out. But already it was beginning to break apart, people drifting away uneasily.

At home, we found Naia at the door to the apartment, and we entered together. I told her to lock the door behind us, as we tiptoed inside. Aiva, however, was awake, peering through the window. She glanced over her shoulder as we entered, her little face pale, her eyes rimmed with red.

"What happened?" she asked.

"No one knows," Naia answered. "I don't even know where Mother is. Did you see her on Level 6, Imre?"

I shook my head, remembering that I hadn't seen her that afternoon, but that was hardly unusual.

"She would have been working in her laboratory," Naia said.

"I hope she heard the announcement," I said, beginning to worry.

Naia pursed her lips. "She did, but she's stubborn, and she hates being interrupted. She says the project is vital."

"Your mother told us about this particular strain of powder that's being refined. Is that what she's working on?"

Naia nodded. "Yes. It's why we went to the Spindle, to the Great Library – to research it."

A connection was slowly dawning on me, and a chill ran up my spine.

Naia made some moth-wing tea, and we each held a cup while we waited. Thaniel was the only one who asked for a refill, which Naia gladly provided. Aiva barely took two sips, and lay back down on the sofa soon after, falling into a deep sleep.

Thaniel, Naia, and I ate a miserable little meal together, of cold rice and dried mushrooms.

Still Liliath did not arrive.

"I'm going to go back to the factory and look for her," Naia said determinedly as she stacked the dishes in the small sink.

"I don't think that's a good idea," I said.

"Who are you to say?" This was as much assertiveness as I'd seen in the girl since I'd met her. "She's my mother, and I'm worried!"

"I'm worried too," I reminded her, though I didn't add, *I have more cause for concern than you.* "But they'll never allow us back into the refinery, not until we're told otherwise."

"Then what are we to do?" she said in despair, with a glance towards her sister, who still hadn't stirred from the sofa. "She should have been home by now. And I'm worried about Aiva."

I twisted my Guild-belt. "I am a guildswoman. I have more chance of being let back inside than you."

She looked at me imploringly.

I did not want to go back to the refinery. I was certain it would put me at risk, and, if the murder of Jark did have anything to do with our arrival, possibly other people as well. But Liliath had been good to us, and we'd lied to her about who we were and what we were doing here. We were responsible for what happened to her as a result.

Thaniel stood up immediately when I told him I was going. "I'll go with you."

"You need to stay here," I told him.

He shook his head. "No. If she's in danger . . ."

At this, Aiva's eyes went wide, and I held up a hand to stop him before he said anything else. "Anders," I said, very slowly and deliberately. "You must stay here. The girls need someone here in case anything happens, and besides, it will be easier for me to get in if I go on my own."

"Give me your Guild-belt," he argued. "They'll let me past –"

"If anyone is out there, looking for you," I said in a hushed, angry whisper, "you'll be walking right into their hands."

"Why would they be looking for you?" Naia queried, her gaze richocheting back and forth between us. "Are you in trouble for something?"

Thaniel ignored her. "They're looking for you, too," he reminded me.

"Yes," I returned. "But I'm less important than you."

He laughed, a sarcastic laugh.

"I am responsible for your safety. Grath is not here. Jark is dead. There is no one else."

He glared at me with red-streaked eyes, then whirled around and ploughed his fist into the wall. The force of the impact made the whole apartment shake, and startled me and the girls. Aiva began to cry, but Thaniel said nothing more, marching into our shared room and slamming the door.

I pressed my palms to my eyes, then slowly let my hands fall to my sides. "Keep the door locked tightly," I said to the girls. "Don't answer it unless it's me or Liliath. This is very important."

"This is to do with Benoi, isn't it?" asked Aiva in a small voice.

I didn't scold her for mentioning it in front of her sister; after all, Thaniel and I had just disclosed much more than we should have to both of them. "Perhaps. I can't be sure."

"Please," she said, desperately, tears pouring from her eyes. "Please don't go."

I kneeled by her side, and reached into my pocket, pulling out the small blue woman. The playing cards and the feather I tucked down my shirt, closer to my heart. The figurine I pressed into the girl's hands. "She will look after you," I told her. "My abuela told me Mary was a kind woman, who looked after those who were also kind and good. Keep her close."

Aiva's delicate fingers shook as she ran them over the worn, chipped paint, the tiny features, the smooth blue cloak. "She's beautiful." She looked up at me, with a look of thanks and wonder that I will carry with me for the rest of my life.

I stood, then, patting her hair; I was worried if I left it a moment longer, I would never be able to leave this small, brave girl.

Naia went to the kitchen counter, and, fishing in a small ceramic container, removed a few bronze coins.

"Who are you?" asked Naia, as she pressed the coins into my hands. I took them without protest, for my own supply was low.

I considered this for a moment. Was I Imre? Lady Arabel? A Daughter of the Pavilion, a whore, a fugitive, the guardian of a Prince?

I gave the only answer I could give. "I don't know."

***

The streets were much quieter now. I found a servitor easily, and told it to take me to the refinery. It did so, with speed, and before I was ready, large, luminescent dome rose up ahead.

The steps were empty, now. In fact, the whole place seemed deserted, and I walked inside unchallenged. My footsteps echoed far too loudly through the grated floor, into the cavernous spaces below. The benches were still covered with the remnants of work. A few masks had been discarded, and since I still had mine, I pulled it over my face.

How was I to find Liliath in this huge maze?

I wandered to the back of the room, where the stairs we'd taken earlier led down to the lower levels. I had only just taken one step when I heard voices. I pressed myself back against the wall, my metrónomo beating fast and irregular.

" . . .any idea," a voice was saying. "We can't just let it go. How long before the impact is felt on the Spindle? Already we have barely enough . . ."

"We are just following orders," a gruff reply came. There were two of them, coming up the stairs, their shadows wavering against the wall.

"The orders make no sense!"

"Then what would you have me do?" I recognised the voice. The man who had spoken on the front steps – the Overseer. "Do you think any of this is my choice?"

"Perhaps not. But do you see where this is leading us?"

"For the sake of the Pattern, man, do you think I don't know the facts and figures? Do you think I don't lie awake at night, running them through in my head? Every turning, more systems fail. My hands are tied!"

"Then we need to start evacuating the Wheel."

"You know as well as I, we can't do that," the Overseer growled. "The panic would destroy us, even if we were able to do it. Putting aside that fact, and the fact that food is already growing scarce, let alone if there are no Ruedans to produce it, you're talking about moving thirty thousand people into a space designed to hold thirteen. In the end, the result would be the same; many, many people would die."

A door opened, closed, and then the voices were gone. I was shaking as I came out of my hiding place. I wanted to turn back, but I still had found no sign of Liliath.

Despairingly, I looked through the doors into the levels I passed. Like the upper floor, they were still lit, with tools and supplies laying where they'd been left, but not a soul was here, only the moths, flittering and fluttering untended. At last, I reached Level 6.

I crossed the empty bay. The trays continued to rotate, slowly, the dust falling in whirling plumes. The creaks and groans of the machinery was much louder as I passed towards the source of the noise. Beyond a metal railing was a slot in the floor, where gears and wheels turned slowly, steam hissing from between them. All of these were connected to one large wheel, from which ran a series of cogs and belts, which in turn made the tiered trays rise and fall.

Behind this was a door into a room, just as dark as the bay, but much smaller. There were several benches, on which sat glass cases, some containing murky liquid, others, hundreds of tiny, fluttering white-moths. Lining the walls were cabinets filled with vials and jars, and to one side, a stack of barrels.

The large wheel just outside the door filled the space with constant, ceaseless sound.

I crossed the room, bending down to peer into one of the glass cases. The moths fluttered frenetically, seeking freedom. I kept to one side of the door and stared through the shadows. Inside, there was nothing to say that anyone had been in the room at all that day.

And even as I thought this, I felt someone behind me.

I whirled, but not fast enough. The hand was around my throat before I could even scream.

I had a panicked flash of the face – Chette's. Impossible! And so it was – for it wasn't a man at all, but Liliath, her expression twisted.

"Don't scream," she hissed, and that was when a blade pricked my neck.

Chapter Forty-Two

"I'm sorry," she said. There were tears in her eyes. "You shouldn't have come here."

Pressed back against the wall, my head twisted slightly to one side, all I could do was look at her. I didn't dare to blink. "What are you doing?" I managed to say, though my throat was tight.

"What do you think?" She seemed annoyed.

"I think you're trying to kill me. But since you haven't actually done it, I can't be sure."

"Is that supposed to be funny?" she said, and one of those tears trickled down her cheek. She shook me a little, the knife paring the top layer of my skin with a sharp jolt of pain. "How can you be glib?"

"It's not supposed to be anything." I tried not to wince. My mask shifted a little over my nose and mouth, making it harder to breathe. "But you're hesitating, and that makes me think you don't actually want to kill me. So, I think I have the chance to at least ask you why."

She took a shuddering breath. "I don't have a choice. No one can know what we do in here. They have Holthe, and they'll kill him if they find out you've seen this!"

My brain, addled from the white-powder, struggled to pit these pieces of information in place. "Your brother. Whose room we are sleeping in."

She nodded, relaxing her hand on the knife just a little. "They took him. Told me to use my knowledge of Horticulture to modify and combine the genes of a moth with that of the Sacred Tree. Not just any plant – it must be the Sacred . . ."

"Why?" I asked, trying to understand, desperate to keep her talking – for while she was conversing with me, she wasn't pushing the knife into my throat.

"The Sacred Tree is the emblem of the Pattern. The Brotherhood revere it. But I suspect there was some more practical meaning, as well. The Sacred

Tree is known for its adaptability. It can be grafted with other plants, and is easily hybridised. My first attempts were failures, producing small, withered things. Still, I was able to refine some white-powder from their stunted wings. The heralds were pleased. They took what I had to offer, and told me I would need to double my efforts.

" 'Go to the Spindle,' they said. 'Research the white-powder in the Great Library. Find whatever you need.' "

She gave a small, disbelieving laugh.

"Naia and Aiva thought it was a holiday. They knew only that Holthe was gone on some mission. I couldn't tell them the truth.

"I did what I needed to do; in truth, I already knew what to research, for as an apprentice I had played with the ideas of combining the cells of plants with those of animals. For a while, it was a test, a challenge, a chance to prove my skills as something other than a Level 6 moth refiner. The heralds had assured me, when I came back, when the powder was ready, they would let Holthe go. But then . . . the barrels were full." She motioned to the side of the room, and there they were, marked identically to the ones we filled every day on Level 6. "They shipped them out, and they told me they had other plans. They would let him go when they were done. They took what I had made, and . . . people started falling ill."

"The white-powder." I closed my eyes. So many in the Lower Tiers had already died. Had they been taking Liliath's modified white-powder, thinking it was the normal type that had been among the people for generations? It could only be so; and yet, there was one unfathomable question.

"Why?"

"I only did what I was asked!" she cried, her eyes full of anguish, as if she was accusing me of blaming her. And, without a doubt, I was.

"What you were asked," I repeated, "Was to kill Jark. Benoi, I mean."

She shook her head. The knife pricked me, deeper this time, and a trickle of blood ran down my collar bone. "No. You're lying."

"She died of your illness. She took some, thinking it the normal variety of white-powder, or some found its way into her apartment, somehow. We found her there." Another thought struck me, one even more terrible. "Aiva was with me."

That poor child. Her red-rimmed eyes, her tiredness and weakness. She had caught the illness, and even now, the malicious seeds were probably taking root in her stomach, her lungs. Even now, she was probably dying.

At this, Liliath let out a cry of anguish.

"You did this!" she shouted.

"No!" I returned with vehemence, my voice slightly muffled by the mask. "Who asked you to create the powder? Who sent you to the Spindle, to the Great Library? They are the ones responsible!"

Liliath still did not release me, but her grip loosened. "The Overseer told me the orders were from the highest," she whispered. "From the Brotherhood itself."

"They care nothing for you." My voice cracked. Thaniel was a threat to the Brotherhood, yes, and they despised me; but this white-powder had already killed dozens, perhaps hundreds. It could kill thousands, as it spread throughout Tierra Mejór. People would use it, unknowingly, breathe it into their lungs. It was a weapon with an immeasurable range. "Or your niece, Benoi, or your brother. They have some terrible plan, and you are only a small part of it. This poison, it spreads unchecked, through the air and through touch."

Ketra.

Ketra, lying so still, her hands folded.

I bit back a sob, and took a slow, even breath, as well as I could through the mask, without pressing my neck against the blade. "I have twice touched an infected victim. Why hasn't it passed to me?"

"I don't know," Liliath cried in despair. "How can I? There is no cure, so perhaps you will become ill, in time! And I, too – and Holthe," she wept. "They'll kill Holthe as well."

I tried to slow my racing heartbeat. I tried to think past the panic swirling through the muddy mixture of thoughts in my mind. Suddenly, Liliath leaned forwards, putting her weight back onto me.

"Then what about you?" she asked. "Are you the one they're searching for? If I hand you over, they will spare me. And Naia. And Holthe . . ."

"I don't know who you think I am," I told her, my voice perfectly calm. I was trying to reconcile this woman, this haggard, anguished woman, with the motherly figure I had known for the past three turnings. There was so little resemblance. Could I ever count on anything, on anyone, again? "But everything I've told you is the truth."

The pressure on the blade eased a little, and I took advantage of this to wriggle sideways. "If you allow the Brotherhood to do this, you will be a murderer. You will kill hundreds, even thousands. Your brother, even if he is still alive, will not thank you for that."

She blinked, then tightened her grip once more. More blood run free from the wound on my neck. "You must destroy the laboratory," I said. "You can't let them do this."

Even as I said the words, I could tell she wasn't going to do it. She would kill me and go back for Thaniel. She could easily raise the alarm. He would probably never have the sense to run, nor the wits to find a place to hide, weak and drunk on powder as he was.

With a deft turn, I whirled away from her. Turn, turn, step – and I was behind her. A movement from the Dance of Greeting and Leaving, executed with perfection that would have made Maestra Tinir proud.

I grabbed the arm that held the knife, but she was stronger. She clenched it tight to her chest, then spun to face me. Her mouth was twisted in fear.

Off-balance, I fell backwards. Even as I tried to right myself, my elbows crashed though the glass. Suddenly, the air filled with moths, the scales from their wings rising like smoke. I clutched my mask to my nose, trying to hold my breath, but they swarmed towards Liliath as if recognising their parent; they covered her face, and she wailed, flailing. The knife fell from her hands, and she dropped to her knees. Her wild eyes already turned red.

I ran for the door, but only got halfway there when she lunged after me. She caught me by my Guild-belt, wrenching me backwards, and we fell to the floor. She was heavier than me, and she tried to use this to her advantage, to pin me to the ground with her weight, but I bucked my hips, tipping her off-balance, then scrambled on hands and knees for the door. Where was it? I could hardly see – the air was filled with powder, and my eyes ran with thick tears. Finally, I found a blank space and hauled myself through. I turned to pull the door shut, but she was already blocking the space, though she looked so much like Jark's corpse, I thought she must already be dead.

And then she lunged at me again, bringing the knife down, right above my heart.

I ducked, but the knife caught my mask, tearing it free.

My bad ankle gave way and I fell into her. Off-balance, blind, flailing, she tottered back against the railing that protected the wheel. And then, almost in slow motion, she toppled over. There was a screech. I couldn't tell if it came from my mouth or hers or was simply the mechanism chewing into her corpse, but I felt a warm splatter of blood.

And then, unable to hold my breath any longer, I drew in air.

The white-powder came with it.

***

I staggered towards the moth trays, white wings fluttering all around me. The door beckoned from the other side of the bay. All I had to do was reach it – but my limbs had stopped obeying me. It felt like I was walking through water, then like my whole body was no more than that. Then I saw the floor, abruptly, and it took me a moment to realise I had fallen.

Red streaks crossed my vision. Blood? I couldn't be sure. The floor felt sodden with it. Except . . . no, it was moist, cool, comfortable . . . not hard cement, but soft grass. The smell hit my nostrils, beautiful and sweet and fresh. Where was I?

Hello again, querido.

I took a deep breath, and with it, my body rose. It was as if a great weight had been lifted. The shadows drew back, and I wasn't on Level 6 anymore. Instead, I stood in a wooded glade, surrounded by trees. Above me opened a sky so clear and blue, I had to blink. This was not any sky I'd seen on Tierra Majór.

"Hello?" I called.

She stepped into the clearing, her dress trailing behind her, her long dark hair curling around her cheeks.

I felt like I knew her.

You do know me, she said, though her lips didn't move.

"I – Where am I?"

She spread her arms. *Here.* She smiled. *I know you, querido, dear one. You want a name. I could give you many names for this place, but none would describe to you where it is, or even what it is. Let us just say that this is a place where we can talk.*

"Talk? About what?" I had a vague notion that something important had just happened, but I couldn't place exactly what it was.

About anything you wish.

"I – I don't understand." I shook my head.

I think you do. She sat, her skirts billowing, and patted the grass next to her. Warily, I joined her. Everything felt very real, even though I was sure this was a dream. *I think you know what is happening.*

"To Tierra Mejór? It is falling apart. But I don't know why." I was distracted for a second by a flitting green-and-blue creature, like a moth, but stunningly beautiful; its wings barely brushed my skin, and then it was gone. "Is that what I'm supposed to ask? Why Tierra Majór is dying?"

All things come to an end, she replied. *At least, those things you can touch; those you can't, they will endure forever, and that is the riddle of existence. For you desire touch, with all your heart, you mortal beings.*

"Is that bad?" I asked her. "It sounds like something the heralds would say."

Not at all. It is what you were made for. And you, my child, more than any.

"There's nothing different about me."

Except that you are here, when no one else is, she pointed out with her enigmatic smile. *Not your heralds. No one, except for you.*

"Well," I said, "am I to let Tierra Majór die? Just sit back and wait for it to happen?"

Is that something you could do?

"No."

Then you must do everything you can to stop it.

"But I just told you. I'm no different to anyone else. And the heralds want me dead. I don't even know why."

Then perhaps that is the question you should be asking.

"I *am* asking! But I don't understand you!" I snapped in frustration. "If I'm supposed to save Tierra Mejór, why would they want to stop me?"

Indeed?

"It is dying. Everything is winding down, in the process of breaking, if it's not already broken. The heralds know it. And they're letting it happen. Why would they want that?"

Why does anyone do anything in this world?

"Power, or wealth. Boredom. Greed."

Then perhaps there is a motive you are not aware of.

"How does that help me?"

Perhaps it doesn't. She rose.

"Wait!" I called after her. "Please! You have to tell me something!"

You already know the answer, querido, she replied, and then she was gone. And so was the clearing.

A man was there. I could barely make out his features, but his eyes filled with relief as I focused on him. Heat prickled my skin, and a smell filled my nose. Smoke.

"I'm a friend. Come!" He pounced on me, dragging me through the clouds of dust. Flames licked the walls, burned my skin.

Then, I was at the end of the street, looking back at the refinery. The dome was huge and bright and beautiful in the night sky. An alarm blared in my ears.

Chapter Forty-Three

The man told me his name – Hillder – and that he was a Green-band sent by Senor Grath, but at first I didn't believe him; in any case, all I cared about at that moment was getting home. And so, with blood leaking into the collar of my guildswoman's shirt, white-powder still in my hair, I ran.

The ampliphones crackled to life.

"Attention. Please return to and remain in your homes. Anyone caught on the streets will be subject to punishment. Serve the Pattern, and keep to your homes."

I had never seen anyone disobey the voice before, but ahead of me, a group was gathering on the sidewalk. "This is intolerable!" a woman shouted. "We cannot be subjected to this any longer. The time has come for equality!"

There were hollers of encouragement, cheers, and applause. Somewhere, a child cried, thin, high-pitched wails.

I kept running. I don't remember how I got to the apartment. In fact, time seemed to move in fragments, with the pieces in between absent; I passed another group of men, and as I watched, one of them picked up a brick and hurled it through a window. The shattering sound echoed that of the glass cases in the laboratory. More cheering followed. Then, everything is a blank, up until the moment I pounded up the steps. I knocked, but when there was no answer, I tried the door. It was unlocked, and my heart sank. I'd told Naia to open the door for no one.

"Naia!" I called. "Aiva! Anders!"

Empty. Aiva was gone from the sofa, and Naia with her. I rushed to the bedroom, but though the contents of our bags had been flung everywhere, he wasn't there. I could have believed that they'd simply gone out, leaving the door unlocked, if I hadn't known in my heart that something was deeply wrong – not just here, not just what had happened in the laboratory, but on Rueda. I returned to the kitchen, looking about helplessly, and found only a plate smashed on the floor. That single sign seemed to speak volumes.

I stood there in the middle of the sitting room floor for what felt like several minutes, but was probably only seconds, trying to force my brain to work. It only occurred to me slowly that the best thing to do was get out of there, as fast as I could.

"Imre?"

I whirled. At first I couldn't believe my eyes, and then my knees gave out and I sank to the floor.

It was Grath.

***

After leaving me with Jark, back on the Spindle, Grath had returned to the Citadel. He had bundled Thaniel into an autocarriage, along with Miguel and Hendrich – the only two he could trust with the task. Miguel himself had driven the carriage, for there was no time to find a replacement automata for the journey.

Having done all he could for now, Grath cleaned himself up in the Prince's suite, changed his clothes, and prepared for what was to come.

The summons came only a few hours later, as he was drifting into an exhausted doze on a sofa. Chancellor Darhn bought the news himself, his old face lined with concern. "There will be a price to pay for this," he said quietly, as he led the way to the lift-car.

Grath nodded. He was expecting nothing less.

Hendrich and Miguel guarded the door, and Grath suspected this was by design. Darhn knew the men were trustworthy, and he wanted them nearby.

The Conclave was half-formed. Besides the vigilar at the door, only those who could convene hastily were there – a scattered handful of Guildmasters and lawmakers – but the Chancellor had arranged for la Reina to be sitting in her rightful place. Beside her sat Benefine, and on her left, Chancellor Darhn. Commander Fedren took the end seat.

And, of course, la Boca, the Mouth of the Pattern, was there, lording over the back of the room. As Grath took his seat, Chancellor Darhn raised his staff. "I call –" he began, but was cut short by a clacking as the seats changed their configuration, la Boca's moving its way to the front.

"This is no time for ceremony," he growled.

The Chancellor glared at him, but la Boca was not cowed.

"Where," he demanded, "is our Prince?"

"It has been decided," said Chancellor Darhn smoothly, "that the safety of the Principe Regente cannot be guaranteed in the Citadel."

La Boca's eyes flashed. He surveyed the small crowd as they reacted to the news with shocked murmurs and gasps. "You mean to say that he has fled, leaving his people, his City, to face the dangers of the quakes and this spreading illness alone?"

"I am saying that the Principe Regente must be protected —"

La Boca stood. His long black cloak billowed behind him as he stepped from his chair down to the floor. Here, he turned to face the chairs. "The Principe Regente, who speaks for us all." His voice was a taunting drawl. "Yet he is not even named Principe Verderaro."

Agreement was evident in the faces of those gathered. They nodded to one another. It was true, after all.

La Boca turned, crossing to stand before the table. Once there, he placed his long, spindly fingers atop it. Leaning forwards slightly, he peered into Chancellor Darhn's sightless eyes.

"Is it not time," he spoke slowly, "that he was named as our future King? Hm?"

The murmuring of the Conclave grew louder.

"Why has la Reina hesitated?"

La Boca shifted, so that his focus was no longer on Darhn, but on the woman sitting beside him, stiff and upright in her chair, her face pale, her porcelain features unmoving. Very slowly, her eyes blinked once, as if struggling to focus on the man before her. Grath tensed. It was all he could do not to look sideways, for that might very well give the secret away.

"Has he proved himself unworthy?" La Boca continued. "Is he unfit? La Reina?" He leaned in even closer. "What say you?"

Grath closed his eyes, reaching for his wristwatch and fiddling with the knobs. The tiny increments of each dial moved the automaton in so many different ways. He'd come to know them well over the past few months, and he could do it with his eyes closed. But he couldn't make the automaton speak. His greatest, most singular failing. He had tried recordings that had been made of la Reina's speeches during her time of health, stored on ancient devices that wrote the voice to black strips of tape, piecing together fragments of speech, enhancing them to make them sound more real. It hadn't worked.

He had known the reckoning would come, had known the ruse would be discovered. But even so, he had hoped for more time, for some solution to arise from that deep part of his mind that was forever churning over, worrying at what was effectively a death sentence. He had never before spoken a parabra so heartfelt as his wish that the automaton would not fail him now.

Under Grath's direction, la Reina tilted her neck slightly to one side, then slowly shook her noble head. At any other time, it would have been enough. The councillors and guildsmen in the room were used to la Reina's silences and vacant stares, aware of her illness, and unwilling to question her publicly, even if they did think this unusual. But today, a simple gesture wouldn't suffice.

La Boca swooped.

He tangled his spindly fingers in her curling blond hair and wrenched. The wig, so carefully sewn from strands of la Reina's real hair, came free as the stiches tore. The porcelain face looked on in shock as la Boca held the wig high over his head, shaking it in triumph as he turned back to the Councillors, who were openly gaping.

"See how you have been deceived!" he cried. "Deceived by these –" sweeping an arm, he encompassed the table – "your leaders, your masters, your councillors! They have lied to you. It is all . . ." here he dropped his voice to a hiss, "*lies*."

The clamour had grown in volume.

"None of these men or women is fit to lead you," la Boca said. "None of them can be trusted. I ask you then. Who has had your best interests at heart? Who has spoken only the truth?"

Herald Benefine shot to his feet. "La Boca!" he cried.

Suddenly, there was a resounding response: "La Boca! La Boca!"

The shocked, dazed crowd rocketed to their feet. They raised their fists and pounded the air.

"La Boca!" they said as one. "La Boca!"

La Boca turned his eyes to the table. He waved an arm, almost casually. "Arrest these men."

Grath had remained sitting, but now he stood. His hand clenched on the hilt of his sword. He could fight, and he would, and damn the odds; but in the end, it would accomplish nothing. No-one in the city would back him now; he had betrayed them all by creating this failing puppet.

Several councillors started forwards, as if hoping to accomplish the deed themselves; however, Commander Fedren motioned them back. His face showed his astonishment, but he was levelheaded to the last.

"Silence!" he roared. "Let cool thought prevail here!"

La Boca stared at him, and it was a credit to the man that he didn't quail, not for a moment.

"They will be taken to the cells," he said. "To await a trial and questioning, to determine the degree of their guilt."

This was not what la Boca wanted – a fair trial was not what he required to seize power. However, the idea of a public spectacle, and one in which he would be seen as the fair arbitrator of justice, did suit his needs. He nodded in assent.

Fedren took Senor Grath's hands himself, twisting an arm up behind his back. "March," the captain whispered in his ear. "Don't loosen your blade, or you're done for. Obey me and I might just get you out of here."

Grath tried to see what was happening to the others. Chancellor Darhn had been swallowed by the crowd. Where was Secretary Allius? Where was the treacherous Benefine? He had a glimpse of Hendrich, who must have been drawn into the chamber by the noise; but he couldn't see Miguel. Grath gritted his teeth, wanting nothing more than to pull his sword from his sheath and cut down these monsters, but allowing Fedren to propel him through the crowd. In the hallway, Fedren turned quickly right, then left. The crowd fell back as the accused were loaded into the lift-car.

The Commander let go of Grath's arm once they were out of sight. "Go quickly, while the ruckus holds. Is there somewhere you can hide?"

Grath nodded. "Watch your back, Commander." He clasped the other man's hand in his own.

Fedren nodded grimly, then turned back to the melee. Grath knew he could waste no more time worrying about what the Commander might face for letting him walk free. He turned and ran.

***

At a house on the edge of the Second Tier, a tidy woman with brown hair opened the door to find a handsome, tall man. Instantly, she seized him by the collar and drew him inside – not without considerable force, it must be added. For a small woman, Risella was formidable.

Glancing out into the street to see if anyone was watching, she pulled the door quickly closed and began to do what she did best – bustle.

She sat Grath at the kitchen table, and put a mug before him, full of tea, then took a canister from a cupboard and doled seven biscuits onto a plate, setting this beside his right elbow.

Then she told him to stay where he was while she set-up a room for him upstairs.

Grath had no problem complying. He picked up a biscuit, but it was like sawdust in his mouth. He sipped the tea instead, but after two gulps, he put his hands on the table and let his forehead drop on top of them.

Imre.

His attention, he knew, should be with the Prince. But it was not. Instead, every thought looped back to the girl, the beautiful girl, who should have faded into non-existence long ago. What was it about her? Why could he not tear his mind from the way her mouth moved into a smile or frown, the clear light in her eyes, the curve of her hips?

He was distracted from these thoughts only by the arrival of Miguel. With him was a man wearing a green-banded hat. "Risella," Miguel said to his wife, who had just returned to the kitchen. "Senor Grath. This is Hillder, an afficianado of the Green-bands."

The man removed his hat with a bow, but his gaze, when he straightened, was troubled.

"Senor Grath will need to hear your report," Miguel prompted, as he sat down.

"A shuttle-train," the man blurted out, shaking his head. "Lifted from the tracks en route to Rueda. A failure – a terrible accident –"

Grath's heart seized.

Miguel rubbed a hand across his sweaty brow. "We don't know. We know nothing for certain. It may not have been theirs."

Grath looked down at his biscuit. He was dimly aware of the conversation swirling about him, but he could barely hear it. A crumb fell from one corner, bouncing on the table.

Finally, Hillder left, and Risella went upstairs to try and sort through some of Miguel's smaller civilian clothes, that Grath might wear them in disguise.

Miguel and Grath sat in glum silence, until Miguel reached for a sweet. Like Grath, he seemed unable to eat it, however.

"They are her favourites," he said. "Coffee biscuits."

Grath replaced his half-bitten biscuit on the plate.

***

The next few days passed in a blur for Grath. While I was cooped up in the moth refinery alongside Thaniel, breathing in white-powder and dealing with Jark's death, he spent his days meeting with Hillder, Miguel, and Hendrich. The three of them bought with them news from the Citadel and the streets. None of it was good.

After discovering Grath missing, la Boca had ordered the immediate execution of Commander Fedren, Chancellor Darhn, and, for good measure, the tutor, Lyndra, who had spoken out in favour of the Prince. It had happened in the Plaza de Lágrima, in front of the statue of la Oráculo, and several hundred horrified and fascinated men and women.

La Boca had then returned to the Pendulum and the Iglesia, leaving Benefine to govern in his stead.

The illness spread. More and more people were dying. There had been more tremors, though none quite so bad as those earlier quakes. Many carrier pigeons were delivering garbled messages, and there were other diseases arising from the garbage piling up in residential areas.

Grath listened to it all, feeling increasingly powerless as the turnings passed. Miguel wouldn't allow him to leave the house, even to help the Green-bands dispense much-needed aid. It was too dangerous, even in disguise. Grath could see the sensibility of it, but felt himself slowly going mad.

That was until one morning as he struggled from nightmarish dreams to wakefulness, he heard a tapping at his door, and Risella entered, carrying a battered-looking carrier-pigeon.

"This arrived at the Citadel for you," she said. "One of our comrades intercepted it and smuggled it out. It's a private message, so rest assured no one has heard it."

"Speak," Grath told it, and from its beak sprung my voice – according to him, the most welcome sound he had ever heard in his life.

*****

He helped me to the sofa, and sat me down. Despite my protests that I was, perhaps, infected with the illness, he bathed my eyes with water. He marched back and forth across the room, then stopped and stared at me for a long while, his hand on the hilt of his sword, then turned and marched again, his boots too loud and heavy for this room, which had always been full of quietness and contentment.

I had blurted out everything in an incoherent stream of words, and he'd listened very seriously.

"But now the Prince –"

"The Prince is safe," he growled. "He's with Guardsman Dillion, at this very moment. Their order are to meet us at the shuttle-train station. It's best if we arrive separately, at different times, to throw off anyone who's been watching you."

I thanked the Pattern. Of course, the only other person the Prince would have opened the door to was a guardia he trusted.

"But then – if the Principe Regente is safe, you should have left straight away. Why come back for me?"

He stared at me. "Do you really not know?"

"No?" I answered slowly, trying to work it out for myself. "Since we met, all you wanted was to have me gone. Now you come all the way back here, risking the life of the Prince, just to find me and take me home? No, Senor Grath, I do not."

"You don't have to," he said grouchily. "Suffice it to say, the Brotherhood have found you – or you have found them. I'm starting to think there is nowhere that will be safe for you, or the Prince."

"Naia," I gasped. "Aiva. Where are they?"

"The children?" Grath looked sorrowful. "One of them was dead. The other has been taken to a safehouse. Hillder organised it. She will be fine there."

"Aiva," I moaned. "No."

I think I would have buried my head in the worn sofa cushions then, and cried my heart out, but there was no chance for me to wallow in sorrow. The benighted ampliphones crackled to life. There was no voice, this time, just the sound.

It rang out through the street below. Almost instantly I heard something crash, then someone's shout. And then the whole apartment began to shake.

Another tremor – or so I thought at first. But then came the explosion, and the glass in the window above me blew in. Grath knocked me to the ground, landing heavily on top of me. Small pieces of glass grazed my arm, and heat – incredible heat! The stench of scorched fabric reached my nostrils.

Already Grath was pulling me to my feet.

My head throbbed with bright red pain. "What's happening?"

"I don't want to be here to find out," he said, as we pushed through the apartment door, and into the stairwell. The smell of smoke hit us, swirling in and out of the open doors to other units, their occupants having already fled. But as I turned to start my descent, I saw a figure coming up the stairs. It took a moment for me to recognise the man's face, but when I did, I let out a small scream.

Grath pushed his way in front of me, and with the sound of a knife on a whetstone, he drew the short sword from its sheath on his belt.

The herald, the same man I had seen at the fete that night, sneered. He was wearing grey worker's garb, his tattoo hidden by the collar of his shirt. He was holding, in one hand, a revolver-pistol. This he raised and aimed straight at my heart.

I closed my eyes. This is how I missed seeing Grath spring at him, covering a drop of twelve stairs, and landing in a crouch only after he'd planted a boot firmly in the herald's chest. The gun went off, and I ducked, opening my eyes to see a hole in the plaster of the wall beside me.

Grath was pulling his sword from the man's shoulder, wiping the blood on the man's worker disguise.

I gaped at Grath. "How did you know he was a herald?"

"I saw the gun. It was an educated guess that he was an enemy. Come on!"

I stepped over the man, whose blood was pooling in the floor beneath him. I was halfway down the next flight of steps when I heard the movement, and turned back just in time to see him move the hand which had not been holding the gun. Something fluttered free.

"A carrier-pigeon!" I gasped, grabbing a fistful of Grath's shirt.

Grath whirled, and charged up the steps, swiping at the fluttering thing with his sword, but the arcing blow fell short. The pigeon rose out of reach, heading for some open window higher up.

Grath took my hand, pulling me down. "There's no use," he said. "We must go."

Chapter Forty-Four

The Calle de las Luces was in chaos. Somewhere nearby, several men had overturned one of the modified conveyance servitors, and were gathering the coins that spilled free. There were others running with packages and belongings, yet others carrying small children; older kids swaggered, cussing and yelling, in the opposite direction, throwing rocks and chunks of mortar and concrete.

The air was soupy with smoke. My streaming, wounded eyes stung, and it was all I could do to keep up with Grath as he led the way. I would never have found the train station alone.

Up above, the stars jumped and whirled. Or was that only my mind? I felt dizzy, weak, breathless; I wanted to tell Grath to stop, or to keep going without me.

I pushed on, instead.

The station was almost deserted, dust blowing across the long grey platform. A lone shuttle-train waited under a swinging sign, its engine chugging and steam billowing from the wheels. There were three carriages attached, but I could see no one aboard through the windows. A man, wearing a Green-banded hat, saw us and waved from further down the platform.

Grath didn't wait around to fill me in. He practically lifted me into the carriage.

It was almost empty, except for Hillder, the Green-band who had led me from the refinery; a man in a guardia uniform; and the Prince.

Grath, standing in the aisle, spoke quietly to the men, while I fell into a seat next to Thaniel, so relieved to see him, I could have hugged him – but he was slumped, turned half towards the window, his eyes unfocussed and his jaw slack. A little trickle of drool dripped from the corner of his mouth.

The Guardsman – Dillion, I guessed – gave a signal through the window to the waiting Green-band. He answered with a salute. The engine hissed and steamed, then started to turn. It couldn't possibly have gone fast enough, even if it was the fastest shuttle-train in Tierra Mejór.

I still could not believe we were safe.

Through the grimy glass, I saw glimpses of men and women shrugging off their shrouds of enforced docility to fight in the streets. I saw an apartment building, much like the one we'd been in, burst into flames. And then it all blurred, and we were racing beneath the impassive stars.

I leaned my head on the Prince's shoulder. He stirred, groggily, and sighed.

"Poor little Aiva," he murmured. "There are so many things that I would change, so many, many things . . ."

In the aisle, across from us, Grath's lips tightened.

"What are we going to do?" I asked him. "The Brotherhood will not let us alone."

"There are places," Hillder spoke up. "Where you can hide. We will send you to the Lower Tiers. There are safe houses there."

"They will find us there, too!" Tears filled my eyes. I was tired, bloody, thirsty, and sore. My mind roiled with that horrible slow murkiness of the white-powder, and Liliath's words echoed in my ears. 'There is no cure, so perhaps you will become ill, in time.' "Besides, how long do we hide? La Boca will have no opposition to prevent him taking the throne if the Principe Regente is nowhere to be found. And the world will tear itself apart in the meantime!"

I began to weep in earnest then. I knew it was because of Aiva, and Liliath, and the white-powder; it was because of Ketra, and Senora R., who would have betrayed me, and because I probably carried on my clothes now the new form of white-powder, that might just kill us all.

Hillder and the guardia looked uncomfortable. Thaniel simply turned back to the window.

Grath, however, met my gaze evenly. "Imre," he said. "We are in this together."

"You're not," I sobbed angrily. "You can promise me nothing. It's always been me, alone. Alone, after my abuela went to the Beyond. After my father, wandering home drunk one night, misjudged his step and fell over a lock gate into the gap between Tiers. Facing my mother after Tomas left for the Abbey, hiding from Vallencino without anyone left to protect me. Dancing my feet to the bone to earn my place among the Daughters of the Pavilion, because I needed it more than any of the other girls, who had families to turn to. And now I'm the one who la Boca hates, and for what, I don't even know! I have done everything wrong. My friends die all around me; strangers, too. Of all the people I chose to ask for help, I latched on to the one who will betray us all – every last person on Tierra Mejór. It's not a coincidence!"

It was a wailing, pitiful voice that bubbled from within me, but for all I despised it, I could not stem its flow.

"No," Grath said gently, taking my hand. I clutched his fingers, a warm, solid anchor against the waves of grief rolling over me. "In the Pattern, there are no coincidences."

For a moment, the train rolled onwards, and I looked anywhere but at Grath.

"Imre –"

"Why did –"

We shared laughter at this. "You first," I told him.

There was colour in his cheeks, soft spots of it tinging his cheekbones. "Imre, I know what you must think of me. I'm the Adviser to the Principe Regente; I was his father's Adviser before that, and his mother's in between. I was the youngest ever chosen for that role, but it's been my life up until this point."

I turned away, as this conversation headed into a territory decidedly unwelcome. More blame would be heaped upon my shoulders. I was the reason his career had fallen apart; the reason the royal family was now in jeopardy. The reason for all things.

"I never wanted it. I was an apprentice in the Tinker's Guild before this, did you know? My father didn't think it good enough for me, and he used his contacts to get me the position at the Citadel. I did what he wanted, to please him, and I thought this would be my life. In some ways, not a bad one. But then, you came charging in like a hailstorm. You have to know how much you've changed things. From the moment I laid eyes on you, lying in that bed in the Pavilion, I felt it."

I looked up, through a veil of tears, and saw him, as if for the first time. His angular face was lined, but they were lines worn from care, not distaste. His eyes were dark, yes, but they were warm, not cold like la Boca's. How had I not noticed them before? His voice repeated itself over and over in my mind. *No coincidences.*

For the first time, the silence between us was not unpleasant.

***

I was drifting towards an exhausted sleep when I heard the noise. It seemed to fill the carriage, coming from behind, and I must have jumped fairly high, for I was out of my seat when I looked over my shoulder.

Grath, opposite me, stood up abruptly, his hand going to his waist, drawing his sword.

A second later, the rear carriage door popped open, exposing the length of track behind us, and dark, murky clouds. Wind whipped inside, carrying dust that speckled my face like hard rain. But the door had not opened by accident. No, it was an automaton that had pulled it open.

This artificial, just like all automatons, shared Feval's face and body. And yet, it looked nothing like Feval.

In place of Favel's broken, blinking eyes, this one had two hard, red lights; they seemed to study me with cold hatred, and that was when I sensed the danger – even before it lifted one of its stiff arms and revealed a revolver-pistol. For the second time in the past hour, I found myself looking at the barrel of a gun. I didn't waste another moment. Grabbing Thaniel's shoulder, I pulled him upright, out of whatever dream he was having, and dragged him after me as I pelted down the aisle. A gunshot thumped behind us. Something struck the wood above my head. I didn't stop.

I wrenched open the door at the front. Wind smacked me in the face, tearing my breath away, forcing me to squint. There was a small gap between this carriage and the next, joined by two metal plates that shifted with the motion of the shuttle-train. Ignoring my trepidation, and the dizzying sight of the tracks racing by under our feet, I pushed the Prince ahead of me. He stumbled, but caught the handle for the door to the next car, pulling it open and ducking inside.

Grath was just behind us. The others, I couldn't see.

Bang, bang. Bang. The shots came from the car behind us, but whether it was Dillion and Hillder firing them, or the murderous machine, I did not know. Grath slammed the door shut, blocking out the noise of the Cosmic Wind, and urged us forward once more.

We didn't hesitate, running down the aisle and crossing into the next car.

There was no door at the front of this one – no further retreat. The side door had a glass panel, and showed the tracks whizzing by; beyond that, the curving edge of the spoke, and the murky grey of the sky. We would never survive a jump at this speed.

Grath, however, was not thinking of jumping, at least, not from the side of the shuttle-train. He stepped up onto one of the chairs, reaching up for a ceiling hatch.

"Hurry!" he growled.

"The others," I protested.

"No time!" Taking my hand, he pulled me up onto the seat, lifting me as if I weighed nothing more than a feather. I gripped the edges, hauling myself up, grateful once more for my dancer's training, and grateful, also, for the physical work of the past few turnings, which had kept the strength in my arms.

As I poked my head into the open air, I became aware of just how fast we were going. I drew my body up, perching in a crouch on the curved, rocking surface. If I let go, I'd tumble straight over the side.

The air was thin. It was hard to breathe, and my eyes still watered. I turned my head, towards the engine. It shook slightly from side to side as it traversed the tracks.

Thaniel's head appeared in the hatch, and I took his hand, steadying him as he clambered up with much less grace than I had. He listed to one side, gripping the edge of the hatch.

"I think I'm going to be sick," he muttered, his voice barely audible over the rushing wind and the hissing engine. Looking at him, in the strange half-light reflected from the silver-specked clouds, I realised that his skin was pale and dotted with beads of sweat. Was it possible he wasn't drunk, but ill?

Grath came up next, sitting on the edge as he pulled the hatch back in place. He'd sheathed his sword, and left it there for now. Then he nodded towards the engine.

It was only then that his intention became clear. To get inside the mechanically-controlled engine.

There was actually not that much space between the carriage and the engine. The shuttle-trains travelled in a fairly straight line, without the need for the segmented cars to turn at sharp angles. Given our speed, we wouldn't need to jump far, only high enough to lift ourselves up onto the slightly higher surface. The motion of the train would do the rest.

Our alternative was waiting for the automaton to reach our carriage. I had no idea how dextrous it was. In all likelihood, it wouldn't be able to get through the hatch, but it didn't need to, if it peppered the ceiling with bullets. We could be shot by accident just as easily as by design.

I jumped.

I landed in a crouch, swaying slightly, then turned back to offer a hand to the Prince. At first, I did not think he would do it, but then that familiar deranged look came over his face. He was still half-drunk, of course, which helped somewhat.

He staggered as he joined me, almost pitching over, but I grabbed the back of his shirt, steadying him. He landed on his backside next to me.

Grath, of all of us, had the most difficulty. He mistimed his jump, and slid backwards towards the gap, his legs going over. My heart in my throat, I reached for him, knowing even as I did so I could never support his weight.

Luckily, he caught a protrusion of metal one-handed, and regained his balance.

Again, there was no time to celebrate. We couldn't stay where we were, or we'd be shaking about like moths in a sack the rest of the journey. Grath motioned to the side of the engine, then carefully lowered himself over, legs first.

There was a ledge for engineers to work on, running along one side, though it was probably only ever used when the shuttle-train was in a dock. An access hatch was at the far end, for técnicos to perform maintenance. All we had to do was make our way along the ledge.

It was a thousand times easier to say it than to put it into practice, with the wheels thundering beneath our feet and the sky racing by overhead, green, marbled with purple and flecked with silver.

It was like balancing on the edge of the world.

Grath's hands guided me into place, and I in turn helped Thaniel over. The engine thrummed under my feet and fingers as I searched blindly for handholds, my cheek pressed to the chill, vibrating metal. Below us were the spinning, screeching wheels, like razor-sharp blades whirring along the tracks. Steam hissed up from between them, stinging my exposed skin. I edged my way step by step, telling myself each time we were drawing closer, until Grath tugged at my hand, indicating that we were there.

The hatch was secured with a simple lock, added long after the shuttle-train was built, probably to protect the inner workings from thieves looking to steal parts and sell them on the black markets. But even a simple lock was hard to manipulate at this speed. Grath, holding on to the engine with one hand, pulled out his sword, and used the hilt to smash the whole thing off. The motion pushed him off-balance, and one leg slipped over the side of the ledge, dangerously close to the spinning wheels; with a grunt, he swung himself back, smashing an elbow into the hatch, which opened easily; he pulled himself in, and I scooted in after him.

Inside, I felt a wash of relief. It was unfounded – we weren't anything close to being safe. The automaton who was following us was still on the train. Though I hoped it wasn't possible, there was nothing to say he couldn't climb through the hatch and follow us in here.

Here was a small space just behind the engine, where Thaniel slumped against the wall, shivering, and we crouched over him. The machinery was spread out in the cavity before us, hot and close and smelling of oil. Pistons pumped and wheels turned. The roaring heat of it stabbed at our skin. Only a small slitted window gave us a view ahead, over the front end of the shuttle-train, the distant shape and the pinprick lights of the Spindle.

"Here." Grath pressed his sword into my hands.

"What?" I squealed. "I can't –"

"Aim and swing the blade. That's all you need to do. You see it – you cut it down. Lean out of the hatch."

"No!" Terror washed away all other thought. But it was a token protest – what was I more afraid of? The automaton finding us here, cornered in this small space, or trying to cut it down with a sword, while it wielded a gun? "It's an artificial. It can probably balance far better than we can."

"I'm sure it can."

"Can we disconnect the cars?" I asked him.

He looked thoughtful. "I don't know. I've never seen the workings of one of these things before. But there is something else I can try – I'm going to have to increase the speed."

"How is that going to help?" I yelled at him, furious.

He waved at me impatiently. I had no choice but to do as he asked, poking my head cautiously through the hatch. So far there was no sign of the automaton, but would I even be able to see it before it saw me? Would I be quick enough to swipe at it with the heavy metal blade before it pulled the trigger? It had obviously been programmed to use a revolver-pistol, and I was more used to brandishing hairbrushes and kohl than weapons.

I chanced a glimpse back at Grath. He was staring with great concentration at the wheels and levers as the whole engine rattled and clattered as if it was going to burst apart at any moment. This cabin wasn't made for passengers.

Grath tentatively reached for one of the levers, then backed away. I could see his mind working as he followed the gear tracks with his eyes, tracing their workings deep inside the engine. I remembered his charts, so meticulous, so neatly labelled. Remembered, too, how he told me about La Reloj de pie. He knew machinery, and knew what it could do.

"How can they have sent an automaton after us so quickly?" I called out.

"The herald in the stairwell loosed a pigeon," Grath returned. "It's likely he sent a signal to someone. Any artificial can be updated with new programming from any of the control stations, as long as you have the correct codes for the crystal and the knowledge to program them. It takes only a few minutes for the new commands to activate."

"Can you use your wristwatch to override it?"

"I can't do that and work out how to control this train at the same time. I'm not an artificial!" He waved me away again. "By the time it updated, we'd be dead anyway. Stand back and let me concentrate!"

I leaned back out of the hatch. Still all I could see was the blue-purple sky, the rushing of stars, the empty tracks that ran alongside ours. If I leaned a little further, I could just catch a glimpse of the rest of the shuttle-train, its silver carriages barrelling along in our wake.

I yanked my head back in, panting. The Viento Cósmico was tearing all the air from my lungs, and spots of grey were dancing before my eyes. Or was this the effects of the white-powder? Or the infection it bore?

Then I saw it.

There was no question in my mind now. Feval had been a "he" from the moment we met, but this automaton had no humanity at all. It was a machine. Someone had programmed it to kill.

It was clambering over the top of the shuttle-train. Its eyes were fixed on me, but it moved with unerring sureness, crouched low as it approached the gap between its carriage and the engine. Where was its gun? Had it lost it, scaling the roof?

It was a step away from the gap when the engine gave a lurch beneath my feet. I grabbed at the edge of the hatch, almost losing Grath's sword. For an instant I saw myself tumbling towards the tracks and under the wheels, pulped just like Liliath.

Then, as a cloud of steam billowed from between the wheels, I pulled myself back inside. And saw what lay ahead. We'd reached the end of the Spoke, and were approaching the section where the shuttle-train would slide onto the rotating tracks of the hub. The engine wasn't going faster – it was slowing. Too slow! We were going to hit them at the wrong time.

The wheels clanked over, and for a suspended moment, the whole engine seemed to roll sideways. Then the wheels gripped the tracks. The same tracks that were already sliding out from underneath the passenger cars. If the engine had crossed over in time, the rest of the shuttle-train hadn't.

I looked back through the hatch. The automaton had realised something was wrong. It was still reaching for the engine, its stiff hand stretched out, but it was a desperate gesture now. And then the couplings pulled too far, too tight, and the carriages were ripped away. The automaton went over the edge, tumbling, vanishing with a noise that never reached my ears.

The engine roared on, steam hissing and sparks flying from the torn couplings as they dragged in our wake.

Chapter Forty-Five

I allowed myself only a few moments to cry for the two men who had been left behind in that carriage, for I did not know, not for sure, that they were dead. There was a possibility that they weren't, and that was what I hoped with all my heart.

Thaniel had lost consciousness, and even Grath looked worried as he bent over him, feeling for a pulse.

"He is ill?" I asked him. "It's the illness, isn't it?"

Grath looked up at me, the truth writ large on his face. We could run no longer; we could not leave the Prince, and without help, he would soon join Jark, and Aiva, and all the others who had already died from this. Although, what sort of help could we get?

We were silent as we waited for the shuttle-train to dock. There was nothing more to say, and no time to say it in; we were exhausted, battered mentally and physically, and in any case, we were at the mercy of the train, which was even now slowing as it pulled up alongside its designated platform, sighing and huffing.

They were waiting for us.

Even as we tumbled free, our hands raised, the vigilar were there. They came at us with raised rifles and revolver-pistols, shouting commands I couldn't comprehend, climbing into the engine to remove Thaniel's limp body, dragging us through the station. People were gathered on the platforms and in the station itself, milling about, confused, for all the boards were blank and someone was calling through an ampliphone that all services had been cancelled. Many migrated to see our partialy destroyed shuttle-train, and point and gasp as they saw the outlaws who had wrecked such havoc.

I hadn't realised I was still clutching Grath's sword until it was wrenched from my fingers. One of the vigilar seized my arms, twisting them painfully behind my back and tying them tightly. I tried to see over my shoulder as I was marched – I did not want to lose Grath, or the Prince.

But lose them I did.

I was taken to a room, which must have been an office, though it was bare now. Here, I slumped to the floor. My clothes, covered in soot and ash, torn and ripped and bloody, provided little protection against the creeping cold of the bare brick wall. My jaw ached, and so did my ankle. My lungs burned. My eyes would not stop watering, and that knot in my stomach was so tight, I thought it must be visible through the skin of my belly.

They let go of me, and I slumped to the floor.

It was for a long time that they left me there. I was desperately thirsty, but when I called out, there was no reply, and I refrained for fear of making it worse.

Finally, after hours had passed, the door opened.

And la Boca came in.

I knew at once who it was. The eyes behind that black mask were the same cold eyes that had haunted my dreams since that day in the hall when they'd searched the crowd for me. He stepped in and drew the door shut, looking me up and down.

I straightened as best I could while slumped against the wall. My hands were numb beneath the tight restraints. Even if he released me, I doubted I could have run – but I would have tried, I would have tried very hard, just to put some distance between myself and that gaze.

He stepped across to me, impossibly tall; then bent down to my level. Seizing my chin between his long, thin fingers, he tilted my head up, so I couldn't do anything except stare back.

"So," he said. "I have you."

Defiantly, through the haze of pain and fear, I held his gaze. Eventually, he let me go with a sound of disgust.

"You should have just died," he said. "It might have saved you."

***

We were returned to the Citadel in the back of a black autocarriage, bundled together like a child's dolls in a toy box. With every turn, I was pushed against Grath, his warm breath tickling my neck. The Prince, for his part, had fallen back into a stupor, lolling against the door, muttering nonsense interspersed with small cries and whimpers; I wondered if he was conscious at all.

I envied his delirium.

We stopped at la Plaza de Lágrima. It seemed the heralds wanted the populace to well appraised, for, though it was late and the air full of an icy chill, people had gathered to see us arrive.

It was then that I began to realise that the lies the Brotherhood had told were many, and as carefully woven as a dart-spider's web. They had taken a page from Jark's book. They had united the people in their hatred of a common enemy; and that enemy was us.

As we pulled into the plaza, the mob lunged for the car. They shouted, and banged on the windows. The carriage rocked from side to side as they pummelled it with their fists. I have never known such terror as when I looked into those myriad fervid eyes.

They would have torn us to shreds, and saved the Brotherhood the trouble, had the vigilar let them.

But no. The spectacle was useful to their purposes, and for the spectacle, the heralds had to keep us alive.

The autocarriage pushed through the horde, arriving at last at the Citadel gates, which were opened by guardia, wielding their revolver-pistols to keep the surging crowd back. Three shots were fired, giving the car enough time to break through, then the gates hurriedly drew closed.

High above, the great airship hung low over the rooftops, like a rasp-wasp about to strike its prey.

Grath's heart thudded beneath my ear, and I felt, for an instant, a strange pang in my own, above that tight knot in my belly. "Stay calm," Grath whispered into my hair. "Stay strong."

The darkness of the tunnel through the wall surrounded us. "When have I ever been strong?"

"From what I can tell," he breathed, "always."

And then we were through, the autocarriage screeching to a stop below the steps – the same steps I'd been carried up by Miguel, all those many turnings ago. This time, a revolver-pistol was pushed between us, separating me from Grath with a jab of hard steel. I was lifted bodily from the car by uncaring hands, and dumped onto the cobbles. My ankle twisted underneath me and I cried out in pain. A guardia bent to help me, but the black shape of a herald stepped in front of him.

"Do not show them pity," he said from beneath his hood. "These are agents of chaos."

The guardia, a young man with kind eyes, gave me a helpless glance, then moved aside, allowing the herald access. "Whore," he hissed, and then he wrapped his hand in my loose, tangled hair and dragged me, painfully, to my feet. Head twisted to the side, every stumbling step an agony as strands of my hair ripped from my scalp, he dragged me behind him, up the steps and into the Citadel.

There were people – I caught glimpses of them, through the shroud of pain, and my knotted hair – servants, guardia, vigilar, Guildmasters, and noblemen and women. They gathered in the shadows, on the galleries, gasping at the sight of the three Agents of Chaos. They did not approach – did not question.

I searched for Miguel, but didn't see him; it was just as well. He would have caused trouble, and I did not want his part in this known, lest he join us in our punishment.

"Take them to the cells," the herald barked, raising his hand to gesture behind me, at Thaniel and Grath.

"Please," I said, as loudly as I could, "the Prince is injured. You must let a healer see him."

The herald shook my head, wrenching my hair. Then he drew back his hand and ploughed his fist into my jaw.

"Imre!" shouted Grath, and for a moment I wondered what he was shouting about, for I heard the crack before I felt it, and it wasn't until I was on the floor that the pain hit. My vision wavered as I looked up at the herald, a towering figure of black.

I felt a strange sense of juxtaposition, then. This man, as terrifying as he was, was nowhere near as fearsome as la Boca. By comparison, I almost wasn't scared of him at all.

Another angry shout from Grath, from further away now, and, dazedly, I supposed that was because they were taking him away from me. There was a sound of a pistol-shot, and then . . .

"Grath," I murmured, surprised to find blood bubbling from between my lips. Inside my mind, I heard the echo of the sound. *No, no, no, no, no . . .* with every ragged breath, this word repeated itself, again and again, and again. I pushed against the floor, trying to see, afraid to see – but the herald gripped my hair once more, close to the scalp, drawing tears. He lifted me, my feet skidding on the marble floor, and flung me into one of the waiting lifts.

I cowered on the floor, coughing blood all over my hands as I willed the pain in my jaw to stop. The lift began to rise, and nausea replaced the pain.

That horrible ride seemed to last forever, as we climbed upwards through all the floors of the Citadel. It was all I could do to keep breathing, as I tried desperately not to think about Grath.

Grath was all I could think about.

The fabric of those dresses between my fingers. The Prince's words: 'Oh, that was Grath.'

The smell of cigarillo smoke as he walked into a room. His eyes, when he showed me his telescope and charts, which told me they were his reason for living.

Seeing his face in Liliath's apartment. Knowing that he'd come back for me.

"Get up," the herald spat, pulling me upright. The doors of the lift slid open, and we emerged into a windswept rooftop terrace. The yellow stone of the Citadel spread out beneath my feet, and the turrets of the many towers pierced the thick, silver-lined clouds. The Cuidad gleamed below, lit up like a mirror of the stars overhead.

I had never loved my city more, and never hated it so much.

Ahead of us hung the huge bulk of the airship. I'd never seen one so close before. It was a strangely elegant device. Like a child's balloon, the elongated gasbag, illuminated from within, bobbed and swayed slightly in the wind, fixed in place with long ropes. The cabin, an angled contraption of polished bronze, hung suspended below. At the rear, three large rotors turned, speeding up with a noise like ripping paper. A doorway in the side was open, a flexible gangway bridging the gap between it and the terrace.

Several men stood not far from us – three more heralds, their black cloaks whipping in the wind, several vigilar, and a guardia. It made no difference who they were. None of them made a move, nor spoke a word of protest.

I was marched across to the slanted gangway. Already the ropes were being cast off, and the airship was bobbing, the buoyant gas eager to rise. If my hands were not tied, I would have clutched at the railing as we crossed the fifty-span drop. As it was, I half-hoped I would fall – it would put me beyond reach of the harsh, clawed hands of my captors.

But my death, it seemed, would not come so easily.

We reached the cabin without incident. Inside it was richly-upholstered in red velvet, the carpets a deep burgundy, patterned with gold. The floor hummed with the thrum of the motors. Several passengers were already aboard, three heralds, and at least two crewmen, wearing the grey uniforms of Palace servants. All eyes turned to me. I tried to walk straight, to stand proud and defiant, but it was all I could do to put one foot in front of the other.

At the front of the cabin was a door, through which lay the cockpit. I caught a glimpse of a console covered with complicated knobs and levers, and a padded chair in which the pilot, a dark-haired man, sat, before I was shoved onto a cushioned seat in the middle of the cabin. A vigilar sat either side of me. The humming intensified – and then with a lurch, the airship began to rise.

My stomach sank. The feeling of weightlessness I'd experienced on the shuttle-train was nothing compared to this. There was no solid ground beneath us, nothing to catch us should we fall. We were truly flying.

I watched through the windows as the darkness enveloped us. Inside the thin walls, the globe-lamps pulsed brighter, creating a bubble of warmth. Despite everything, I felt myself drifting towards sleep.

Chapter Forty-Six

I dreamed, I think, though it could only have been a minute at the most; I woke, to the reality of a nightmare.

A hand appeared in front of me, holding a glass of water.

A vigilar on my left stood, smacking the hand away, spilling droplets onto my ruined trousers. "Not required."

The herald – for he was a herald, oddly enough – who had held the water out to me steadied the glass, waving it insistently in front of my face. The vigilar on my right spoke up. "Remember what la Boca said. She's no use to anyone dead."

The herald in front of me tilted the glass, pressing it to my lips, and I drank greedily. The cool water soothed my burning throat, eased the pain, and washed some of the drying blood from my lip. It was pure heaven. "Thank you," I gasped after I'd drained it.

He nodded and left.

***

I know, now, that it took three hours to reach the Pendulum, but it felt much longer. The airship did not travel left nor right, instead rising straight up, using the rotors and tillers to position itself beside the Tether so that when the needle swung past, it would be in the right place to dock.

I could see nothing through the windows, but I heard and felt the change in the engines, and the solid *thump* of metal joining metal. Then the airship was finally still.

The two vigilar hauled me upright. I stumbled between them through the door, following the three heralds, out into the cold wind. It had a voice, that wind: it moaned, long and low, as if singing some unending, tuneless, sorrowful song.

Around us were the shredded ruins of old airships, those that had broken down until they were unusable. They looked so much like skeletons dressed in tattered rags!

I caught glimpses, in between them, of great machines – huge pipes, funnels, vents. Steam billowed from some, water trickled from others. These were the machines that spread clouds across our sky, created the atmosphere in which the air we breathed circulated.

But this sight was soon surpassed by what was before me.

The Iglesia.

It was made of dark stone. I had imagined it as a child, thinking that, swinging outwards as the Pendulum did at the end of its Tether, the heralds must surely walk up the walls, with the ceilings rising ahead of them as the walls should. Of course, the force of gravity created by its motion as it circled the Spindle ensured the ground was beneath us. My body knew no different, but my mind was disconcerted. When I glanced over my shoulder and saw the Spindle below, I reeled, and so I focused instead on what was before me.

We were at the bottom of a long set of steps that wound up between craggy boulder-like forms of black metal. At the top of this mountain were the jagged spires of the Iglesia, flecked with the small slitted windows. The Iglesia was a dark reflection of the Citadel – beautiful, but terrifying.

The climb was interminable. My weakened body would not cooperate, so I was mostly dragged. The air was thin and scarce, more so than even on the Wheel, and my lungs, already raw from the effects of the white-powder, burned with the strain. All the while the Cosmic Wind grew louder and louder, filling my ears and my head, so I could not think.

We reached a dark square doorway, fronted by two rows of dark columns, one set rising from a balcony above the others. They leaned inwards, giving the impression of the ribbed mouth of a giant creature. The winds whistled across the piled sections of the church, finding their way between the turrets and caught by the buttresses, wailing over the central, squared-off dome and its single, pointed spire. Then, just as I thought my head would burst – we were through, and the moaning quietened.

Inside was a vast atrium. It thrust upwards through the building, the ceiling a hundred spans high. Ahead, set into the apse, was a window of stained glass, depicting La Grulla rising from the dust and fire of Old Earth, her wings spread wide, and Tierra Mejór spinning above, her shape unmistakably elegant. The nave was empty of pews, and the transepts leading to either side were darkened spaces full of shadows. Above, the ceiling was vaulted with ridged girders of steel. At its highest point was a perfectly circular hole, ringed with gears that moved an iris that could obviously open or close at the will of its operator.

Below, where the transept crossed the centre of this vast space, attached to nothing and floating of its own accord, was a great machine. I recognised it at once; the model for Grath's telescope, yet different in shape and design.

A singular tube, made of thick, heavy brass, it seemed to defy all laws as it held its position without any visible means of support. Instead of angling on the bottom to accommodate the user, it projected its image straight down, onto the floor, which was polished stone, painted with markings, measurements, increments, symbols, all circling one another, incomprehensible to one such as me.

Gradually, I became aware of dark eyes peering from the recesses. heralds, who had gathered to observe their rites or speak their parabra, or perhaps simply to see me arrive. They stood me here, the two who held me, and two others came forwards. Wordlessly, systematically, I was divested of my boots and jacket, then patted down brusquely.

I expected, at any moment, to lose the two things I had left, of all my possessions; the feather, and the playing cards.

I cannot say how they missed either. But miss them they did, for they backed away and nodded to my captors.

I was taken, footsteps echoing like pistol-fire, through a side door. Steps curved up to one side, and I was back in the icy wind. More steps, these carved from steel, and set into the side of the cuppola – I was high from the ground already, the squared dome to my left. The stairs became shallower as they bridged the space between the spires; there was no railing, and if I looked over the edge, the grey metal rocks beckoned me to let it all go.

My head pounding, my heart racing, and my ankle feeling as if a thousand iron spikes were driving through it, I climbed; when I stumbled, my bare feet losing their grip on the stairs, I was pulled onwards with a rough jerk, my arm twisted, or a hard slap delivered to my cheek or ear. Up and up, until finally there was a clank of metal and a door, made of heavy iron and fitted with a small barred window, opened. I was in the very top of one of the spires. Here, the heralds unbound my hands, and I nearly screamed at the pain of the blood rushing back into my fingers.

They shut the door behind me and locked it.

I looked around. A pile of rags in one corner. A bucket which I supposed was a privy. And a scuttling of tiny feet – roaches.

I pressed my prickling hands to the door. The metal was freezing, and solid enough that it didn't move even when I shoved it. I traced the edges, but there was barely a gap. I peered through the barred embrasure at the whole lot of blue-grey-black sky – and not much else.

The walls were just as solid, constructed of stone joined with metal studs. In some places, the metal struts protruded, but they were fixed solidly in the stone.

There was a small window, in the wall opposite the door. It was unbarred; it needed no deterrent, for there was nothing beneath save the sheer wall of the spire, the slanted roofs of the other sections of the Iglesia, the jutting rib-bones of the buttresses, and the rocks below. Perhaps it was meant to give those prisoners who despaired one last option – to fall to their deaths.

I crossed to the bundle of rags, and kicked it with my toes. The cloth fell away, revealing yellowed bones, still covered with bits of sinew and green-grey tissue. The stench of rotting flesh hit my nostrils and I doubled over, vomiting up what little was left in my stomach.

Then I began to cry.

***

The window showed me the cold distant lights of the stars. Here, without so much of the atmosphere to shield them from view, they could be seen most of the day, except when la Grulla was directly overhead. The wind moaned on and on, so loud I thought it would drive me mad. It caught in the spire rooms like mine, whirling around, creating a hollow sound like a great set of organ pipes.

Nothing grew here, on the Pendulum. Among solid metal and stone, no blade of grass, no speck of lichen, no moss could find a home.

I gauged the passage of time by the rotations of the Pendulum in relation to the stars, and the occasional glimpses of la Grulla. Of course, the Pendulum swung more slowly than the Spindle turned, and la Grulla's light was sporadic, showing twice in one turning, and not at all in the next; so, there was no way to accurately tell day from night. Instead, time became a series of events, of movements, and thoughts, and realisations. I found that even the stench of death was something one could get used to – or sleeping on a cold, hard floor – or that pain waxes and wanes, just like the orbit of la Grulla.

Added to this was another torment. I discovered the addictive power of the white-powder.

The craving was inoffensive at first, an unobtrusive creeping at the edge of my thoughts. It grew slowly, until it felt like dart-spiders scuttling over my brain, stabbing behind my eyes with their barbed stingers. I pressed my palms to my cheeks, and moaned.

I woke once or twice to a sound at the door. There was a gap, through which a small bowl could be pushed through. The bowls contained rotten food; mouldy fruit, bread, yellowed raw vegetables, often all mixed together.

I had no appetite. All I wanted was the white-powder, and in any case, I would never have considered eating the disgusting mix.

I paced my cell instead, groaning, pressing my hands to my cheeks, my temple, my metrónomo; it wasn't long before I turned my fingers into hooks and gouged my skin with my nails, drawing blood. The pain still did not make the craving go away.

I kneeled and tried to speak my parabra.

"I am part of the Pattern. The Pattern is within me. My every breath is a part of the whole. My every movement . . ."

The endless tune of the wind soon drove the thread of my prayer from my mind. I was cold, but I burned. I had no protection against the wind except my thin shirt and skirt, and injured, I shivered constantly. On the third day, I began to force myself to eat the slops that were put through the door, if only to give my body something to do. I soon learned that no more would come unless I placed the empty bowl back in front of the slot.

Slowly, the words of my parabra changed their tone.

"I ask that the Pattern protect and guard Miguel and Hendrich. I ask that the Pattern look to its faithful servant, the Prince. Heal him. He is misguided, but he serves the Pattern with all his heart and soul. This I know."

"I'm not worthy," Thaniel said to me. "That is why the poison took hold in my soul. I did not value this life, and looked always to the past, to the sky, to what was beyond."

I whirled, but though I'd heard his voice clearly, he was not in the room.

"My Prince," I said, sadly. "I'm sorry."

I reached the curved wall, and placed my fevered forehead against it. "And Grath," I murmured. "Dear Aurelia, I ask, as your servant, I ask you . . . Grath, oh Grath . . . please, do not let him have died because of me."

There was no answer from the Pattern. I did not feel its benediction, nor any sense that it recognised me at all. It seemed, in this place that was supposed to be the Pattern's domain, that I was farthest from it than I had ever been.

I spoke to myself, and to other visitors. My mother was there, once, telling me I was late returning with the bread she wanted. My father, grinning at me from beyond the window. The pile of bones became a man, and he told me he was Holthe, Liliath's lost brother.

I even saw a small street-fox, edging its way through the shadows. When I tried to pat it, it bit my fingers with a painful nip, and I retreated, holding my wounded hand, to the opposite wall, there to curl into a fetal ball.

I had been there, by my reckoning, four turnings when there was a noise outside the door. "Imre," said a voice.

Assuming it to be another trick of my mind, I ignored it.

"Imre," came the voice again.

"Stop it, stop it, stop it!" I shouted at the window, at the song of the wind beyond. "I don't want to hear you!"

"Imre. Please."

Perhaps it was time for a meal. I wasn't hungry, but it would provide something to latch my whirling thoughts onto, and that was a welcome distraction. I stared intently at the slot in the door, waiting for the appearance of a bowl, but instead saw a dark shape through the bars.

I pressed myself against the metal. A herald's veiled face peered back at me. How could it be? No one here would call me by name.

"Please. Tell me you are unhurt."

"Who are you?" I said at last.

"Do you really not know me?" asked the voice, and I did, I did know him.

I laughed. It was another hallucination. "Tomas?"

Was it really him? I dared not hope, and yet – his eyes. Behind me, la Grulla breached the horizon, filling the tower with brilliant silver light. Suddenly, it was so clear. How could I have mistaken his eyes? They were filled, now, with compassion and sorrow and horror.

"I couldn't believe it when I saw you on the airship," he said in a hurried whisper, as if he afraid of being overheard. "Oh, Imre, what have you done?"

"What have *I* done?" I repeated in disbelief. "Nothing!"

"You would not be here if you'd done nothing. The worst criminals are sent to the spires."

The worst criminals . . .

"I've done *nothing*, Tomas. How can you believe those lies? You *know* me!"

"I know you as a Pavilion whore," he said sharply. "I know you as a woman, unclean, who would twist the minds of good men from their service of the Pattern. That's what I know."

"Then why did you bring me that glass of water?" I accused him with a laugh. For it had to have been him.

He didn't answer.

I pressed him, my voice urgent, for I could feel my lucidity slipping away as the desire for the white-powder pulled me back under. "Tomas, you have to help me. Please. I have something very important to do."

"No." He turned his head away. "I won't listen."

"Then why did you come?" I almost shouted. "Why did you come to see me at all?"

" 'Confront those things you fear, and if you walk away, you may find you are stronger.' "

The quote from the *Sacred Text* rang emptily in the spire room. I had once thought the words of la Oráculo to be unshakably, inviolably true, but now? La Boca twisted them to his own ends; people's prejudices and ideas could warp their meanings. "You fear me?" I called after him.

He shook his head, and I sensed he was slipping away. Grasping the bars as I would grasp his hand had I been able, I begged him with every ounce of my soul.

"Tomas. I am here because la Boca wants to take the throne. He will do anything, anything at all to prevent La Reina from naming Prince Thaniel as her heir. He has developed a poison, and he intends to spread it across Tierra Mejór. Already, people are dying from it. I've seen it with my own eyes."

"You're lying," he said, glancing back to the door, though he did not approach again.

"Tomas – la Boca seeks to rule. He might have already begun. At any cost!"

Tomas returned to the door, then, slapping his palms against the hard metal. "Don't snare me with your lies," he spat. "Don't tempt me to evil with your words! I won't listen!"

"Tomas!" I called, but he was gone. I curled my hand to a fist and hit the door in frustration. My knuckles jarred on the metal, bleeding and grazed. For a long moment, I stood there, looking through the small gap at the dark sky.

And then I went to the window.

The wind howled as I leaned out as far as I dared. The drop was incredible. There was no flat ground below, only tumbled rocks, and then . . . nothing. The Tether, bending slightly as it arced towards the hub. The Wheel, looming hugely as it spun below. The Spindle, so distant now! And above? I craned my neck. Above, la Grulla, shining her light down on me.

I took a breath, and folded myself through the gap.

My hands were useless. Numb with the cold, and sore where I had hit the iron door, they seemed to have stiffened to claws. As best I could, I wrapped them around a protruding lump of metal on the sill, then eased myself into the gap.

I slipped, then, my bare foot skidding out from under me. I could see it, so clearly, my death; I would fall, pulled by a gravity, which, if lesser than I had known my entire life, would still dash me against those jagged rocks without mercy. Yet even as I felt it, my hand reached up, and somehow managed to find some purchase. I clung there, precariously, swaying in the wind. My tenuous grip, which I could not even feel, was all that kept me from plummeting free.

I had time enough to realise I couldn't hold my own weight forever. A serene and calm acceptance came over me. I would let go, and none of this would matter. I could absolve myself of responsibility for all this. And then I heard a noise from above. It could be nothing other than the door to my chamber opening. There followed a curse, in a rough voice:

"Chaos be damned!"

A rough hand seized my collar, pulling me upwards. The fabric pulled and strained as I was hauled back up, and dumped, unceremoniously, on the cold floor. My eyes focused on a spilled bowl of the sloppy, rotten stew. Obviously, having come to deliver my food, the herald had seen the empty room through the embrasure.

I lay there, clutching the smooth floor and trying to breathe.

"Foolish girl. Your death awaits you! You seek to make it come sooner?" A foot kicked me, hard, in the gut. I barely felt it for the tremors running through my body.

"We'll see."

He left me again, alone, except for the skeleton of the man in the corner, and the ghosts of my thoughts.

Chapter Forty-Seven

As I lay half-dozing, I felt another quake. It was only a shaking of the floor, transmitted from far below, on the Spindle, by the Tether. The Iglesia barely moved. I pressed my palms to the smooth tile, and counted the seconds until it stopped. It happened again, twice, each time with less of an interval in between.

I could only imagine what was going on in the world below.

**

After this, la Boca came for me.

I felt him before I saw him outside my cell; a dark, looming shadow. He stood there for a long time at the small door window.

"You had to die," he said at last. "You understand that, don't you?"

My voice was hoarse, roughened by the cold and the constant struggle for breath in the thin air. My hands were raw from scraping at the door, my cheeks covered with dried bloody marks from my fingernails, which it seemed my body had not the strength to heal.

"I *don't* understand. *You* are the one who has committed murder. Every death on Tierra Mejór, from that terrible white-powder. And how many more, when you take the throne?"

"You are wrong," he said. "They died, and will die, because of you."

"No." The ache stabbed at my heart. "No. It is not. My fall did not cause this. You've observed the slowing of the world through your telescope. You know it as well as I!"

"You were supposed to be aboard the second shuttle-train," la Boca said. Beyond the window, the wind whipped at the hood covering his face, teasing me with vague snatches of the man beneath – the line of a jaw, a glimpse of dark hair. "Before that meddling woman met you and had you board with her. It should have been you who died, among those many, as the carriage broke apart against the Tether.

"We arranged for the dart-spider to be smuggled in. We paid that whore of a girl to make sure you were stung. She didn't take much convincing. You must have made some enemies during your short years, Imre.

"When *that* failed, we hired another man to kill you. What a depraved, ugly little man he was; stupid, too. He found his way into the Prince's apartment, but he was too idiotic to make that work. The automaton, aboard the shuttle-train as you escaped Rueda. At every turn, when you should have died, you lived. And it is on your conscience now that the world ends."

The tears had begun at his first words, more and more welling up, spilling over. I made no noise as they fell. Perhaps he wouldn't see them, through the small window.

A part of me resisted the implication – that I had killed the people aboard that shuttle-train, that I had brought about the Prince having to flee, and thus, his exposure to the tainted powder. That part of me knew that it was la Boca who was responsible for these actions. But it was a small part, and it was losing ground to the looming thought that, no matter how I defended myself, all this had started with me. "I suppose you released the white-powder in the Estate, too."

He shook his head. "That was their own doing. Only a few guards ever manned it when the Principe Regente was not there. It could get rather dull, I suppose. It was just bad luck that they bought the altered powder. But again, *you* survived."

He moved to the side, reaching for something, then held it up. Sparkling a little under the smattering of stars, the glass vial looked so small, so innocent, very like the vial Thaniel had given me, full of violet perfume. Inside was a small sampling of the white-powder. My mouth watered and I craved it, with every inch of my body, but at least it was a dull ache, now, like feeling the lure of a distant fire and knowing it would clear the chill from your bones, but knowing too that the walk to reach it would kill you. It was the wrong type of powder, in any case. It was the deadly strain of Liliath's.

"You want it, don't you?" la Boca murmured, in a soft, lilting voice. "After all that time on the Wheel, you must be addicted to the stuff. But this type won't have any effect on you. Unlike the others – the woman, whose laboratory you destroyed; your Green-band friend; that child."

How did he know all this? To this day, I can't be sure, except that he believed he was a God, and his power and influence was so widespread that he might as well be.

"Why not?" I croaked. "Why didn't I die?" La Boca shifted, slipping the vial back beneath his cloak. "The altered white-powder will not kill everyone. Only those who are not worthy."

Thaniel. Thaniel was ill. Had he caught the illness while nursing Aiva? Would he die, now, because of it? Perhaps these questions were irrelevant, and he was already dead, a small brown bulb protruding from between his lips.

" 'Pray beneath the Sacred Tree, those who are worthy, and you will be lifted by its branches.' " It was a line from The Words of la Oráculo. " 'But those who are Scions of Chaos will only feed the roots.' The Sacred Tree will feed on the flesh of those who are sullied and unclean. Those who are left," la Boca continued, "are those who will be worthy of starting a new world."

I stared at him, uncomprehending. "*I* am alive. I breathed in the modified white-powder, and I live yet."

"Yes," he said. "And the reason for that is clear. I am to kill you myself, with my own hands, and thus restore Tierra Mejór."

"What?" I laughed, incredulously. "You think that killing *me* will stop the machines of Tierra Mejór from falling apart?"

"You are a Scion of Chaos," he enunciated, as if explaining something to a small child. "You spoiled the Pattern, and worse than that, you flaunted it before me. Dancing, at that Chaos-damned Ball, taunting me . . . But I know, now, why it was done. It had to be this way. You showed me that the time is now. That Tierra Mejór was ready for rebirth."

He paused for a moment, stroking the veil above where his mouth might be.

"There are too many of us, and more and more are being born each day. Even the Council knows it's not sustainable – they just won't admit it. Why do you think they're trying so hard to disband the Green-bands?" He laughed. "I have a great respect for them, you know. Those little men and women running around, painting their slogans and getting themselves shot for their cause, pretending to make a difference in a world they know they can never change. But *I* can. I know what Tierra Mejór needs – it needs less of us, less vermin making demands on its precious resources, less wanton procreation, less selfish, greedy souls sucking at its perfect Inner Core. I'm only doing what is right by the Pattern."

A shocking little part of me, deep down inside, believed him. His words rang true; I'd heard them before, had I not? Yes. Tierra Mejór needed to be reborn if it was going to survive. "Then why not simply implement a limit on the number of children born, such as they have on Rueda? You could propose it to the Conclave . . ."

His shadowed eyes were full of scorn. "The system works on the Wheel because they're all of them kept in line with constant management. Time consuming, and ultimately ineffective. How many of them are truly serving the Pattern in their drudgery?" He shook his head. "It wouldn't work on the Spindle. They see too much of what the Upper Tiers have, and they have not. How long would it be before they revolted? No, it's much better this way – and fairer. The Pattern has guided my hand in this, Imre."

I stepped back, shaking my head, aghast. "You can't mean this. The white-powder doesn't *select* anyone. It's affecting those on the Lower Tiers because they're the ones addicted to the vile stuff!"

He ignored me. "You cannot possibly comprehend the hand of the Pattern, whore – at least, not yet. But *I* have. A new era is coming. And you are to see it happen, before I send you to the Beyond."

I could not see his mouth, but I could tell that he was smiling.

***

Another full turning must have passed. I looked down from my window, craning my neck, to see the Wheel passing overhead, marked by the bright glint of fires. How many people were dying in the riots, in the quakes? The knot in my heart burned with them, and I writhed with the pain of a thousand white-hot spikes of agony – I finally realised what they were, these pains; they were punishment. They were the deaths of good people at the hands of dark forces. Each one, I would feel, like a red-hot needle.

'Can you not see how people will love you?'

I wept at the memory of Bethery words. She was wrong. Those who loved me, I hurt; my sisters, whom I had betrayed; Tomas, whom I had turned away from me; my Prince, who lay unmoving, unconscious, possibly already dead from the tainted white-powder; Miguel, Hendrich, Feval, all wounded and damaged, fighting to defend me. Liliath, who had betrayed me. Aiva, who had paid a price too big for one so young. Naia, whose mother was torn from her. So many others, who I'd never met, but who, thanks to me, would know only the terror of their world's destruction.

Still the wind moaned.

I slept, and when I woke, I saw a face at the door again. It was not la Boca.

"Tomas," I croaked.

"They are going to execute you," he said, his voice stiff.

"And you're going to let them. In your eyes, I deserve this, do I not?"

He bowed his head.

"Look down," I told him. "Look to the Wheel, and the Spindle. You can see the ruin. People are dying, and more are going to die, yet. You have to help me, Tomas."

His eyes, the only part of him that I could see; but I couldn't tell what was in them. I thought I knew him so well, but . . . no, the joke was on me.

"I can't, Imre," he said at last. "You've made your choices. I've made mine."

"Tomas. Please!" I banged on the door, loud enough to make him jump. My knuckles, coated still with dried blood, split open once more; a bright streak of red smeared across the iron. "Think of Mother, if no one else!"

It was the wrong thing to say, the wrong challenge to throw. He hated her as much as I did. He reared back from the door. "No," he said. "I will never think of her. She is dead to me." And then he was gone.

Chapter Forty-Eight

I paced my cell. I did not sleep – I could not. There was no chance of it, for the ache in my heart. So many deaths. What made it worse, oh so much worse, was that my craving for the white-powder had dulled to a dry irritation. Without that burning need, my continued existence seemed pointless, making me long for a resolution, any kind, even death.

I did not weep, for I couldn't any longer.

I abandoned my parabra. This was worst of all. But I was certain, as I spiralled through those dark places, that Aurelia had forgotten me. The words I spoke would never reach her ears.

I could not eat or drink. The bowls sat, untouched, in the slot below the door.

When I became too numb to walk another step, I sank to the floor, where I stared with glazed eyes at the pile of bones and rags in the corner.

When they came for me, I was ready. I felt nothing as they opened the door. I didn't struggle as they took my arms, binding them behind me with a thick cord. I allowed them to lead me, moving like an artificial, down those steps, into the Iglesia.

All was silent, until seven chimes rang out. Here, in the heart of the Iglesia, they were louder than I have ever heard them. The Tether, my broken mind realised, must amplify the sound, like a plucked guitar string; and here the heralds assembled for the dawn regimen.

Cloaked and hooded, they gathered in the aisles of the chamber, moving with precise steps, taking their allotted stations, as I was led to stand in the apse, before the stained-glass window. The colourful light fell around me, the only brightness among the black robes and dull metal and stone. I did not look up, into those faceless masks, but instead watched the dance of the stars and planets across the great floor. The chimes finished, and the Cosmic Wind sung in the silence.

La Boca stepped from the shadows, standing opposite me, framed by the open door. He turned as he took in the sight of those loyal heralds, each in their designated space.

"We are ready to begin," he said. "Everything is in place. The white-powder has been dispersed. Already, people are succumbing."

"It is as it should be," the heralds intoned.

La Boca broke from his place, then, and crossed the floor. The projected planets were eclipsed by his shadow. With a swift, predatory movement, he gripped me by the hair and pulled me upright, forcing me to look at his disciples. "This girl is an example of everything that we are leaving behind. An example of depravity which we want to excise. This is why we will cleanse Tierra Mejór, and begin anew."

He held aloft the small glass vial he had shown me before. Inside were the tiny white scales. Why did he have it with him? The powder was already being distributed among the people of the Wheel and the Spindle. Its only purpose here could only be as a display, a sickening show of his incredible power.

With the other hand, he hauled me into the centre of the chamber. I stumbled, unable to keep my balance with my hands tied, and went down, covered in the light of the planets. I squinted, but could barely see the dark silhouettes crowded at the edges of the chamber through the brightness of it all. Where was Tomas? Was he watching this, believing with all his heart that this was the right thing to do?

"Five hundred years ago, our people tried their best to destroy their world. Through imperfection, through allowing chaos to reign, they bought disaster on themselves. We, the chosen few, fled, and left behind those who were weak and unworthy. In thanks, we have performed the *Dance of a Thousand Steps*, every year, for five hundred years. This year, this girl, this fallible human, ruined the Dance. The Pattern has been compromised. Now, we feel its effects – our machinery is breaking down, our people are discontent, our crops are afflicted with blight and our people go hungry, all because this harlot *fell*. She profaned the Dance. Then she sought to ingratiate herself into the company of the weak-minded man who would rule our world. She had the audacity to address the Conclave. Having wrapped him around her finger, she even fled with the Prince, hiding like a drain-rat in the shadows! For this, we must punish her; the Pattern demands it!"

He wrenched on my hair, tilted my head; there was no pain in that, only in my heart. I looked up into his face, but beyond him, I saw the curved glass of the lens as it flickered and glinted. The wind moaned. And the planets . . . they danced.

He let go of me, and I fell sideways, bracing myself with my bound hands. I knew what he was going to do, and even as the thought formed in my mind, he backed away towards the edge of the chamber.

He held the vial loosely, almost casually, in one hand.

"This powder," he said, "is the beginning of the cleansing. We are immune, my Brother heralds and novices; our piety and devotion to the Pattern will keep us safe. But the rest of the population must be culled. Only those worthy of survival will join us in a new world."

He stood, and smiled. I knew it, then, with soul-freezing certainty; he expected the powder to choose the unworthy among his own heralds just as he did the rest of the population. Did they know anything of this?

I could almost see it, the white-powder, forming a cloud around me, spreading outwards towards the other heralds. They would be able to do nothing except breathe it in. The powder would have no effect on me, but this was la Boca's punishment: not my own death, but the deaths of everyone else in this room. He wanted me to watch others die before he killed me.

There was enough power in that vial that they would die in an instant. As quickly as Jark, or even more so. And they would all be at risk, including Tomas.

A sense of calm came over me. Not the terrible bleak numbness I had felt before, but rather, a warm sense of knowing that everything was exactly where it should be, in its own place, its own time. This was the Pattern.

Hardly knowing what I did, I pushed myself to my feet. And into a dance.

Among the stars and planets, I whirled – around los Amantes, the Lovers, around Nuevo Saturno, the Yellow Planet, across Constanza, the bright blue gaseous nebula. Their light bathing me, I stepped and jumped. I danced to the music of the Viento Cósmico, and all around me, the heralds clamoured and shouted in outrage and incredulity.

I danced.

It should have been awkward, with my arms bound behind my back. I should have stumbled and fallen. But I did not.

The coldness and pain ran out of me. Everything was bright, light, beautiful. A swirl of leaves blew past me, and I felt grass under my feet, and rich, soft earth; the kiss of the warmest sunshine upon my face.

And then I saw her.

She came forward, her face lit in a smile. "You found me," I said, not so much in surprise as in joy.

She took my face in her hands, and kissed me. I tasted sweetness on her lips – nectar from some fruit I had never encountered. Then, taking my hands, she danced with me.

I knew you would come again, querido.

"I'm sorry," I said. "I have come, but I have failed."

Why do you say this?

"Because the heralds have already released the new white-powder. People have taken it. They are dying."

The way of mortals is to die. While you might fight it, you must know it is your reason for being. You will spend more time not-being than you ever will being.

"I would rather believe my reason for being is what I do while I'm alive!" I said stubbornly.

Aurelia – for I was sure, now, that it was her – smiled at this. *And that is why you Dance.*

"That is why I Dance," I agreed. And then I realised I had known what I needed to do all along.

She nodded, and all of a sudden, I was back in the chamber. La Boca had grabbed my collar and swung me to the ground. Pain seared through my weak ankle. He held the glass vial in one hand, clenching it now, and he was furious, trembling.

"You did it," I whispered. "You did everything to make sure I would die, and you failed every time you tried to make me fall. Except the first. You made sure, on the day of the Fiesta de Tiempo, that I couldn't complete the Dance."

A glint in those eyes, and he whispered back as the wind tore the words to shreds before they reached the ears of his followers. "It wasn't personal, whore. A misplaced stone, where there should be smooth cobbles. A Dancer would never expect it, in the precision of her Dance, but the exactness of the steps meant it was certain. The Dance would have been ruined, no matter who they chose as la Grulla." He flashed a triumphant smile. "It was the will of the Pattern that it was you."

And then suddenly, as if the hand of the Pattern itself had reached down, a tremor surged through the room and he was flung aside. He tumbled on the floor, rolling over, once, twice; his hood came free, and with it, the veil over his nose and mouth. Beneath it was a close-fitting leather mask, like the one Ollender and his team had worn when the entered the Core, but the violence of the throw had knocked it away, and it hung loose and useless from its straps.

I saw him, in that instant, this man who was the Mouth of the Brother-hood, who was supposed to speak for the Pattern. He was not tall, as I had thought him in his robe of office. He was not fine-featured. He was plump, his pale skin veined with blue, sagging under his eyes and chin. His eyes were watery, beady. Scared. His mouth was open in horror.

He looked down at his hand. The glass vial had smashed when he'd fallen. From the fragments, tiny wispy clouds rose, drawn in on his breath.

Everything stopped.

And then, he began to cough. A terrible sound, one I'd heard before as Liliath choked on those Pattern-forsaken spores. Blood spattered his hands and the floor. And then, a small bright tendril, impossibly green in this dead place of stone and metal, unfurled from his mouth.

La Boca clawed at the growth, ripping it free and flinging it from him. But another followed, and another: too fast. The roots had taken hold in his throat, and were making their way into his lungs, his stomach. Already, a cocoon would be growing somewhere inside him, and in it, a little white moth. La Boca slumped forwards, and fell to the floor. The blood from his mouth spread across the stone, darkening the planets. I might have been mistaken, but in that shape, I saw a bird.

And then I looked up, and it was Tomas standing over me, over the fallen shape of la Boca. He took my hand, pulled me upright. "Imre! Do not breathe!" he said urgently, trying to pull me away and cover my mouth with his sleeve. "I beg you, hold your breath!"

"It's all right," I told him dazedly. "I am immune. But pull your hood over your nose and mouth, by the Pattern!"

Tomas already had his veil covering his face, and I hoped that would have been enough to keep him out of danger. He pushed back his hood now, draping it over his mouth and holding it there with one hand.

In the shadows of the pillared aisles, the heralds dithered. Some pushed forward, as if to help their fallen leader, but they hesitated, unsure. They had not expected to find their leader cheating them by wearing a filter mask. Even now, the white-powder was seeking the eyeholes in their hoods, the gaps in their sleeves.

I had no doubt that he'd never meant to release the white-powder in this chamber. It had only been meant for those below. Some would survive – but most who used it would not. It didn't matter whether they were chosen or not. He'd changed his plans when he brought me here, however. He wanted me to see this, and he didn't care what it cost.

I did not know why he had hated me so much.

But his mask revealed to them who their leader truly was. A charlatan, a pretender. They'd followed him blindly, believing that what he said was true – that their faith and purity would protect them. Now they saw that he was nothing more than a man, a misguided man who couldn't even be sure of his own immunity to the deadly drug.

Tomas took my hand. I felt it, his familiar, fine fingers clasping mine gently. He pulled me behind him towards the door.

We burst into the cold, windblown air, still clutching one another tightly. It could not have been my imagination that the Viento Cósmico was stronger, that the wailing song was louder; it was. It tore at my hair, my skirt, threatening to fling me aside. Tomas's grip that kept me steady. As we ran, he tore off his hood, and tossed it aside into the rocks, where it tumbled and vanished.

We ran down the steps, stumbling, just as we had run through the orchard as children. We were breathless when we reached the yard of ruined airships, bobbing up and down on the myriad currents and eddies. The craft that had bought us here was gone, the dock empty; our only chance were the derelict airships.

A quick glance over my shoulder showed that the heralds had noticed our escape. They came like a swarm of insects, pouring out of the arched doorway and racing down the steps. I had never seen such chaos!

"Stop! In the name of the Pattern!" one of them roared, and then the others took up the cry; but the wind battered them, pushed them back, and the strength of their words was snatched away.

We did not wait to see what would happen should they reach us. Tomas pulled me across to an ancient, rusted gangway. As he shoved me towards it, telling me in no uncertain terms that I was not to think about falling through the rusted, crackling metal, he bent to tear at the ropes. I didn't have time to worry; I scrambled across the flexing metal bridge, and through the door. Tomas had succeeded in loosening the restraints, and bounded in after me.

How he kept his presence of mind, I have no idea. Once inside, he reached back and pushed the rusted gangway from the lip of the door. It held for a moment before the strong grip of the Viento Cósmico caught it, flipping it up, and whirling it down into the open air below.

The pipes and vents protruding from the bottom of the Pendulum became visible. There was no sign of the white-powder, but I knew even now it must be spilling through the Iglesia, making its way into the filtration systems. I had to hope it would disperse too widely to do any damage before it reached the Spindle and the Wheel, but it was a slender hope. The heralds had by that stage reached the bottom of the steps. Seeing that we had succeeded so far, in this insane plan, they redoubled their efforts. There were shouts and curses, and an attempt to fit in another plank, but we were already drifting away. And then, I could barely make them out. As pleasing as it was to see the distance widening, it wouldn't help us if we kept drifting.

We could hit the side of the Iglesia, or even drift out beyond the atmosphere. We needed power, but who knew if this ancient hulk could still even fly?

I surveyed the cabin. It was a wreck. The seats were torn, their stuffing collected in clumps on the floor. Ragged sheets of dull red upholstery hung from the ceiling, like the innards of a great beast. The windows were pitted and cracked.

I turned to the cockpit. To my shock, instead of an empty pilot's chair, I saw a silver-plated automaton, its legs crumpled in a heap below the control panel.

My first thought was that he must surely be dead, for how could his crystals still hold power? Clearly, this craft had not been used in decades. My second thought was that it would be the work of moments for anyone on the Pendulum or the Spindle to reprogram him. In a flash, I saw those piercing red eyes of the murderous machine on the shuttle-train.

"Imre!" Tomas grabbed my arm, obviously sharing my fears. "Come away –"

And the automaton turned its head.

Its eyes were bright, pulsing blue. Rust stained its chin, but its torso seemed to be in good shape. Perhaps the thin air had preserved it.

"Greetings," it said, its voice calm, with only a hint of a crackle. "We appear to be drifting. Would you like me to pilot you down to the landing dock at the Citadel?"

"That would be lovely," I said, warily. At any moment, I knew, its program could be updated, and it could turn on us. We were entirely at its mercy.

"Imre, help me. We can get it out of the chair between the two of us," Tomas spoke urgently in my ear.

"And then what?" I hissed back at him. "Can *you* pilot an airship?"

He rubbed a hand over his face.

"I can pilot for you," said the automaton. "However, at present, I can not go anywhere. My left arm became inactive some time ago." It did not turn, its gaze fixed through the forward window, its eyes blinking rapidly.

With a backwards glance at Tomas, I squeezed into the tight space of the cockpit. The forward view was of the Spindle, and beyond, the arc of the Unknown. Or Space, I corrected myself, as Feval would rather have called it; space, full of other places and possibilities.

"Do you know what you're doing?" Tomas said.

"Of course I do!" I snapped, then almost laughed, for Tomas had no idea what I'd been through in the past months, and no reason to expect I knew anything about automata.

I fumbled the rings at the automaton's shoulder, trying to remember how the Green-band had disabled Feval's arms in the basement. I found the rings, but they were stiff with rust. I clenched them hard between my fingers, jiggling them with all my strength; sharp metal cut into my skin, but a moment later, the shoulder clicked into place.

"Do you need your legs to pilot?" I asked him.

"I do not. There was a time," he added – and this one, I decided, was definitely a *he* – in what was a tone very like Feval's, "when I considered harvesting the parts to repair the rest of me. But once I had detached them, it seemed a pointless exercise."

"But you could have left the airship," I said.

"Imre!" Tomas called to me. "There is no time for this!"

"I've never had cause to leave the airship," the automaton said, his head tilting curiously. "Why would I? I perform my function here in this chair."

"Your function is whatever you wish it to be," I told him. "What is your name?"

"Name?" he repeated. "I suppose it would be Pilot."

"That is a function, not a name. You should choose one that suits you."

The ring slipped into place under my fingers, and there was a whirring sound as he circled it, like a dancer stretching during a warm-up routine. His flickering eyes turned to me, twin points of blue light. "A name?"

There was a thump on the side of the airship, and the cabin swayed. "Imre! Make him fly us out of here!" Tomas yelled.

"Gilgamesh." I smiled. "Your name should be Gilgamesh."

"I know that name," said the automaton. "It is the name of a brave and daring hero. I am no warrior."

He had heard the name because Divon knew it. Good. He would know the story behind it, then, and the reason he would be deserving of it. "Being a hero is merely a function, if you would prefer to look at it that way," I countered. "Your name is what you are."

The automaton's eyes blinked, and I was almost certain there was a smile in his voice. "I have never encountered a human such as you."

Something heavy hit the side of the cabin, hard enough to knock me off my feet. I caught the door, as Tomas yelled something unintelligible. Through the door, I saw him grabbing a dust-covered decanter of what must be very old wine from one of the sideboards, and hurling it through the open door into the massed heralds gathered on the dock; the airship door, still open, swung closed at the airship's pitch tilted.

"Will you fly us down to the Spindle, Gilgamesh?" I asked the automaton.

"That is the first time anyone has given me a choice," he replied.

"It must be a choice," I told him. "And I'm offering it to you, because if you agree, you will be aiding the enemies of the people you've known as your masters."

"If I choose not to help you," he mused, "what will you do?"

"We can do nothing. They will take us prisoner, and what happens after that I cannot say, except that I wish very strongly to avoid it. You are our very last hope, Gilgamesh."

His eyes blinked off and on again. "Then I will do it."

I breathed a sigh of relief as he moved his hands expertly across the panel, flicking a switch, pushing a button, turning a dial. The deck shook beneath my feet as the engines hummed to life, and then settled to a constant vibration as the huge rotors reached their peak speed.

Slowly, the airship eased away from its mooring. There were more shouts, and another loud thump; glass shattered in one of the cabin windows, and the Cosmic Winds whipped in through the small opening, tearing at the red drapes, making the gold tassels whirl in the sudden rush.

We picked up speed. I left Gilgamesh and went out into the cabin and, bracing myself against the angry wind, looked through an unbroken window. There, gathered on the platform at the bottom of the stairs, were the heralds. I was glad to be away – words could not express how glad! – but still, the thought that they were trapped now on their Pendulum, facing the ravages of the white-powder, filled me with regret.

What could I have changed? How could I have made this play out differently?

Exhausted, I flopped down on one of the padded chairs. The comfort of the velvet was almost unseemly, after all I had endured.

"Imre," Tomas said quietly, as he sat beside me. "Can you ever forgive me?"

I bridged the distance between us, and was glad to do so. How I had missed him! It had been so long since I had been able to touch him. I let my head rest on his shoulder. "There's nothing to forgive."

"The heralds have told us, time and again, how wrong it is that women should sell themselves. To lay with multiple partners, to accept payment for it. That the city should profit from the vice." He sighed. "And yet, I knew you were pure of heart, Imre. I knew you were kind and good. I knew your beauty as a gift from the Pattern."

I replied to this wryly. "Or a curse."

He wiped the tears from my cheeks with his sleeve. "A curse? I think not."

"When people look at me, they do not see what's inside. They see someone they can have and use. They like my beauty because they find pleasure in it."

"There will always be people like that in this world," said Tomas. "But there are those who see beyond, as well. Are you telling me there is no one whom you care for?"

"Well," I drawled. "There's you, of course."

He laughed. "I meant in the romantic sense."

In the romantic sense. The sense of two people who fit together as no one else does. I had denied it for a long time, telling myself it was not so; but there was only one answer to that question.

I nodded slowly. "Yes."

"I always hoped you would meet someone like that. And is he good? And kind? Does he put you above all others?"

"He does," I said. "Though he doesn't always show it."

Tomas smiled. "Then I'm glad you found him."

"Me, too," I murmured into his black robes.

The descent was interminable. I slept, and woke, and slept again.

I dreamed, but it was only half a dream – the rest was memory. I was back in the Chamber of the Iglesia, which was planted with the verdant plants of the Citadel gardens. I was looking up at Aurelia, who was also la Boca. 'A misplaced stone, where there should be smooth cobbles. A Dancer would never expect it, in the precision of her Dance, but the exactness of the steps meant it was certain. The Dance would have been ruined, no matter who they chose as la Grulla . . .'

Again, the words echoed around and around that garden that was not a garden.

'A misplaced stone, where there should be smooth cobbles.'

At one point, I was torn from a panicked, formless dream, to see the Wheel arcing overhead. A trail of flame was ripped from it, tearing free as it burned out in the thin oxygen. I clutched my hands to my heart.

I sat up, looking for Tomas. He wasn't in the gondola. I saw him through the door into the pilot's cabin, which had been left open. He was standing behind the automaton, looking through the front viewport, and, as the airship dipped suddenly and sharply to one side, I realised what had woken me.

The Tether whipped by the side windows, missing the airship by what must have been the breadth of a hair. I braced my hands on the seat, afraid to look, yet unable to close my eyes; the huge cable, its intertwined strands so close I could have counted them, was being shaken like the string of a child's kite at the Day of the Fiesta de Tiempo.

"I must apologise," Gilgamesh said loudly and politely. "This will be a little rougher than usual."

Tomas looked over his shoulder. His face was white, and he was holding on to the back of the pilot's chair with a death grip. "Imre –" But in the next moment we were both flung to the floor as Gilgamesh wrenched the controls. Again, the airship jerked to the side, narrowly missing the wildly swinging cable. We spiralled crazily for a few seconds, the blood rushing to my head and throwing bright sparks before my eyes. I clutched at the seat vainly, and then, all of a sudden, we were level and flying normally. The Tether passed us, continuing into the distance, the Pendulum swinging at its end.

"Another quake," I said. A redundant comment. Neither of my companions paid attention: for beyond the windows, I could see the roofs of the tallest buildings on the Spindle.

We were coming into dock at the Citadel.

Chapter Forty-Nine

I would learn, later, what had happened to the Principe Regente and Senor Grath since I had been dragged from the entrance chamber of the Citadel.

As I had travelled in the airship, the heralds had patted them down for weapons and devices. They'd taken Grath's wristwatch, then hauled them both to the lowest levels, below the Great Library, which Miguel had told me about on the day we'd met Divon. They were awful, dank, dark, and so deep underground that the noises from the core of Tierra Mejór resonated through their walls – screechings, thumps, and the constant rumble of the burning fire.

There were few prisoners in here, but of them, three were Green-bands, two men and a woman; this, Grath knew, for he himself had ordered them locked up here.

The cells were made of iron bars. The prisoners could reach one another through them, for they were cruelly small. Often, fights broke out over food and clothing. This solved the issue of what to do with many of the more hardened inhabitants, for often they would murder one another.

Grath had always felt shame at what he knew took place there. But they were buried, deep beneath the Citadel, and like all things out of sight, they were difficult to remember in the light of day.

Grath has told me, he will never forget them now.

"What are you planning for us?" he demanded, as he was pushed roughly along the corridor between the cages. The floor was hot, so hot, it burned him through the soles of his shoes, and the air was stifling.

"That is for la Boca to decide," the herald holding Grath's bound hands told him.

"The Prince needs treatment," Grath snarled. He had no idea if this was true or not, but it seemed wise to try anything at all at this point. "The illness he has is contagious. You might even have infected yourselves by touching him!"

The herald gave a sniff of contempt as he pushed open one of the cell doors. "The illness affects those who do not follow the true Pattern."

With that, Grath was hurled into the cell, hitting the hot stone floor hard. Oh, if only they would give him back his sword! He would run these men through in a heartbeat . . .

But as he struggled to his feet, the door was slammed shut. A complicated lock clicked, and the herald pressed his thumb to the external pad. Grath had calibrated these touch-locks himself. They would never break, and without his wristwatch, he couldn't override them.

"You, on the other hand," the herald leaned through the bars to gloat at the helpless Grath, "might find proximity to be an issue."

With this, Thaniel was dumped into the adjoining cell. The Prince was limp, his pallid skin almost translucent.

"My Liege," Grath called as the heralds left them alone. "My Liege. Awake. You must . . ."

Thaniel's eyelids fluttered. "Grath," he rasped. "Where is Imre?"

Grath struggled upright, slipped his wrists underneath his feet, and began working on his bindings.

"Where is Imre?" repeated the Prince. "Please, tell me she's safe . . ."

Safe. Imre was anywhere but safe; she had never been safe in her life. The girl attracted trouble like a magnet attracted iron filings. It was probably better that she was further away from the Prince now . . .

Grath fought down a welling of an incredible, deep despair. The only person he could see in his mind was me, my face flushed as I worked in the garden, terrified and shaking as I looked down at the body of an assassin, defiant and foolhardy as I glared at Jark in the basement where we were kept prisoner. Why, he asked, why? He had never wanted, never asked for this.

He left off his task and leaned back against the wall.

"My Liege," Grath answered at last. "I do not know."

***

Their turnings passed much in the way mine had. The Prince seemed to worsen every hour. His breathing was shallow, and Grath was sure this wasn't helped by the constant heat. Water, when it was passed, occasionally, through the bars, was tepid and filthy. The food was worse.

They were fed perhaps once a day, by a stonefaced vigilar. Grath did not know this man, but when he attempted conversation, the vigilar would refuse to pass Grath's bowl through the bars, instead taking it with him as he left. Grath soon learned that if he wanted to eat, he wasn't to question, cajole, or try to talk sense to the man. He was obviously in thrall of the Brotherhood, and probably paid handsomely for his stoicism.

Through a combination of pulling and chewing, Grath had managed to free his hands. He spoonfed the Prince as best he could through the bars, but most of the time Thaniel refused to, or could not, swallow it.

Grath could feel his own strength draining from him. The food was poor, and there was never enough. The heat was intolerable. And further down, the other inmates made their own entertainment, already having been driven half-mad by their conditions.

The woman insisted on singing.

> "La Grulla rises every morn,
> Silver-white, with feathers so light,
> Carrying courage twixt her wings,
> To sink at eve, and rise again . . ."

The man next to her, however, recognised Grath.

"So!" he would call, rattling the bars. "How goes it in your cage this day, fine Senor? Is the food to your liking? The bedding to your satisfaction? How goes it? It's not polite to sit in silence while your hosts are trying to make conversation! Answer me!"

"I remember you," Grath told him once. "You derailed a rotor-tram. A neighbour informed the vigilar, for he heard you boasting about it at a night-café. Three people were killed, one of them a child of four."

"It was all for the cause!" the man retorted. "A *good* cause! See how our machines are failing? It would have happened eventually, anyway! No one knows how to fix them – we've lost that knowledge. At least this way, people heard about it. They were speaking of it on Rueda! They'll be talking about it long after I'm gone! They will know that la Rebelde is the only true leader of the people!"

Grath leaned against the bars of his own cell. The man believed that his message had been heard, that the means of it justified the end. Grath knew better. People would speak of it, but they would hate the man who had done it, and any cause he put before them.

"I am a hero," the man cried. "A great hero! La Rebelde himself couldn't have done better!"

Having met Jark, Grath doubted very much that la Rebelde had condoned such an action. The fact that the man was turned in, possibly even by the Green-bands themselves, instead of being hidden and protected, said as much.

Yet another prisoner was silent, staring through the bars of his cage. His beard was long, his hair a tangled mess. He said nothing, and barely moved, even to eat and drink.

With the Prince worsening with every turning and the cell so small, he could barely take two steps in any direction, Grath thought he would soon go mad. He had fiddled with the lock several times, trying to rewire it, but here, his own competency with devices worked against him. The locks were infallible.

And then the third prisoner, the silent man, died.

The illness came upon him quickly. One hour he was fine, the next he had slumped to one side. From his mouth, a tendril unfurled, cupping a small brown cocoon.

The woman began to shriek wordlessly, and soon the first man had joined in.

"Let us out! Let us out! I don't want to die!" This went on for hours, the screaming and wailing and desperate sobbing. Grath covered his ears with his hands and pressed his back against the wall, silent.

And then came the footsteps.

They were much heavier than the vigilar, and Grath thought at first it might be one of the heralds. It was not, however, a robed form that came into view as he stood up. Instead, it was Miguel, in his black and grey guardia uniform, carrying a long metal bar.

Seeing Senor Grath and the Prince, still, though barely, alive, Miguel's face broke into a sigh of relief. "Hendrich!" he called over his shoulder. "I have them!"

All at once, the man and the woman started clamouring. "Help! Help us! Please!"

"Miguel." Grath leaned through the bars. "What's happened?"

"The illness spread among the heralds," Miguel replied. "Most of them died within the last few days. An airship arrived with more, and those fell ill even quicker. Hendrich and I have been lying low, pretending to be loyal and trying to get down here; but the unrest in the streets has grown. Even the vigilar have deserted, running home to protect their families, or to loot the wealth of the Citadel. Just this morning, the remaining three heralds fled, unable to keep control any longer."

He passed something through the bars – Grath's wristwatch. Grath gave a grim smile as he held it close to the lock and began to work the dials. In moments, it clicked, and Miguel shoved it wide open.

"Get us out of here, guardia," Grath growled.

Chapter Fifty

They had seen us coming.

The gangway folded out as soon as we docked. With a clang, the clamps locked into place. Tomas took my hand, leading me down. We passed by the forlorn airship which had taken me to the Pendulum. It was empty, floating beside us at the dock, and the airbag hung crookedly, the undercarriage coming free at the rear. I doubted it was able to fly.

Our city, the Cuidad, spread out around us. Fires were burning, cinders floating on currents of air. The sky, usually murky, was covered with thick ashy clouds, tinged red with the reflection of the flames. Above, the Wheel loomed like a dark shadow, and even as I watched, some molten debris dropped from it, spinning as it was pulled in by the forces of motion, crashing to the ground on the distant side of the Cuidad.

It was the end of the world.

I didn't care. I was looking at the group of people who had seen our airship soaring downwards, and come to meet the occupants, whom they had assumed would be heralds.

Some few guardia, in torn, ragged uniforms, faces blackened with soot and bruises. They held revolver-pistols and rifles, all of which were levelled at this airship full of supposed enemies. They fairly quivered with tiredness and fear. Among them, Grath, Miguel, Guildsman Ollander, and Hendrich. I saw only Grath, his sword held across his body, ready to defend his fellows.

Do you remember what I said, of recognising those moments in which history is written? Well, I shall say only this: I recognised this one. It may not have been some grand decision that changed the course of the future, nor an instant so profound its effects were felt throughout the Unknown.

And yet – it was.

Grath was the first to break from the defensive group, while the others still gaped, clearly wondering when the hoard of evil heralds would appear from the broken door behind us.

He dropped his sword as he crossed to me, his steps slow and steady at first, then quicker as he reached me. I thought he was about to scold me. A protest was on my lips, but he stifled it, pressing his mouth to mine, his arms coming around me, gathering me close. I had never felt a body so rigid and hard, yet yielding; I had never felt a body that fitted so perfectly with mine.

And I knew, then, with that kiss; I was capable of love. It was not with Bethery, not the Prince. Not with anyone in the world except him.

The pain that had plagued me, that cold, hard knot deep inside, it melted and vanished.

He pulled away for a moment, and I looked up into his grey eyes, and saw what had been there all along; not disgust, not revulsion, but possessiveness, yearning, desire. He brushed my hair from my face. His touch was tender and loving, possessive, fierce; he was everything, everything at once. He gathered me to his chest.

But even amidst all this, I could tell something was not right.

"Where is the Prince?" I asked.

"Imre," he breathed, and he could say nothing more.

***

None of the lifts were working, and some of the shafts were empty gaping holes. We took the stairs. Most of the servants had fled. They had gone home to their families, I supposed, or tried to find somewhere safe. Did they know that nowhere was safe? We passed a contingent of vigilar, and they stopped and saluted Grath.

"Get out of here!" Grath growled, but the men looked confused. "Protect the people on the streets. Stop the rioting, if you can. If you can't, protect your families and get help to those injured or ill. Go!"

Finally, they disbanded.

Grath turned to the rest of the vigilar and guardia who trailed behind us. "That goes for you, as well. We can't do anything now except try to protect the defenceless. Go, now."

Guildsman Ollander, with a final look at me, went, and so did the Chancellor. Miguel and Hendrich refused.

Grath, looking impatient and resigned, led the way onwards.

Tomas, jogging behind Miguel and Hendrich, was gawking in awe at the grandeur of the Citadel. He had probably seen it only in part, for he'd boarded the airship, but now he was able to view it properly. "This is where you've been living, Imre?"

I nodded, smiling. "But I much preferred my garden house."

"A garden house," he murmured. "Yes, of course you would."

***

We came in through a side door to the long, curved passage that led to the back door to the library and into La Reina's chamber.

The cold was just as I remembered it.

Here, the Príncipe Regente lay on his back, alongside his mother. Through the thick glass of the case, his face was slack, his skin pale, blue veins showing under his skin.

I rushed towards him, but Hanna, who I had not seen before, stood up from a chair and caught my arm. Beside her, Doctor Oren was crouched at the base of the casket, examining the workings behind a raised panel.

"It had to be done," he said, sadly, standing up, his old knees creaking. "The scales of these new white-moths are unlike anything I've seen before. They infect the tissue, take root, and, like a parasite, turn the body into a system that will reproduce more moths. The process can take hours or days, depending on the level of exposure and the vigour of the host's immune defences. The chamber will keep him alive, and quarantined, slowing all his responses to the point of near-death. But without a cure, we cannot risk waking him."

Tears stung my eyes. "No, no, no." I couldn't believe it. I'd gone through all this, and still I had not succeeded in gaining the Prince his rightful throne.

"Is there no cure?"

"I have never encountered anything like it," Oren said. "I would need to study the origins of these modified moths."

"The lab on the Wheel was mostly destroyed," I told him numbly. "And Liliath, the woman who created it, is dead. I – I killed her myself."

He fixed me with that patient gaze, but this time there was something like admiration behind it. I shook my head, for I wanted no approval, not for this.

"Unless I know its origins, I doubt I will be able to cure it."

"Liliath," I gasped. "She bred the moths using knowledge she gained from the Library. She told me she came here to research it!"

Oren pressed two wizened fingers to his lips. "Yes," he said. "Of course."

I turned to the guardia. "Divon. You must find him. He knows the Library better than anyone!"

Looked back to the case which held the Prince, I reached out a finger to touch the cold glass. But before I could make contact, the floor trembled, and something in the distance exploded with the jangle of shattering glass.

The danger was not past. Having faced everything I had faced, having defeated la Boca, having survived this long: it all seemed laughably pointless. Tierra Mejór was still falling to pieces around us; we were still doomed. We'd been doomed from the start, perhaps from the moment we had landed here, with la Relojero leading us down from la Grulla's back onto this, our new home.

Had she really only delayed the inevitable? Had she known that the children of the Companions would live only another five hundred years, before they, too, were destroyed? Surely, surely she had some other plan. Why else did we enact the *Dance of a Thousand Steps* every year, to ensure good fortune?

Except for this year.

A misplaced stone, where there should be smooth cobbles.

I gasped, then gripped Grath's arm. "I have to get to the Square."

To his credit, he didn't ask me why, but turned and led the way out of the chamber, telling Oren to stay where he was and wait for Divon; Miguel and Tomas followed.

Since none of the lifts worked, the way up was a long one. Miguel knew the way to the stairs, but even as we climbed, they shifted underneath our feet, small pieces crumbling away. A loud noise boomed overhead, making us all duck for cover. A cloud of smoke billowed down the stairs, covering us from head to toe. When we reached the top, we realised the cause; a whole section of the hallway ceiling had collapsed. Broken furniture, plaster, and stone impeded our progress.

"This way," Grath said grimly, pointing behind us.

We rounded the corner, and found another pile of debris blocking a doorway. Suddenly I knew where we were, for it was the Oak Door, with its beautifully carved tree; the door that led into the Den. The door that was never locked, now blocked completely.

In near-unison, Grath and I rushed to the door. I hauled on a piece of stone, unbelievably heavy, only to have it roll towards me, nearly crushing my toes. Grath had seized a large wooden beam, and dragged its impossible weight to one side.

Miguel didn't have that kind of patience. Heedless, he leaped into the pile like a wild animal at its prey. He tossed aside pieces of fallen masonry and plaster, and in under a minute, had cleared enough of a path to barge at the door with his shoulder. It splintered near the hinges.

Inside the common room were several huddled women – I recognised Audren, Misthra and Laisa among them, as well as the three small children, Xith, and even haughty Jardine. They were terribly frightened, cowering behind the couches and tables. "Is anyone hurt?" I called.

Slowly, one of the figures stood. It was Bethery – of course it was. "Imre," she breathed. Without another thought, she ran to me and hugged me tightly, spinning me around. "I tried to get them out through the window," she said as she set me down. "But they wouldn't listen. They were too scared of what lies out there. Weren't you?" Here she turned, setting her blazing gaze on them, baring her teeth in contempt. "You are like little mice, too frightened to move!"

No malice coloured her words. The fact remained, she could have left herself, for she wasn't afraid to climb through a window and face the outside world. Reading my thoughts, she smiled bitterly. "I couldn't leave them here, could I? If they wouldn't leave, neither would I. I had to stay."

I looked at the women, who were still staring in shock at my bloody, dirty dress. "Listen to me, you can't stay in here. It might have been safe, once, but it is no longer. The Citadel is being shaken to pieces. It's too dangerous – the ceiling might fall. You have to come with us."

I looked at them. None of them were moving.

"I know how to fix this," I continued, desperately. "I know what to do. I can make the quakes stop, but you can't stay here, where it's not safe. You must come now!"

Bethery turned back to the cowering group, glaring at them each in turn. "Come on, you cowardly little girls! Are you really so arrogant you can't follow a Daughter of the Pavilion? Would you rather choose death?"

Jardine was the first to come forwards, clutching her daughter, the small girl who had played houses of cards with me by the fountain. The child carried her ragged, stained toy under one arm. "Take her," Jardine said, in a querulous voice, holding the girl out to me. "Make sure she's safe."

Pressa gave a small wail, clutching tightly at her precious Scothe.

I didn't take the small girl. "She needs her mother," I told Jardine firmly.

"We are sisters," Bethery added. "We go together."

And one by one, the women came.

They passed me, looking at big Miguel with over-awed eyes, like children themselves. And behind me, Tomas looked astounded at the ranks of beautiful women dressed in scanty silk clothing. His cheeks turned red and I had to laugh at him. But he didn't hesitate before picking up the little girl, and taking the hand of one of the small boys as we hurried down the hallway.

I found Bethery at my side. "I don't know how you think you're going to fix this, sugar," she whispered in my ear.

"All of this happened because I didn't complete the Dance," I told her. "I realise that now. What is happening to our world began years ago, but to fix it, the Dance needs to be completed. All I have to do is make those final steps. I promise you, it will change everything."

I hoped I was right. Oh, by the Pattern, how I hoped! Aurelia's words still resounded in my ears - *and that is why you Dance* – but now? Oh, now I was scared. For there was a chance, a very good chance, that I was not –

that my deluded mind, starved of sleep, ravaged by drugs, and deprived of a decent meal, had merely dreamed the solution.

Still, we had nothing else to try.

In reminder, the walls quivered around us, as if made of matchsticks, not stone. We ran through the hallways, down a wide set of steps which I now recognised, through an arched door, and into the light of day – such as it was. The smoke was thick enough that even with la Grulla overhead, it looked like twilight.

Ominous grumblings from the building we'd just left dogged our steps. We couldn't stop here. I pushed the women around me across the small courtyard and through the long tunnel under the wall, out into the Plaza de Lágrima.

We burst out into the square. And there it was, the statue of la Oráculo. He stood just as he always had, but his tears had dried. The tracks where they had run were white over his cheeks.

I walked around the empty base, looking for the spot where I was to have finished the Dance.

And there it was, the stone, slightly raised above the others. I wouldn't have seen it as I Danced in my flowing white feathers. Neither would anyone else.

It bubbled up from within me, terrible sorrow for all that had happened, for all that was now irretrievably lost. And terrible joy, for what I had found; Tomas, who was here by my side, as he should be; Miguel, my steadfast friend and guardian; Grath. Grath!

I took a deep breath, and . . .

I Danced.

I turned first towards Bethery, pulling her close to me, and she responded with a surprised, incredulous laugh, brushing a hand over my breast as she did so. Step, step, leap – I twirled away, then, and gripped Tomas's hands, his slender fingers matching my own. Step, step, turn – I danced around Miguel and Hendrich, their strong, muscled bodies stumbling and awkward when trying to be graceful. I whirled around Grath, feeling his heat, his gaze on every part of my body, marvelling at the Dance, marvelling at me; for there was no difference, in that moment. I *was* the Dance.

Around the statue I danced. Past the three stains of smeared blood that had not been washed away. I jumped from symbol to symbol, from the open book to the house, to the rising sun of the Physician, to the anvil, to the tree, to the moon of Aurelia.

Seven steps. Step, step, step. Step. Step. Step. Step. Each one marked by the ticking of my metronómo.

And then I was back where I started, standing on the slightly raised cobblestone, that with the crescent moon. The sigil of Aurelia, whose guild did not sit at the Conclave. For a moment, I almost lost my balance once more. The cobblestone was cleverly tilted, and so small, that there was little room for error. La Boca had done his work well. I could see that anyone walking the square might have found themselves off-balance – let alone a Dancer, whose movements must be so precise.

My ankle twinged as I landed, pain lancing all the way through my body. But I was prepared, this time. I did not fall.

And yet, nothing happened.

My chest heaved as I looked up into the eyes of the statue. Blank, they gave away nothing. La Oráculo's hand reached for me, empty, beseeching. And then I realised I had not completed the Dance at all. The feather!

I almost laughed. I reached into my bodice and pulled it free, that ruined, crumpled, filthy thing, then placed it reverently in the palm of the statue.

There was a sigh, like a breath of wind on a hot day. The feather fluttered, and my heart quivered with it, my throat clenching at the thought that it might simply blow away, as all the feathers had, over the centuries. But I knew this was right – this was the missing step, which la Boca's plan had prevented me from taking. It hadn't mattered that I'd fallen, not at all; if I'd placed the feather, I might have saved us.

Again, a moment in time when everything hinged on one action. La Boca had only sought to spoil the Dance, to show the world that the Dancers were damned by the Pattern, that our very way of life was a sin. Instead, what followed showed that he'd almost condemned us all to the very fate he'd tried so desperately to avoid – our complete annihilation.

The statue awoke.

La Oráculo rose up. His bent knees straightened, his hands clenched, one curling tightly around the feather. He turned his neck stiffly from side to side.

He was not a statue at all, but an automaton.

I had never taken the time to study him closely. His casing was white, unlike any other artificial I had seen. It had been weathered by the rain and wind, stained green in parts where moss and lichen had taken hold, but his joints were smooth, barely noticeable. He had been crafted beautifully, his clothing moulded onto his exterior, the long flowing cloak hanging down his back and the tunic finished at his waist with a belt. Loose trousers were tucked into his high boots, all of it part of the same smooth structure as his hands and face. Each strand of his hair had been shaped in realistic curls. I had never seen the like, and I could almost feel Grath's admiration radiating from behind me.

"Many long years have I slept," he said, his voice gentle, slightly crackled, like a kindly grandfather's. "Waiting for this moment."

Around me, the others shrunk back. But I didn't move with them. Instead, I stepped forward. "Every year, for five hundred years, a Dancer has placed a feather in your hands. Why have you only awoken now?"

"Because the weight of five hundred feathers was needed to wake me. It is time, when it was not time before."

He tilted his head to the sky, and then I saw it: la Grulla. So crisp and clear was she! I could make out the feathers on her wings, and feel the breeze as she passed. A gasp went up from my group. How had she come to be so close?

A moment later, she was gone, disappearing over the horizon.

"She will circle," la Oráculo said. "Until she lands."

"How –"

"This is the way it was meant to be," la Oráculo interrupted me, as if he already knew my question. "La Relojero did not build Tierra Mejór to last forever. It was a waystation on the greater journey, and that journey is only beginning."

I gaped at him.

Behind me, echoed Grath's heavy step as he came to stand at my shoulder. "A waystation?"

"This is not your terminus, and it was never meant to be," la Oráculo told him. "It was a safe haven, and it's served its purpose."

"But where are we to go?" My heart raced. "Where, in all of the Unknown, are we to find our home?"

"Where it has always been," la Oráculo said, and did I imagine it? Or did his white lips turn up in a smile?

"Old Earth." I smiled back.

La Oráculo nodded.

Chapter Fifty-One

I shifted in my sleep, surprised to find cool, clean sheets under me, a crinkly pillow beneath my head, and a thickly-woven blanket trapping warmth against my skin. I was almost dazzled by the brightness of the room, though no globe-light lit it; it was simply la Grulla's light, streaming in through the window.

I knew this bed. It was the same one I had woken in after my fall. The one where Ketra had languished, then breathed her last.

I remembered, only then, firm hands guiding me through the darkened Pavilion last night. Feverish with wakefulness, my body and mind saturated with adrenaline, I had protested against sleep until I was horizontal. Then, I had lost all choice as unconsciousness took me.

"Good morning," said a voice from the chair near the door. My eyes, still unused to this brilliant light, focused on Senora R. She was dressed in drab plain cotton robes, looking as solid and steady as a rock.

I pushed back the covers and swung my legs over the edge of the bed, so very aware of my rumpled hair and the smudges on my cheeks. I had not bathed since leaving Rueda. I was no longer a slender, graceful Dancer, worthy of a place in the White Pavilion, but a skinny, wiry girl-woman, her beauty marred, and the fate of Tierra Mejór on her hands.

"Imre," Senora said sharply, forcing me to meet her gaze.

I did so with trepidation, uncertain what she could want with me. The last time I had seen her, she'd been ready to hand me over to la Boca. Would she scold me? Ridicule me? Point out that she never should have chosen me to dance as la Grulla, or even that she had never sent a carrier-pigeon to tell me my application to the Pavilion had been successful?

Instead, she stood, crossed the space between the bed and her chair, and reached out to touch the scar on my neck with gentle fingers.

"Do you remember the day you came to me, child?"

I nodded. Of course, I remembered it.

"I asked you," she went on, "if you could dance to the glory of the Pattern. Do you remember what you said?"

I shook my head, my hair trailing messily across my shoulders.

"You told me, '*I can Dance*.' "

I flushed with embarrassment. "I was impertinent –"

"You were truthful." Those eyes – they were hard, critical, but filled with depths of compassion. "That was why I accepted you."

I bowed my head, tears pricking my eyes but she gripped my chin with her fingers – the lines around them showed where her heavy rings had once sat – and raised it. Then she kneeled before me.

"Forgive me," she spoke to the ground at my feet. "I can ask it, even if I know I'm not worthy."

I was mortified. I slid from the edge of the bed and crouched before her, gripping her hands, pulling her back to her feet; her old knees creaked and clicked. "Senora R., you did what you did to protect my sisters. I couldn't have asked you to do anything else." Still, she would not look at me, so, throwing caution to the winds, I gathered her to my chest, surprised that her head barely reached my chin. "You are forgiven, you are forgiven," I said, again and again.

***

The Pavilion was changed. The workings that had made the rooms spin, the scents fill the air, the projected images function, had all slowed or broken. But despite all odds, some rooms remained in operation; the Valley Room, for example, still held a soft breeze, and the chirping of birds. No one entered, for the tranquil scene was unnerving amid the chaos outside.

Senora R. had insisted that every room be thrown open, the kitchens emptied, and food, water, and clothing distributed among the refugees.

The Prince had not wakened. Oren had done the best he could with his limited equipment and hastily-read passages in the Library books, before the Citadel had become too unstable to be safe. But without access to proper equipment, and with parts of the Library already inaccessible even to Divon, his attempts were frustrated.

Feval and Divon had helped move the heavy caskets from the cellar. Both the Principe Regente and La Reina were now housed in the Room of Roses at the Pavilion, covered by heavy protective sheets and guarded by sentinela. Grath's disguised automaton, however, had been missing when he returned to the Citadel to fetch the ice-caskets.

I moved through them, astonished at how many people could fit in these rooms, normally so spacious, now littered with belongings, makeshift beds, and discarded rubbish. Servitors moved about, attempting to do their job by cleaning and serving food, carrying blankets or towels, but it was clear the task was too big for them to manage.

My sisters – for such I still counted them – I found huddled in one dormitory.

"– cannot claim such a thing!" The voice was high-pitched, argumentative. Rehina.

"Do not question me," answered another – Firelli. "I tell you, this comb is mine!" A sound of a scuffle, then a sharp slap. "You'll break it!"

A frustrated cry followed, and as I entered, I found Sharquen throwing herself down on a bed, her face red with fury. Firelli was holding a small silver comb, with Rehina at her side, hands on her hips. Yui stood aways off, hands over her mouth. My sisters were all in their night-robes, and they looked somehow childlike.

Seeing me, they stopped and stared.

"Imre," spoke Carla, who I hadn't seen until that moment. She was sitting on the bed nearest the door – Ketra's bed. Her eyes were rimmed with black; it wasn't kohl, this time. This bruised darkness came from exhaustion and pain.

Had I imagined a warm welcome home? That they would throw their arms about me, and whisper that everything was all right, that I was one among them again? Had I thought I could make some grand speech, about all I had overcome?

I did not know what to say to them, and they did not know what to say to me. I suddenly wished I had never come.

I almost turned to leave without a word, but one question I had to ask. "Where is Vahn?"

"Oh, Imre." Carla's voice trembled.

It was thus I learned that Vahn had died during the second tremor. She'd been crushed by a falling block of masonry, probably at about the same time I was fending off the Concerje in my cage.

There were tears as Carla told me, the argument over the comb forgotten, at least for a time. But there were reproachful glances, as well, barely hidden. They blamed me.

Sisters I might still count them, but whatever they thought of me, I could only be sure of one thing: that I was no longer one of them.

I went next into the bathroom we'd once shared. The tiles on the walls had cracked. No one had cleaned or tidied in a while, and there were bunched towels on the floor, discarded dresses, and a broken bottle of scent had left a pool of dark, sticky liquid on one of the benches.

I stood before one of the hand basins and peered at my reflection in the smeared mirror.

The first thing I noticed was my cheeks. They were sunken, hollowed. My eyes were surrounded by black circles. My hair was ragged and messy. I was thinner, much thinner than I had ever been, but I was no longer slender – I was skinny.

Carla followed me. She stood behind me and looked over my shoulder into the mirror.

I made a small, self-deprecating gesture. "I wanted to see the damage," I said wryly.

She lifted my hair, letting the unkempt golden curls slide through her fingers. "We are none of us what we used to be."

"Don't say that," I begged her. She, for one, looked just as beautiful as ever. I hate to think it, but perhaps even more so, for her haunted expression lent a quality of depth that had been missing before, in her carefree, cheerful bearing.

"It is true, and you know it better than all of us. What place is there for a Dancer, in this world?"

"Is that why they hate me?" I asked.

"They don't hate you." Carla wrapped an arm around my neck, pulling me tightly against her. "They fear you. If we're to survive, we must become something else, something more. They are reminded of this every time they see you. You intimidate them."

I lifted a hand so I could wrap it around her wrist. "And you?" I asked her, my eyes locking with hers in the mirror. "Are you intimidated?"

"Me, most of all," she admitted, kissing the side of my cheek and slipping through the door, back into the darkened bedroom.

Chapter Fifty-Two

A turning passed, and another, in which we lived in abject terror. The tremors worsened. A great plate of the earth itself had ripped free on Third Tier, taking houses and buildings, and countless souls with it as it spiralled into the Unknown.

We huddled together as best we could, caring for one another, sharing our limited food supplies. And hoping against all hope that the illness would burn itself out. There seemed to be no reason behind those who died and those who survived. A youngest child would die, while her siblings looked on. A husband and wife would die in one another's arms. An old man would bathe the perspiration from his granddaughter's forehead while she lay prone on the ground, eyes rolled back in her head.

Every turning, la Grulla drew closer, and as she soared overhead, the wind from her wings blew tiles from the rooftops and flattened small trees.

The Green-bands, though their efforts were previously conducted in subterfuge, were experienced at organising and distributing essentials. Nathuin, Alen, and Jornel did their best, gathering supplies from the Citadel, distributing them among those who needed them, but every day it became more and more dangerous to enter those shaking ruins. The Librarians were busy salvaging what they could from the Great Library, but so much had to be abandoned when the second floor collapsed almost entirely, blocking most entrances. Feval and Divon, meanwhile, worked to stack what had been retrieved into crates and boxes.

To be sure, Commander Fedren and Chancellor Darhn were missed. Their skills in organisation and knowledge of the Cuidad would have been an asset. As it was, Vice Chancellor Mardrey, Guildsman Ollander and Secretary Allius, and Guildswoman Terreth of the Artisans, were busy cataloguing and distributing what supplies could be salvaged, and trying to put together a hierarchical group of leaders, as well as a force of former vigilar to stop the looters. To the people they selected, they gave Green ribbons, for this had become the symbol for aid. In all, however, the populace was well-behaved, and there were very few real issues.

In the afternoons, as people rested from the morning's work and their scant meals, the minstrels played for us. Pherie had lost her harp, but in her ingenuity, she had fashioned an instrument out of a broken chair and some viol wires. The flautist, Pielo, accompanied her, and joyful music filled the rooms of the Pavilion, spilling through the windows into the streets beyond.

And we waited – for what, we didn't exactly know.

There was little time for rest in between treating injuries, and distributing food and clothing, and still people who had inhaled the white-powder continued to die in their hundreds. We did all we could to ease their passing, but it was a horrible job, for, though Oren and all the healers were doing their best, we all knew there was no hope of a cure. They died, and the tendrils of those awfully beautiful plants arose from their mouths – sometimes ears, or even navels – and allowed more moths to be born in only a matter of hours, spreading the white-powder further and infecting more people. There was widespread panic, and terrible despair while we waited to see whom among us would be taken. But some did survive, and gradually the number of deaths began to fall.

The last vestiges of the illness passed, leaving those who were left to mourn them: hollow-eyed, distant, half-wishful of following their loved ones into the Beyond. Mothers, lovers, brothers, so many were left behind.

At least I was kept too busy to think, and used this busyness to search the crowd for people I had lost.

Naia, for one. Adina and Paje. My mother.

It was a hopeless task. There were so many, and they weren't all housed in the Pavilion. Many more cowered in the buildings surrounding us, in the shops and night-cafés; wherever there were beds, or food.

I was hurrying to fetch more bandages for a man with a broken leg when Grath pulled me into a corner, and there kissed me, running his hands possessively down my body. He pushed my dress from my shoulders, passing his hands over my skin, his fingers finding the small, slowly-healing scratch where Liliath had put her knife.

He pulled back, and pressed something into my hand. I looked down, amazed to find a tin box of coffee biscuits. "Where did you get these?" I asked him, adjusting my dress. And then, "How did you know they're my favourite?"

"Just eat them, and enjoy them," he said gruffly. "And if I catch you sharing them with anyone else, I'll . . ."

"You'll what?" I challenged him.

He pulled me back to him, cupping my cheek with his hand, looking deep into my eyes. I knew he saw it – that, despite the here and now, the incredible exquisiteness of this present moment, despite the healing of my scars and injuries, the terrible things I had seen and done would be, forever, marked inside me.

He knew it, and he wanted to share the burden. And he knew he could not. For there was more for me to do yet. Aurelia had as much as told me that.

He kissed me again, quickly, sweetly. "Put it from your mind. For this moment, be here, with me."

I kissed him, and I was.

***

As I hurried back to my task, away from this stolen bliss, Bethery cornered me.

"I see you have found your man," she accused.

"Oh, Beth." Sadness welled up in me. I looked down at my tin of biscuits. "I am sorry."

She smiled, dropping the accusatory act. "I've had many lovers." She shrugged. "I'll have many more if we make all make it through in one piece. You, sugar, are meant for one great love."

There were tears in my eyes as I hugged her. "I thought you said everyone would love me."

"It's true. But you will only ever love one." She pulled back and looked into my eyes. "Are you sure of him?"

I nodded, and I couldn't help smiling.

She nodded across the room. "And what of your secret tryst with your herald-boy?"

"Tomas?" I laughed, looking past her to where he sat. "I do love him, deeply, but it's love of a different nature. We spent our childhood together, first on the Third Tier, before he was accepted into the Abbey; I found him again a year later, when I was accepted into the Pavilion. He is my half-brother, born of my mother and a Ruedan man."

Bethery looked back at Tomas, who was holding some small child, rocking him to sleep. There was a wicked glint in her eyes.

***

The streets had changed.

They were full, now, of garbage, stinking piles of it. Some servitors still remained in operation, and you could find two or three sometimes determinedly digging away at a heap of discarded clothing, or some flattened boxes, or rotten fruit – but the task was too much. It was a futile task, but no one had the time or energy to devote to shutting them down.

The windows of the shops were smashed, by looters or by the quakes, it matters not. The dark interiors were like open mouths, desperate to be filled with the glories they had once held.

I walked the Calle del Corazón one afternoon – I say "afternoon" but as la Grulla closed in, our days were only two hours long at most. I was tracing the path of the *Dance of a Thousand Steps*, through a lock gate – with a nervous, hurried step, for they had been known to shift suddenly and without warning, leaving a person with a foot on either side of the path – and up to the Citadel.

Many of the plants I had loved were dead, killed by the changeable temperature and the ash in the air, or ripped from their beds as la Grulla passed overhead, her wings creating winds too strong for them to stand against.

I had thought, when I first came, that I would go to my garden house and gather my things. But as I reached the gardens, I did not think I could stand to return. The little house might be in ruins, the eddy-lake still and dark; it might have been looted, my fine dresses stolen by those who thought they might be valuable. What use, really, were beautiful dresses now? What use my face paints, my kohl? You could not eat cosmetics, and the clothes were too flimsy for work.

I would rather hold the memory of my little house as it was, a happy place.

Instead, I found my way to the statue of la Grulla.

Here was la Oráculo.

He was sitting on the bench, as Thaniel and I had done. His white exterior gleamed with a sudden flash as la Grulla vanished over the horizon. His eyes, which were very human in that they did not glow, but unnerving in that they rarely blinked, settled on me.

"People are dying," I said to him.

"If la Grulla had landed when she was supposed to, most would have been saved. That was la Relojero's plan. Five hundred years – no more. This is what I told her."

"But some would still have died in the quakes and tremors," I said. "And the malfunctions of equipment have been happening for many years."

"Just as many as those on Old Earth were left to their fate. This is the way of mortal things. I am an interpreter." I could swear I heard a sigh in his voice. "I read the Pattern, translate it. I don't make it. I would have saved them all, if I could."

La Oráculo looked at his palm, where I had placed the feather. I was wrong to accuse him, if that's what I was doing. He had been linked to the Core – he had known that the machines were breaking down. He had kneeled in the Plaza for hundreds of years while all around him people were born, grew old, and died. He had watched the execution of Chancellor Darhn, Commander Fedren, Councillor Lyssa. He had witnessed the cruelty and inevitability of dozens of lifetimes.

"Oráculo, how did we all come from seven people? The Companions cannot be father and mother to us all!" And now that I'd started, I couldn't seem to stop. The words tumbled out of me, questions upon questions. "And, la Oráculo, if you are an automaton, who built you? Where did you come from? Why did you tell us not to be curious about the Core of Tierra Mejór, or about the stars around us? Did you know –" here, I took a gulping breath, a slight sob coming from inside me, "Did you know it would be me who woke you?"

That was one question I wanted answered, more than all others. La Boca had told me it might have been any one of my sisters who failed to put the feather in la Oráculo's hand. But if it was, would they have kept the feather, as I had? Would la Oráculo have ever woken up? Would la Grulla have been called down for us?

La Oráculo, when he spoke, sounded slightly amused. "My story will be told, I promise you that. As for the Words I left behind – they, too, were necessary, but these are both questions for a later time. Suffice to say it was necessary. As for your last, only the Pattern knows how it came to be you, Imre. But I couldn't think of anyone more suited to the task."

I looked away, uncomfortable. I had made a mess of things, and I didn't deserve praise. "If I'd worked it out sooner, I could have saved people. I could have stopped la Boca."

"We all had our part to play. La Boca had his own role. Things do not often happen without reason, Imre. La Boca was misguided in his faith, and I do not condone his actions. But he was as the rest of you were – afraid of the future. If he had known that la Grulla would decend, would he have played his part differently?" La Oráculo lifted his white hands. "And if he had, what would that mean? Perhaps someone else would have taken up his mantel. Perhaps it would have been worse. Perhaps, if la Reina had not fallen ill, all this could have been avoided. It's best not to start down the path of reordering history."

"Will you lead us?" I asked him.

He shook his head slightly. "I am no leader. Only an adviser. This has always been my role."

"Prince Thaniel may die, or he may never wake. Even then, the Queen may die before naming him as the Príncipe Verderaro. Things are working well for now. But what will happen when la Grulla lands? Are we to board her, as the Seven Companions did? Who will lead us then?" I sighed, looking out at the garden, wishing I could simply pick up my tools and plant something. I didn't ever want to leave it behind. "How can we be sure there's anything left of Old Earth to return to?" I asked him. "Five hundred years have passed! Everything is so uncertain, and we're just supposed to . . . to trust in the Pattern?"

La Oráculo looked away from me for an instant. I wondered if he was capable of tears, for he seemed about to shed them now. "This," he said, "is the way of mortals."

I pressed him, but he would say no more.

***

And then the airships came.

Tattered and ruined they were, in worse condition than the one we had stolen. They were barely habitable, but, as the only course left to the heralds, they took them.

Some arrived with all on board dead, white-moths spilling from their mouths. Some came with only a few survivors. They docked atop the Citadel towers, though at least two crashed, broken beyond repair, into the Tether. The heralds who did arrive safely tumbled from the gangways, wide-eyed, barefaced, their hoods abandoned, scarves tied over their necks to hide their tattoos. We did not turn them away. It was a mark of the courage of the people of the Cuidad that they shared with them their shelter and food.

It was Gilgamesh who flew many on that perilous journey. The automaton refused to be removed from his chair, but a técnico had refit his legs. He lived up to his name, fearless as he rode the wild cosmic wind, ferrying the black-robed men from the Iglesia down to the relative safety of the Cuidad.

Chapter Fifty-Three

La Grulla landed on the bluff at the side of the Avenida de las Estralles, the Avenue of Stars, where Feval, Ollander, and I had stopped that day in the autocarriage and pondered the mysteries of the Unknown. "Space," he had called it, and now more than ever that seemed to ring true.

She flew slowly, but with precision and poise, just like the graceful bird I had danced in the *Dance of a Thousand Steps*. She was huge, larger than I ever imagined, but she did not lumber like some heavy machine; the ground crumbled beneath her clawed feet as they stretched out, flexing under her weight, but the effect was one of supreme, grand elegance.

She was no machine. Somewhere deep within her breast beat the heart of crystal, which la Oráculo had given to la Relojero, and her body was made of millions upon millions of glass feathers, fluttering and tinkling in the breeze.

Her huge wings folded silently into her sides. She lowered her long neck and gracefully tilted her head to one side, creating a ramp that led up onto her back.

People came. They came with their families and without; they came weeping with sorrow and with joy. Some came fearfully. Some did not come at all.

As horrified as this left me, I could understand, too, the fears that kept them in their familiar houses as fire rained down upon their roofs. I knew that paralysis, and how it could leech into one's limbs, into their mind, until a person could not move for the fear of facing the darkness of the unknown.

I knew it – in a bloodstain shaped like a bird taking flight, in the horrified face of a woman I had grown to love and respect, in the sight of a shuttle-train, lifting as if by magic into the sky, only to be smashed to pieces.

I knew that fear. And ultimately, I could not decide for them. If they would stay, they would die. I may rail against it, but, like those who refused to follow la Relojero, it was their death to choose.

***

I boarded with a golden cage full of the Prince's finches, a pack of hacer julepe cards, a half-empty tin of coffee biscuits,and Grath, holding my arm.

Behind us came some tens of thousands of men, women, and children.

I looked among them for Naia, but did not see her. I had no idea if she had survived, the last remaining member of her family. Even now, as I sit here, I hope to find her among those we took on board. I hope, too, that I will find Paje, and Henny, and even Ibban, the man who had loved Liliath for that one night.

We brought with us servitors, broken as they were, and a few of the sentinela. One or two of the shambling automata from the Room of Roses were able to make the journey, but most had shut down, dust and dirt from the explosions and collapsing buildings having finally worn them out. Gilgamesh was there, as well as Feval and Divon.

La Grulla's neck was covered with small feathers. Though they looked soft, they, too, were made of hard crystal. As we walked up that long sloping ramp, light began to glow from within her, glittering and glinting under our feet. Inside the cage, the birds began to sing. Beside me, Grath squeezed my hand.

We climbed.

The light grew brighter and brighter. As we reached la Grulla's back, the crystal feathers lengthened. Some were bigger than two or three men atop one another, some taller still; they were canted at various angles, creating walls and partitions. We passed through a curving archway, and found ourselves on a gallery, overlooking a great chamber. It was white, the ceiling laced with fine feather-fronds, the walls glittering, full of that clear light.

There were tables below, and cushioned benches, in the colours of soft cream, brown, and grey. I couldn't tell what materials they were made from – velvets softer than any I'd ever seen, shining metals with an ice-like patina, polished dark wood that must have come from trees twice the size of any I knew. Everything was dust-free, perfectly preserved in the crispness of the Unknown.

The floor of this platform was slightly curved, and provided us with a view of the rest of la Grulla's interior. Shaped like the bottom of a boat, it swept away from us, curving downwards and then back up towards her tail.

Beyond this platform, there were towers, of varying heights and sizes. The biggest, and most central, stretched all the way to the ceiling, and others around it in a ring were by turns elegant and slender or short and squat. Seven of them in total, they were bridged by walkways, some covered, some open to the air and bare of railings. All at varying heights, they created airborne streets over the cavernous space below.

Above, through the latticed gaps of the feathered walls, I saw the black of the night sky.

Behind us came the others, gasping when they stepped onto the shining white floor. People descended the gallery by way of the ramps swooping down like two curved wings, there to mill about, touching the walls with wonder, looking up at the high ceiling. Most of them had never seen such opulence.

Me, I would have settled for my tiny garden house.

"It is wondrous," the refugees said, over and over again. "A miracle of the Pattern."

There were other levels, we would soon discover; reached by doors made of some fine white metal traced with swirling etchings, and which hissed open when we approached. There were berths, in which were comfortable crisp white beds, two or four to a room. There was a large chamber in which the food we had so carefully packed and stored could be prepared – and, I would learn later, large bays were more food could be grown and harvested. There was an open space for exercising.

And, in one of the furthest towers, an infirmary, complete with several white beds, workbenches, cabinets filled with glass bottles, neatly labelled, their contents appearing unspoiled. But most intriguing of all were the strange flat, blank screens set at angles into benches and walls.

This is where la Oráculo led me, and I had Feval and Divon bring the Prince and the Queen in their caskets down here immediately. Doctor Oren had sworn Hanna to secrecy, and they had barely left the caskets for a moment in all the days we waited. Here, there were alcoves, divided from the central room by arched windows.

Seeing this room full of foreign, peculiar equipment, Oren and Hanna were entranced.

"What are these machines?" I asked Doctor Oren, as I touched the strange, dull screens. "Can they help us? Does one hold a cure?"

"That I can only hope," he replied. "We have precious little else to try. We have lost so much – all those books in the Great Library. The knowledge of lifetimes. I only hope we have gained some time."

"We are alive," I reminded him. "I choose to hope. La Relojero has led us this far – surely she had hidden some secrets here, in la Grulla."

Divon was surveying the panels and controls at one of the workstations. "I do recall some references to devices such as these in several archaic texts. I believe, if I study them, I might be able to make them work."

We shared a glance between us, Hanna and I; even dour Oren's drooping mouth lifted a little as he watched Divon tap at the controls. I did not speak my worry that once we left the orbit of Tierra Mejór, and the influence of the crystal centres within its core, that Feval and Divon might lose their stored memories, and with it, their undeniably distinct personalities; we all shared the same apprehension.

Yet, we had hope, and we clung to it.

Chapter Fifty-Four

There was time, in the end, for many things before la Grulla was ready to leave. The Green-bands, both new members and old, were busy. Thankfully, the populace was too, so didn't think to ask too many questions, though what we would do without Thaniel, now that la Reina's automaton double had been exposed, was an issue we would have to face soon enough. The provisions we had brought with us needed to be sorted. The injured had to be treated. Many, many people needed to be consoled, brokenhearted at leaving behind relatives, houses, fortunes – and their dead.

I do not know how any of these tasks fell to me, but they did. And I did them, running from one dilemma to another. There were no more turnings, no more days and nights, for la Grulla's splendour was all around us now, her feathers simplifying and refracting the light of the stars – it was hard to find a reason to rest, let alone sleep, so I kept working. It helped me keep my mind from other matters, matters which were harder to think of. It also gave me a chance to look, for I still hoped to find those people I had lost.

And one in particular.

Mother.

La Oráculo was by my side, at least, and it was to him I deferred, even above Secretary Allius – whose coffers were exchanged, now, for crates of books and moth-meat.

"La Relojero's companions," I found myself talking to him, as he helped me shift a few heavy containers of different-sized boots that had been rescued from Hillier's Fine Fashions. "They numbered seven. But la Grulla has room for us all – or even more. Was this part of her plan?"

La Oráculo moved his lips in an approximation of a smile. "It was. La Relojero only ever wanted more children to return home, to fill Old Earth with new families, new guilds, new ways of thinking. It is your task, now, to do as she wished."

"Is this part of the story you will tell me?" I asked him slyly, only to have him lift his hands in mock surrender.

"There is time for that yet."

I thought of the many varied people who had boarded la Grulla. We were a motley bunch, picked from all the different paths of life. How would we work together, after the shock of what had happened wore off? After a journey of months, or years? Would we make the right choices, even after we reached Old Earth?

La Relojero had believed we would.

I wished I could have her faith.

As I left the side room where we'd been working, I intended to make my way back to the chamber through which we'd entered. It had been named the First Chamber, and had become a kind of base for operations. There were boxes of bandages and medicines which I wanted to make sure arrived in the infirmary, for those still nursing broken bones or burns. I walked the length of an undulating corridor, stopping with a smile as I saw Grath standing at the walls. He had a cigarillo in his hands, but it was burning unheeded. Beside him two younger men, the age of most apprentices, were making quick notes as he spoke.

" . . .some kind of field of force that exists between these 'feathers,' " he was saying. "Somehow, keeping the vacuum outside, while the pressure of air within remains constant."

Even as he spoke, he prodded the gap between the feathers with the tip of his cigarillo. Ash fell as it came in contact with some invisible barrier.

Seeing me, he turned. He did not smile, but there was an energy to him that I'd never seen yet, not even in the Clocktower, or his telescope room. I thought for a second he would let me pass without a word – perhaps embarrassed in front of his new pupils. Instead, he turned quickly on his heels and gripped me by the waist, kissing my cheek.

I felt the prickle of his beard, the warmth of his lips. I laughed, once, and steadied myself against his solid chest; he released me, and pressed something into my hands. It was a small book, bound in red cloth, full of thick creamy paper; and a pen, almost brand-new.

"What are these for?" I asked him.

"It seems to me we've lost more knowledge than we can ever replace," Grath said. "It's time now to begin anew, to record what we can, and let others know what occurs on our journey."

I almost gave the gifts back to him. I didn't want this task! And yet, even as I opened my mouth to refuse, my fingers traced the edges of the pages, and I knew – even if I did not want this, I must do it. Perhaps this was the will of the Pattern. Perhaps this was why I had endured everything I had – that I could record it in this journal.

Grath turned back to his work with a sideways glance so intense I felt it burn through the layers of my clothing. "Pay attention!" he barked, but his pupils continued to nudge one another, hiding giggles behind their hands.

*****

So it was that I was in the First Chamber when La Grulla unfolded her wings.

Some others had gathered here – Miguel, and his wife Risella, in one corner, waved to me. I passed Hillder, directing a man towards the bathroom facilities. There was Jardine, scowling at a scant meal of moth-meat while little Pressa bounced on her lap. A few other, whom I did not recognise; most others were spread throughout la Grulla, exploring, eating, enjoying the myriad comforts after days of privation and hunger. I took a seat at one of the tables, tapping my pen against the first blank page of my book.

I think I had the first words in my head when I felt a sudden jolt. It startled me, making me think another quake might be about to occur, but no; it was a different movement, much more controlled, as if something in motion deep beneath the floor had suddenly sped up.

The neck of the bird retracted, slowly tilting upwards until the way in or out was blocked out our last view of the murky grey sky. Those around me gasped and murmured, clutching at the walls, the seats, or at one another with the mixed fear and exhilaration of children leaping from a rope-swing, uncertain of where they would land.

Beyond the outer walls, the great wings moved away from the sides. The mechanisms were smooth; there was no grinding of gears, no shrieking of metal. In fact, I would have felt better if there was, for this effortless movement seemed far too powerful.

And then we lifted.

I left my seat and walked to the edge of the room, steadying my steps, prepared to feel ill-at-ease – but there was no need. The smooth, curving floor did not tilt beneath me. Some force had adjusted, making it feel flat. I pressed my hand to the wall. The feathers were sharp, and dug into my skin, but I could feel no breeze from the outside. As Grath had said, some force, some magic of the feathers, kept everything outside, and the air in.

We rose carefully, steadily, as the wings razored smoothly up, then down. Again, faster; we ascended further. Moths tumbled in my stomach, but it all seemed so purposeful, so safe, that it was difficult to credit my nervousness.

With a pang of sorrow, I thought of Thaniel, locked in a casket in the infirmary, somewhere between life and death. He should have been here to see this. Travelling across the stars to find Old Earth; this was his dream.

If I looked down, I could see through the gaps in the feathers the Citadel, half-crushed as if by a careless boot; the carrier-pigeon spires, most snapped like broken needles; the shuttle-trains, abandoned on their tracks, small as caterpillars on the branches of a tree. The White Pavilion, miraculously intact, its beautiful towers a single, lonely reminder of everything I had thought my life should be – and everything it was not.

I could see Tierra Mejór, broken, flaming, falling gently and silently apart.

But I didn't look down, not at all. I looked upwards, to the stars, the planets, and the blackness of the Unknown, and what was to come.

***

I walked slowly back to our room. Grath and I had chosen a berth at the top of one of the nearer towers, nestled on an angle at the very top of a long set of stairs. It was windowless, but this, for privacy rather than anything else, suited us perfectly. The door was designed to open with the touch of a thumb to a small sensor, just like the one in the pen below the Pavilion. It hadn't taken Grath long to train it to recognise two sets of prints, using his wristwatch programmer – nor how to exclude anyone else reprogramming it for their own prints.

In the room was a pit in the floor, into which was fitted a sunken bed. It was small, probably made for one person with a little room to spare, but we – honestly! – didn't mind sharing the space. A small alcove in the wall provided steaming water from a sluice in the ceiling, which ran out through a drain in the floor, which la Oráculo had told us recycled every drop through complex evaporating systems so that la Grulla could provide water endlessly. Standing under it was like basking in a warm rain, and we had tested it twice already, both of us in that tight space, skin to skin.

On one of the shelves, I had placed my pack of hacer julepe cards. Only one was missing, still, as far as I knew, wedged in the door of the terrace room; though quite possible, the room was a head of rubble, now. Beside these was the box of coffee biscuits, an indulgence of which, on Grath's orders, I must eat at least three before bedtime.

Grath slept with his short sword against the wall, within easy reach of the bed, and insisted on fashioning and fitting a second latch to the door that could be locked from the inside.

"Surely all that is past, now," I pleaded, though I knew we couldn't provide any such guarantee. La Oráculo had said this was only the beginning, and of course, he would know more of such things than I. He had lived innumerable years in La Plaza de Lágrima. Before that, he had lived who knew how long, gathering intelligence, storing knowledge, computing data, and analysing information. He had made the prediction. He had travelled with la Relojero across the Unknown. I trusted la Oráculo, more than I trusted anyone, to lead us home. But there were so many questions. How long would the journey take? A thousand days, like the journey to Tierra Mejór? What would happen between here and there? Would we face the trials la Relojero had faced? Would we survive? Was there anything left of Old Earth to return to?

I had so many questions, but I was determined, now. I was not going to stop asking them. La Oráculo owed us answers, and I would get them. I would demand his story.

As I opened the door now, my book clutched to my chest, my eyes instantly sought out Grath. He was standing, dressed in a fresh suit of soft greys – there were many such garments, kept in sealed drawers in one of the many chambers deep inside la Grulla – he looked handsome. His beard was newly trimmed, though where he had found a razor or scissors I did not know; his hair slightly tousled as if he had been sleeping.

He was truly so very beautiful.

Looking at him, it was easy to push aside my dark thoughts and worries for tomorrow. "Waiting for me?" I asked him lightly.

"It seems so," he replied with slight amusement, and he slipped his arms around my waist, pulling me close. I stepped into him and rested my head against his broad shoulder, smelling his scent – cigarillo smoke, the slightest hint of perspiration, and the clean scent of his new clothes. He took the book from my hands and dropped it to the floor. The pen rolled away, but I did not care.

Together, we rocked back and forwards, our motions becoming more deliberate, harder, faster as the heat intensified. We shed our clothes like leaves from the trees at the end of the warm-season, tumbling into the bed.

He was everything I had wanted, and more besides. The hard, flat planes of his chest, curiously hairless; the beauty of his lean, powerful muscles, bunching and moving beneath his skin. His grey eyes, so deep and dark and kind – the eyes I had seen lift me from danger so many time – they fixed on me, and only me. I did not represent anything to him except myself. I knew it, and with it came a surge of wonder and fear and excitement.

He ran his callused hands down my body, tracing the line of my spine, the curve of my hips, sweeping beneath my thighs, into the warmth and moistness there. I gasped, pushing into his hand, wanting more; he gave it, willingly, eagerly. In turn, I grasped his erect pene, stroking it in the way I had learned, but had never wanted so much to put into practice. He moaned, in turn reaching up to tangle his hands in my hair, tilting my face up to receive a kiss that had the heat and power of Old Earth's sun.

We danced together, the Dance of Love, as we soared among the stars.

Acknowledgements

This book has had a troubled history. When I first began writing it, I thought it would be a straight-forward fantasy. I had no idea it was going to end up being a clockpunk sci-fi novel with romance and robots. As such an unusual book, most publishers didn't know how to take it. A few liked it but couldn't work out how to market it; finally, it came to the attention of one publisher who loved the premise and the characters and was more than happy to take it on.

Unfortunately, this publisher ran into several logistical problems, and were unable to keep publishing their amazing catalogue of books. *The White Pavilion* was released as an ebook without any marketing and sold only one copy. The promised paperback was never produced, and after a few unhappy emails, the rights were reverted back to me.

After a conversation with Hague Publishing's Andrew Harvey, I sent him the manuscript, stipulating that it 'wasn't a submission (unless he loved it)'. He came back to me to say that he would be happy to publish it, and I'm so, so pleased that this was the case. I'm glad *The White Pavilion* has found its home alongside *The Bridges Trilogy* at Hague Publishing.

So, first of all, thank you to Andrew! Your enthusiasm for this book when I had lost all hope of it ever being published is so appreciated.

Thank you, as always, to my husband for putting up with my long hours at the keyboard and for not getting mad when I sometimes have to yell 'can't talk, writing'. Thank you to my gorgeous children, Rydyr, Quinn and Whitley, who are all beginning to love storybook worlds as much as I do. And thank you to my mum and dad for buying me books and feeding my belief that I could, in fact, be a writer.

Thank You

Thank you for reading THE WHITE PAVILION.
We hope you enjoyed it.

If you would like to be kept informed of further releases by Ruth Fox,
or other new books from Hague Publishing, why not subscribe to our
newsletter at:

www.HaguePublishing.com/subscribe.php

And if you loved the book and have a moment to spare we would
really appreciate a short review. Your help in spreading the word is
gratefully received.

About the Author

Ruth Fox is the author of many books, including the award-winning *Monster-boy: Lair of the Grelgoroth.*

She has a Bachelor of Arts/Diploma of Arts in Professional Writing and Editing, and loves to read science fiction, fantasy, romance, adventure, young adult, adult, literature, old books, new books, and everything in between.

She lives with her husband, two cats and three very adventurous sons (who also love books) in Victoria, Australia.

You can find more information about her other books on her website at:
https://rfoxclair.wixsite.com

or on Facebook at:
https://www.facebook.com/RuthFoxAuthor

Hague

Publishing

www.HaguePublishing.com

PO Box 451 Bassendean
Western Australia 6934